PRAISE FOR THE COL

“[A] gripping novel of suspense fro. ls layers of intersecting stories, each one integral to the overall story of the Mills family and their small-town secrets. Readers will want to see more from this author.”

—*Publishers Weekly*

“Elliot succeeds in creating both a thrilling mystery and a fascinating character study of the people inhabiting these pages.”

—Bookreporter

“With her riveting, narrative-driven, deftly crafted storytelling style as a novelist, Kendra Elliot’s *The Last Sister* will prove to be a welcome and enduringly popular addition to community library Mystery/Suspense/Thriller collections.”

—*Midwest Book Review*

“Suspense on top of suspense. This one will keep you guessing until the final page and shows Elliot at her very best.”

—The Real Book Spy

“Every family has skeletons. Kendra Elliot’s tale of the Mills family’s dark secrets is first-rate suspense. Dark and gripping, *The Last Sister* crescendos to knock-out, edge-of-your seat tension.”

—Robert Dugoni, bestselling author of *My Sister’s Grave*

“*The Last Sister* is exciting and suspenseful! Engaging characters and a complex plot kept me on the edge of my seat until the very last page.”

—T.R. Ragan, bestselling author of the Jessie Cole series

"Thriller Award finalist Elliot's well-paced sequel to *The Last Sister* opens at the home of fifty-two-year-old Reuben Braswell, a devotee of conspiracy theories, who's lying dead in his bathtub . . . The twist ending will catch most readers by surprise . . . [and] fans will look forward to seeing characters from the author's other series take the lead in future installments."

—*Publishers Weekly*

"Elliot skillfully interweaves the various plot threads, and credible, mostly sympathetic characters match the lovingly described locale. Fans of contemporary regional mysteries will be rewarded."

—*Publishers Weekly*

AT THE RIVER

ALSO BY KENDRA ELLIOT

COLUMBIA RIVER NOVELS

The Last Sister
The Silence
In the Pines
The First Death

MERCY KILPATRICK NOVELS

A Merciful Death
A Merciful Truth
A Merciful Secret
A Merciful Silence
A Merciful Fate
A Merciful Promise

BONE SECRETS NOVELS

Hidden
Chilled
Buried
Alone
Known

BONE SECRETS NOVELLAS

Veiled

CALLAHAN & MCLANE NOVELS

PART OF THE BONE SECRETS WORLD

Vanished
Bridged
Spiraled
Targeted

ROGUE RIVER NOVELLAS

On Her Father's Grave (Rogue River)
Her Grave Secrets (Rogue River)
Dead in Her Tracks (Rogue Winter)
Death and Her Devotion (Rogue Vows)
Truth Be Told (Rogue Justice)

WIDOW'S ISLAND NOVELLAS

Close to the Bone
Bred in the Bone
Below the Bones
The Lost Bones
Bone Deep

AT THE RIVER

KENDRA
ELLIOT

Published by Montlake, Seattle

www.apub.com

ISBN-13: 9781662511844 (hardcover)
ISBN-13: 9781662511851 (paperback)
ISBN-13: 9781662511837 (digital)

Cover design by Caroline Teagle Johnson
Cover images: © Kornelia Rumberg / ArcAngel; © Victoria Hunter / ArcAngel; © Xinzheng / Getty

Printed in the United States of America

First edition

For my girls

1

Ollie was minding his own business when he heard the woman scream.

Enjoying the sunny December day, he had taken Shep snowmobiling in Oregon's Deschutes National Forest. His dog adored the rides in the snow as much as Ollie. Bungee cords fastened a small wooden crate behind Ollie's seat, and he had shoved a small dog bed in it for padding. Shep loved his crate and had only leaped out once, as Ollie slowed when a rabbit dashed across their path and Shep had been inspired to pursue.

A sharp command had immediately stopped the chase.

Ollie and his riding buddy had seen tons of animal sign on their snowy forest road journeys. Rabbit, elk, bear, cougar, and coyote. Man-made ruts in the snow indicated other snowmobiles and four-wheel drives had gone before him, but he rarely encountered another vehicle. They passed the occasional narrow lane that vanished among the tall firs, possibly leading to a cabin or two but most likely leading to nothing at all.

The old snowmobile had been an impulse buy. Something rare for Ollie—he was extremely frugal with his money, having lived several lonely years with none. The unit's engine had been shot, the paint scratched, the body dented, and the windshield missing. But Ollie had seen the possibilities. He'd bought it for a song, and he and his guardian, Truman, had spent long hours rebuilding the engine and replacing other parts.

He'd considered following in Truman's law enforcement footsteps for a career, but Ollie struggled a bit with the necessary social skills to deal with the public's problems; he'd much rather talk to animals.

His twentieth birthday wasn't far off, and he felt as if he should have a better plan for his life by now.

I'll think about it later.

He and Shep were speeding through a twisty section of snow-packed road when Shep started to thrash in the crate behind Ollie, knocking him in the back several times. Surprised and concerned about his dog, who usually sat quietly, Ollie slowed and cut the noisy engine.

A woman's shouts filled the quiet forest.

Ollie spun to look behind him.

Fifty yards away, a woman ran toward him, her boots sinking in the white powder between the tracks of the snowmobile.

Shep must have heard her.

Not taking his gaze from the approaching woman, Ollie pulled off his gloves and snapped open the small storage space before him on the snowmobile. His fingers closed around his bear spray.

It's just a woman.

Doesn't matter.

Ollie was cautious. Truman wanted him to carry a gun for protection, but Ollie refused, preferring his bear spray. He couldn't shake the image of aiming a gun at another person, and Truman had taught him never to aim his weapon unless he was prepared to shoot.

Ollie couldn't mentally prepare for that.

"Do you have a phone?" she yelled as she came closer, panic in her tone.

Ollie estimated she was in her forties. She had long, blonde hair that stuck out from under a red knit cap, and she wore a heavy green coat and black snow boots, but her pants were thin like yoga pants. Her eyes were wide and very blue, and she panted between words.

Shep stood in his crate, two paws balanced on the back edge, his tail wagging at a happy tempo. His posture was relaxed but interested. Ollie always tuned himself to his dog's reactions, using Shep's behavior as a barometer for the situation.

"There's no reception out here," said Ollie, his hand still on his bear spray but not lifting it.

Stopping about six feet away, the woman covered her face and burst into tears.

"Are you okay?" Ollie asked, spotting what appeared to be blood on her white mittens. "Are you hurt?"

"My husband is missing. I woke up this morning and he was gone and there's lots of blood on the floor and the door was wide open," she babbled, wiping her nose with her mittens, her voice cracking as she breathed hard. She was a small, desperate figure in the cold winter air.

She's genuinely terrified.

Ollie closed the storage lid and stepped off the snowmobile after a quick scan of his surroundings. Shep's behavior still showed no concern, so Ollie approached the woman. "You don't have a vehicle?"

"Our SUV is gone! There's no internet or landline and my cell phone is useless. Can you give me a ride?" Her eyes pleaded with him, her breath coming in quick, panicked gulps. "Something must have happened to him. I don't understand why he didn't wake me up if he was hurt."

It didn't make sense to Ollie either.

She brushed a mitten over her wet eyes. "I was walking out to the road to try to flag someone down when I heard your snowmobile and ran but you'd just passed by."

"Shep heard you," Ollie told her, gesturing at his dog. "Do you think your husband got injured and drove into town?"

She sucked in a deep breath. "No. I think someone hurt him and took him away. We must have been followed to the cabin." Her eyes turned serious. "He has a lot of enemies," she said softly as she looked at the blood on her mittens.

A chill ran up Ollie's spine.

What kind of man has enemies like that?

2

Truman Daly parked his four-wheel drive along the snow-covered forest road behind two Deschutes County sheriff SUVs. A black Explorer was in front of the county vehicles, and Ollie's snowmobile in front of that. Ollie stood nearby, his constant shadow, Shep, at his feet. Truman blew out a breath of relief at the sight of the teen. Several miles back, near the main rural highway, he'd spotted Ollie's truck with the homemade snowmobile carrier sitting in a small clearing.

Earlier Ollie had called Truman to report a missing man, and in turn Truman had immediately called the county sheriff's office. As the Eagle's Nest police chief, Truman knew the location wasn't in his jurisdiction, but he came anyway. Ollie was his son.

Sort of.

Ollie had been an eighteen-year-old orphan living alone in his grandparents' cabin in the middle of nowhere, completely cut off from society. He'd rescued Truman from men who'd kidnapped and beaten him, and then Ollie had nursed him back to health in his primitive home. Truman owed him his life.

He'd welcomed Ollie into his own home, and now, a year and a half later, they were a tight family of four, including Truman's wife, Mercy, and her niece Kaylie. And too many pets.

Truman couldn't imagine any other life.

Ollie was more than capable of taking care of himself in the snowy forest—more than anyone Truman had ever met—but Truman had a parent's instinct to show up. And Ollie could be a little naive. Kaylie had done a good job incorporating him into the real world, but he had a lot more to learn about people.

Truman strode through the snow to the teen. "You good?" he asked, scanning Ollie from head to toe. He wasn't the undersize teenager Truman had first met in the woods. He'd filled out and grown several inches—a result of regular meals and balanced nutrition. Truman blinked at the figure standing before him, realizing Ollie had become a man right under his nose.

He'll be twenty soon.

Ollie nodded. "The detective asked me to stick around for a bit. She's talking to Sara at the house." He gestured down a narrow lane that vanished in the woods.

"Sara?"

"The woman who stopped me." Ollie's mouth tightened and concern showed in his eyes.

"What exactly happened?" Ollie had given a clear account on the phone, but Truman wanted to hear it again. Often witnesses later remembered additional details.

The story Ollie told him was exactly the same. He'd driven Sara out to the main highway, where he had picked up a signal on his phone. The woman had first tried to call her husband's cell, but the call had gone straight to voice mail. Next Ollie had called Truman. He'd known he needed to contact the county sheriff but figured Truman could make things happen more quickly.

"Sara said they were on a working vacation," Ollie continued. "But I didn't ask what she and her husband do." The young man's brows came together. "I didn't like what she said about her husband having enemies." He met Truman's gaze. "But I feel she's telling the truth."

Truman nodded, reserving judgment. Ollie was observant but had been fooled by liars in the past.

A Deschutes County deputy appeared, striding around a curve of the snowy lane that led to the victim's rental cabin. "Detective Marshall wants to talk to you now," he told Ollie after he greeted Truman. "Don't walk on the tracks." He pointed at the tire prints on the narrow lane.

Ollie lifted a brow at Truman, a hopeful question in his eyes. "Yeah, I'll come along," Truman told the young man. The two of them headed down the road, keeping to the sides, breaking their own paths in the fresh snow. Truman noticed a single line of footprints had already marred the tire tracks. Sara had walked out to catch Ollie, so Truman suspected those were hers. The tire tracks were lightly covered with a layer of snow, but Truman believed a forensics team could identify the type of tires. "You didn't drive the snowmobile to the house?" he asked Ollie.

"No. Sara was positive her husband wasn't there, so I thought it was best to preserve the scene. We waited at the road until the deputies and detective showed up."

"Good thinking."

As I should expect since he lives with me and an FBI agent.

The two of them walked for several silent minutes, breathing the crisp air. It hadn't snowed overnight in Bend, but apparently it had up here in the Cascade foothills. Discovering the time of the snowfall could tighten the window during which the husband had vanished.

Assuming the woman is telling the truth.

The house came into view. It was a small A-frame cabin that reminded Truman of Mercy's original hideaway, which had also been tucked deep in the national forest. Hers had burned down the year before, and they'd built a bigger one in its place. The tire tracks led to a rectangular spot near the cabin where the snow was less deep. Clearly a vehicle had sat there for a period while it snowed.

Three people were in front of the cabin. Detective Noelle Marshall excused herself from the woman she had been speaking with, who Truman assumed was Sara. Sara waved to Ollie, and a deputy said something to her, pulling her attention.

Truman had worked with Detective Marshall a few times, and her skills had earned his admiration. The tall blonde woman knew how to dig into a case and find answers.

"Hello, Chief," she said.

"Morning, Detective."

"How are you doing?" she asked Ollie, eyeing the young man with her dark-blue gaze. Detective Marshall was very direct. Truman didn't know her personal history, but he suspected her heavy coat and boots were out of his pay grade. Every time he'd met her, she'd reminded him of a photo in a catalog of understated, expensive clothing. Today it was a winter-activities catalog: perfect but casually styled clothes with a polished appearance.

Unlike most detectives he'd met.

He knew Mercy highly respected her and had told him that if she were blonde, she'd want Noelle's striking shade of platinum. Truman had been taken aback at the comment, completely unable to picture his wife's black hair as blonde.

"Fine." Ollie reached down to pet Shep and stared at his boots.

Truman grimaced. Ollie had suddenly gone shy in the detective's presence. He'd gained a lot of confidence since he'd moved in with Truman, but this woman with a badge clearly intimidated him. Which was odd, considering that Mercy carried a badge, and Ollie often poured out his soul to her.

Maybe he would do better if I wasn't here.

Truman could see why Ollie would defer conversation to him since he was in law enforcement. If Truman hadn't been there, he knew Ollie would have stepped up to the plate. Maybe his instinct to immediately come to the scene had been wrong.

I shouldn't hover.

Parenting was hard. Especially since he had started with an eighteen-year-old.

"Tell me again what happened," Noelle said to Ollie.

He launched into his story for the fourth time. Truman was pleased to see he held the detective's gaze as he talked. She nodded as he finished and then glanced at Truman. "You got a minute to look at this scene? I'd like another perspective."

"Sure." Surprise went through him. He had no jurisdiction in this location. "What's wrong?"

"I'm trying to make sense of the boot prints inside."

"If you need tracking or print explanations, Ollie is the person to ask," Truman told her. He'd seen Ollie follow invisible tracks—invisible to Truman, anyway—for hundreds of yards.

Next to him, Ollie straightened almost imperceptibly.

"It's an odd story," Noelle said. "Husband Rob Newton is a podcaster of conspiracy theories and true crime, according to his wife. He was here doing research on a story. Sara says he's received a lot of hate mail and threats for several of his stories, but this is the first time there's been a physical altercation."

"She thinks his disappearance is tied to one of his podcasts?" asked Truman.

Noelle nodded. "But it feels like poor odds to me. They live in Bakersfield, California, so an attack in response to his story in a national forest a thousand miles away seems unlikely. It makes more sense that her husband drove away for some reason."

"But didn't tell his wife he was leaving?" asked Truman.

"Weird, right?" Noelle paused. "Lotta blood."

Truman understood what she hadn't said out loud. There was a chance the wife had done something. Immediate family members were always the first suspects, and the majority of the time, one turned out to be the criminal.

Truman glanced at the woman—Sara—talking to the deputy. Even though she wore a thick coat, she'd wrapped her arms around herself as if struggling to keep warm. She wore black gloves that were clearly too large, and Truman recalled that Ollie had mentioned on the phone that her mittens had blood on them. They must have been bagged as evidence. She wiped her eyes and cheeks and her shoulders slumped. She seemed genuinely upset.

Truman hoped she hadn't harmed her husband.

But the odds are against it.

3

FBI special agent Mercy Kilpatrick zipped up her coat and squinted at the tall structures in the remote electrical substation in Oregon's Wasco County. The silver framework was impressive against the rich blue sky, the color of which gave no hint that it was thirty degrees outside.

She dropped her gaze and again studied the bullet holes in the substation's transformer. Hundreds of shells had been left behind. The shooters had methodically focused on the right equipment to cut power to three small communities.

Two sets of boot prints were still visible in the inch of crispy snow near the shells, and wide tire tracks indicated a large vehicle had been parked close by. The station's chain-link fence with barbed wire across the top could not stop bullets from high-powered rifles.

How will they prevent another attack?

"This is the second county substation to be damaged in a month," said Ray Anderson, the Wasco County sheriff, as he watched workers from the Bonneville Power Administration assess the destruction.

Mercy had read the report on the previous substation sabotage. Tens of thousands of dollars in damage had been done in an identical assault. An agent out of the Portland FBI office had investigated the first scene, but after the second attack, the Portland Special Agent in Charge had turned the case over to the Bend office, which was a little farther from the county attacks but closer in terms of community. Wasco County was five times the square mileage of the county containing Portland, but it had a thirtieth of the population.

And was red versus the blue of Portland.

Mercy knew Anderson had been the county's sheriff for only a couple of months. He appeared to be in his early thirties and seemed young for the position. He had a baby face under a stained straw cowboy hat, but his heavy-duty Carhartt jacket was pristine. When he moved, it was with purpose and an air of authority, his demeanor calm and collected. She wondered if he had developed it to offset his youthful appearance.

Gusty winds kept blowing Mercy's long hair in her mouth, so she fished in her pockets for a ponytail holder. "You haven't heard any gossip or whispers of who might have done this?" she asked as she bound her hair. No arrest had been made in the first substation attack, and she felt the odds were good that this had been done by the same people.

He scowled and shook his head. "None. People are tight lipped around here. I've only lived here a few years, so people still see me as an outsider."

"It's a pretty county," Mercy said. On the drive up the hill to the station, she'd had wide views of the Columbia River. The blue sky had been reflected in the water, and with the white layer of snow covering the hills, it had created a stunning sight.

But the harm to the substation had an ugly element that went beyond physical destruction.

It was the *why* of the harm.

Sheriff Anderson crossed his arms. "This was done by assholes trying to make a point."

Mercy had come across assholes before; this time she believed they were accelerationists.

Accelerationists were a small segment of domestic terrorists. They believed the federal government was irreparably corrupt and tried to accelerate its demise by creating chaos and political tension. The idea behind harming the federal substations was to show that the government was incapable of protecting itself and the public. Sometimes they used the blackouts they'd created to commit burglaries or arson, further proving the government couldn't keep its people safe and driving the public to rebel against it.

Their primary goal was a new government that would rise from the ashes of the old.

The logic was twisted.

It was based in racism, violence, and chaos.

The sheriff glared at the substation. "This kind of behavior angers me. Don't these people know they're risking lives when they do this? They cut off heat to homes with small children and babies. Senior citizens. People dependent on medical equipment who can't afford a backup generator. BPA is working on rerouting power from another station, but it'll take another twenty-four hours. There are safeguards in place so communities aren't completely dependent on one substation, but they told me that replacing the equipment could take a year because of supply chain issues."

Mercy sighed. "It hurts people. It's not just a hunk of metal being damaged; affecting the community is the goal. This probably wasn't done by some drunk locals shooting for the fun of it. I'll collect the shells and have them run through NIBIN. Maybe we'll get lucky." The National Integrated Ballistic Information Network was a database that stored characteristics of bullets and casings used in crimes.

"I've got some equipment in my vehicle to get better pictures of the boot prints and tire treads," she said. Anderson followed her to the back of her Tahoe, where she searched for a can of gray primer paint and some evidence rulers. It was unlikely that a forensics team could arrive before the sun melted some of the snow. She'd do what she could.

She'd never had to collect forensic evidence when she worked in Portland. There was always someone available who'd been specifically trained. But since she'd transferred to Bend, she'd started adding more and more tools of the trade to a large kit in her Tahoe. Too many times she'd been in the middle of nowhere with no one to respond and needed something documented correctly.

"Why did the FBI send a different agent this time?" Anderson asked, giving her a frank look.

Mercy had been expecting the question. She squatted next to the clearest boot print she could find and lightly sprayed it with the primer, which would help it show up better in photos. Ideally a cast of the print would be taken, but she didn't carry impression materials because she hadn't mastered the skill. "I've dealt with groups who do things like this, so Portland decided to hand it off. I understand how these groups think . . . as odd as their logic is." She set one of the rulers by the print and took several photos. Then she repeated the action with another boot print that had a different tread.

Mercy had grown up off the grid in Central Oregon. Her family had been preppers, and she'd been surrounded by a lot of antigovernment and anti–law enforcement rhetoric as a child, but her parents had never encouraged violence or destruction. Mercy had left home at eighteen after clashing with her father and eventually become an FBI agent. A federal law enforcement career. A job that went against everything her family believed.

She still wasn't sure if an element of pursuing the job had been getting back at her father.

More than two years ago, she'd been involved in an investigation in Eagle's Nest, Oregon, that had brought her back to her hometown and face-to-face with the family she hadn't spoken with in almost fifteen years.

The investigation had also crossed her path with that of Police Chief Truman Daly. Now her husband.

After patching things up with her family and realizing she wanted to put down roots where she'd grown up, she'd accepted a position with the Bend FBI field office and never looked back.

She was happy and content. Two feelings that had evaded her for years.

Mercy had no tolerance for domestic terrorist groups that used destruction to make their point. The damage to the substation could be fixed, but the surrounding small communities would pay the price by having their lives turned upside down.

"People have faith that when you plug something into an outlet, odds are that it will work," Mercy stated. "And if electricity goes down, they believe it will be fixed as quickly as possible. Most people can't afford to pack up and move into a hotel when their power is out."

She moved to the tire tracks in the snow and sighed. She wasn't a forensics tech. A complete forensics investigation of the tracks would involve multiple measurements to find the spatial relationships among the tires. She decided to focus the best she could on the treads. The vehicle had swung in a circle, giving her clear views of each tire tread. She sprayed long sections of each one, added her rulers and stretched out her tape measure, and then photographed them.

I can't do much more.

"Those who are most at risk are the ones the assholes are trying to influence," said the sheriff. "The shooters want the community angry. And believe me, I've received an earful ever since the power went down last night." He grimaced. "As if I have the ability to fix the substation." He looked at Mercy, a hopeful question in his eyes. "Think this was organized? Part of me hopes it was drunk teens being stupid."

Mercy hadn't ruled out the "drunk teen" possibility. Or the "drunk adult" possibility either.

She took a deep breath. "Two attacks in a month, and there've been other substation attacks across the US. I'm leaning toward organized . . . but I'll look into all possibilities."

"Good." Sheriff Anderson eyed the tire treads. "I wouldn't mind catching these guys in the act. I'd lock them in jail without heat. Tell them the power is out and see how they like it."

The sheriff's cell phone rang, and he took a few steps away. "Anderson," he answered.

Mercy turned to watch the workers weigh the damage. She'd taken all the photos she could and spoken with the BPA office. The tread photos could be used to identify the tire make and show any oddities in the treads, such as depth-of-wear indicators, rocks trapped in the grooves, or noise-treatment characteristics. But unless she had a vehicle to match the treads to, the information wouldn't be immediately helpful.

She also had shells and bullets. But without the weapons to match them to, she was in the same boat—although they might match the ones left at the previous substation attack. At least then she'd be able to confirm the attacks had been made by the same people.

She suspected the best lead would come from the community. Someone would brag. And someone who'd lost power would be annoyed enough to report them.

"Are you *sure*?" Anderson said into his phone. He turned back and met Mercy's curious gaze, his eyes wide. "I'll be there in ten minutes." He appeared stunned as he ended the call.

"Problem?" she asked unnecessarily.

"Yeah." The sheriff put the phone back in his pocket and blew out a deep breath. "Looks like the county got its first murder since I've lived in the area. Guess my luck ran out."

"Need another pair of eyes?" Mercy offered, feeling sorry for the rookie sheriff.

"Would you mind?" he asked, his gaze hopeful. "I'd appreciate it."

"I've got what I need here. Lead the way."

I'll check the murder scene, give him some advice, and then head back to Bend.

4

"There are two other sets of boot prints besides Sara's smaller ones, right?" Detective Noelle Marshall asked Ollie as he studied the back-and-forth tracks that went down the side steps to where the missing SUV had been parked. The covered porch on the cabin had stairs that went straight out from the front door and another set on the side that led to a parking area.

"Yes," said Ollie, feeling the weight of Noelle's and Truman's gazes. "Her tracks only go to the front steps. She didn't walk down these side ones." The two sets of tracks in the deep snow near the SUV's empty spot were evident to him, but he wondered what he'd find inside the cabin. Detective Marshall had said the bloody prints were a jumbled mess.

Thick white flakes had begun to fall. "Dammit!" Detective Marshall swore as she looked up at the sky. "Just what I don't need. Good thing we already took photos out here. I requested a forensics team, but I don't have an ETA yet." Her tone wasn't happy. Some overnight snow had already lightly lined the boot prints, and now there was a chance the prints could disappear for good.

Animal tracks were Ollie's specialty from years of hunting when he lived alone. When he had found human tracks back then, he'd made every effort to avoid contact. He hadn't tracked many humans but had found they were easier than animals. People automatically followed the path of least resistance and left more physical clues behind than deer or rabbits.

"It's pretty obvious," said Ollie. "Two people. Both went up and down the side stairs a few times and over to where I assume the rear passenger door of the SUV was. One eventually circled around the front of the vehicle to get in the driver's door, and the other got in the front passenger door." He pointed at where footprints had created a messy area where he believed the rear door had been. "Looks like it took some maneuvering to get someone—or something—into the vehicle here. Lots of steps in a small area."

Ollie moved his boot close to one of the clearer prints. "I wear a size twelve. These look comparable, so I think it was two men."

"Or a woman wearing a man's boots," added Truman, glancing back at Sara.

Ollie shook his head. "I don't think so. Look at how deep these prints are and compare them to Sara's prints." He pointed at her smaller boot prints, which went to the back of the cabin. "They're much shallower. The wearer weighs less."

"Sara said she circled the cabin calling for her husband," added Noelle. "Her path is pretty obvious. And she said she went searching for him even though there was no sign in the snow that he had walked away from the cabin. She said she was frazzled and scared with no clue what had happened. I already took her boots and other shoes for evidence. Gave her the rubber boots I keep in my vehicle to wear."

"A woman wearing a man's boots and helping to carry her husband's body could make these deeper tracks that lead to the vehicle," Truman pointed out. "The extra weight from the body."

Ollie flushed. "I didn't think of that."

"That's because I'm used to thinking like a criminal." Truman shrugged one shoulder. "You're not."

"True," Ollie admitted. He generally tried to see the best in everyone.

"So I can't rule out the wife yet," said Noelle in a quiet voice.

"Did they rent a car?" Truman asked the detective. "I think they track their vehicles."

"It was the victim's own Jeep Cherokee, so I put out a BOLO for a fifteen-year-old black Cherokee with California plates."

"Where is the vehicle the assumed kidnappers arrived in?" asked Truman.

"That's my question too," said Noelle with a grim frown. "We did an initial search of the area but haven't turned up any evidence of a second vehicle."

She and Truman exchanged a long look, and Ollie wondered what they were thinking.

Think like a criminal.

How would I arrive here and leave no sign?

"Park out on the road—you can tell a few vehicles have gone by—and then walk down the center of the long drive," Ollie said. "Make certain to drive over the footprints as I'm leaving. A little tricky to cover them all, but not impossible."

"Good possibility." Truman nodded at him.

"Or they were inside the cabin from the very beginning," added Ollie. "Came with Sara and her husband."

Noelle pressed her lips together. "My thought too." Her gaze strayed to Sara, several yards away.

That would mean that Sara is involved and lying.

The thought made Ollie uncomfortable. He'd believed her story, but now he was wavering.

The detective took a deep breath and eyed Ollie. "Ready to look inside? You okay with blood?"

He'd seen lots of animal blood—that was no big deal. But the worst time he'd dealt with human blood had been when Mercy's niece Kaylie had been shot by a killer who'd thought she was Mercy. His hands flinched as he remembered his terror and the warm wetness of her blood as he applied pressure to the entry wound on her abdomen.

Kaylie had lived. But Ollie had been convinced she'd die.

Not long before that, he'd found his tutor, Bree Ingram, after she'd been tortured and some of her fingers had been chopped off by a man from her past. Ollie briefly closed his eyes, trying to put the image of Bree's dripping blood out of his mind. Queasiness stirred his stomach.

He noticed Truman watching him closely.

He remembers.

"I'm good," Ollie told the detective, meeting her gaze.

There are no bodies inside. Just blood.

Noelle didn't look confident at his reply but gestured for him to follow her up the steps to the cabin. He walked along the very edge, automatically avoiding the boot prints left on the snowy stairs. Some of the prints had faint reddish-brown spots.

Blood.

Earlier his mind had classified the spots as dirt.

Ollie followed, Truman behind him. At the top she handed them blue cloth booties, and he slid them on.

"Here are some gloves, too, but I don't want you touching *anything*, got it?" Her dark-blue gaze held his.

"Yes, ma'am—Detective."

Why did I say that?

Truman snorted. "You're making him nervous, Noelle."

"Good." She grimaced at Truman. "You convinced me to have a kid look at evidence. I'm the one who should be nervous. I'll probably lose my job."

Ollie straightened. "I don't want you to lose your job. I don't need to look." He moved his gaze from her to Truman.

Noelle tilted her head as she studied him. "My brain hurts from studying the tracks inside. I feel like there's something I'm not seeing.

Usually the forensics techs help me see patterns, but who knows when they'll get here, so for now I'm using you two."

"Been there," said Truman. "We'll look for a few minutes and not touch anything."

Noelle opened the cabin door and stepped inside. Ollie paused at the threshold.

That smell.

The metallic scent of blood. A hum sounded in his ears.

He looked back at Sara. Several yards away she stood next to the deputy, watching them, her face expressionless.

Do I believe her?

Besides the scent of blood, the cabin smelled a little musty, but it appeared well cared for inside. The owner had painted the A-frame walls white but left the supporting beams with a simple clear varnish. It helped brighten the cabin, which was surrounded by fir trees. The building was one big room with stairs on the left that went up to a partial loft. Through the loft's railings, Ollie could see the side of an unmade bed.

In the center of the main room was a large woodstove. Its black pipe chimney passed through the loft to exit through the angled walls. Against the back wall was a tiny kitchen with cheerful blue cabinets. Two small couches with yellow and blue throw pillows and a huge braided rug sat in the center of the big room. The only sound within the cabin was the occasional creak of floorboards beneath their feet.

The cabin would feel inviting if not for the copious amounts of blood covering the wooden floor near the stove and on the rug. Bloody tracks and large, long smears led to the door. Ollie placed his feet carefully, avoiding the blood. Most of it had dried to a rust brown, but thicker red spots reflected the light. He knew they would be gooey if touched.

He swallowed hard, keeping his gaze down and avoiding eye contact with Truman and the detective as his ears continued to buzz.

He immediately spotted two sets of boot prints and some barefoot prints.

Clearly there had been a struggle near the woodstove. Smudged prints and wide swaths of smeared blood covered the floor. He could make out handprints in the blood too. Grasping, searching, struggling handprints and streaks.

He fought back.

"If the two kidnappers were working with Sara, then why did she stay behind?" Truman asked in a quiet voice. "She could have vanished along with them instead of facing the police."

"Maybe they refused to take her," said Noelle. "Double-crossed her."

"If that had been done to me, I'd tell the police as much as possible, so they would catch them," said Ollie.

"But that would incriminate you. You can't explain the two men without admitting you were involved," said Noelle.

"Easier to deny everything from the beginning," added Truman. He looked up at the loft. "I assume that's where Sara slept. How could you not hear a struggle down here?"

"There's no blood on the stairs or in the loft," said Noelle. "If Sara isn't involved, then the attack happened down here. Even the heaviest sleeper would wake if someone was attacked next to them as they slept."

"What's that fuzzy noise?" asked Truman, looking around. "Is it from the kitchen?"

"A thing by the bed upstairs," said the detective. "I think it's a white noise machine."

"I thought my ears were ringing," admitted Ollie. The sound reminded him of a *Star Trek* episode. It was like the constant low background noise of the *Enterprise* passing through space.

Now it was all he could hear.

"Can it be turned off?" asked Truman, scratching in one ear with a finger.

The detective jogged up the stairs. The noise stopped, to Ollie's great relief.

"I didn't notice before," said Noelle as she came down the stairs. "But there are little foam earplugs on the nightstand behind the white noise machine. Looks like someone snores."

"If the snorer was Rob, that might explain why Sara didn't hear a struggle down here," said Truman.

"Or was it someone planning ahead?" countered Noelle. "Creating reasons the attack couldn't be heard?"

Every discovery raises more questions.

Ollie refocused on the blood, specifically the bare footprints. They were all partial prints with no rhyme or reason, as if someone barefoot had been struggling. Lots of smears with toe prints as if he had been trying to get a purchase. Ollie studied one large spot, convinced he was looking at a texture from fabric. Maybe the victim's shirt or pants.

Ollie maneuvered past the stove and squatted to shine his cell phone's flashlight on a dried round spot. "I think this is a toe print. It's got the patterning you'd expect from the skin of a toe." A couple of feet away was another, more faint. He followed the occasional fading spots into the kitchen. "Based on the short stride length, I'd assume it's Sara. Looks like she tried not to step in the blood but couldn't completely avoid it." He looked at Noelle. "Do you know how tall her husband is?"

"I'll ask." The detective headed outside.

"Can you tell where she went in the kitchen?" asked Truman.

"No. This is the last print I can make out," Ollie said, pointing at an almost invisible print where the wooden flooring changed to the kitchen's linoleum. He studied the tiny kitchen. It was pristine. No blood. He rejoined Truman near the woodstove, keeping his gaze on the floor. "Even though she's small, she could have leaped over most of this when she came out of the kitchen," Ollie said, demonstrating with an easy jump of his own. He walked toward the front door, which Noelle had left open. Beside it were a series of hooks for jackets and a shoe tray with a man's pair of heavy boots.

Ollie bent over near the tray, staring at a light blood smear on the wooden floor. "Possible heel print?" He traced his steps back to the heavier mass of blood smears and pointed near its edge. "That's a bare heel. And it's on top of the long, bloody skid that leads to the door—which I assume is from Rob being dragged. If the heel print is Sara's, Rob had already been dragged out. I think she came out of the kitchen, leaped over the blood, but caught some with her heel and then put on boots by the door."

Truman crouched next to him, using his own cell phone's light. "The question is, Was that immediately after they took Rob away or hours later?"

"I think the struggling bare footprints in the blood are the victim's. They're big like a man's foot," said Ollie. "And there are only two sets of boot prints. I guess one set could be Rob's, which would mean he walked to the Jeep—which doesn't make a lot of sense, considering it appears he was dragged out of the cabin."

"Maybe it's not Rob's blood," said Truman. "Could be one of the men we're assuming attacked him. Maybe Rob held a gun on the second attacker and made him drive away with the bloody first attacker in the back seat."

Ollie stared at him. "But Rob's boots are still here."

"How do you know they're his?" asked Truman, playing devil's advocate.

"That would indicate Rob knew what was happening . . . and either Sara is in on it or clueless." Ollie frowned. "I'm starting to not like it when you bring up different angles."

"Welcome to police work."

"Rob is six foot one," said Noelle as she reentered the cabin. "And Sara added that he's around a hundred and sixty pounds. That'd make him pretty slender, right?"

"Yes," said Truman. "Did Sara have socks on when you took her boots for evidence?"

"No. She was barefoot. It would make sense if she pulled on her boots and dashed outside."

"Did you notice blood on her feet?" asked Truman.

"I didn't think to look. I don't remember anything obvious."

"How did your boots fit her?" asked Ollie.

"She's swimming in them. Tiny feet. I wear a size nine. She's probably a six or even smaller."

Ollie knew nothing about women's shoe sizes but gleaned enough from Noelle's comment to be certain that the large partial footprints that appeared to slide in the big mass of blood weren't Sara's.

"I believe two attackers in boots carried out Rob," said Ollie. "Why would an attacker be barefoot? I think Rob made the struggling barefoot prints. Sara passed through the scene later. Her few small prints are faint and inconsistent because a lot of Rob's blood had already dried." He looked at Noelle. "That's my amateur opinion."

She nodded, her gaze still on the blood.

Truman gave him a discreet thumbs-up.

Ollie's stomach churned as he looked again at the scene where something horrible and violent had happened.

Maybe law enforcement isn't for me.

5

It wasn't the most gruesome murder scene Mercy had seen. In fact it was relatively mild.

The male victim lay on the Columbia River's rocky shore several miles east of The Dalles. Mercy suspected he was in his forties or fifties. It was hard to tell because he lay on his side, half his face pressed into the rocky bank, and Mercy didn't want to move him until the ME had taken a look. His arms were tied behind his back, and there was a cloth gag in his mouth. He was dressed in boxer shorts and a white T-shirt. His throat had been slit.

A large X of black electrical tape covered his mouth.

The scene was at the bottom of the sloped riverbank, adjacent to a steep boat ramp, and a small crowd of onlookers had shown up to gawk. A few boats dotted the river despite the cold temperatures.

The body had been discovered by two thirteen-year-old boys who had ridden their bikes to the boat ramp's dirt parking area and rigged some jumps with boards. One of the boys had wiped out in some nearby brush, rolled down the hill, and come face-to-face with the body.

Now the two boys waited up top with their parents, unable to see Mercy, Sheriff Anderson, and the two Wasco County deputies as they studied the scene. When the deputies had first arrived, they'd moved all the onlookers up the bank and behind the brush so they couldn't see the body.

But the ones who'd arrived early had gotten an eyeful.

Mercy noted that although there was plenty of blood on the dead man's shirt and boxers, there was no blood on the rocky beach around the victim. Wherever he'd been killed, it hadn't been in that exact spot. Anderson had one of the deputies working a small grid pattern of the immediate area, scanning for evidence and blood.

The second deputy was taking photos. He'd started wide, taking shots of the entire scene as he walked in a circle, slowly working his way closer to the body, getting every angle. As he got closer, he zoomed in on details. Mercy had watched him for a few minutes, pleased that he was so thorough. Anderson had told her he didn't have the budget for forensics technicians in his small county, so his deputies were continually educated about preserving crime scenes and collecting evidence.

No ID had been found near or on the body. None of the onlookers had stepped forward to say they knew the man.

"Thoughts?" the sheriff asked her as they studied the body.

"I wish there were some homes or businesses nearby. Some camera views of passing traffic would come in handy," she answered. "With the lack of blood near him, I believe he's been dumped, but did they originally intend to put him in the river? His clothes are dry. Possibly they planned to come back with a boat and sink him out in the water. This riverbank seems an odd place to leave a body; it's exposed to anyone on the water or using the ramp. Most people would attempt to hide it. Maybe the boys showing up interrupted their plan."

"It's risky to plan to return," said the sheriff.

"They might have had no choice."

"What do you think of the black tape on his mouth?"

"It's personal," Mercy said slowly. "I doubt it was placed when he was alive because it wouldn't have stopped him from speaking or making noise—a gag would be needed for that. Or else a few strips of duct tape.

I suspect it was placed after he was dead. The killer making a point—I don't know if it was a point about the victim or making a point to us."

Anderson nodded. "My thoughts too. Might tie in with leaving him in his underwear. That feels deliberate or maybe even unnecessary. The tape is obviously unnecessary."

When they'd arrived at the scene, she'd asked one of the deputies to photograph the license plates of the vehicles and boat trailers in the parking area. And then to get the best pictures he could of the nearby boats in the Columbia River and of any other boats that passed. Possibly the killer was sitting in one of the boats, frustrated that they hadn't returned to the dump site before the police arrived.

"How long do you think he's been here?" Anderson asked.

"I'm no medical examiner, and the cold temperatures will have slowed down any decomposition, but frankly I think he was probably murdered last night—maybe at some point overnight. He looks . . . fresh." She stumbled over the word, wishing a better one had come to mind.

Sheriff Anderson made a pained expression at her word choice. "I'd thought the same thing."

The boats on the river seemed to have moved closer, and Mercy spotted a man on one with binoculars pointed their way. The sheriff followed her gaze and moved to stand between the body and the water, trying to block the boaters' views.

"I really want to cover him up, but I know that risks destroying evidence," Anderson stated.

"If you could rig a screen of some sort to block the view from the water, that would work."

"I don't have anything in my vehicle to do that. At least the brush and bank block the view for the people up top." The sheriff checked the time. "The ME won't be here for another hour." He turned to the photographing deputy. "Take my spot. Try to keep the boaters' views to a minimum. We're going to talk to some people." Then he trudged up the bank, Mercy behind him.

"The old-timer in the blue cap looks like he has something to say," said Mercy in a low voice as they crested the rise. He hadn't been there when they arrived and now pushed to the front of the small group of people, an expectant expression on his face.

"I want to talk to the boys again first," said Anderson. "Then we can send them home."

"Look at the two women with the dog," said Mercy, watching them from the corner of her eye. "They seem like the type to notice everything that's going on. I'll start with them. You take the boys."

"Sheriff!" The man in the blue cap waved.

"I'll be with you in a minute," Anderson said as he strode toward the boys and their two sets of parents.

In spite of his cap, thick white beard, and mustache, Mercy could see the annoyance and impatience of the man who'd tried to stop Anderson. She joined the two women standing apart from the small group. One held a white Pomeranian in her arms. Mercy was amused to see the dog wore a pink jacket and booties. The women appeared to be in their seventies or eighties and were heavily bundled up in matching coats against the cold but wore running shoes instead of winter boots. They were nearly identical in face and build, making Mercy wonder if they were twins.

"Good morning, ladies. I'm Special Agent Kilpatrick. Can you—"

"The FBI?" The woman who spoke wore bright-red lipstick that stood out sharply against her pale skin and white hair. "Was he a wanted man? Do you think he's the victim of a serial killer?" Her gaze was eager and deeply curious.

"Let her speak, Marjorie!" The woman holding the Pom nudged her in the shoulder. "I told you not to jump to conclusions."

"I watch TV. I read books," stated Marjorie, glaring at the other woman. "I know the FBI doesn't show up unless something big is going on." She turned back to Mercy. "What happened?"

"Someone has died," Mercy said, keeping her answer vague, still wondering if they were twins. The woman with the dog didn't wear lipstick, but she did wear startlingly thick fake eyelashes that almost reached her eyebrows. "Do the two of you live nearby? Have you seen anything odd happen around here in the last twenty-four hours?"

"We live exactly seven-eighths of a mile away," stated Marjorie. "We walk down here every day. Cold weather doesn't keep us from our walks."

"Unless there is heavy snow or ice," added the woman holding the dog. "We don't walk in that."

"That's true," Marjorie reluctantly admitted while shooting a glare at her for the small contradiction. "But that's rare. We've only had one ice storm, and this is the most snow we've had so far this winter."

"But there was that year where we couldn't walk for two weeks, remember that?"

"Yes, but—"

"Ladies, I'd appreciate it if you'd tell me if you've noticed anything unusual in the area." Mercy figured that if she didn't put a halt to their tangent, they'd continue arguing.

"Those two." Marjorie jerked her head at the two young boys talking with Sheriff Anderson. "They're going to kill themselves riding their bikes off those ramps they built. You can hear their shouts almost all the way to the house. I should have a talk with their parents." She shook her head and clucked her tongue. "Kids these days."

"Kids these days," echoed the other woman.

Mercy eyed the homemade bike ramps. They were less than a foot high. Her brothers had built ones that were easily five feet high when they were the boys' age. Owen had broken his arm and twice broken his collarbone.

"No unusual adult activity?"

The two women exchanged a pointed glance. "We came across Dean Porter parked down here in his pickup the other day." Marjorie leaned closer to Mercy, her eyes serious. "The woman he was kissing wasn't his wife," she said in a loud whisper.

"Not his wife," repeated the other.

Mercy wished she'd interviewed the man in the blue cap first. She handed the women a business card and wrote down their full names and phone numbers and was pleased to learn her guess about them being twins had been correct. "Contact me if you think of anything else."

"Aren't you going to tell us what happened?" Marjorie's eyebrows arched.

"We don't know what happened yet," said Mercy. "You two enjoy the rest of your walk." With a smile she left them and headed to the impatient man in the hat.

"Good morning, I'm—"

"I need to talk to the sheriff." He pressed his lips in a tight line, his pale-blue eyes dismissing her as he eyed Anderson, who was still speaking with the boys and their parents.

Mercy bit back her annoyance. "I'm Special Agent Kilpatrick." She showed him her ID.

His gaze flew to the identification as his mouth formed an O. "I thought you were the sheriff's assistant."

"No," Mercy said firmly.

I knew I should have worn my FBI jacket.

"What did you want to tell the sheriff? Did you see what happened?"

"I didn't see anything. But I heard those boys found a body at the water. Made me curious."

"News travels fast," Mercy commented.

"Not much happens around here," he told her. "So when it does, people talk."

Mercy was about to end the discussion. The man was simply a nosy local.

He stepped closer, and she could see every crazy hair in his thick white eyebrows. Beneath them, his eyes were worried. "I heard it's a male. Is that true? How old?"

He'd moved into her personal space, so she took a half step back. "Yes, it's a man. Probably in his forties or fifties. We don't have an identification."

He seemed to deflate. "Not a teenager?"

"No. Is someone missing?" she asked sharply.

"Not that I know of . . . Just wondered if it was happening again."

Her senses went on alert. "What was happening again?"

"Well, it's been a long time." He scratched his beard. "Any chance this person is tied up in their underwear and their throat has been cut?"

Mercy blinked.

He heard that through the gossip.

His eyes lit up as he searched her face. "I'm right! And believe me, no one told me *anything* about him! I'd only heard that there was a murdered man on the banks. But he's not the first dead person to be found in that same spot just like that. Those two sisters didn't mention that?" He jerked his head at the women she'd just spoken with. "They lived here back then. Maybe it slipped their minds."

I sense he's being honest.

"When . . . Who?" Mercy's brain spun.

He scratched at his beard as he thought. "It's probably been twenty years now since those five teenagers vanished one night. Two of them were found right on this bank. Only one of them was dead, though . . . and the other three kids were never found. You really need to do your research," he added with a frown. "I expected more from the FBI."

"Excuse me a minute." Mercy headed toward the sheriff as she ran a quick Google search on her phone. She halted, staring at her screen.

The man hadn't lied.

6

"I used to teach English at the high school in The Dalles," the older man with the white beard told Mercy and Sheriff Anderson after they sent the small crowd of curious onlookers away. His name was Ted Weir, and he sat on the bumper of the sheriff's SUV, his coat pulled tightly around him. "I knew all the kids in our school. Whenever something happened with teenagers, I paid attention."

"But the missing five teens weren't from around here," said Mercy. "They were from the Bend area."

My area.

After verifying Ted's comment about the teens found in the exact same spot and situation as their victim, Mercy had given the sheriff a quick update, and they'd pulled Ted aside for an interview. Mercy had found that online information about the old murder was sparse. Most of the articles simply repeated the same facts over and over. The case had long gone cold.

"That's true they weren't from here," said Ted. "But teachers tune in when something big happens to kids, even outside our circles. We want to prevent it from happening to *our* kids or at least learn from the tragedy. It was a big mystery how those five teenagers disappeared. They'd gone on a camping trip—I think it was for high school graduation. And it's *still* a mystery since only two of those five ever turned up, one dead and the other claiming to have no memory of what happened." He leaned closer to Mercy. "I believed the poor teenager who survived. His mother said he was completely different than when he vanished. I can still picture her crying on TV. I felt bad for her, but at least she got her son back. Three other families still don't know what happened to their kids." He paused and rubbed the back of his neck, looking thoughtful. "I think I read that the survivor died a couple of years ago. I don't recall that any of the others have turned up. It was twenty years ago, so I coulda missed an update here or there."

Mercy had a sense of déjà vu while she listened to Ted speak. She would have been around fourteen when it happened, so she could have read about it or heard about it on the news at some point.

Maybe I read about this cold case at work?

Missing kids fell under the FBI's investigative umbrella.

She was pretty sure she'd heard the story before. The disappearance of five local teenagers would catch anyone's attention, but the element that two of the teenagers had shown up on the banks of the Columbia River wasn't familiar. Mercy was eager to dig through the old investigative reports, but first she wanted to hear what else Ted Weir remembered.

"Let me get this straight," asked Anderson. "You came down this morning because you heard that there was a dead body on the banks, and it reminded you of when two teens were found in that exact spot twenty years ago?"

"Yes, sir," said Ted. "It's the sort of story that sticks with you. Not much happens around here."

Sheriff Anderson shifted his feet, and Mercy suspected he was wishing less had happened that day. Between the substation attack and a murder, his plate was overflowing. She doubted he had more than six or seven deputies, and without detectives, he had to take the lead on important investigations. Truman had the same problem in Eagle's

Nest. Tiny department. Tight funds. But at least he could reach out to the Deschutes County Sheriff's Department for assistance. It was a good-size department and could lend manpower or forensic services.

"What do you remember about the two boys that were found?" Mercy asked Ted.

"Like I said. Tied up. Wearing nothing but underwear. Throats slit and lying almost exactly where you found that poor man today." Ted's gaze went past Mercy, his eyes distant as he remembered. "It's a miracle the second boy wasn't dead. Probably would have been in a few more hours. The important blood vessels in the neck had been missed. The murderer had tried, and the survivor definitely lost a good amount of blood, but not the way the dead boy had. The survivor probably passed out from the shock, and the killer thought he was dead."

Mercy wanted to ask if he remembered whether they'd had tape over their mouths but decided to hold back. She didn't want that fact entering the gossip chain. It might come in handy later.

A black SUV pulled into the parking area, and Mercy was pleased to see medical examiner Dr. Natasha Lockhart behind the wheel. Mercy and the sheriff gave Ted their cards along with the usual spiel that he might hear from them later and that he should call if he thought of anything relevant.

"Do you know Dr. Lockhart?" Mercy asked Anderson as they crossed to the SUV.

"I met her once when a child drowned." The sheriff kept his eyes straight ahead, and Mercy sympathized. Children's deaths were the hardest.

The petite medical examiner was getting gear out of the back of her vehicle when the two reached her. "Afternoon, Mercy. Sheriff Anderson." Dr. Lockhart hefted a bag and shut the rear hatch. "Damn, it's cold. The wind is making it ten times worse. What do you have for me?"

The sheriff led them down the ramp and several yards east to the scene.

"How's that husband of yours?" the ME whispered to Mercy as they tailed the sheriff.

Mercy grinned at her. "Truman's good."

"Isn't your first wedding anniversary this month?"

"Yes."

Natasha sighed. "I still haven't met someone who isn't bothered by what I do. Most vanish two seconds after they hear I cut up bodies for a living."

"I can understand that," Anderson said sourly as he trudged along the bank, his back to the women.

Mercy met the ME's amused brown gaze and tried not to snort.

Not appropriate to laugh when there is a murdered man nearby.

But the three of them were in careers that dealt with the ugly and horrid side of human life almost every day. Talking about normal things while facing rough scenes helped them keep their sanity. Witnessing the horrors that humans did to one another built up inside. Letting off steam was necessary.

Mercy knew law enforcement officers who had been exposed over and over to the frailty of the human body. It created a sucking hole inside them, affecting other parts of their lives. One was a crash investigator who had attended more than sixty fatal vehicle accidents over a number of months. Every time she caught up with him, he seemed more easily angered and more distant, his walls growing higher. His job wasn't supposed to have him attending so many fatals in a short time. But there was a shortage of law enforcement personnel, and someone had to show up.

Mercy couldn't imagine the real-life nightmares he'd seen, over and over.

Shit like that rotted the soul.

She liked Dr. Lockhart. The ME was about her age and was sharp and always upbeat. Mercy felt she had a healthy outlook for someone who dealt with the macabre every day.

They reached the deputy standing guard near the body. "Jerks," he said with a tip of his head toward the boats on the water. There were fewer now, but they'd moved closer. The second deputy was still searching the area but had progressed much farther down the beach.

Dr. Lockhart circled the body, taking her own photos as Mercy and Anderson silently watched. She squatted and felt his limbs, checking the joints' ranges of movement. She gently probed the wound across his neck, peering closely, and nodded to herself as if she'd seen what she expected. She gently touched the tape over his mouth but left it alone. Her fingers rapidly ran across the victim's skull, palpating and exploring, and then slid between his head and the beach, and she froze with a small catch in her breath. She frowned and felt the rest of his skull again, slower this time, taking care to feel every square centimeter.

Mercy saw dark, sticky blood on one finger of her glove that hadn't been there a few moments before.

"Help me lift the head and shoulders a bit," Dr. Lockhart directed the deputy as she took a small flashlight from her bag. It was impossible to roll the body onto his back with his hands tied behind him. Mercy and Anderson moved to stand behind the ME, wanting to see from her point of view.

The deputy knelt and levered up the victim's shoulders while the doctor balanced his head and pointed the flashlight. The body was stiff and in full rigor.

A mass of dried blood coated the right side of his head, his blond hair in thick clumps. She nodded at the deputy and eased the head back to the ground.

"They got him twice," said Dr. Lockhart. "The cut throat and a gunshot to his right temple."

"He was shot?" Anderson blurted in surprise.

Mercy was surprised too. The way the victim had been left, on his side, there had been no sign of a gunshot wound. The blood in his hair she'd attributed to the damage to his throat.

"I can't find an exit wound," said Dr. Lockhart. "And the entry is tiny. Most likely a small caliber and the bullet is still inside. I've seen it happen several times."

"How long has he been dead?" the sheriff asked bluntly.

"Why does everyone ask that?" the doctor asked in a sarcastic tone, with a gentle smile to take the sting out of her comeback. "Rigor is set, but I'll look up the temperatures for the last twenty-four hours and—"

"Cold," said the sheriff. "Too damn cold right next to the water."

"But he wasn't killed right here," added the ME, gesturing to the lack of blood on the ground. "So you need to keep that in mind. I'll take a liver temperature and give you a window. Give me a minute."

Mercy stood and stretched her thigh. She'd been shot in the leg more than a year and a half ago, and her muscles had instantly ached when the ME said "gunshot." She watched the sheriff's face as the doctor lifted the victim's shirt to make a quick cut and slide a thermometer into his liver. He was stoic, his gaze never leaving the doctor's hands.

I wonder if he's ever seen that done before.

Anderson had formed a favorable impression with Mercy. He'd shown concern for his residents and didn't let his ego get in the way of her assistance. He'd had two investigations dumped on his plate that day and was taking them in stride.

Dr. Lockhart removed her gloves, set them on the body, and then started tapping on her cell phone. Mercy saw she was checking the overnight temperatures and then doing some quick calculations.

"I estimate he died between eight p.m. and two a.m.," said the ME. "But don't quote me until I run some labs and get a firmer window," she added with a direct gaze at the sheriff. He nodded in understanding.

A chime came from the doctor's phone, and she opened a text. "Transport's here. Can you give him a hand with his equipment?" she asked the deputy.

"When can you do his autopsy?" asked Anderson.

"I believe I can do it tomorrow morning. At the very latest, the following morning."

Impatience rolled off the sheriff as he turned to Mercy. "Can I request assistance from the FBI? After speaking with Ted, I feel like this case might be bigger than it appears."

Mercy agreed. "Especially if this involves children. We'll be more than interested in helping." She'd take the case straight to her supervisor. And make certain she was assigned. She was itching to dig into the details of the disappearances and murder.

"Children?" asked Anderson. "The two found were probably eighteen since it happened near their high school graduation."

"Still kids in my definition. And it's a cold case. Time to get some fresh eyes on it."

Anderson held her gaze as he pointed at the body at their feet. "*This* death is the one I specifically want assistance with."

"Absolutely," said Mercy. "But I agree with you . . . I think we're going to find a bigger case here than we expected."

7

It overtakes my dreams.

That haziness. The confusion. Their faces.

Are they friends? Or enemies?

I think I know them.

But I'm scared for them. I'm scared for myself.

Then suddenly they're gone. All of them. And I know something horrible has happened to everyone.

Is it my fault?

Tall, tall trees. Pines, I think. I smell dry, dusty dirt.

Is it possible to smell in a dream?

I remember beer. Joints. Doritos.

Then I see Colin. He's furious. No, he's terrified. He's both.

He's screaming at me, telling me to stop lying.

Lying about what?

I should know. It's important.

He grabs my arms, his eyes wide as he shakes and shakes me.

Don't tell anyone, he screams.

I promise over and over that I'll never tell. And he slowly backs away, his angry gaze holding mine. I'm petrified but also overwhelmingly gratified that I recognize him.

I know him.

I surge awake, pulling myself out of the familiar nightmare.

The pain in my head is crippling, and I fumble in the dark for my pills and the ever-present water bottle on my nightstand. I swing my legs out of bed and sit there, trying to slow my heart and breaths so I can take the pills.

It's pitch-black outside and in my room, but I don't want a light. The light will destroy the dream remnants that still spin in the dark. I want to hold on to them as long as possible, but they inevitably fade as I stare into the dark.

And I'm left empty.

I dig two pills out of the vial, pop them in my mouth, and take a swig of tepid water as I try to pull up the images in my brain, but it won't cooperate.

"Colin." I say his name out loud. I can't see his face anymore, but I know his name.

I keep their photos buried in a box in my closet. I could look at his photo if I wanted.

I don't want to.

My heart continues to pound, and I take deep breaths. Anxiety races through my nerves.

Always anxious. Always. It never stops.

I have many prescriptions to fight it, but it's never fully gone.

It's always under my skin, ready to jump out.

Human faces are my biggest triggers.

It's hard to venture outside when the world is so full of strangers.

I never know who wants to hurt me.

8

As Truman drove back to Eagle's Nest, he called Mercy.

After leaving the bloody cabin crime scene, he'd reached an area of cell service and his phone had lit up with texts. Three from Mercy.

She'd been checking in, and her texts hadn't carried a concerned tone, but Truman knew she had been worried because she couldn't pinpoint his location on the phone app their family of four used to keep tabs on each other. It wasn't perfect, and Central Oregon had a lot of data black holes, but it gave some peace of mind.

Mercy had vanished the previous summer. The app had shown Truman her last known position, most likely saving her life.

No one in their family complained about the lack of privacy.

"Good morn—no, good afternoon." Mercy's voice sounded through the speakers in his vehicle. He knew she was also driving. He'd checked her location before calling and seen she was on the highway heading south from the Columbia River toward Bend.

"I just got your texts," he told her. "I was with Ollie, and you know how that area is."

"You went snowmobiling with Ollie?" she asked.

"No. Little snowmobiling got done. That kid had quite the morning." Truman told her how Sara Newton had flagged down Ollie, and then the news about her missing spouse and the bloody scene in the cabin.

"The husband is still missing?" Mercy asked sharply. "What's he look like?"

"Six one. Thin. Blond hair. He's thirty-nine."

"Shit. I think I found his body in The Dalles this morning. My John Doe ticks all those boxes. I'll call Detective Marshall."

Shock rolled through Truman. "You found a body? At the substation?" He knew she'd headed out of town to look at the damage.

"No. Wasco County's Sheriff Anderson got a call while I was with him, and I went along for support. He'd never dealt with a murder before."

"It's a small county," Truman admitted.

"I'm going to tell Jeff that the FBI needs to assist on the murder case. Anderson's department doesn't have many resources," Mercy said. "The weird thing is this body was found in the same location and position as two teenagers years ago, and those kids are a cold case linked to three more missing teens."

Truman didn't know what to say as his mind absorbed that the missing podcaster had turned up on Mercy's watch.

Maybe it's not him.

"Is Ollie okay?" asked Mercy. "He has a knack for stumbling into odd situations."

Truman agreed. Some people attracted predicaments while minding their own business. Ollie had experienced more than his fair share of surprises.

"Yeah, he's holding up. Detective Marshall utilized some of his tracking skills, and I think he was proud of that."

"Have you had *the discussion* with him yet?" Mercy asked.

He grimaced. "Not yet. I will. This morning didn't present the right time."

Truman was nervous about having *the discussion*. Ever since Ollie had come to live with him, Truman had made it his mission to find a record of the young man's parents. Ollie's grandparents had told him his parents died in a car accident when he was three. Truman had searched police records and newspapers, seeking a reference to the accident. Or any trail of Ollie's parents.

And come up empty.

Several factors made the search difficult. The first was that Ollie's last name was Smith—or so he'd been told. His parents' names had been David and Kathy Smith—or so he'd been told.

Truman couldn't find a record of either person. There were lots of David Smiths and Kathy Smiths, even some who were married to each other, but they weren't in the right age range or hadn't died in a car accident or weren't related to William Smith, Ollie's grandfather.

Truman suspected Smith wasn't Ollie's last name—or anyone's last name in his family. Ollie's grandfather had been a sovereign citizen. They were notorious for believing that they were not citizens of the United States and were above all its laws. Many changed their identities. It wouldn't surprise Truman one bit to learn that everything Ollie had been told about his relatives' identities was untrue.

He'd updated Ollie every time his search hit a dead end. The teen had wanted to hear about every avenue Truman was pursuing. But Truman swore Ollie's gaze grew more distant and he asked fewer questions with each update. Truman had started to keep the results to himself. The teenager didn't need to hear of each failure.

Ollie wouldn't talk about his feelings on the topic. Both Truman and Mercy had gently prodded but been rebuffed. "It doesn't matter," Ollie said after every dead end. "You're my family now."

It hurt Truman's heart.

A year ago, a plan had sprouted in his mind—something he wanted to do very badly, but he'd always been too nervous to approach Ollie about it. At first Truman had wanted to wait until he found a record and hopefully some pictures of Ollie's parents. But it appeared that might never happen.

Now he worried Ollie would think he was suggesting it because Truman felt sorry for him.

That couldn't be further from the truth.

Ollie was his son in every way but a legal one. And Truman wanted to adopt him.

He's practically a man.

Truman didn't care. He loved Ollie, and this was a way of showing him.

But he found it hard to raise the issue in light of the unknowns about his birth family.

"You need to ask Ollie about adoption," Mercy said. "I know he's going to be thrilled you want to do it. He's family."

"What about Kaylie?" asked Truman.

"That's different. My niece belongs to me, and she knows it," said Mercy. "We've always been Kilpatricks." Kaylie's father's dying wish had been for Mercy to take care of his daughter.

She's done a damn fine job of it.

"Kaylie has asked me a few times if you planned to adopt Ollie," said Mercy.

"She has? I didn't know that. Do you think Ollie brought it up with her?"

"I asked her. She said he hadn't."

"Maybe I should wait until the DNA results come back."

Am I procrastinating?

Truman didn't understand why he might be stalling. He wanted more than anything for the boy to legally be connected to him. He and Mercy had agreed they didn't want to have kids, so there wasn't going to be another son or daughter.

Ollie and Kaylie were their kids.

"I hope we're doing the right thing with the DNA," said Mercy.

The remains of Ollie's grandfather had been recovered the previous year. He'd been murdered by other sovereign citizens and buried on their property along with two other victims. When Truman's search for Ollie's parents kept coming up empty, he'd requested DNA be extracted from the hard tissue samples kept by the lab and compared to Ollie's.

The empty search for Ollie's parents had made Truman wonder if he was even on the right track. So he'd gone to the source of what Ollie knew about his history: the grandfather.

Truman had taken cheek swabs from Ollie and Kaylie at the same time. When they'd asked what he needed it for, he'd simply said, "You never know." The teenagers had exchanged a look and asked no more questions. Living in a law enforcement family had made extra precautions commonplace. "Maybe you should look into those trackers they implant under the skin," Kaylie had joked.

It's not the worst idea.

Truman had thrown away Kaylie's swab and sent Ollie's to be compared to the DNA extracted from his grandfather's tooth.

He felt guilty about going behind Ollie's back. He was toeing an ethical line—he'd probably blasted right over it. But if he turned out to be wrong about the DNA, he didn't want Ollie waiting several months to only be disappointed.

"Do you want me there when you talk to him?" asked Mercy.

"Will you be offended if I say no?"

She laughed. "Absolutely not. I know this is between you two. I'd wondered if you needed moral support."

"No, I need to bite the bullet and do it. Not sure why I've hesitated so much."

"It's not like you're eliminating any of his past or his roots. You're adding to his future and confirming he always has a place with us."

Truman appreciated that she'd said *us*—not just him. "I love you a lot, you know."

"I know. And right back at you. Hey." Her tone went up. "Maybe you could ask Ollie about the adoption on his birthday. It's right around the corner. Your offer would be an amazing present."

"That's a good idea." Truman tried to picture the conversation. "I'd still want to talk to him alone, though. And I don't think of it as an offer; I'll be asking something of him. I wouldn't call it a favor . . . maybe more of a gift. It's almost a present for me."

"No, it's not just for you. It would be special for *both* of you, but I think it's bigger—in a good way—for Ollie than you realize."

Why am I nervous to ask him?

Stop overthinking. Now.

"Don't forget to call Noelle Marshall," Truman told Mercy, changing the subject. "I don't think she could be more stunned than me that you may have found her missing victim."

"Right? What are the odds? I'll call her right now."

They said their goodbyes, and Truman continued to drive back to Eagle's Nest, returning to overthinking and pondering if he should hold his question until Ollie's birthday. He would have the DNA results by then.

I hope my suspicions about his grandfather are wrong.

9

It was almost dinnertime when Mercy met Detective Noelle Marshall in her office. When she'd called Noelle, she'd had to leave a voice mail about the possibility that she'd found her missing victim. Noelle had called back thirty seconds later, asking if Mercy was serious. They'd exchanged information and photos, and both women were convinced that Rob Newton was the dead man on the banks of the Columbia River. She'd asked Mercy to attend her evening interview with Sara Newton but to come early to talk first.

Mercy hung her bag on the back of a chair in Noelle's office and shrugged out of her heavy coat. As she shook hands with the detective, she abruptly remembered Truman's shocked face when Mercy had said she'd like platinum-blonde hair like Noelle's, and the memory triggered a big grin.

"What?" asked Noelle. She gave Mercy a side-eye as she rounded her desk and sat in her own chair.

Noelle's chair wasn't crappy standard department issue. It looked comfy with its soft black leather, headrest, and adjustable arms. The detective must have bought her own.

"I once told Truman that I was considering your hair color. He almost swallowed his tongue."

"Ha!" Noelle gave a wide smile with perfect teeth. "That would be a big change from your black." She leaned forward, a confiding look in her eye. "My real color is a boring dirty blonde. I've been platinum since college." She turned to her computer, still grinning, and slid her keyboard closer. "I've been writing up notes on the Rob Newton investigation for the last hour, so I haven't looked up the case you told me about from two decades ago. I think we need to focus on Rob Newton at the moment anyway." She turned her screen so Mercy could read.

Mercy didn't see anything she hadn't already heard about from Truman. Except that Rob Newton used the pseudonym John Jacobs for his podcast.

"I'll show you his website." Noelle clicked and wrinkled her nose.

Mercy immediately understood Noelle's expression. His site was called *They Were Wrong* and appeared to target lovers of conspiracy theories. As she read the sensational title of each episode, it was clear that Rob loved to tell his audience about "the other side." Most of his episodes were about deaths. Each one exposed alternative theories about what had happened. Noelle clicked on a sample to listen.

Rob's voice was butter. Mercy met Noelle's gaze in surprise. He wasn't the loud and obnoxious shock-jock type Mercy had expected; he sounded professional. His enunciation was perfect and his tone cool and collected.

It was his assertions that were off the wall.

Noelle stopped the sample, a podcast about a solved child abduction in Atlanta, and Mercy ached to hear more. Noelle raised a brow. "What do you think?"

"I think I could listen to him read the phone book."

"Right? He wasn't what I expected either."

"How popular is he?"

"I checked his social media and did some quick Google searches. He's not huge, but he does all right. I noticed a lot of his podcasts cover solved cases, but if you read the summaries for each one, he introduces different angles and shines a light on whether investigations were handled appropriately. I imagine law enforcement doesn't number among his fans."

"I bet he has female fans," said Mercy. "That voice." Her shoulders twitched in reaction. "Where are he and Sara from?"

"They currently live in Bakersfield," said Noelle. "But they're both originally from Oregon. I'm not sure exactly where, but Sara said she had family in Portland. They were doing research here for a podcast."

"Do they make a living doing that?" Mercy asked while scanning the screen.

"Sara said she works remotely for a medical insurance company, so it isn't their only source of income."

Mercy took a closer look at the episode titles, recognizing a few murder cases that had made national news. And been solved. No doubt there were some people unhappy with Rob casting aspersions on the outcomes. "He's had threats in the past?"

"Sara said he's received threats through social media—"

"And I always told him he needed to be cautious. People would say horrible things." Sara Newton finished the sentence in a monotone as she stood in the doorway.

Noelle and Mercy stood simultaneously, but Mercy was closest and offered her hand. "I'm so sorry about your husband." Sara Newton's striking eyes were bloodshot and puffy, her blonde hair loose around her face. She seemed numb. Mercy indicated the chair next to her, and Sara stared at it for a few seconds before she took a seat. Mercy wondered if she was medicated.

"Who brought you here?" she asked Sara, hoping she wasn't driving.

"My aunt. She drove over from Portland a few hours ago. She's in the waiting area." She stared at Mercy blankly. "Who are you?"

Mercy introduced herself.

"You're the FBI agent who might have found Rob." Sara looked at Noelle. "You said you wanted me to identify him from a picture. I can't fully believe it until I see for myself."

Mercy took out her phone. She had a photo of Rob that showed his face from one side. The slit throat had been cropped out and the blood on the other side of his head wasn't visible, but the color of his skin and lips showed he was dead. Mercy's heart was in her throat as she showed the image to Sara.

Sara glanced at the photo and then jerked her gaze away. She drew in a deep breath and held it as she looked again for longer. She closed her eyes and slowly exhaled. "Yes, that's him." She pushed Mercy's hand away and sat back in her chair, tears streaming from her eyes. "What happened?"

Noelle and Mercy exchanged a look. "We aren't sure yet," said Noelle, moving the tissue box on her desk closer to Sara.

Sara took one and wiped her cheeks. "You must know how he died. It had to be bad. I saw the blood in the cabin." Her voice cracked.

Mercy set her hand on one of Sara's, and the woman closed her fingers around it. "We don't have a cause of death from the medical examiner yet, but I can tell you his throat was cut. I saw photos of how much blood was in the cabin and suspect it happened there."

"While I was sleeping? It makes no sense." She looked from Mercy to Noelle, her gaze begging for answers. "How could I not hear someone kill my husband? It looked like a slaughter in the cabin." She pressed her lips together, appearing nauseated.

Noelle reached under her desk, grabbed her garbage can, and brought it around to set next to Sara in case she vomited. Mercy had already taken note of a second garbage can near the office door. She'd seen multiple people vomit during stressful interviews and liked to be prepared.

Noelle leaned against the edge of her desk in front of Sara and Mercy, studying the woman.

"I'm really sorry for your loss," Mercy told Sara, holding her gaze. "I can't imagine what you're going through."

I sort of can.

Her brother Levi had died in her arms after being shot.

"We appreciate you coming to talk with us," added Noelle. "I know this is the last place you want to be and how hard it is to talk about so soon, but we need your help to find out who did this to your husband."

Sara gripped Mercy's hand tightly. "I want to help. Ask me anything. I know your first question is who I think could do this, but my answer is that I don't know. Yes, Rob had people who hated him and threatened him, but to us they were faceless names on the internet. Rob said the messages mostly came from fake accounts. If he was worried about someone in particular, he never mentioned it to me."

"Can you give us access to all his social media accounts and email?" asked Noelle.

"Yes," she answered simply. "I know his passwords."

"What about snail mail? Did he receive any threats by mail? Or phone calls?" Mercy asked gently.

"Not that I know of."

"What about visits to your home? Any problems there?"

Sara blanched. "No. Rob worked hard to protect our privacy. He never told anyone involved with the podcast his real name or where we lived."

"I assume family members and friends knew about his show," said Noelle.

"Yes. People we trust." She blinked rapidly, and Mercy suspected she'd realized someone they'd trusted could have leaked Rob's identity. Or done the crime.

"Someone knew you were here," Mercy prodded. "We'll need a list of everyone who knew you were going to be at that cabin. You said Rob was here researching a story. If you could list who he has talked to in the area, that would be helpful too. I imagine his research notes will also help us know who he's talked to."

Noelle turned to pick up a notepad and pen from her desk and handed them to Sara. "Also list any stores or stops the two of you made since you've been here," she said.

Sara awkwardly held the notepad and pen as if she didn't know what they were for. "We had to be randomly targeted," said Sara, her gaze pleading with Mercy to agree that was what had happened instead of the killer being someone she knew.

"That's always possible, but we need to consider all angles."

The murder seemed personal to Mercy. Rob Newton had been killed and then taken to a specific spot for his body to be dumped. And an X had been placed over his mouth. It made sense now that she knew he was a podcaster. Someone had wanted him to shut up.

Why didn't the killer dump him in the woods?

Why go through the trouble of removing his body from the cabin?

The killers had traveled two and a half hours to leave the body where someone would find it.

It felt like a message.

Was it a message from an angry wife?

Mercy wanted to eliminate Sara as a suspect but hadn't found evidence to do so yet. If Sara was involved, she'd had help. The large boot prints at the cabin indicated two more people. Sara could have been involved and never left the cabin.

"Did you or Rob bring any weapons on this trip?" Mercy asked. "Knives or maybe guns?" So far the knife that had been used to cut Rob's throat hadn't been found. Mercy had deliberately held back that he'd also been shot in the head. She hadn't wanted to pile that information on a grieving widow who'd just heard her husband's throat had been slit.

And she was keeping it quiet in case she needed an ace in the hole to weed out suspects.

Sara shook her head. "We don't own any guns. We have kitchen knives, of course, back home, and there is a set at the cabin, but they're so . . . dull . . ." Sara paled, and Mercy worried she'd vomit this time, but the woman held herself together.

I hope she's not involved.

If she was involved, Sara was a very good actor.

Or a sociopath.

"How is your marriage?" Noelle asked. "Everyone has their ups and downs; how would you categorize yours?"

Sara stared at her, anger simmering in her eyes for the first time. "I know you have to ask that question," she said slowly, never taking her gaze from Noelle. "And I understand you need to eliminate me as a suspect. Our marriage is—was—fine and has lasted fifteen years. It's not perfect, but we were both in love and content. I believe Rob would have answered the same," she said firmly. She bent her head to work on her list.

Mercy and Noelle exchanged a look. Noelle lifted one shoulder the tiniest bit.

She's not positive Sara is involved either.

Sara lifted her head, glancing from Noelle to Mercy, suspicion in her eyes. "Do I need a lawyer?"

"Did you kill your husband?" asked Mercy, sincerity in her tone.

"No!"

Mercy shrugged. "Then a lawyer is up to you."

Get a lawyer!

But Mercy wasn't about to say that. She wanted to interview Sara as much as possible before a lawyer stepped between them and put a halt to the questions. It was a delicate balance. She knew Sara wanted to appear open and helpful to the police. After all, her husband had been murdered.

Rule number one if your spouse has been murdered: get a lawyer.

But Mercy and Noelle weren't legally required to educate their witness.

They also weren't required to tell the truth in interviews, but Mercy tried to anyway. Unless she felt she had no choice or a suspect really pissed her off.

"How was Rob's attitude the last few days?" Noelle asked after Sara had finally written a list of names and places. "Was he nervous about anything? Upset?"

Sara thought for a few seconds. "Not upset. He was excited. He'd wanted to work on this story for a long time. He'd done lots of research, but I think he was mainly excited because he'd lived here when it happened."

"What is the story about?" asked Noelle.

"Missing teenagers. I think it's been about twenty years since five from here vanished while camping."

Mercy's blood pounded in her ears.

Noelle held Sara's gaze, and her hand tightened on the edge of the desk. Mercy knew the detective was struggling to appear as if she'd never heard about the five teenagers.

"Camping?" Noelle asked, using the repeat-the-last-word-as-a-question technique to keep the interviewee talking.

Mercy used it when she couldn't come up with something to ask.

I bet Noelle's brain is spinning as fast as mine.

They both knew Rob Newton had been left in the same place as two of those teens. But neither of them had considered that Rob himself had somehow been involved. Yet.

I'm definitely considering that now.

"Yes," said Sara. "I don't remember exactly where they went camping—it was somewhere near the Columbia River, but the location is in Rob's notes. One of the campers was murdered and another almost died. The other three were never found."

Sara looked at her list and added something. "I forgot I made a Safeway run a few days ago."

Noelle finally met Mercy's gaze, and shock ricocheted between them.

Was Rob killed for something in his research?

10

The next morning Truman swore as his SUV slid on a small patch of ice, catching him off guard. He'd been focused on a mental to-do list, but the Tahoe immediately regained traction. Truman slowed as he continued down the main street of Eagle's Nest, making a mental note to have one of his men gravel the shaded spot. The county was in charge of keeping the tiny town's roads clear in the winter, but it was quicker to have one of his men handle it.

He parked in front of the Eagle's Nest Police Department, noting that Lucas's and Ben's vehicles were present. It was Samuel's day off, so Royce must already be on a call.

I need to hire another officer.

Officer Ben Cooley was in his seventies and still going strong, but the department was already a bit shorthanded, and Truman wanted to be prepared when Ben decided to retire. He'd keep Ben on as long as the man wanted to work. And Truman knew Ben's wife liked having her husband out of the house. The officer moved slower these days, but the community knowledge stored in his brain was priceless.

The department's average number of calls had steadily increased since Truman became chief more than two years ago because Central Oregon had attracted more residents. More people were working from home and had decided that an area with more than two hundred sunny days a year, snow sports in the winter, and tons of summer water sports was the best place to live.

Not to mention it was gorgeous. Snow-topped mountains to the west and high desert to the east. The air smelled cleaner here. Tourists came year round and, to the local residents' dismay, swelled Central Oregon's population, but there was still a good quality of life.

Truman's town of Eagle's Nest wasn't much of a tourist attraction. It was thirty minutes from Bend, where most of the visitors swarmed. In Bend they found good restaurants, an arts and music scene, a wide variety of shopping, and nice hotels. In contrast Eagle's Nest was a former logging town. The mill had closed decades earlier, and now most of its residents were ranchers and farmers. The main street had a couple of diners, a post office, a city hall, a little movie theater, a lovely bed-and-breakfast in an old Victorian home, the tractor dealership—where gossip was a bigger commodity than tractors—and, of course, Kaylie's Coffee Café. The best coffee and baked goods in town.

Besides the coffee shop and the B and B, there weren't any draws for tourists. Truman liked it that way. The previous summer, the town had been overrun with national and international media and treasure seekers from every state when clues to a $2 million treasure hunt had been shared online and Eagle's Nest pinpointed as the jackpot's location.

The crowds had driven Truman nuts.

Truman kicked his boots against the steps to dislodge the packed snow and then strode in the department's front door, unzipping his heavy coat. The comfortable warmth relaxed him, and he lifted his nose and sniffed, looking around. Something smelled like Christmas.

"What do I smell?" he asked Lucas. The burly young man was the most efficient office manager / dispatcher / receptionist he'd ever met. He kept the office—and all the officers—running smoothly. Truman felt lucky to have him and was thankful Lucas had no interest in becoming an officer. He'd be irreplaceable.

"I've got some cinnamon sticks and other spices simmering." Lucas indicated a little hot plate on his desk. "And Sandy brought over that wreath," he said, pointing across the office. "One of the heating vents is blowing on it, making the pine scent even stronger." He considered the cheerful wreath. "It'll dry out faster, but frankly I think the scent is worth it."

Truman agreed as he took off his thick coat.

"Morning, Chief!" Ben appeared from down the hall, three gingerbread men in one hand and a giant cup of coffee in the other.

Truman recognized the cookies as one of Kaylie's seasonal designs at her coffee shop. She kept his department in sugar with her baked experiments and day-old goods.

"Morning, Ben." Truman looked at Lucas. "Where's Royce?"

"He's out at Will Sheridan's place," Lucas told Truman. "Will's missing two horses."

"I told him to check near the creek where it runs through the neighbor's spread," said Ben, speaking through a mouthful of cookie. "They usually turn up there."

"You don't think someone took them?" asked Truman.

"Nah. Old Will Sheridan is pretty forgetful these days," said Ben. "I have no doubt he left a gate open. He never remembers to check for them near the creek either."

"Does he have someone to look in on him?" Truman frowned, not liking the idea of the old-timer alone on the remote farm.

"His daughter's nearby. She must be out of town, or she would have handled it."

"Maybe you should check on Will," Truman told Ben. "Royce sometimes misses things."

Ben nodded, understanding in his eyes. Royce was young and easily distracted and often didn't see the forest for all the trees. He might not notice if Will's kitchen had no food or his health was suffering. Ben set down his coffee and turned to grab his jacket.

Truman went down the hall to his office. He hung his coat on a hook and set his cowboy hat carefully on a shelf as his mind wandered to the previous day's bloody cabin. Mercy had updated him and Ollie last night about her interview with Sara Newton and how Rob had been researching a murder investigation from twenty years before. And had ended up dead in the same spot as the victim.

Fascinating.

Ollie had asked Mercy if she believed Sara was involved in Rob's murder, but Mercy had told him it was too soon to know. Truman knew the young man hoped she was innocent.

Truman wasn't holding his breath.

He dropped into his desk chair and moved the mouse to start his computer. He'd nearly emptied his inbox when the intercom beeped.

Truman hit a button. "Yeah?"

"There's an abandoned vehicle near Grandma's place," said Lucas. "Want me to have Ben go there next?"

Grandma was Ina Smythe. She was Lucas's grandmother and had manned the front desk at the Eagle's Nest police station for decades before she trained him to take over.

Truman always enjoyed chatting with Ina. She knew more about Eagle's Nest's residents and gossip than Ben. Probably because she'd been sticking her nose in everyone's business all her life.

"No. I'll go. Ben's on the other side of town."

On his way out, Truman backtracked and grabbed some of the gingerbread cookies to share with Ina, knowing she'd have coffee ready.

Ten minutes later he knocked on her door. Her cane thumped inside, and she peeked through the window. Happiness filled her face, and she immediately opened the door.

Peeks to see who's there but doesn't ever lock the door.

Small-town life.

"Truman! I was expecting one of your men. Give me a hug."

He bent to hug her. As usual she smelled of coffee and floral lotion. He'd known Ina ever since he was a teen spending the summers in Eagle's Nest with his uncle. She and his uncle Jefferson had been close friends—very close. When the police chief position opened up, she had suggested Truman for the job. He had been more than ready to leave California for a slower-paced life.

"I brought cookies," he said.

"Thought I smelled gingerbread. You're lucky I just made a pot of coffee."

There was always a fresh pot of coffee in her home.

"I didn't see an abandoned vehicle out front," he said as he followed her into the kitchen and sat when she pointed at a chair.

She set a big mug of coffee in front of him, and he put the four cookies on a napkin. She took her own seat at the little table with a sigh, releasing her ever-present cane, which handily stood on its own. He knew her knees hurt.

"It's not out front. It's actually on Linda Bonner's property—that's the home east of mine. I noticed it'd been there since yesterday and gave her a call. She can't see it from her windows. She said she didn't know whose it was, and her son also knew nothing about it. I told her I'd call it in. She has enough on her plate." She dipped a gingerbread man's head in her coffee, and Truman did the same.

There wasn't much that missed Ina's attention. Truman wasn't surprised that she'd spotted an unfamiliar vehicle on *someone else's* property and known enough about that neighbor to offer help.

"You know her, right?" Ina scowled at him. She considered it part of his job to know every Eagle's Nest resident.

Luckily, he had Ina to fill in the holes in his knowledge. He ate his cookie's arms as he thought. "Um . . . Linda Bonner? The name is familiar, but I can't put a face to her."

I have no idea who that is.

Ina's expression shifted into instruction mode. "Her husband died right before you moved to town. Sweet woman. Comes from a good family. But she's as introverted as they come. I don't think she goes out much except to buy groceries. Luckily there's no grocery delivery service here, or I suspect she'd never leave the house. I wasn't surprised she hadn't noticed the vehicle since she stays home so much. Her son's no help. He can't drive."

Truman ran the name Bonner through his mental list again, wondering if the Bonner boy had lost his license to a DUI. The name sounded familiar, but he wasn't positive. "I'll head over there in a minute. Would you let her know I'm coming?"

"Of course." Ina pulled a cell phone out of her pocket, slipped on a pair of readers from the tray in the center of the table, and proceeded to tap out a text as he drank his coffee.

I don't think I've ever received a text from Ina.

He was a little hurt but realized they enjoyed chatting together so much that phone calls made more sense. If her neighbor was as introverted as Ina said, a text was more appropriate.

She set down her phone and fixed her eagle-eyed gaze on him. "Now. Before you go, tell me what you're getting your wife for your first wedding anniversary. Some men are clueless when it comes to gifts."

"Mercy's not very typical." Truman shifted in his seat under her scrutiny. "I built her a greenhouse last year as a wedding present. She acted as if I'd given her a ten-carat diamond ring." He paused. "That's a bad analogy. She'd have no use for a ring like that."

"Exactly."

"We agreed no gifts." He braced himself, aching to hide behind his coffee cup.

Ina simply stared at him. Her silence more painful than any scolding.

"I know, I know," he said. "I'm planning a nice dinner out. We never have time to go out. Our schedules rarely line up, and usually Kaylie cooks something anyway. She's teaching Ollie to cook. He's getting pretty good."

"Don't change the subject. Dinner out and what else?"

He wanted to squirm. "Frankly, uninterrupted time alone is what we both would appreciate the most."

"So a hotel room in Bend. At least two nights. Buy some fancy champagne. Those kids can manage without you."

"That's a good idea." It was. He was surprised he hadn't considered it. "I'll set something up."

"Does she like chocolates?"

"Yes and no. She likes the chocolate but dislikes the guilt from eating it. Sometimes she buys those nasty ninety percent dark chocolate bars. I think she does it to keep the kids and me from eating them."

Ina snorted. "Then what's her favorite treat?"

Truman thought. "Pita chips."

"What the hell are those?"

"They're like crackers . . . but made from pita bread."

"Boring. It's your anniversary, not a picnic. What else?"

"She really likes them," Truman said. "Her eyes light up when she sees them in the grocery store."

"Hmmm." Ina didn't look convinced.

"Hotel, champagne, and pita chips," said Truman, liking the idea more and more. "Trust me, it'll work."

"I'll take your word for it. Now that I've gotten you straightened out from that no-gifts nonsense, you can go handle that vehicle." She waved a hand in the general direction.

"I'm on it." He stood. "Thank you for the coffee—don't get up. I can see myself out."

She braced herself with her cane and stood. "I'm not so decrepit that I can't see a guest to the door."

They slowly made their way to the door, and she surprised him with a hug and a kiss on the cheek. His heart warmed with affection for the woman who'd been his "mom" when he spent summers in Eagle's Nest with his uncle.

"One of the best decisions I ever made was making you move here and be chief."

"I like to think I had some input," said Truman.

"A little bit," she said with a wink. "Now look that way. See the vehicle?" She turned him to the left.

Truman squinted and spotted the metal roof of something dark behind the trees. A stretch of tall pines and brush separated the two properties and mostly hid the vehicle. He would never have noticed it. But he wasn't surprised that Ina had.

He got in his Tahoe, turned it around, and headed back down Ina's long drive. He turned east on the main road and drove for about a hundred yards, then took the next driveway. He drove a little ways up the gravel road, spotting the vehicle about a dozen feet off the road with its front end buried in the brush.

He hit the brakes.

It was an older Jeep Cherokee.

He held his breath as he checked the license plate against the BOLO for Rob Newton's Jeep.

It was a match.

11

Before he walked around the Jeep, Truman took a dozen photos that included the thin layer of snow on the ground. He'd called Detective Marshall and sent her an image of the vehicle that showed the license plate. Then he'd texted Mercy and sent the same picture. Both women would arrive in about a half hour.

The light overnight snow had almost hidden the Jeep's tracks. Only the faintest impression was visible leading off the driveway. The footprints were completely gone. He knew the snow on the hood and roof would melt the moment the sun hit it.

He peered through the driver's window. The gas gauge showed a quarter of a tank, so the vehicle hadn't been abandoned because it had run out of gas. There could have been some other mechanical difficulty, but Truman suspected it had simply been dumped.

Not the best place to leave a getaway vehicle. Like Rob Newton's body, it had been easily found.

He moved to the rear window on the driver's side. The glass was lightly tinted, and the cloth bench seat had a large dark stain.

Rob Newton's blood.

He checked the cargo area. There were a couple of items that looked like a case for traction chains and possibly a road emergency kit. Most likely they had been there before the Jeep was taken. Overall the vehicle was quite clean and neat inside.

Except for the large stain on the rear seat.

Truman eyed the door handles. No blood. No doubt the killer's hands had been bloody after they'd loaded Rob in the Jeep, so they must have wiped them down.

He was tempted to see if it was locked, but he'd wait for Noelle and Mercy. He hadn't seen anything inside that required him to immediately get into the vehicle. Noelle had ordered a crime scene team but didn't know when it would arrive.

This wasn't his investigation. It belonged to Deschutes County and the FBI.

But damn, he was interested. The fact that it appeared to be tied to the disappearance of some teens long ago stoked his curiosity even more.

There were no vehicle tracks present up the long driveway, not even faint ones that had been buried by snow, so it appeared Ina's neighbor hadn't driven past the vehicle. Truman couldn't see her house from the Jeep because of the curve in the driveway.

He left his Tahoe and walked up the drive, checking each side for any possible evidence. The house appeared as he rounded the corner. It was a small ranch home like Ina's. Probably built in the 1970s. Both homes sat on multiple-acre lots, backing up to a dense wood.

It looked quiet, as if no one was home.

He made his way to the front door, knocked, removed his hat, and made sure the police department logo was visible on his coat.

After a long moment, the door opened. "Good morning, Chief."

Truman recognized her . . . just barely. Linda Bonner had bobbed gray hair with several purple streaks near her face and a warm smile. A gentle, happy energy hovered around her, and he liked her at once. He was certain they'd never spoken before, but he felt as if he'd seen her in the diner or maybe the grocery store. The purple hair seemed familiar.

"Morning, Linda. I wanted to ask you about the black Jeep Cherokee down your driveway."

Her smile widened. "The one I had no idea was there until Ina told me. I didn't walk down there since she said she'd report it, and I thought it might not be the smartest idea for me to peek in the windows if some drunk was sleeping inside."

"Good decision."

"I don't know anyone with a black Cherokee anyway."

"It's been reported missing." He decided not to inform her that it was tied to a murder investigation. Detective Marshall could tell her if necessary. "It'll be removed later today. A few more of us will look it over first."

"Is it blocking my driveway? Not that I need to go anywhere today."

"No, it's into the brush a bit." He remembered Ina had mentioned a son. "Is your son home? Does he know anyone that drives a black Cherokee?"

Linda turned. "Devin?" she shouted behind her. "Can you come here for a second?" She turned back to Truman. "Would you come in for a cup of coffee?" she asked politely.

"Thank you, but I just had one at Ina's."

"The coffeepot is always on over there," said Linda. "She's a good neighbor. Really looks out for everyone."

Truman grinned. "That's a polite way of saying she's in everyone's business."

Linda's eyes lit up. "But she always has good intentions."

A man appeared behind her. Devin Bonner was tall and appeared to be in his forties. He had his mother's warm brown eyes but was pale—beyond the normal Oregon winter paleness—making Truman wonder if he'd recently been in prison. But Ina would have mentioned that.

Assuming she knew.

Ina had said the son didn't drive. Truman wondered again why his license had been pulled.

"Devin, I don't think you've met Police Chief Daly before," said Linda.

The man hesitated for the slightest second and then held out his hand, a tentative smile on his face. "I don't think so."

Truman shook his hand. If he hadn't been watching Devin so closely, he would have missed the hesitation.

Something has made him cautious of law enforcement.

He'd look up Devin as soon as he returned to his vehicle.

"Nice to meet you, Devin," said Truman. "Do you know anything about a black Jeep Cherokee being left on the property? It's partially in the brush about halfway down your driveway."

"Sorry, Chief. I don't. I guess we should call a tow truck." He glanced down at his mom.

"The police are having it towed. It was reported . . . stolen?" Linda looked to Truman for confirmation.

"Yes. They think it disappeared the night before last."

Linda frowned. "If they dumped it here, then they left on foot or had a ride waiting. I haven't heard or seen anyone around in the past couple days. I wonder how long it's been there."

"Do you have any cameras on the property?" asked Truman. "Or know if your neighbors do?" All the homes along this road sat far back. If a neighbor had a camera, it was unlikely that it captured the road. But he'd still ask around.

"No cameras here," said Devin.

"We don't know if the neighbors do," added Linda.

Ina's home had cameras. Truman knew because he'd installed them. So he also knew that none of the views covered the long distance to the street.

"Okay, thanks for your help," said Truman, handing Linda his card. "Let me know if you think of anything. You'll probably hear from a Deschutes County detective too."

They said goodbye, and Truman headed back down the drive.

He rounded the corner and spotted Detective Marshall getting out of her vehicle. She waved at him and then put her hands on her hips as she studied the Jeep.

"We meet again," she said to Truman with a wry smile. "That's two mornings in a row."

"Sorry it's not under better circumstances."

"I disagree. I think today is an awesome circumstance. You found my missing Jeep." She pointed at his boot prints in the snow, which circled the Jeep. "I assume that's you?"

"I took pictures before I walked around, and I didn't notice any blood on the handles. I'd guess they wiped it down. I haven't checked to see if it's unlocked."

Noelle put on vinyl gloves. "I don't know how long the crime scene team will take to get here. Last I checked they were still tied up in Redmond. Film me?"

"You bet." He started recording.

Noelle used one finger to tug on the passenger door. It opened. "Well, hello," she said to the empty interior in delight. "Thank you for leaving it unlocked for us." She shined her flashlight over the dash, seats, and floor, then bent down to see under the passenger seat. Next was the glove box. It held what Truman expected to find in a glove box: receipts, owner's manual, and ice scraper. No gloves. Noelle didn't touch anything and backed away, leaving the box open. "Can you get a closer shot of the contents?"

Truman stepped forward. Beneath the metallic bloody scent, the Jeep had a musty smell, as if water had leaked inside for many years, and he caught a faint whiff of cigarettes. "I didn't smell cigarette smoke at the cabin, did you?"

"No," said Noelle. "No ashtrays inside or out on the porch either. Maybe the Newtons bought it from someone who smoked. I didn't ask Sara how long they'd owned the Jeep."

She opened the rear passenger door and caught a breath. "Oh." She stilled, taking in the bloodstained seats. Both of them stood silent, viewing where someone's life had ended.

The tinted glass had mitigated the sight of the bloodstain when Truman peered through it earlier. Now it was crystal clear. The majority of the dark stain was on the seat behind the driver's, most of it near the back support. Truman could picture Rob lying there, the last bits of his life seeping into the seats of his Jeep.

"Does that mean his heart was still beating when they put him in here?" Noelle asked softly.

Truman knew that dead men don't bleed. It made sense. Once the heart stops pumping, there is nothing to drive the blood. "Maybe gravity did it?" he asked. "If they quickly put him in here and positioned him in such a way that the cut at his throat happened to be lower than the rest of him? That seat slopes down toward the rear. I think the rest of the stain is transfer from the blood on his clothes."

"Maybe." She checked under the seats and in the doors with her flashlight. "Let's do the other side."

She took a longer time studying the driver's area. She peered closely at the steering wheel, and Truman knew she was looking for blood, hoping the crime scene tech could find a fingerprint in it. She was silent for the rest of her efficient search, which unnerved Truman a little. Noelle always had something to say.

The sound of a vehicle announced Mercy's SUV turning into the drive. Right behind her was the crime scene van. Both of them parked away from the scene, and then Truman watched as Mercy strode up the drive. She was dressed in black from head to toe. Boots, thick leggings, and a heavy coat with a hood. Her usual winter weather wardrobe. Her hood was edged with black fake fur, the one thing that wasn't utilitarian about her clothing. As she drew closer, her green gaze met his, and she smiled.

Truman felt a tiny flutter in his chest and grinned back.

My wife is stunning.

She gave him a kiss on the cheek and greeted Noelle, and the two immediately put their heads together to look at the back seat. Truman couldn't help but compare them. One black haired, one platinum. Both tall. But Noelle projected a poised, energetic, and confident in-your-face presence. Mercy projected confidence with a calm, intense bearing, and when her gaze fell on you, it felt as if she could read all your secrets.

Both were talented investigators.

The crime scene tech joined him, a camera around her neck and a duffel in each hand. "Morning, Chief."

"Hey, Angela. Nice to see you."

She set down the duffels and fiddled with her camera. "Looks like I'm the last one here."

"We've been careful."

"Uh-huh," she said noncommittally, deliberately eyeing the footprints around the Jeep and its open doors.

"I swear. I took photos before anyone got near."

"I'm teasing," she said, with a glint in her eye. "You know what to do. It's other law enforcement that blunders their way through a scene." She shook her head. "They don't think." Mercy and Noelle reluctantly moved away from the Jeep, and Angela raised her thirty-five-millimeter camera and started shooting, taking wide shots from several locations.

Truman watched for a few moments, pleased to note he'd done exactly the same thing.

Mercy and Noelle joined him.

"Anything?" Truman asked.

"Nothing new," said Noelle. "You already talked to the property owner?"

"I did. Linda Bonner. I told her she'd hear from you too. How is Sara holding up?"

"I spoke with her briefly this morning. Her aunt wanted her to go back to Portland with her, but I asked that she stay in town a few more days. I'm hoping forensics gives us something from the cabin or the Jeep."

"Or from Rob," added Mercy, checking her watch. "His autopsy starts soon. I plan to be there. I started going through his website and social media. He gets people riled up. Most of the comments on his social media are inflammatory. People angry that solved cases aren't reopened when Rob has presented such clear evidence." She made quote marks with her fingers as she said the last two words.

Truman and Noelle sighed simultaneously.

"If you two need to get to the autopsy, I can stay here with Angela," Truman said.

Mercy looked at Noelle. "Ready?"

Truman noticed Noelle was suddenly uncomfortable.

Someone doesn't like autopsies.

He couldn't blame her.

"Would you mind if I went back to the office?" asked Noelle. She grimaced. "I nearly cracked my skull several years ago when I passed out during an autopsy. I didn't realize I had a problem being in there until my vision tunneled. This morning I was checking out the case files on the old disappearances when Truman called. I want to dig into those."

"Okay by me," said Mercy. "We can touch base when Dr. Lockhart is done." She gave Truman another quick kiss and squeezed his hand, holding his gaze. "See you tonight."

Best part of being married. I see her every night.

12

Ollie jerked the wand. The feathered cat toy jumped, and three of the kittens lunged after it. He was sitting cross-legged on the floor in the kitten room, passing time until he needed to leave for work. He usually spent an hour or two each day playing with the foster kittens or even stretching out on the floor to nap with them.

Kaylie had filled the room with cat condos and carpeted shelving. As they grew older, the kittens learned they could run and leap along the shelves around the entire room near the ceiling. More than once a kitten had tried to drop onto Ollie's shoulder as he came in the door. There were also cushy perches attached to the windowsill, where the happy kittens melted as the sun shone in.

Kaylie's current foster litter had five solid-black kittens. She had to use colored collars to tell them apart, but Ollie had figured out their subtle characteristics the first day. A different head shape. Four white hairs. Eye color. Tail length. A pink toe bean or two.

Being with them was therapy.

Something about being covered with little purring balls of fur made everything better.

The kittens helped mitigate the disappointment from his online searches for his family. Truman and Mercy didn't know he spent hours on the computer looking for what had happened to his parents, but

Kaylie did. Truman was already frustrated with his own search, and Ollie didn't want to make him feel any worse, so he kept it to himself. Truman looked discouraged every time he told Ollie about his lack of results.

Having the last name Smith had made everything harder.

I should stop looking. I have a family already.

But he wanted to know. He couldn't remember his parents and had no pictures. There was an odd-shaped hole in him, and he ached to fill it.

The door opened, and four kittens barreled past him. Kaylie managed to snatch the fastest and shut the door before anyone escaped.

They'll escape one of these days. Onyx will be first.

The male kitten was the biggest and most curious. Ollie believed the kitten preferred him over Kaylie.

"Where's Olive?" Kaylie asked, scanning for a purple collar.

"At the window."

The kitten was sunning herself, limp in ecstasy from the warmth. Kaylie dabbed a bit of goo on both her eyes. She was so used to the daily antibiotics, she didn't even move. Kaylie put the cap back on the tube, and Ollie felt her study him.

She was his best friend. He had good male friends, but he couldn't tell them the things he told Kaylie. When he'd first gone to live with Truman, he'd had a huge crush on Kaylie and hated her boyfriends. Now he was still annoyed by her choice of boyfriends, but the crush was long gone. She'd become his sister.

"What's wrong?" she asked as she joined Ollie on the floor. Two kittens immediately crawled in her lap, but Onyx returned to Ollie, boosting his ego.

He scratched Onyx under the chin, turning on the purring motor. "The usual."

"Still nothing?"

"Another deep rabbit hole that went nowhere."

"I really think you should leave it to Truman and Mercy."

"I know." He kept his gaze on the kitten.

"Has Truman told you what he's doing for Mercy for their anniversary?" she asked.

He looked up. "No, what?"

She wrinkled her nose. "I'm asking you, you dork."

"He hasn't told me anything. Mercy hasn't mentioned anything either."

"I'm worried they aren't going to do anything. They're both so . . . practical. It's their first wedding anniversary. That is big!"

"I'd think a fiftieth anniversary would be big," said Ollie. "Lasting through twelve months of marriage isn't that big of a deal. It's probably the easiest year of all of them."

Kaylie's glare should have fried him on the spot.

"You know I'm right," he argued.

"It's the romance of it. Not the number of years. It's something that should be celebrated."

"I don't think it's any of our business," said Ollie. He didn't understand why Kaylie seemed so swept up in something that didn't involve her. "Let them do whatever they're going to do." He frowned. "Actually, Truman just said something about them being gone for two nights later this month. The weekend he mentioned to me is over their anniversary. Sounds like they have something planned."

"You didn't ask?"

"It didn't even register until right now that it was their anniversary."

"Sheesh. Trust me. When you get a girlfriend, pay attention, okay? Anniversaries are important. First month, second month. That sort of thing." She continued with her lecture about how to be a good boyfriend, covering texting etiquette and his shoes.

Ollie silently nodded a few times. He'd stopped listening after "Sheesh."

With Kaylie, it's easiest just to agree.

13

When Mercy arrived at the medical examiner's office, Dr. Natasha Lockhart was in the middle of a thorough scalp-to-toe exterior exam of Rob Newton. Pleased she hadn't missed much, Mercy quickly gowned up and added booties, gloves, and a mask before she joined the pathologist. The autopsy suite was cold, the lights were bright, and the smell was . . . not great. A unique blend of industrial disinfectant, decay, and raw flesh.

Rob Newton lay on a raised-edge stainless steel table on wheels. In the past Mercy had seen the tables rolled to connect to the big stainless steel sinks along the back wall. Assistants could rinse a body right on the table with the heavy-duty sprayers, and the water would drain into the sink. There were also several drains in the floor of the room. Easy cleanup.

Above the body hung a scale, waiting for each organ to be individually weighed. There was also a microphone so Dr. Lockhart could record her findings and a close-by smaller table covered with metal tools and instruments.

"Good morning, Mercy," said Dr. Lockhart. Only her eyes were visible behind her mask and face shield. Popular country music played loudly in the background, a change from Dr. Lockhart's usual '90s rock.

"Morning, Doctor," said Mercy. She pointed at the small but powerful speaker pod on a shelf. "Did you lose a bet?"

"Yes, she did," said the medical examiner's assistant. "I bet her I could do more push-ups in sixty seconds. So we get to listen to country all week." She sang along with the music. "'Don't wanna scoot the boots with no body. Get straight tequila drunk on no body.'"

"You only beat me by three push-ups," Dr. Lockhart said pointedly, turning a sharp gaze on her assistant. "And I'd just had a big lunch."

It appeared the doctor didn't like to lose.

Or she really didn't like country music.

Her assistant winked at Mercy, and she suspected the woman wore a big grin behind the mask.

"Anything interesting yet, Doctor?" Mercy asked, studying the body, trying to figure out why Rob looked different to her today.

Dr. Lockhart was examining the scalp, separating every inch of hair, peering closely through her loupes. She stood on a low, long step that went all the way around the table. She was tiny, and the tables didn't lower enough for her to work comfortably. Her happy assistant stood next to her, recording the pathologist's findings on a clipboard. "Besides the bullet hole in the skull and the cut throat, nothing new yet. A few old scars. Two tattoos. Birthmark. His X-rays don't show much except an old break of his right radius." She looked under each eyelid and moved on to look in his mouth with a dental mirror. "Clearly manner of death is homicide. He didn't cut his own throat with his hands bound behind his back or have a wound like that occur in an accident. Mechanism of death will most likely be exsanguination."

"What about the gunshot wound?"

"I believe that happened after the victim was dead—I still need to confirm. So cause of death is most likely the cut at his neck." She paused. "It still could be the gunshot. I'll know more when I'm done."

"You removed the black tape. Was there anything in his mouth?" Mercy had wondered if something placed inside would give insight toward motive.

"There was nothing. You'll have the tape to process for evidence."

Disappointment went through Mercy. "Do you have nail scrapings?" There had obviously been a big struggle at the cabin. Mercy hoped Rob had captured some evidence of his attacker.

"I have them set aside for you," said the assistant.

Mercy suddenly realized why the man appeared different—besides that he was fully naked. At the river he'd been on his side, his legs pulled up, his arms tied behind his back while in full rigor. An uncomfortable position. Here, lying flat on his back, he looked . . . relaxed.

As if a body could look relaxed during an autopsy.

Dr. Lockhart picked up a scalpel and started her Y incision. She cut from each shoulder to the bottom of the sternum and then straight down to the groin. The openings weren't made with one easy slide of the scalpel. She had to go back over each cut a few times to get through the muscle to the bone. Then she cut back the flesh flaps created by the Y and exposed the ribs.

She studied the ribs for a few moments, touching each, checking for breaks, before reaching for the rib cutters.

I hate this part.

Mercy would rather watch the scalp be pulled back and the skullcap removed than listen to each snap of the ribs from what were essentially pruning shears.

After cutting each rib at the sides of the chest, Dr. Lockhart lifted out the breastbone with parts of the ribs attached. Now she had access to the organs.

Mercy wondered at which point during an autopsy Detective Marshall had fainted. Mercy had seen it happen a few times. Usually it was the men. The big men. She'd heard of assistants placing bets on who they thought would go down during an autopsy when a number of people were present. She watched as Dr. Lockhart examined each organ, weighed it, sliced into it to peer at the undertissue, and then set aside samples of each organ. Mercy knew this portion of the autopsy would take a while.

Her mind wandered, speculating on what information they could gain about Rob's death from this autopsy. He had two traumatic wounds that could have caused his death. Both indicated homicide. She couldn't think of what else could be relevant from all the other steps of the autopsy procedure. They already had his identity.

Toxicology?

That had the potential to reveal something. Maybe he'd had a sedating drug in his system, something that might allow him to be quietly overpowered in the cabin without his wife waking up.

Maybe Sara was drugged.

Mercy swore to herself, wondering if it was too late to find anything in a blood draw or urinalysis for Sara. "I'll be right back, Doctor." She headed toward the doors so she could make a private call.

"You good, Mercy?" Dr. Lockhart asked in an anxious tone.

"Oh, yeah. I'm not sick. I need to make a call." She stripped off her gloves and tossed them in the appropriate bin near the door. In the hall, she opened a text from Truman that said Rob's Jeep had been towed to Deschutes County's evidence lot. She sent him a thumbs-up and called Detective Marshall.

"Is the autopsy finished already?" Noelle asked as a greeting.

"No. I had a thought. Can we get a blood draw and urinalysis on Sara Newton? What if she slept through her husband's attack because she was drugged?"

Noelle was silent for a long moment as she processed the implications. "We'd be looking at this case differently if she was. Is it too late for drugs to show up in those tests?"

"I don't know. Can't hurt."

"I'll call her. She might refuse, you know."

"Has she hired a lawyer yet?" asked Mercy.

"Not that I'm aware of. A lawyer would definitely challenge this request."

"Tell her we're worried she was drugged."

"I'll let you know what she says."

Mercy ended the call and went back into the suite, grabbing another pair of gloves from the boxes just inside the door.

Not that I ever touch anything in here.

Or want to.

Dr. Lockhart had moved to the head and was making a cut in the scalp across the back of the skull from ear to ear.

Mercy studied the table of tools. Autopsies didn't use that many small, delicate tools. The contents of the table looked as if they came from a hardware store or a restaurant supply store. Or like a torturer's tools in a movie. There was a manual bone saw that could cut through a small tree trunk and a hammer with an evil-looking hook on the opposite end to help remove the skullcap. Next to it was a chisel to also help pry off the skullcap.

She glanced back to the pathologist just in time to see her peel Rob's scalp from the back of his head and rest it inside out over his face, leaving the bony top of the skull exposed. Dr. Lockhart paused for a long moment, studying one side of the skull, and Mercy moved so she could see the bullet's entrance wound. Two cracks radiated outward from the small hole. The assistant was ready with a camera and took several shots.

"Thoughts?" asked Mercy.

"Small caliber. The stippling on the scalp was light, indicating the gun wasn't up against his head, but it's hard to estimate the distance of the gun. A lot of factors to consider. The fact there's no exit wound means the bullet quickly lost energy inside the skull. That *could* be because he was shot from a distance."

"At least we'll have the bullet, no matter how poor of a shape it's in."

The doctor didn't answer as she reached for her Stryker saw. Mercy stepped back to the edge of the room. She didn't have the head covering or the eye protection that the doctor and assistant wore. The saw had a tendency to create a cloud of bone dust even with its attached vacuum. The room's ventilation was excellent, but she didn't like the idea of wearing bone dust in her hair if she stood too close.

She showered after autopsies. Even though her skin and clothing were covered, the scent of the autopsy suite clung. At least it seemed to. Wafts of the scent would pop up throughout her day if she didn't change and shower.

Dr. Lockhart turned on the saw and started to cut from the top of the skull down to an ear and around the back. Mercy wished for noise-canceling headphones. By itself, the saw sounded like a large, rough dental drill. When it was held to bone, the tone was higher and identical to the noise inside her head when she had a cavity worked on. The doctor made a matching cut on the other side. At the back of the head, she took some extra time as she created a pointed notch in the bone. It would help her replace the skullcap after she removed the brain.

She set down the saw, and Mercy sighed at the lack of noise and the return of the music. The doctor struggled a bit to lift the skullcap and had to use her chisel to pry it up. She gently lifted the ivory arc and set it on the tray her assistant held ready. Then she turned her attention to the brain. Mercy moved back to her close position and saw the damage from the bullet. Dr. Lockhart carefully removed the brain from the cranial vault, turning it and checking each side. She slid her pinkie into the bullet hole. "The bullet is still inside."

Mercy knew she'd have to wait for that piece of evidence until the doctor could dissect the brain. She checked the time. "Are the preliminary blood and urine labs finished?"

The assistant nodded. "I'll get them." She left the room.

Full toxicology labs could take weeks. Every organ's tissue sample would be tested at an off-site lab, but Mercy knew the doctor ran quick preliminary tests to check for any immediate red flags. Samples of all fluids—blood, bile, urine, and vitreous humor—were also sent to labs for in-depth testing.

The assistant returned, a page in her hand. "He has an indicator for benzodiazepines."

I might be right about him being drugged.

She clamped down her sense of triumph. Rob Newton could have been taking a benzodiazepine for any number of normal reasons. For insomnia, anxiety, or panic attacks, or as a muscle relaxant. She'd ask his wife what prescription medications her husband used.

She might not know. Some people hide them from their spouse.

"You can't tell which specific medication, correct?" Mercy asked.

"No. But we can with more tests," said the assistant.

Dr. Lockhart scanned the lab page. "Nothing else appears out of the ordinary." She met Mercy's gaze. "We'll see what further testing turns up."

"I should go," Mercy said, starting to strip off her protective wear. "Let me know when you have the bullet."

"You'll have a preliminary report from me late tonight."

Mercy eyed the medical examiner. "You shouldn't have to work after hours."

Behind her shield, Dr. Lockhart's brows rose. "And you don't?"

"Touché," Mercy admitted. "I guess we both do what's needed to find answers."

"Exactly."

Mercy said her goodbyes to both women and threw her PPE in the bin. Outside she took in deep breaths of fresh air.

"Shower," she muttered to herself. "Then find out if Sara agreed to the lab tests."

Will Sara's tests show the same benzodiazepine?

14

Hair slightly damp and with the much more pleasant scent of a burger hovering—she'd eaten one on the way to the Deschutes County Sheriff's Department—Mercy made her way through the building to Noelle Marshall's office. She felt a little guilty that she'd easily eaten a burger and fries after attending an autopsy but shrugged it off. She carried two eggnog lattes, one for herself and one for Noelle.

Perks of the holiday months. Seasonal flavors.

A note was taped to Noelle's door. *M—I'm in conference room 3.*

Mercy had no idea where that room was, so she asked a passing deputy, who stared at her drinks like a caffeine addict instead of making eye contact. He pointed down the hall, telling her to take the first right. She eventually found the room. Noelle had propped open the door, but she shut it firmly after Mercy entered and set down the drinks.

"That smells amazing," Noelle said as she took the lid off one, closed her eyes, and inhaled, a dreamy smile on her face. The tall detective had changed clothes since they met earlier at Rob's Jeep. She wore low-heeled boots with black jeans and a deep-turquoise-colored sweater that Mercy immediately coveted. Her hair was in a perfect bun on the very top of her head. It was a style Mercy had tried, but it had given her head an unflattering shape. On Noelle it made her more powerfully statuesque.

Conference room 3 was small but had a table, several chairs, and two large whiteboards on the walls. Several office storage boxes lined one side, and five large binders were stacked on the table. A well-used yellow pad with several pages turned over was at Noelle's chair.

"The latte is the best thing I've smelled today," Mercy said as she took a seat next to the detective.

Even better than my burger and fries.

Noelle's dreamy expression vanished, and her nose twitched. "I'm not surprised."

"What part of an autopsy gets to you?" Mercy asked after taking a sip.

Noelle drew in a breath as she thought. "Well, I've only attended one, so it's not so much a certain part. My problem was it was a floater who'd been in the water a long time. I can still see it . . . and smell it."

Mercy nodded in sympathy. "Those are hard." Her experience with floaters had also been rough.

"Anything new turn up during Rob's autopsy?"

"His preliminary lab shows benzodiazepines in his system," said Mercy. "Further tests will pinpoint exactly which one. Did you ask Sara about getting tested?"

"I called her, and she agreed to the test. I played up the angle that we were concerned she may have been drugged. I think the idea surprised her," said Noelle. "She admitted that she'd slept a little later than usual that morning but didn't recall being tired when she woke. But she pointed out that her nervous system went into overdrive as soon as she saw the blood on the cabin floor."

"Anxiety and shock would have pumped her full of adrenaline, possibly offsetting a drug effect. Especially if it had been administered the evening before. Did you happen to ask her if Rob takes any prescription medications?"

"I didn't. I did check the list of personal items found in the cabin. There weren't any prescription medications on it for either one of them."

"Once Sara's labs come back, we can decide whether or not to tell her about the medication in Rob's system." Mercy thought back to the autopsy, sifting through details she thought Noelle needed to know right then. "The bullet was still in the brain when I left. We should have it soon."

"If it's like other bullets I've seen after they've gone through a skull, it'll be almost unrecognizable."

"At least it's something."

"Speaking of something." Noelle straightened her shoulders and flipped back the sheets on her yellow pad. "I've found some interesting things about that old case," she said. "I guess I should say *cases* since it involves five people." She met Mercy's gaze, a glint in her eye. "There's one *big* connection you haven't put together yet."

"What?"

"I'm not going to tell you just yet," Noelle said, grinning. "It deserves a buildup."

"Make it fast."

What could be bigger than Rob Newton researching a crime and ending up like one of the victims?

Noelle slid her yellow pad closer to Mercy. "Twenty years ago, these five high school students went camping to celebrate their graduation." She tapped a list of names. "Four guys, one girl. All from the same Bend high school. The girl, Mia Fowler, was dating Colin Balke, and friends say the two went everywhere together."

"I wonder how his friends felt about that," said Mercy.

"There are a ton of friend interviews, so we should get a pretty good picture. Mia and Colin are two of the three who were never found, along with Alex Stark. The big story Rob Newton was researching was to figure out what happened to these three teens and present it in a podcast." Noelle gestured at the storage boxes. "Of course Rob didn't have access to the case notes and evidence that we do. I haven't dived into his personal research yet, because I wanted to review the actual facts of the case before reading his point of view."

"Good call," said Mercy.

Noelle opened one binder. "This is Mia."

The teenager had a wide smile and cheerful blue eyes. It was a face that would stick with Mercy. The photo had been professionally shot. Most likely her senior picture.

Noelle turned a page. "And Colin and Alex."

Also professional photos. Both boys looked happy. "So young," muttered Mercy. "I just can't see them taking off and starting a new life somewhere. Something horrible happened to them."

"All five were missing for five days before the other two boys were found at the river's edge." Noelle flipped back to the picture of Mia. "And the boy that died hadn't been dead for five days. The medical examiner's report said he had died the night before he was found, so they were either held somewhere or hiding somewhere. If Colin and Alex—and Mia—did something bad to the two friends that were found, I can understand why the three took off."

"How long were they supposed to be camping?"

"Two nights. When it got late on the third day, one of the moms called the other boys' homes and confirmed that none of them had returned yet, so she called the Wasco County sheriff. Deputies were sent out that night, but no one was certain of the exact location. The campsite wasn't found until the next day."

"What evidence was found at the campsite?" asked Mercy.

"I haven't looked at the evidence myself yet, but the summary essentially says there was no sign of violence at the site and all their gear appeared to still be present. Even the trucks they drove up in were parked nearby. One detective is quoted that it looked as if they had simply walked away."

"And left their trucks behind? From what I know, little can separate a high schooler from their vehicle."

"Also lends some credence to the suspicion that something bad happened to the other three," added Noelle. "How could they vanish so cleanly unless someone took them? If the other three teens were running after hurting the other two boys, surely they would take at least one vehicle."

"Running away would take a lot of planning or dumb luck." Mercy sighed. "There is a ton of evidence to go over . . . *Now* can you tell me about the big connection you found?"

Noelle nodded and pulled out the other two boys' photos. She tapped one. "Tyler Hynd was the boy who died and was found in the same spot and body position as Rob Newton."

Tyler had freckles and warm brown eyes. Mercy's heart ached for his family.

Noelle held up the other photo. "This is the boy who survived." She covered the list of names before Mercy could see which one Noelle hadn't mentioned yet.

Annoyance twinged through Mercy at Noelle's game. "And?"

"Remember Rob Newton's Jeep?"

"Of course."

"The property it was found on belongs to Linda Bonner." Noelle uncovered the names. "Our survivor, Devin Bonner, still lives there with his mother."

Mercy's annoyance vanished. "That is huge! There's no way that vehicle was abandoned there as a coincidence." Her mind raced, trying to find all the implications. "But wait . . . The guy from yesterday—Ted Weir—said the survivor died a few years ago."

Noelle shook her head. "Linda's husband died three years ago—he was also named Devin. Ted must have confused the two."

Eagerness spread through Mercy. "We have a witness!"

Noelle nodded solemnly. "We do."

Something is wrong.

"What am I missing?" The detective wasn't showing the level of excitement that Mercy was feeling.

Noelle pressed her lips together. "Devin has no memory of what happened. I haven't read his interviews, but the summaries are disappointing. He couldn't remember his graduation ceremony, let alone going camping."

Mercy deflated. "And the follow-ups over the years?"

"No change. He's been contacted every few years to see if he recalled anything."

"When was the last contact?"

Noelle flipped to the front page of the binder, where various detectives working the cold case had logged their contact with Devin Bonner over the last twenty years. "Eight months ago."

"Sounds like it's our turn to talk to him. Maybe the recent death will trigger something in his memory."

"We need to dig through this first. I'm not talking to him without knowing everything that happened."

"Agreed," said Mercy. She looked at the boxes and then checked the time. "It's too much to go through today. How about we plan on talking to him tomorrow? I think we'll be here late tonight."

Noelle nodded. "It is a lot. Want me to set up an interview?"

"No." Mercy thought for a few moments. "I'd rather surprise him. Let them think we're there to talk about the Jeep—which is true. Then bring up the connection to the old case and watch for the reactions."

The detective's eyes glittered. "I like the way you think."

15

I always know her in my dreams. I know her by her hair and her eyes. Her voice. Her laughter.

I can smell her scent. She always smelled faintly of sunshine and the outdoors. It's fresh and warm. When I meet her gaze, I'm happy.

We're all close friends. Ribbons of good memories intertwine between us.

We've promised to stick together for life.

Alex is there. Tyler. Colin.

The five of us hold up our beers, and I feel warmth. It comes from my friends as much as the campfire.

"Can there be five musketeers?" asks Alex.

Tyler and Colin make fun of him. But I understand what he means.

We're bonded.

We've all had our struggles. Some of us more than others.

Especially Mia.

We're stronger together.

Nothing can tear us apart.

But something did.

16

Starving, Truman strode down the main street with his gaze locked on the diner's sign a block ahead. After Rob Newton's Jeep had been towed away, Truman had gone to help Ben turn around the traffic that had been blocked by a jackknifed semi that had hit a patch of ice on the highway. And then he'd spent several additional hours assisting vehicles that had tried to get around the semi on their own and were stuck in the snowbanks on the highway's shoulders. Nearly every vehicle had been from out of state, belonging to someone traveling for the winter break. Everyone was cranky. Those drivers. Their families. The semi driver. Even Ben had gotten short with those who weren't listening to his instructions.

Truman had kept hoping an Oregon state trooper would show up to assist, but they were spread thin in his part of the state. There were too many vehicles on the roads statewide, their drivers determined to get to their holiday destinations.

Everyone was busy and in a rush.

By the time Truman checked in at the police department, he was beat. Lucas had taken one look at his face and told him he wasn't immediately needed, so Truman's grumbling stomach had become his priority.

Eagle's Nest was quiet, and he wasn't surprised to see fewer vehicles than usual parked on the streets. The locals usually didn't let a little snow stop them from going about their business, but today's low numbers showed caution. A small ice storm had happened before the light snow. No one liked to mess with ice.

He wished the tourists had stayed off the roads too.

Inside the diner he took a seat at the counter. Only one other person was there. An old-timer instead of the usual three or four who liked to spend the afternoon in a booth drinking free coffee refills. The waitstaff didn't mind them. The seats wouldn't have been used anyway. Truman nodded at the man in the booth, and the old-timer held up his coffee cup in acknowledgment.

A woman appeared behind the counter. "What can I get you, Chief?"

"I'm surprised to see you out front, Marion," said Truman. The diner owner rarely waited tables, preferring to stay in the kitchen. She was somewhere in her seventies and was missing two lower front teeth. Her white apron was stained with dried egg yolk and what he hoped was ketchup.

"Shorthanded. My sister's got a bug." She looked at him impatiently, pen and order pad in hand, and raised an eyebrow.

Marion didn't have a good table-side manner. Another reason she stayed in the kitchen.

"Turkey club," he told her. "To go," he added after realizing he didn't want to eat with her watching him.

Maybe that's why there's a shortage of old-timers today. Not just the icy roads.

"Fries?"

"Slaw."

She turned and headed for the kitchen. He would have liked a glass of water while he waited, but since he wasn't eating in, he didn't ask.

"Are you Chief Daly?"

Truman didn't recognize the woman who'd sat on the stool beside him. She seemed to be a few years older than he, and a hint of an accent told him she was originally from somewhere in the Midwest. He didn't know if she was a transplant or a tourist.

"Yes. Can I help you? Forgive me if I don't recognize you. I do try to know everyone from around here."

She smiled faintly. "You wouldn't. I'm from out of town." Her accent was even more pronounced. "I'm a friend of Rob Newton's. I understand you're investigating his death." Her voice caught the littlest bit on the last word.

"I'm not," said Truman, surprised to hear Rob's name. "His case is being handled by the Deschutes County sheriff." He didn't mention the FBI's interest in the case—saying *FBI* always prompted too many questions. "I'm sorry for your loss."

"Thank you." She glanced down for a long second before meeting his gaze. "But you were at his cabin. And you found his Jeep."

Small alarms went off in Truman's brain. "What's your name?"

"Paula Jupp."

"Well, Ms. Jupp. If you have questions, you should contact—"

"I know why he was visiting here, Chief. Several times he and I discussed the story he wanted to cover. When I saw on his social media that he'd passed away while in Oregon, I knew I had to come. I live in Saint Paul."

"Saint Paul, Oregon, or Minnesota?" He suspected he knew which city.

"Minnesota."

"His death was announced on his social media?" Truman frowned at the thought that someone would share that news so soon. "Did his wife post that?"

"I assume so. I don't know who handles his social media. It didn't say he was murdered. I found that out after making some calls."

"You didn't ask Sara if she made the post?"

Paula looked away. "I'm not friends with Sara—just Rob."

Were they having an affair? Why else would someone travel halfway across the country?

"Rob told me several times about those teenagers who'd vanished when he was in high school. He was obsessed with getting to the bottom of the story. He didn't think the investigators had dug deep enough back then. He believed there was some sort of cover-up, and he was determined to use it for one of his podcasts."

"How did you hear that I found his Jeep and was at his cabin?" He studied Paula Jupp, wondering if she was a conspiracy theorist. They were Rob's target audience, so it made sense.

She shrugged, not meeting his gaze. "Like I said, I made some calls. It's a small town. People talk."

But you're not from here. And I just found the Jeep this morning.

Truman ran through a mental list of who could have known about the Jeep and talked. There were quite a few people, including his own officers; the Bonners, who owned the property; the crime scene tech; and the tow truck driver. But how did a stranger from out of town get that information so quickly?

Keep her talking.

"How long did you know Rob?"

"Several years. He was a good man." Her brown gaze met his. "Who killed him?"

"I don't think they have an answer to that." Her sudden directness surprised him.

"Who do you *think* killed him? Clearly it had to be someone involved in the old case he was researching." She leaned forward the tiniest bit, still holding his gaze.

"What do my thoughts have to do with anything?" asked Truman. "It's not my case." He wanted to cut her off and just walk away, but he suspected Mercy and Noelle would want to talk to her. Unless she was a fruitcake.

"You were there. Your opinion is relevant."

"I wasn't there when he died. Anything I said would be speculation."

"So you do have an idea. Who do you suspect?"

Paula threw questions at him as if he were a dartboard. Something wasn't quite right with her. She'd begun meekly talking to him, but now she was a hungry hawk.

"Here's your sandwich." Marion set down a brown paper bag and slid Truman's check across the counter. She eyed Paula. "You here to eat?"

Again, Marion's table-side manner is lacking.

Truman set a few bills on the check, including a generous tip.

"I'm just talking to the chief," Paula said.

"Hmph." Marion headed back to the kitchen.

Truman stood, gathering his bag. "If you have questions or information, you need to contact Detective Marshall."

"I wanted to hear your side of the story."

"It's not a story, and I don't have a *side*." He'd grown annoyed with her persistence and nosiness. He took his hat from the other stool and put it on.

She's as nosy as . . .

"You're a reporter, aren't you? Not a friend of Rob Newton's. You're just fishing for information." He snorted, now pissed at himself that he hadn't immediately spotted the type of person she was. "Have a good day." Truman turned to leave.

"I'm not a reporter. I'm an investigator." She grabbed the side of his jacket.

He immediately spun, knocked her arm away, and dropped the paper bag as he protected his weapon, which had been inches from her hand.

Her mouth dropped open as she froze, shock in her eyes.

"Don't *ever* grab a police officer. Especially from the back."

"Oh my God. I'm so sorry—I wasn't thinking." Her face flushed red.

He believed her. But he wasn't about to turn his back to her again.

"Problem, Chief?" Marion had returned and now stood a few feet behind Paula. The outline of Marion's hand showed through the big pocket of her apron, and Truman realized she held a pistol.

Everyone carries here.

"We're good, Marion. Just a misunderstanding." He waved her off to emphasize she wasn't to get involved.

"Hmph." She removed her hand from her pocket and returned to the kitchen.

Truman refocused on Paula. "What kind of investigator?"

She opened her mouth and closed it, still flustered. "I have a podcast too," she finally muttered.

"In other words, a reporter."

"But I do know—I did know Rob. He told me things. He was scared to start the story. That's why he put it off for so long." She rattled off her words, trying to hold his attention.

"Scared of what?"

Paula hemmed and hawed. "I'm not sure."

She's lying.

"Do you have a business card?" Truman asked. He wasn't going to give her information; he wanted to know exactly who she was.

Her eyes lit up. "Yes." She immediately removed one from the back pocket of her jeans.

It was warm in his hand, and now he had her name, email, and phone number.

Her podcast was called *Paula's Pursuit of Truth.*

"You showed up so fast because you're in the same business."

Peddling conspiracy theories.

"Yes." Horror suddenly filled her face. "You thought—no—we're not. We've never . . . He's married. I would never—" She covered her eyes. "Shit. It wasn't like that. We met online about eight years ago, when we were both starting out. We message or talk every week. He's just a work friend, I guess you'd call it."

Truman removed one of his cards from his pocket and wrote Detective Marshall's name on the back. "Give her a call at the sheriff's department. She might be interested in what you know." He picked up his sandwich bag and headed toward the door. Setting one hand on the door, he turned back to Paula. "Why don't you order some food? Marion could use the business, and I think you owe her for not shooting you in the back."

He had the pleasure of seeing her mouth fall open again as he left.

17

Truman ate the turkey club sandwich at his desk. According to the clock, the sandwich was more dinner than lunch. His enjoyment of it was slightly spoiled by the encounter with the nosy podcaster. He had her site up on his computer and was going through it as he ate.

Paula's podcasts were very similar in tone to Rob Newton's.

Will more "investigators" be coming to town?

He could see how the murder of one conspiracy theory podcaster would motivate others to dig into the story. Truman was glad it was Noelle and Mercy's problem, not his. He took the last bite of his sandwich and had started to lift the slaw from the bag when he realized there were two containers left. He pulled out both and stared at a thick piece of carrot cake in the second.

He knew cake wasn't included with the sandwich.

A smile turned up the corners of his mouth. He didn't think the cake was a mistake.

Glad I left a good tip.

He suspected Marion was one of those people who appeared tough on the outside but were actually mushy on the inside. But she wasn't so mushy that she wouldn't use her pistol.

He wondered if the usual staff also carried while waiting tables. He hadn't noticed any weapons in the past, but that didn't mean they weren't there.

Truman opened the clear cake container and took a bite. It was fresh and the cream cheese frosting was perfect. He finished it in a dozen bites and was no longer interested in his coleslaw. He shoved everything back in the bag and checked his email.

There it is.

Ollie's DNA results. A twinge of guilt washed over him for going behind the teen's back. But he didn't want Ollie to worry about his results until there were some facts. Truman took a breath and opened the email. Quickly scanning, he felt his heart sink to the floor. It stated there was no chance that the two submitted DNA samples came from related people.

He leaned back in his chair, a million thoughts racing through his mind.

The first being that he had to tell the teenager.

Ollie deeply loved his grandparents. Truman had learned that early on. The only mementos that Ollie had from them were a few old, battered novels and ancient textbooks that had a special place on a shelf in his room. His grandparents had raised him well. He was compassionate and had a strong sense of right and wrong.

How will this news affect him?

They were still his grandparents. They just didn't share his genes.

What if there was an error in the testing?

It was possible. But the lack of a match along with his inability to find any trace of Ollie's parents made Truman believe no error had been made.

For the hundredth time he debated sending Ollie's DNA to a genetic database and seeing where relatives popped up. And then he talked himself out of it for the hundredth time. He couldn't do it without asking. It was Ollie's decision. Possibly this news about his grandparents would lead him to do it on his own.

He called Mercy.

"Hey," she answered. "I'm with Noelle. We're digging through the old cases of the missing teens."

"Ollie's DNA shows he is not related to his grandfather. At all," he stated bluntly.

Silence.

"Oh, Truman. I'm sorry. That poor boy. This is going to crush him."

Truman ran a hand over his face. "I have to tell him, and I don't want to."

"He deserves to know. Could there have been a mistake?"

"Of course, but I think it makes sense considering the black hole of my search for his parents."

"Well, you said you wanted results before you asked to adopt him. I guess it's time."

"I'm still worried he'll think I'm doing it out of pity."

"He might. But he'll believe me when I tell him you've been talking about this for months."

I hope so.

"How was your afternoon?" Truman asked, wanting a break from the emotional discussion.

"Not bad. I'm getting a good picture of the old cases, and guess what?" Her voice rose in excitement.

"What?"

"Remember how there was a survivor?"

"Yes. You said a witness told you he died a few years ago."

"Nope. Alive and well. The survivor is Devin Bonner."

Truman's mind struggled for a split second to pinpoint the name. Then it slammed into place. *"From this morning?"* he asked. "Where the Jeep was found?"

"Yes!"

"Rob's Jeep on his property can't be a coincidence."

"That's what we think too. We're planning to talk to him tomorrow. What was your impression of him this morning?"

"His mother, Linda, was very pleasant." Truman thought back. "But Devin was hesitant when he realized I was law enforcement."

"I think that's normal for everyone," said Mercy.

"True. He was very pale and thin. His skin was sort of translucent, you know? It made me wonder if he'd recently been in prison, but I think Ina would have mentioned that. I meant to look him up this morning but forgot when you and Noelle showed up."

"He doesn't have an arrest record," said Mercy. "We also couldn't find a current driver's license for him. His previous one expired around fifteen years ago."

"Ina mentioned he doesn't drive. I assumed he'd had it taken away."

"He could have lived somewhere else. Maybe Europe or Central America?"

Devin Bonner hadn't looked like a world traveler to Truman. He'd given off recluse vibes. "He moved slow," Truman said, remembering the man walking up behind his mother. "Moved oddly, now that I think about it. Almost like he had just woken up." He thought of Devin's brown, lively eyes—so much like his mother's. "Mentally he seemed coherent."

"All the case follow-ups say Devin Bonner still has no memory of what happened back then. I guess we'll form an opinion tomorrow at his interview. We're not giving them a heads-up that we're coming. I want to see how he reacts when we ask about the old cases."

"Why would Rob's Jeep be on his property? I have a hard time believing Devin left it there. And there's no way he could have been one of the attackers at Rob's cabin . . . He didn't look strong at all."

"Maybe he was injured in the fight at Rob's cabin," said Mercy. "That could account for him being pale and moving slowly. And being thin doesn't mean someone isn't strong."

"If he's one of Rob's attackers, does that mean he's trying to cover something up? Did Rob get too close to something and realize that Devin was involved in the disappearance of the other three?"

Mercy was quiet on the other end of the line. "Devin was tied up and almost died," she said slowly. "I've seen the photos. There's no doubt in my mind that someone wanted him dead back then. So maybe he knows something and killed Rob to protect that secret—but who would he be protecting? Himself?"

"He could have been involved in something and then the other three turned on him," said Truman. "Maybe he's stayed silent all these years to protect himself from them. Or whoever."

"That would mean he's lying about not remembering," said Mercy. "This is making my head hurt. If Devin didn't put the Jeep there, did someone leave it there as a message?"

"If he doesn't remember anything, he's not going to understand the message," said Truman.

"How can he not remember?" Exasperation filled her tone.

Truman knew it was a rhetorical question. No matter what had happened, there was no doubt Devin Bonner had been through a traumatic situation. People who experienced those situations frequently had blocked memories. "Wasn't he beat up too? Could he have brain damage? Or maybe the loss of blood created some damage. There's plenty of reasons, both physical and emotional, why he can't remember."

Mercy sighed. "I know. Hopefully his interview tomorrow is helpful. Although, digging through these boxes, I now have a whole list of people I want to talk to."

"Have you retraced Sara and Rob's footsteps since they've been here?"

"Yes. Using Sara's list, Noelle sent deputies to each location to check video to see if they were followed. So far we've only heard back from the places that don't use video. It's going to be a needle-in-a-haystack search. Sara doesn't remember exact times they were in certain stores. And Rob went cross-country skiing on his own several times. Sara didn't know where."

"Make sure you look for Devin in those videos too."

"Definitely. It would be interesting if they turned up in the same place."

"Does Sara know Devin?" asked Truman.

"I haven't asked. We plan to interview her again. We'll definitely talk to Devin first, though."

"I had a visitor today. Paula Jupp. She's a podcaster that claims to know Rob Newton and says he talked to her about the case he was digging into. I gave her Noelle's phone number."

Mercy's voice was distant as he heard her ask Noelle about Paula Jupp.

"Noelle says she has four voice mails she hasn't listened to yet," Mercy said, returning to her phone. "Jupp could be one of them."

"Paula told me Rob was scared of something."

"Why did she come to you?"

"Good question. I think she thought I'd be an easy source of gossip or information. Small-town police, you know. I set her straight. She tried to make it sound like she was here out of concern for Rob, but I think she's working on her own story for a podcast. I do believe she knows him, though. They're part of the same crowd."

"Sounds like we should talk to her. I'll add her to the list."

"Do you have memories of when the five teenagers disappeared?" Truman asked.

"Not really. I've tried to recall, but I would have been about fourteen, and we didn't have a TV." She sighed. "I really need to get back to reviewing this case. I might be late tonight. I'll let you know."

"Want me to bring by dinner?"

"That'd be lovely. I'd like enchiladas, please." She laughed. "Noelle is emphatically agreeing."

"Got it. I'll see you later. Love you."

"Love you too."

Truman hung up the phone and realized the DNA email was still open on his screen, reminding him that he had a tough discussion with Ollie coming up. He'd almost forgotten about it during Mercy's discussion of her case.

I better pick up enchiladas for Ollie too. He's going to need them.

18

Ollie's mouth watered as the spicy scent of Mexican food reached him.

"Where's Kaylie?" Truman asked as he set the carryout bags on the kitchen counter.

It'd been nearly an hour since Truman had told him he would bring home dinner. Ollie had tracked Truman with his phone, watching him stop at the Deschutes County sheriff's office to drop off Mercy's dinner first. Ollie had stared impatiently at his screen as Truman spent fifteen minutes with his wife.

Ollie popped open one of the boxes, and steam rushed out. The food was still hot. "Kaylie is staying at Michelle's tonight. I'm on kitten duty."

"Great! It's a guys' night, then," said Truman as he unpacked the other two boxes. "Kaylie can have her food tomorrow."

"Unless I take it for lunch," said Ollie. "I didn't tell her you were bringing dinner. She'll never miss it."

Truman snorted. "You're willing to risk that? She'll know somehow." He joined Ollie on the tall stools at the raised counter, and they both dug into their food. After a few minutes of companionable silence—except for the crunch of tortilla chips—Truman cleared his throat. "I've got something I want to discuss with you."

He sounds serious.

Ollie set down his fork, his stomach suddenly tight.

“First I’m going to apologize for going behind your back.” Truman picked at his enchilada and then turned to face Ollie, his gaze sober.

What did he do?

“I didn’t know how long it would take, so I didn’t tell you. I didn’t want you stressing about results while we waited.”

“Results for what?” Ollie struggled to speak. He’d never seen Truman so intent before.

“I sent in your DNA . . . and your grandfather’s DNA for a comparison.” Truman put his hand on Ollie’s shoulder. “I’m sorry, son, but you’re not related to him.”

Ollie searched Truman’s eyes.

A faint hum sounded in his ears as he tried to process the words.

He wasn’t my grandfather.

“He’s *still* your grandfather,” Truman said, as if he’d heard Ollie’s thought. “Love formed that relationship, and that can’t be taken away. You simply don’t share any crumbs of genetic material.”

“Maybe the lab made a mistake,” Ollie said, his brain swirling with questions. “That happens. I know samples can get mixed up. And there were two other bodies that were found at the same time as his. It’s got to be a mistake.”

My grandfather wouldn’t lie to me.

“I had the same thought. But we had a positive ID on your grandfather—you helped with that by identifying his boots and belt. And he was the only one found in his age range. The others were much younger. I traced back every step of the handling of his DNA. There wasn’t a mix-up.”

“But we had a funeral for him in a real graveyard after he was found. Did you dig him up to get his DNA?” Ollie’s voice cracked as he imagined someone disturbing the grave. He visited the graveyard every few months to have a private chat with his grandfather. Update him on how his life was going and tell him how much he missed him.

"He wasn't exhumed," Truman said. "Since he was a murder victim, he had an autopsy. They kept some bone and tooth samples."

"Is that normal? Do they always do that?" He'd been told his grandfather's remains were fully skeletal. He squeezed his eyes shut, hating the image in his brain.

"I think they usually do, but I specifically requested it at the time."

Ollie's eyes flew open. "Why?"

Truman grimaced. "I didn't have a plan back then, but because of the circumstances of his death, I wanted to have evidence available in case it was needed for some reason."

Ollie picked up his fork and set it back down. His appetite was gone. Even the chips and salsa had lost their appeal. "Now what?"

"Well, that's up to you. You know there are genetic databases where people register their DNA. You could request a kit and see what happens. Some people on these sites keep their identities private, while others want to contact new relatives. You'd decide how you want to handle it. It could come to something. Or nothing."

"I've thought about doing that while trying to find my parents. But they'd died before those sites got popular, so I doubted they'd be in there. I guess some of their relatives could be. But how did I end up living with my grandparents if I'm not related to them?"

"I'm following up on the possibility that you're biologically related to your grandmother. Maybe your grandmother had your father before marrying your grandfather. Or . . ."

Truman didn't finish the sentence, but Ollie knew.

Or she cheated on him.

"I did finally find a record of their marriage—I'm pretty sure it's them. Your grandfather used the name Smith, which I never could verify was his real name. Anyway, her last name on the record was Webb—but that could be from a previous marriage, because I haven't been able to find a birth certificate under that name, but sometimes in rural areas they simply can't be tracked."

Ollie felt a tiny lift of hope. Truman had a good point. Just because his grandfather wasn't related to him didn't mean his grandmother also wasn't.

"It's possible your parents weren't named Smith. Your father could have been a Webb or something else. I'm going to start searching with that." He paused. "We could start with comparing your DNA to your grandmother's."

When Ollie moved in with Truman, Truman had asked if he wanted his grandmother moved to the same graveyard as his grandfather. Ollie's grandmother had been buried in the woods ten years before, not far from his grandfather's cabin. Ollie had said no. He couldn't imagine disturbing her resting place, and his grandfather had told him she loved that particular spot in the woods. It was a long trip to visit her, and Ollie didn't think his grandfather minded that he'd been buried where Ollie could easily visit. He talked to both of them when he went.

"I don't want to dig up my grandmother for a test," Ollie said. *"I hate this."* He grabbed a napkin and wiped his eyes. He wanted the subject to go away.

I wish Truman had never brought it up.

"I don't know where I came from," Ollie blurted.

"There was a lot of love there, right? That's what is important."

"Yeah." Ollie kept his gaze on his food.

Truman squeezed his shoulder. He hadn't let go of it the entire conversation. "Look at me for a second."

He looked. Truman's eyes were slightly wet, but he smiled, care and affection in his gaze. Ollie knew he was someone he could always trust. He was lucky to have Truman in his life.

Karma?

He'd rescued Truman from the same men who had killed his grandfather. And Truman had rescued him right back.

"You know I've always considered you my son," Truman stated.

"Yeah." Ollie did know that. Truman sometimes called him *son* and always referred to him as part of the family.

"I know you're a man," Truman continued. "Another year or so and you'll even be legal to drink." He paused and held Ollie's gaze. "But I'd like to adopt you."

Ollie couldn't speak, joy and confusion ricocheting through his brain.

He's serious.

"Can you do that if I'm over eighteen?"

"Yep."

"Do I have to change my name?"

"That's completely up to you."

Ollie ducked his head, unable to hold Truman's gaze anymore. Truman had been a father figure for a long time. But Ollie had never allowed himself to think of him as Dad.

"This has been on my mind for over a year," Truman said. "I wasn't sure how to ask you. Was worried you might feel I was cutting you off from everything you'd ever known. Like I said, they're still your grandparents. Nothing can change that."

"What about Kaylie? Are you going to ask her too?"

Truman took a deep breath. "I love Kaylie, but she lost her father pretty recently. That bond is still very tight, and she's got Mercy and her other aunts and uncle. I have no doubt she knows how I feel about her. But for you and me . . . It's different between us. We don't have anybody here. Mercy and I don't plan to have kids—you two are our kids. I've talked to her about this, and she loves the idea. And she agrees with me about Kaylie. This is for *us*. But only if you want it too."

Ollie was quiet for a long moment. He'd dreamed of his parents for years. It was probably typical for any orphan to have fantasies that their parents weren't really dead, that one day they'd simply show up and be overjoyed to see their child. In the past he'd felt guilty about such daydreams; he'd had his grandparents and should be thankful. It was selfish of him to wish for parents. But he'd always had an empty space in his heart.

And now Truman had offered to fill that space.

"You promise you're not offering because of my DNA test?" He forced himself to look Truman in the face, needing to see his eyes as he answered. Truman had already stated that he'd wanted to adopt him for a long time, but Ollie needed to hear it again.

"Hell no," said Truman. "I'm asking because I love you and I want this." He cleared his throat. "I hope you feel the same way."

"I do." Then Ollie snorted. "That sounded as if I'm getting married."

Truman laughed. "Nope." He flung his arm around Ollie's shoulders and pulled him to his side in a tight squeeze. "You're sure about this?"

Ollie had never been more certain of anything. "Yeah. I've sometimes wished you were really my dad."

"Thanks, Ollie." Truman shook his head. "Never saw myself having an adult son. This means I skipped the hard parts of raising kids, right?"

"I don't know about that."

"We'll keep looking for your parents. This won't stop that hunt. Like I said, we've got some different avenues to research now that I have a surname for your grandmother."

"Okay." Ollie needed to make a decision about the DNA registry.

But not today.

He took a big bite of his enchilada and grinned at Truman. His appetite was back.

In fact he felt the best he'd felt in weeks.

19

"Maybe we should have called first," Noelle told Mercy on their way to interview Devin Bonner. It was midmorning. Mercy was driving and looking forward to questioning Devin.

"Truman said they don't leave the house much. And I think the element of surprise will be in our favor," Mercy said. "Most likely they'll be home."

"Wonder why they don't leave."

"Ina told Truman that Linda is very introverted."

"I'm definitely not like that," said Noelle. "Being around people energizes me. I love it."

"Can't say it energizes me," said Mercy after thinking for a moment. "But I don't mind it. I also don't mind being alone." But she couldn't imagine barely leaving the house. She needed to be in the outdoors a few times a week. Maybe Linda and Devin did outdoor activities.

From their research the previous evening, Mercy and Noelle had found little more on Devin Bonner. He had an Oregon ID card, but no driver's license. The title to the house was solely in his mother's name. He had some credit cards and a good credit score but no employment records.

"Where's his income?" Mercy had asked. "He has credit cards but no income. It doesn't appear Linda works either."

"They give credit cards to almost anyone," Noelle had said. "And he lives at home, so expenses are minimized." She'd shrugged. "The house is paid off, and Linda draws Social Security. Although I can't imagine that's enough for the two of them. Maybe her husband's death left her with a nest egg or life insurance."

Mercy turned off the highway and took the long driveway to the Bonner house, passing the place where Rob's Jeep had been discovered the day before. All their footprints and the tire tracks from the tow truck were still visible. It hadn't snowed since the Jeep had been found.

She had studied Devin's ID card photo, comparing it to the senior photo in the case file. The current ID photo didn't project the energy his eyes did in the graduation photo. In the ID he smiled a bit, but his gaze seemed empty.

Not that anyone's ID photo is good.

She parked, and the two of them walked up to the door. Mercy noticed large boot prints in the snow that went to the door and then walked back down the driveway, and she figured they were Truman's from the day before. No one had shoveled the snow from the short walkway or the three steps up to the front porch. Noelle rang the doorbell.

And they waited. She rang again. A full minute went by.

Noelle looked at Mercy and shrugged.

"Maybe they're not home, but there aren't any tire tracks leaving the garage," Mercy said under her breath as she scanned for cameras. "Now I hear something." She smiled pleasantly at the peephole.

The door finally opened. It was Devin Bonner, and he looked curiously at them, uncertainty in his gaze.

Truman was right. Thin and pale.

"Good morning, Mr. Bonner," said Noelle. She introduced herself and Mercy as they held up their identification.

"I don't know the two of you," he stated, but there was a bit of a question in his tone.

"Correct," said Mercy. "We were here yesterday collecting evidence from the Jeep but didn't come to the door."

"Right," said Devin. "Mom said someone else might stop by with questions. Do you have business cards?"

The women each dug out a card. Devin took them. He eyed Mercy's card and then took a long look at her. Then he did the same with Noelle's card. Mercy found it odd.

Our photos are on our IDs, not our cards.

"Please come in." He took a step back to allow them to enter, and Mercy realized something was wrong with his left arm.

He was wearing a sweater, but the way his arm hung and the cramped look of the fingers told her something wasn't quite right. She was reminded of the late senator Bob Dole, who had lost the use of his right arm.

"Thank you," she said as she passed him. "Is Linda here?"

"Yes, she's out feeding the deer. She should be back in a few minutes. It's part of her morning routine. Have a seat." He gestured—with his right hand—at a formal dining table to their right. "I just made coffee. Would you like some? I also have tea."

"We'd both love some coffee," Mercy said, before Noelle could speak. She wanted a minute alone with Noelle to compare observations.

She and Noelle took seats, and Mercy watched Devin leave and turn a corner into the kitchen. His pace was hesitant, as if he had no confidence in his balance when he walked.

"He's handicapped in some way," she said in a low voice to Noelle. "That explains why we were finding so little work information and no driver's license. I wonder if it happened twenty years ago."

"The records indicated he'd been beaten pretty bad. I remember mention of a broken arm and head injury. But the cold case check-ins don't mention anything physically going on."

"I bet all the contact was over the phone," said Mercy.

"You're probably right."

Dishes clinking and liquids pouring sounded from the kitchen.

"Should we help?" asked Noelle.

"I think he would have asked if he needed it," said Mercy, thinking of her sister. Rose was blind, and her siblings had learned long ago that she would ask when she needed help. Mercy's sister could do almost everything but drive. She taught preschool, cared for her toddler, and kept the books at her husband's lumberyard.

Devin appeared a minute later carrying a tray with three coffee mugs, sugar, and cream. He held it with his right hand but balanced it on the raised forearm of his left arm, his left hand dangling like an empty, forgotten glove.

He can move the arm a bit. But not the hand.

He set down the tray and handed each woman a mug. Mercy's was from Glacier National Park. Noelle's was Bryce Canyon National Park, and Devin's was Yellowstone.

"Have you been to all these parks?" Noelle asked, holding up her mug.

His face lit up. "Yes. Each summer we pick one to visit."

"Have a favorite?" Noelle asked.

"Impossible to say," said Devin with a grin as he took a seat. "Each one is stunning in its own way."

Mercy agreed.

The interior of the little ranch house was clean but very dated. The living room had a worn sofa, two easy chairs, and a woodstove that was putting out a lovely heat that reached the dining room table. Devin fit in with the interior. His clothes were neat but slightly shabby, and his brown hair needed a trim. He'd laid their business cards on the table in front of him.

"Did you find the owner of the vehicle from yesterday?" he asked, a mild curiosity in his eyes. "Why is the FBI involved with an abandoned vehicle? Is it tied to a bigger crime?" He glanced at Mercy's card, as if verifying that she was the FBI agent, and then looked to her to answer the questions.

"It's possible it's part of a crime the FBI is looking at," Mercy said, keeping her answer vague. "Yesterday Linda told the police chief that you didn't see anyone around? What about for the previous twenty-four hours?"

"No one," said Devin. His forehead wrinkled as he listened to her questions; he appeared very focused.

"Have you heard of or been contacted by someone named John Jacobs who has a podcast?" she asked.

He thought for a second. "I don't recognize the name."

"He's tall. About forty with blond hair. He might have used a different name. Rob Newton."

"No one has contacted me recently. How far back should I be considering?"

"A week or so," said Noelle. "Although he might have contacted you by email or phone at any time."

"I don't remember anything like that." He paused. "I don't interact with many people."

After speaking with Devin for a bit, Mercy hadn't seen any evidence of brain damage from twenty years ago that affected his speech or comprehension. Her interview with Ted Weir at the crime scene had given her the impression that he might have some. She was sympathetic about his physical limitations and wondered if they were why he didn't interact with people. She found him intelligent and personable, and quite likable.

She still planned to ask him about the old crime, but she wanted to talk to Linda too.

"You said Linda is feeding the deer?" Mercy asked after glancing at the time. "How long does that take?"

Devin shrugged. "Depends if some of the deer are waiting. Two of them will let her pet them, so if they're there, she'll stay and watch for a while."

"Are people supposed to feed them?" Mercy asked.

Devin grinned. "We've had many discussions about that. She gets her way."

"What's the issue?" asked Noelle, looking from one to the other.

"They become dependent on being fed and stop foraging," said Mercy, as Devin nodded.

"My mom weans them off the feed in the spring," he said. "Slowly cutting back on the amount of food. She sticks to feeding them during the winter and only feeds enough to supplement. They still need to forage this time of year."

"Would you mind if I went to get her?" Mercy asked. "It's close, right?"

"That would be great," Devin said. He pointed at the glass slider at the back of the house. "It's not far. Just go out that door and head directly north toward the woods. There's a well-worn path once you reach the trees. It starts near the shed."

"How far up the path does she feed them?"

"Maybe a hundred yards?"

Mercy slid her chair back, slipped on her coat, and left while Noelle started a conversation about Bryce Canyon. Outside she immediately spotted footprints in the two-inch-deep snow leading across the backyard toward the shed Devin had mentioned. She followed the prints, stepping in them with her boots that weren't meant to be worn in snow. She had good hiking boots in her Tahoe, but she decided against changing.

She passed the shed and immediately spotted the dirt path. The canopy of the tall pines had kept the snow from reaching the ground in the woods. It felt colder under the trees, which blocked the blue sky and sun. Probably twenty-five degrees in the shade. Keeping an eye out, she walked several yards and then called Linda's name. She knew better than to surprise someone in the woods. Some people would shoot first and ask questions later.

Mercy called again. Ahead she finally spotted a clearing and stopped as a dozen deer darted away. One halted to stare at her. Mercy didn't move, enjoying the quiet moment.

Is that one of the tamer ones?

She could just barely see the doe's nose quiver as she tried to scent Mercy. The deer finally ran off after the others, and Mercy pushed on. "Linda! Hello?"

There.

Mercy burst into a sprint, her gaze locked on something orange. Someone—she assumed Linda—was on the ground. "Linda?"

She slammed to a stop. "Oh, *shit*!"

The small woman was on her back, her eyes closed. Blood seeped into the dirt and pine needles around her. Blood streaked her orange jacket, and more ran from the corner of her mouth.

Did the deer trample her? Or did a cougar attack?

Breathing hard, Mercy quickly scanned the clearing and didn't see any predators. Her weapon was under her coat at her ribs. She unzipped her coat in case she needed to reach the gun quickly and dropped beside the woman. "Linda! *Are you okay?*"

Stupid question.

Mercy shook the woman's shoulder as she said her name. She was relieved to see Linda was breathing—although the breaths were shallow and rough—and then was instantly anxious that she wouldn't breathe for much longer. Mercy opened the woman's ripped coat and pulled up her shirt, trying to find the source of the bleeding, and realized she'd been stabbed several times.

A human predator did this.

She spun on her knees in the dirt, checking for the attacker. Still nothing.

I've got to stop the bleeding.

Mercy pulled out her phone and was relieved to see she had service. She called Noelle.

"Mercy?"

"Linda's been stabbed," she said rapidly. "She's still alive but barely. I need my medical kit from the Tahoe. It's the small black duffel in back. We're up the path that Devin described. *Run!*"

She hit END and then called 911.

20

After calling 911, Mercy ripped off her coat and used it to apply pressure to the wounds.

"Shit." She only had so many hands, and there were at least seven bleeding stab wounds. She prioritized and pressed on the heaviest bleeders. Her shins grew damp where she knelt, Linda's blood soaking into her pants.

She's so tiny, and she's lost so much blood.

"Hang on, Linda. An ambulance is on its way."

She didn't respond.

Her breathing sounds were getting fainter and more irregular. Her lips were tinged blue.

Probably a punctured lung.

Mercy checked the woman's pulse. It was fast. The heart was trying to compensate for the lowered oxygen level in the blood. "You can do this!" she told Linda. "Not much longer now."

I hope.

She estimated Linda to be in her seventies. Her age and small stature were working against her.

"Mercy!"

"Up here!"

Noelle tore into the clearing, Mercy's medical kit in her hand.

"Oh, damn!" Noelle dropped to her knees and opened the duffel. "What do you need?"

"Take my place. Press here and here. I'll find what I want."

They switched, and Mercy dug in her bag, immediately pulling out a thin black package. She ripped it open, and her hands shook as she peeled the clear covering off a thin, rubbery, highly adhesive round bandage. She spread it over the stab wound she suspected had penetrated a lung. She pressed on the sticky bandage, making a tight seal, and then paused, watching and listening to Linda's uneven breathing. It didn't change. "Crap!" Mercy took the second round piece from the pack and covered a second stab wound where she thought she'd seen an air bubble exit, sealing it tightly.

Linda's breathing hitched and seemed to slightly improve.

Thank God.

"I think I got it. Lift one hand, Noelle." Mercy opened a different package, pulled out a strip of hemostatic gauze, and crammed it into the heavily bleeding wound. "Now press on that." She did the same thing to the cut under Noelle's other hand and then did the others, stretching her fingers to press on the gauze. The product's makers claimed to stop heavy bleeding with sixty seconds of pressure.

I should start fluids next.

But she wasn't ready to take pressure off the bleeding.

"Look at her hands," Noelle said in a low voice.

They were covered in nicks and slashes.

Defensive wounds.

"She fought him." Mercy's heart ached for the woman.

"Which means she saw him," said Noelle. "We'll catch the bastard."

"Where's Devin?" asked Mercy, glancing back down the path as sirens sounded in the distance.

"I told him to wait out front and direct the paramedics. Hey. I think her lips are pinker."

Mercy agreed, her heart still pounding. "I managed to seal the lung puncture."

"You need to make me a medical kit."

"It's saved a few lives." Mercy shuddered, remembering how Kaylie had almost died from a bullet wound. Mercy's quick actions and kit had saved her life. The same had happened when her partner, Eddie, had been shot.

All her family's vehicles carried a similar kit.

I hope I never need to use it again.

◆ ◆ ◆

Mercy tried not to pace in the hospital waiting room, but she had energy to burn.

Why was Linda attacked?

Was it random? Or connected to the Jeep left on her property?

She hopped up out of her chair and strode across the room to look out the window. She stood there, fingers tapping the windowsill, not focused on anything outside. All she could see was Linda's blood seeping into the dirt. The EMTs had looked grim as they started fluids and took her away.

Linda was in surgery, and there had been no updates. Devin sat in the waiting room staring straight ahead, seeming detached, occasionally touching the faint scars that crossed his neck. Mercy and Noelle had tried to talk to him, but his answers had been short and curt. They'd finally left him alone.

His father died a few years ago. Now this.

Mercy had noticed he'd shuddered a few times as they entered the hospital, and she'd wondered if he had bad memories from his father's or his own experience. She'd driven him and Noelle to the hospital once she'd cleaned up and changed her bloody pants and boots, swapping them for the extra clothes she always carried in her Tahoe. Along with clothes, she carried emergency food, water, tools, and fuel. And her precious medical kit. They made up her GOOD bag. Get Out Of Dodge.

I'm always ready for shit to hit the fan.

Truman strode into the waiting room, Ollie right behind him. He went straight to Mercy and enveloped her in his arms. She took a deep breath and tried to relax her shoulders and spine. His heavy coat smelled like the outdoors. Fresh snow and crisp, cold air.

"What the hell is going on?" he asked in a low voice for her ears only.

"I'm going to find out."

"You think it's related to Rob Newton? And those old cases?"

"I don't have any proof, but I suspect so. I don't believe in coincidences. There is too much happening all at once."

"But why try to kill Devin's mother? What could she have to do with *anything*?"

"I don't know. Maybe she saw something or knows something." Mercy turned her head to see Devin. Ollie had taken the seat next to him and was showing him something on his phone. Devin's emotionless zombie gaze had lightened. "Ollie's a good kid."

Truman looked at the two. "He is. On the way over I mentioned that Devin might need some help since his mother seemed to be his foundation. I was just talking out loud, feeling bad for the guy. I didn't tell Ollie to do anything." He turned back to Mercy. "Did you question Devin?"

She sighed. "Not yet. He was practically mute on the drive here."

"If he wants his mother's attacker found, he'll answer questions."

"True. Noelle went down to the cafeteria. When she gets back, we'll get started. I know there's a small meeting room down the hall. I'll see if it's being used."

"I'll go check." He gave her a quick kiss. "You look like you need to sit down."

"I can't sit still."

"Try again." He left to check on the room. Noelle came in as he was leaving, carrying a tray with four big paper cups of coffee and a white bag. Truman spoke to her briefly and she nodded, her gaze going to Mercy.

Mercy glared. No doubt he'd told Noelle that she needed to rest.

Noelle offered him one of the coffees. He shook his head and headed down the hall.

She approached Mercy and held out the tray. "I grabbed as many as I could carry. I figured too much is better than not enough when it comes to caffeine."

Mercy took one. "Let's take Devin down the hall for that interview. He's had some time to get his bearings." She eyed the white bag in Noelle's hand. "What's in the bag?"

"Everything. Several sandwiches, fruit, yogurt, and shortbread." She shrugged. "I can never pass up shortbread, although I have low expectations for hospital cafeteria shortbread."

"Sounds perfect to me." Mercy set her coffee on the windowsill and took the two others to Ollie and Devin. "Here." The men automatically took the cups. "Ollie, we're going to take Devin down the hall to talk for a while. You sticking around?"

Ollie exchanged a look with Devin. "Yeah, I'll be here."

"Noelle has sandwiches if you'd like one." Mercy held his gaze and jerked her head in Noelle's direction.

Ollie got the message and jumped up. "Sandwich sounds good."

Mercy took his seat. "Devin, Detective Marshall and I need to figure out who did this to your mother. There's a private room where we can talk."

He nodded. "Detective Marshall," he repeated, staring at Mercy.

He's still a little foggy.

Truman reappeared and gave Mercy a thumbs-up. He joined Noelle and Ollie, who were looking through the sandwiches.

"Let's go." Mercy stood and looked expectantly at Devin.

The man slowly stood. It was more an unfolding of his tall, thin body. His withered left hand dangled, a reminder of something that used to be.

"What was Ollie showing you?" she asked. They had been intently watching something on Ollie's phone.

"New *Star Trek* series. I'd heard there were a few new shows but hadn't seen any of them. We don't get the right streaming service."

"You a fan?" Mercy knew Ollie was. Kaylie had introduced him to the original *Star Trek* and he'd binged his way through every episode of every series and every movie. And then watched them all again.

"Big-time fan. Ollie is nice," he said as they left the waiting room.

"He's my husband's unofficial son."

Confusion crossed Devin's face. "Unofficial?"

"Soon to be official," she said. "He'll be legally adopting Ollie."

"Ollie's an adult, isn't he?" Devin suddenly sounded uncertain.

"He's almost twenty. It's more symbolic than anything. It's important to the two of them."

"That sounds nice," said Devin. A woman walked down the hall toward them, and Devin smiled warmly at her. She appeared slightly startled but nodded and gave a tentative smile.

He seemed to deflate as she passed, exhaustion catching up with him. Understandable with the emotional toil his mother's attack must be taking on him.

"Here we are." Mercy opened the door. Inside the small room was a round table with a half dozen chairs. An old TV sat on a rolling rack in the corner. Two boxes of tissues were on the table, and Mercy suspected the room was often used for delivering bad news.

"Have a seat." Mercy glanced back to see if Noelle had followed them. Not yet.

Devin sat and put his coffee on the table. "Would you tell me your name again, please?"

"Mercy."

"Mercy Kilpatrick. The FBI."

"Yes. Detective Marshall is the one with the sheriff's office." Mercy wasn't surprised her name had slipped his mind after the horrible morning.

Maybe he still has memory issues.

When she'd spoken with Devin in the morning, he'd seemed focused and intelligent. But she had noticed how often he'd glanced at their business cards when they talked at his home. Her heart sank as she wondered if he still remembered nothing from his abduction and near-murder twenty years ago. "I'll get Detective Marshall. I'd thought she would follow us."

She met Noelle halfway down the hall.

"Sorry, Ollie couldn't make up his mind about a sandwich. I finally made him take two." Noelle had her own coffee and the white bag.

Mercy's stomach growled. "Hang on a second before we go in," she said quietly. "I think Devin still has memory issues. He just asked my name, although he remembered my last name once I said my first."

"It's a good sign that your reply prompted him to remember your last name. We've got nothing to lose by asking questions," Noelle said with a shrug.

Mercy agreed, and they went to join Devin. He eyed Noelle as she set out two yogurts and a huge stack of napkins. "Crap. I forgot spoons for the yogurt."

"Thank you, but I'm really not hungry," Devin said, still watching Noelle. "Do either of you have a pen and paper I could borrow?"

"I do," Mercy said, reaching into her bag for one of the notepads she always carried. She slid it across the table along with a pen. His left arm was awkwardly in his lap, and he picked up the pen with his right, moving the pad into place with his elbow. He immediately wrote down her name and something below in cramped handwriting she couldn't read upside down. He eyed Noelle. "Noelle," Mercy prompted, deliberately only giving her first name.

"Noelle Marshall. Deschutes County sheriff detective," he stated as he wrote it out. "Sorry. My memory is horrible sometimes." He looked at Mercy. "The *Star Trek* guy?"

"Ollie Smith."

"Thank you." He made several notations under Ollie's name.

Mercy met Noelle's gaze, and Noelle gave a subtle nod.

I start.

"Devin, did you notice anything unusual with your mother this morning before she went to feed the deer? Did she do anything she doesn't usually do?"

His brows came together. "Like what?"

"Something not in her daily routine. Did she get any calls? Talk to you about something odd?"

"Are you suggesting my mother was going to meet someone where she feeds the deer?" Shock filled his eyes. "Like she was attacked by someone she knew?"

"Most attacks are personal," Noelle said.

He shook his head, denial in his eyes. "No one would want to hurt her. Everyone loves her. She's a gentle, happy person."

"Who are her closest friends?"

He thought for a moment. "Ina Smythe, who lives next door. Katy Lowrie lives a couple of miles away. They talk."

He remembered those names.

Mercy wrote down Katy's name. She already knew Ina very well. No doubt Ina had made a dozen calls after hearing the ambulance that morning and had discovered what had happened. Ina would probably receive an update on Linda's current condition before Devin.

"Any threats to you or your mother recently?" asked Noelle.

"Threats?" He looked from one woman to the other, anger building in his face. "Of course not. You should be searching the woods behind our house instead of talking to me about things that have never happened."

"A crime scene team is working the area, Devin," Mercy said gently. "If there's something that leads to your mother's attacker, they'll find it."

"Then why are you questioning me?"

Mercy opened her mouth and closed it. She'd been about to recite her usual line: "We need to eliminate family first." But then she'd realized she'd never asked herself if Devin could have attacked his mother.

He took forever to answer the door this morning.

But his left arm is weak. He's unsteady on his feet.

Or is that what he wants us to believe?

If his mother wasn't expecting him to hurt her, it may have given him an advantage in the attack.

She swallowed, trying to come up with something that didn't indicate the path her brain had sped down.

"Because you were the last person who saw her," said Noelle, filling Mercy's silence. "That's always the first person we talk to." She kept her gaze on Devin. "And that's two unusual events at your place in two days."

Devin blinked and straightened in his seat. "Unusual? I can't see how an abandoned vehicle is that out of the ordinary. Or has anything to do with us."

Mercy took the plunge. "Devin, the Jeep belonged to Rob Newton. He was killed two days ago and left tied up on the banks of the Columbia River."

She didn't think it was possible with his pale skin, but Devin's face went white.

"Rob Newton—a.k.a. John Jacobs—was the podcaster I asked you about in your home earlier today. He was doing a story on you and your four friends' disappearances twenty years ago when he was murdered."

Devin's mouth opened the tiniest bit, and his eyes rolled back in his head as his body went limp. Mercy and Noelle unsuccessfully lunged for him as he fell out of his chair.

The sound of his head hitting the floor rattled through Mercy's bones.

21

Truman glanced up at the sound of people running down the hall. Several hospital employees in scrubs tore by the waiting room.

"Somebody die?" mumbled Ollie, sitting next to him.

Truman strode to the waiting room door in time to see the employees turn into a room far down the hall, near where Mercy was interviewing Devin Bonner.

Or is it the same room?

He'd jogged halfway there before finishing the thought. He stopped at the open door. The little room was packed with people, and Mercy and Noelle had stepped back against the walls as four employees worked on Devin, who was on his back on the floor.

"I'll get a wheelchair." A tall man in scrubs darted past Truman.

"I'm okay! I'm okay," Devin kept repeating, trying to sit up. One of the women made him lie still.

"Have you eaten today?" asked a woman in pink scrubs. "Do you pass out often?"

"He hit his head *hard*," Mercy told them. "I'll be surprised if he didn't crack his skull."

"Get him to the ER. He's going to need some scans," said the woman keeping him from sitting up.

"No, I'm fine," argued Devin.

"Did you land on your arm?" asked the man. "Did you hurt it?"

"No." Devin's eyes were wide as he stared from face to face. "That's how it always is. Useless."

He's terrified.

Truman wasn't sure if the fear had come from Devin rarely leaving home or if he didn't leave home because of the fear. He suspected the latter.

"Excuse me, sir!"

Truman stepped out of the way as a wheelchair was pushed into the room. Devin was slowly helped to his feet and immediately put in the chair, panic on his face.

He was peppered with more questions as they wheeled him away, and Noelle followed after a hushed word with Mercy.

Mercy moved to the hall to stand beside Truman to watch the group leave. "What happened?" he asked her.

"I told him how Rob Newton's body had been found while investigating the old case, then I saw the whites of his eyes, and he went down before either of us could reach him. Poor guy. He didn't like those people fussing over him at all."

"What will he do if his mother dies?" came Ollie's voice.

Surprised, Truman and Mercy turned around. Ollie must have followed without his noticing. The teen looked stricken.

He knows what it's like to lose all your family.

"We don't know that Linda will die," Mercy said, but uncertainty touched her tone.

"Even if she doesn't die, he'll be living alone for a while, which I doubt he's ever done," said Ollie. "I wonder how much day-to-day stuff his mom does for him. He can't drive, right?"

"Right," said Truman as the three of them walked back to the waiting room. "He'll probably need someone to stop in once a day to check on him. Bring groceries. Make sure he's eating. Some sort of home health aide, I guess. Linda might need that, too, when she gets out."

If she gets out.

"I'll do it," said Ollie.

"No," said Truman at the same time as Mercy. "That's really kind of you, but you don't know the extent of—"

"I don't mind," Ollie said earnestly. "I helped my grandfather when he broke a leg. It's not a big deal. Besides, Devin's cool. We get along well enough, and he likes some of the same books and video games that I do."

"I thought you were talking TV and movies with him," said Mercy.

"That was part of it."

"You only talked with him for, what? Ten minutes, if that?"

Ollie shrugged. "He needed someone to talk to."

Mercy's brows shot up as Truman remembered that she'd said Devin would barely speak to her and Noelle on the drive. He doubted they'd asked him about his favorite books or movies.

"You've got two jobs; you don't have the time," said Truman, worried Ollie didn't know what he was getting into.

Would it be safe? His mother was attacked.

Maybe they could stay somewhere else.

"I think I'm done working at the car dealership. I've waxed and detailed enough cars for a lifetime," said Ollie. "The people are nice, but I don't see any future there since I don't want to sell cars. I love working at the sports warehouse, though," he added quickly. "I think that's a better use of my time. I like working around all that outdoor equipment, and I could move up if I wanted."

"Devin Bonner?" A woman in scrubs stood in the doorway, her hair covered with a bright-yellow floral surgery cap.

"He just went to the emergency room," said Mercy, stepping forward to read the stitched name on the woman's scrub top. "Dr. Prescott, you're Linda Bonner's surgeon, correct?" Mercy held out her identification. "FBI Special Agent Kilpatrick. I'm investigating her attack."

Truman bit back a smile at Mercy immediately identifying her role in front of the surgeon. Otherwise the doctor would insist on speaking only to family—as she should.

"I heard law enforcement found her," the surgeon said, eyeing Mercy's head-to-toe black clothing and boots. She looked like an outdoorsy ninja—not an FBI agent.

"Yes, that was me. How is she doing?"

"Why is Mr. Bonner in the emergency room?" asked the surgeon, scanning the three of them, still hesitant to discuss medical details with nonfamily members. Her gaze stopped on Truman, and he silently held out his law enforcement identification.

"Her son had a fall. I think he'll be okay. His mother?" Mercy prompted.

Dr. Prescott pressed her lips together, her gaze troubled. "I've done what I can. It's up to her, but I'm guarded about her prognosis. She lost an excessive amount of blood."

"I know," said Mercy softly. Truman put his hand on her shoulder, knowing she felt she should have done more for Devin's mother.

"She also had a severe head trauma. I'm not sure if she fell or was hit in the head—but I'd put my money on the latter. Who packed her wounds?" asked Dr. Prescott. "I pulled a lot of material out of them. I was told one of the officers did it."

"I did."

The doctor nodded, respect in her eyes. "Nice job. She wouldn't have made it to surgery if that and the chest seal hadn't been done."

Truman felt a small vibration go through Mercy, and she exhaled. "I did what I could. Hopefully it was enough."

"I hope so too," said Dr. Prescott, sincerity in her eyes. She shook Mercy's hand, took the proffered business card, and left.

Mercy put a hand to the small of her back and stretched. Her spine popped three times. "I'm exhausted." Ollie ambled off to sit in front of the TV at the far end of the waiting room.

"Take a seat," Truman told her. "I'll go grab what you left in the other room." He walked down the hall, and in the little conference room, he put the yogurts back in the paper bag and picked up a yellow notepad.

Must be Devin's writing.

Under Mercy's name and title, he'd written *Saved Mom. Tall with long, black hair. GREEN eyes. Pretty.*

Truman didn't disagree. Her eyes had also caught his attention when they first met.

For Noelle, he'd written, *Tall, gold-white hair pulled up, intimidating but nice.*

He chuckled. Noelle rarely held back when she had something to say. For their short acquaintance, Devin had summed her up nicely.

There was an entry for Ollie too. *Young. Big teeth. Kind. Star Trek.*

He frowned at the mention of Ollie's teeth. They were rather prominent, but at least they were white and straight. It seemed an odd thing to list.

The man had admitted to Mercy he had memory problems. The note making was obviously a much-needed tool for him.

Back in the waiting room, he handed the notepad to Mercy. Sympathy flashed in her eyes as she read it.

"I guess we should return it when he comes back. Clearly he struggles."

"Did he say anything about the cases from his past?"

"No." Mercy grimaced. "He passed out on the first question. But I did ask about his and his mother's morning. He was fine with those questions." She glanced at Ollie, who was engrossed in a TV show about whales, and lowered her voice. "Stupidly I'd never considered if Devin could be his mother's attacker until that conversation."

Truman realized he hadn't either. "We're both slacking. Until he's ruled out, he has to be considered. He was there."

"I've been fooled a few times by faked physical limitations," she said grimly. "But everything I've seen so far with Devin seems genuine. If it's not him, it would have to be someone who knew where his mother fed the deer—or had watched the house a few times. Devin said she did it every morning."

"Or it was random," Truman said. His brain argued against the statement, but it couldn't be ruled out. Yet.

Mercy's phone rang. "It's Jeff." She stepped into the hall to answer the call from her supervisor.

Truman looked in the white food bag and dug around for the shortbread cookies he'd spotted earlier. Disappointed, he realized there were none left. He was pretty certain he'd seen Noelle slip a few pieces into her pocket. He settled for an orange instead.

Eat when you have the opportunity.

His training officer had frequently emphasized that rule when he was a rookie cop. Meal breaks were rarely on time and often nonexistent. The pace in Eagle's Nest was a little slower than during his early years in California, but the rule had stuck with him.

Mercy returned. "I need to go. There's been another substation attack."

"They're getting cocky," said Truman. "You'd think they'd have concerns that security had been stepped up after the first two."

"What security?" asked Mercy with a shrug. "The government won't put armed guards at these remote stations. Maybe some different fencing and some cameras, and that won't happen overnight; it'll take time." She checked the clock. "Can you and Noelle figure out what to do for Devin when the emergency room releases him? Ollie's offer was generous, but he might be taking on more than he realizes."

"We'll take care of it. I wonder if they'll keep him overnight because of his head injury."

Mercy shuddered. "I can still hear it hitting the floor." She gave Truman a quick kiss and hug and strode to the door.

He smiled as he watched her walk away.

Yep. She's pretty.

22

As she drove back to Bend from the electrical substation, Mercy thought over the destruction she'd seen. The damage was similar to that at the one she'd investigated in Wasco County two days earlier. Again, someone had known exactly where to aim to destroy. And like the other substation, this one had been surrounded with easy-to-shoot-through fencing and was on a remote dirt road with no other buildings around for miles.

The attacks weren't sly and well thought out; they were blunt and primitive. Accomplished by someone who knew only how to create damage by shooting. As if they'd been told "Shoot here," and so they had.

She wondered if tire treads, shells, and bullets would match the evidence from the first two attacks, in Wasco County. Today's substation destruction had been in Crook County, an hour northeast of Bend. As before, she'd found two sets of footprints and tire tracks from one vehicle. She'd gone through the same steps of evidence collection that she had at the previous location. If everything matched, at least they'd be able to tie the attacks together and build a big case once they caught the perpetrators.

But first she had to find the suspects.

It could be more than two people. It could be a group that carries out attacks by only two people at a time.

"Accelerationists," she said out loud in her Tahoe.

Back at the Bend FBI office, Darby Cowen, the data analyst, was pulling together everything she could on accelerationist activities in the Pacific Northwest. Substations were currently their target of choice across the nation. They were easy to strike, the attacks needing little strategy or skill.

"Or it could be drunk copycats with guns," she muttered.

Mercy pulled into the Deschutes County sheriff's parking lot and sighed as she turned off her Tahoe. It was nearly dinnertime, so she and Noelle would be eating takeout in the conference room again. They'd agreed they needed to put in several more hours of work that evening. It felt as if they'd worked on Rob Newton's murder two weeks earlier instead of the day before, and they'd only scratched the surface. Between the substations, the Newton murder, and Linda's attack, Mercy felt overloaded.

I suspect Linda's and Rob's cases are connected.

Somehow.

Hopefully the work she and Noelle did on the Newton murder case would help with Linda's case.

Attacked by the same person?

Maybe.

She headed into the station. Truman had called earlier and said that Linda's status hadn't changed. "But the surgeon says that every hour she makes it is a positive sign." He also told her that Devin had been released and that the ER doctor had insisted he not be alone because of the head injury. Ollie had offered to stay with Devin overnight to keep an eye on him.

The doctor had verified that Devin had little use of his arm and had some balance and generalized muscle weakness issues. Truman and Mercy agreed the chance of Devin being Linda's attacker was very slim.

"Is the Bonner house safe for Ollie to stay there?" Mercy had asked. After all, someone had tried to kill Linda on the property.

"After a lot of persuading, Devin agreed to stay in a hotel for a couple of nights," Truman had told her. "Found one with a kitchenette and extra bedroom so that he and Ollie won't get in each other's way. We're going to pick up some things from his house and head over there. I think Ollie's sort of excited about it. He and Devin talk to each other like a couple of movie and gaming geeks."

Please let Devin's mother survive.

The two of them only had each other.

Mercy found Noelle sitting cross-legged on the table in the department's small conference room, studying the board of Rob Newton's crime scene photos. She hopped down as Mercy entered, and Mercy gave a tentative sniff. The room smelled like fish—but in a good way—and she spotted the large bag from a seafood restaurant.

"Spinach salad?" she asked hopefully, suddenly craving greens after a day of nothing but coffee and processed food.

"Yep," Noelle said proudly. "With salmon. Truman told me what to get you."

Mercy tried not to drool. She pulled the salads out of the bag and handed one to Noelle. "Oh, there's bread too!" Her stomach growled. The restaurant had the best bread. She broke off a hunk and slathered it with butter from a little gold foil wrapper. Without even taking off her coat, she flopped down in a chair and chewed. "Where are we at?" she asked around big bites of the ciabatta. "I feel like a ton of things have happened since we dug into the old cases yesterday."

Noelle snorted. "That's putting it lightly." She picked up a binder. "Yesterday you finished reading the victims' family interviews, and I went through the friends' interviews—"

"Which all essentially said the same thing: they didn't have theories as to why the kids vanished." Mercy frowned. "I find it hard to believe that no one knew *anything*. People talk. Teenagers brag."

"Today we can start going through the evidence reports."

Mercy sat up as a thought occurred to her. "What was Rob Newton doing during that time back then? His wife said he'd gone to the same high school and had always talked about the case."

"I saw a yearbook in one of the boxes. Maybe that will give us an idea," said Noelle, taking a lid off a box on the table. Mercy picked the closest box on the floor and quickly searched through it. No luck. She opened the second.

"Got it." She returned to her chair and opened to the index in the back of the heavy book.

Noelle moved to look over her shoulder.

"Page sixty-three," Mercy mumbled, flipping the pages. She found the right page and scanned the color senior photos, wanting to try to find him without looking at the names. It was easy. Rob Newton looked the same but with plumper cheeks and thick-lensed glasses. "This is the only picture, according to the index. I guess he didn't do clubs or sports."

She flipped back to the index and looked up the other five teenagers. Each one had at least a half dozen page numbers listed after their name.

"Busy kids," said Noelle.

Mercy checked Devin's pages first. He'd played basketball and baseball and belonged to a few business-type clubs. He appeared confident and happy in each photo. A contrast to the hesitant man she'd met the day before.

Mia and her boyfriend, Colin, had been prom queen and king. The other boys had played at least two sports each, and Mia had been the senior class vice president. A candid shot showed the five of them standing on a lunchroom table, arms linked and laughing. Devin was on an end, his free arm high in the air. "Like we read in the interviews, these five were good friends. It appears they were well liked too."

"That's the impression I got from the friends," said Noelle. She reached for a binder, checked the spine, and then chose the one next to it. "Here are the friend interviews I read." She shuffled through them. "A lot of upset teenagers saying they didn't understand how this could happen—wait." Noelle stopped on one near the end. "This statement is from Rob Newton. I didn't notice the name on it yesterday. I think after reading thirty interviews that all said the same thing, I'd stopped paying attention to the names. Dammit."

"Does his interview say anything different?" asked Mercy. "I'm a little surprised he was interviewed. From looking through the yearbook, I got the feeling he didn't hang around the same crowd."

Noelle scowled as she read. "Like the others, he raved about how nice they were. Said Colin was his next-door neighbor who he'd known since he was five—that's probably why he was interviewed."

"So Rob wasn't just researching some kids who vanished, he was covering the story of a friend and neighbor he'd known a long time. Why didn't Sara mention that? Did he keep it from her, or did she simply not bother to share it?"

"Did we get her lab work back yet?" Noelle moved to her laptop and started tapping.

"I haven't seen it."

"Here it is! Just came through an hour ago." She opened an attachment and started scrolling through the results of Sara's blood tests. "No . . . no . . . wait . . . you were right! She's positive for benzodiazepines too!" Noelle's eager gaze met Mercy's. "Now what the fuck does that mean for our case?"

Mercy thought for a moment. "Either she took them and didn't want to tell us, or somehow she accidentally took them and didn't know, or she was drugged by Rob or another person and didn't know it. It's not clear cut at all. But it does help explain why she slept through what was clearly a struggle in the cabin."

"We need to talk to her again," said Noelle, making a notation. "For now, back to the older cases and their evidence reports."

Mercy buried her focus in the case of Tyler Hynd, the boy who had been found dead on the riverbank. She studied his autopsy report. Unsurprisingly the cause of death was the cut at his throat, which had resulted in exsanguination. "No gunshot to the head like in Rob's murder," she commented. "If their killer had done that, Devin probably wouldn't have survived. He was lucky he survived the sliced neck. There was no black tape over their mouths either." Tyler had been covered in bruises of different shades, and his wrists had shown various signs of being bound—not bound only at his death.

Tied up and beaten during the days they all went missing.

His digestive system had been completely empty, and he had been dehydrated.

No food. And insufficient water.

She'd once read that a captor not feeding a captive meant their death had been planned. Why waste the food? Mercy wasn't sure she fully agreed. Perhaps a captor tried to weaken their victims by withholding food.

Why wait five days to kill them?

There were too many possible answers to her question. It could have been to inflict some suffering. Or maybe the captor was waiting for something. Maybe it had started as the five running away together but had gone sour.

But why run away? By all appearances the kids had good lives.

She wondered if Devin would agree to hypnosis. Maybe that could tap into his memories. Her description of how Rob had been found dead on the riverbank had clearly resonated with Devin in a huge way, and she planned to talk to him about it again. In a location where he couldn't injure himself.

Using surprise as an interview strategy backfired.

Mercy moved on to the evidence found at the campsite. Hundreds of photos. She flicked through them, pausing here and there. Beer cans. A half-empty vodka bottle. A few joints. Enough junk food to fill a 7-Eleven. Two older Chevy pickups were parked nearby. One belonged to Tyler Hynd's grandparents and the other was Colin Balke's.

I still don't believe a teenager would leave their vehicle behind.

The investigators had been unable to tell if the teenagers had walked away or been picked up. The campsite was adjacent to many hiking trails, and there had been hundreds of prints that crisscrossed and went in every direction. No one from the public had come forward to state they'd encountered the five teens on trails or seen them leave in another vehicle.

"How do you kidnap a group of five people in the wilderness?" she wondered out loud.

Noelle, who was reviewing evidence collected from the kids' bedrooms, lifted her head. "At gunpoint? Threaten to kill one if any of them fight back?"

"I can see that part being handled by one person, but to manage five captives for that long? I'd think you'd need at least two people."

"It's not impossible with one. Both Devin and Tyler had been restrained, so I assume they probably all were. You could have one of the kids tie up another while you held a gun on them."

"Why not just shoot them at the campsite?"

"Too loud? Someone might hear and investigate? It would be pretty hard for one person to shoot all five. I'd imagine they'd scatter after the first shot. Or fight back. There's a lot of possibilities here. Or maybe they wanted something from these kids."

"We need to find the motivation to understand what happened."

"If we knew the motivation, we'd probably know our killer," Noelle pointed out.

"True. The motivation usually involves sex or hate or money somehow," said Mercy. "There weren't any ransom demands."

"That the investigators knew of. Let's have the parents' financials reviewed again," said Noelle. "They were looked at back then, but maybe someone was blackmailed later on. Or has been sending money to one of the missing kids, who is in hiding for some reason."

"Good call." Mercy made a note. "If that is true, it would mean there's a big web of concealment and silence going on."

"There is a big web," Noelle said grimly. "But we don't know who created it."

23

It felt like a guys' night in.

There were pizza and soda, video games and movies. Ollie had flopped down on the cheap sofa in the motel room with two slices of pizza while Devin sat in a chair at the tiny table with the pizza box. Ollie entered Truman's log-in credentials for a streaming service and searched for the new *Star Trek* series. He'd already watched the entire thing twice but was more than happy to watch it again. He wanted to see Devin's enjoyment of the show. The man's eyes had lit up when Ollie first described it.

True fans stuck together.

Devin was more relaxed than he had been in the hospital waiting room. After passing out and hitting his head, he'd been incredibly tense in the ER. The doctor had told Truman that Devin was having short-term memory issues. "He looks at my name badge every time I come in and silently mouths my name as if committing it to memory," the doctor had said. Truman had told him that it wasn't a new issue and wasn't related to Devin hitting his head.

In the ER, when Ollie had first seen him after his fall, Devin had looked confused but forced a smile. When Ollie grinned back—trying to make him more comfortable—recognition had crossed Devin's face. "Ollie," he'd said with some relief. After Ollie had learned that Devin had struggled with Mercy's and Noelle's names, he'd been proud that Devin had remembered his.

He'd been surprised to hear that Devin was an Xbox fan. With limited use of his left hand, Ollie had assumed video games would be out of the question. But when they'd stopped to pick up some things at Devin's home, Ollie had spotted the Xbox and asked if he played, and then Devin had shown him the single-handed controller that he used with his right hand. "I ordered it online. A guy custom-makes them," Devin had said.

Ollie was embarrassed he hadn't considered that. Of course an adaptation was available. They'd packed the controller and console. Devin didn't have the newest *Call of Duty* game, so Ollie had asked Kaylie to bring it to the motel with his own controller and his stuff so he could spend the night. Truman had dropped them off at the motel and left after stopping at Devin's. He had been needed at the police department, so Kaylie would bring Ollie's toothbrush and clothes.

Ollie and Devin had been watching the new show for ten minutes. "What's with his hair?" asked Devin. "Even for *Star Trek* that's a weird choice for a main character."

"I have no idea," said Ollie. "Its height drives me nuts."

Someone knocked loudly at the motel room's door, making both Ollie and Devin start.

"That's Kaylie," said Ollie, jumping up from the sofa. "I guarantee it." She always pounded on doors.

Ollie pressed his eye against the peephole. Yep. Kaylie. She had his backpack slung over a shoulder, and he wondered what clothes she'd packed for him. His cheeks burned as he realized she'd had to pack him some boxers.

She was his sister . . . but still, he didn't want to go through her underwear either.

He opened the door, and she breezed by him. "I smell pizza."

Kaylie rarely lacked confidence.

She stopped short when she saw Devin. "Oh, *hey, Devin*!" Familiarity rang in her tone. "I didn't realize Ollie's roomie would be the two-decaf-vanilla-lattes guy!"

Devin stared blankly at her for a moment, and then uncertainty filled his gaze, and he lightly touched the side of his nose. "Kaylie?"

Kaylie's smile faded. "I'm sorry to hear about your mom." She shoved the backpack at Ollie and moved forward to put a hand on Devin's shoulder. "I hope she'll be okay."

He knows her from the Coffee Café.

Ollie watched them chat for a moment, recalling how Devin had touched the side of his nose when he saw Kaylie. Her nose stud must have triggered his memory of her name.

Devin looked at Ollie. "My mom always drops me off at the Coffee Café when she goes grocery shopping, and I get drinks for both of us. Kaylie is almost always there. It's weird to see her somewhere else."

"She's the owner," Ollie said, always proud of the success Kaylie had made of the shop her father had left her.

"I didn't know that." Devin seemed a little embarrassed about not knowing that fact.

"I don't usually tell people unless it comes up," said Kaylie. "And that most often happens when a cranky customer demands to talk to my boss." A look of satisfaction crossed her face. "*Then* I tell them I'm the owner."

Ollie was a little surprised to hear that Devin was a regular customer at her shop. He'd gotten the impression from Truman that the guy rarely left home. Maybe the coffee shop was the one exception.

Devin pointed at the other chair at the little table. "Want some pizza? We've got more than enough."

"Absolutely." She pulled out the chair and helped herself to the biggest piece. A blissful look crossed her face as she ate. Then she glanced at the TV, where Ollie had paused the show. "Is his hair supposed to look like that?" She wrinkled her nose in her usual Kaylie way.

"Yes," said Ollie.

Devin's phone dinged with a text. He read it and immediately set the phone down as different emotions flickered across his face.

"You good, Devin?" Kaylie asked. "Was it about your mom?"

"Not my mom." He cleared his throat, shooting a quick glance at Ollie. "It was that FBI agent. She wants to set up an interview time for tomorrow. That's who I was talking to when . . ." His words trailed off, discomfort filling his gaze.

"You mean Mercy?" asked Kaylie.

"Yes."

"Did you know she's my aunt? I live with her and Ollie. And her husband, Truman, of course."

Devin looked at her in surprise. "I didn't know that. Small world, I guess." He shifted in his chair. "When we talked this morning, she said that a man . . . a man—" He stopped abruptly, stress crossing his face, his hand touching the pale scars at his throat. "I don't want to talk about it." He quickly picked up his soda as if he needed something else to do with his hand.

Kaylie exchanged a glance with Ollie. They both knew Devin had passed out when Mercy mentioned the man who'd been murdered and left at the river. They also knew that Devin had been found in the exact same position twenty years earlier and barely survived.

I don't think we should talk about it if he's uncomfortable.

But looking at Kaylie, Ollie knew she had no such qualms.

"Mercy is trying to find the person who killed that man, Devin," Kaylie said before Ollie could stop her. "She's very smart. I think if she can solve his case, it may indicate who hurt you when you were my age."

She impressed Ollie with her sensitive tone and sincere expression.

Devin's right hand began to shake, and he set down his drink. The hand continued to twitch, and he buried it in his lap.

"It's okay, Devin. Just talk to her. I don't think she'll ask anything you haven't been asked before," said Kaylie, leaning across the table to hold his gaze.

"I can't remember anything from back then—that's the problem. Everyone thinks I'm hiding something or don't *want* to remember. *That's not true!* I'd give anything to be able to tell them what happened and who they should arrest, but I *can't*."

Ollie stayed quiet, realizing Kaylie had tapped into something with Devin and he shouldn't disturb the flow. Kaylie was like that. Straightforward but caring. People always responded in a positive way.

"Then tell her that," said Kaylie. "She'll understand. She's not going to call you a liar or make you try to come up with a story that's not true."

"The cops in the past . . ." Devin shuddered. "And other people said horrible things about me. Everyone thinks I'm a liar."

"Which people?" asked Kaylie.

"I don't know!"

Kaylie held up her hands in a "Calm down" gesture. "It's okay, Devin. I believe you, and Ollie does too. Mercy will be the same way."

Devin stared at his hands in his lap. "But sometimes I think I do know. Sometimes I dream that it's happening all over again, and it's so clear. But when I wake, every bit of the knowledge is gone." He raised his wet gaze to Kaylie's. "I think I know, but I can't figure out how to find it in my head."

Kaylie nodded slowly, sympathizing.

Ollie continued to stay quiet.

A killer's identity is locked away in his brain.

"That makes sense," said Kaylie. "Obviously you were there and saw what happened, but I don't think you can force it out." She was quiet for a long second. "These were good friends of yours, right?"

Devin nodded.

"Tell me a good memory about one of them. Something from before. Did you play video games with them too?" She gestured at his controller on the table.

He fingered the controller. "It was a PlayStation. Usually at Colin's house. All four of us would play there. That was before he dated Mia."

"Who was the best player?" asked Kaylie.

"Alex," he answered promptly. "Kicked butt at everything. I swear he had superhuman reflexes."

Ollie studied Devin. It was hard to picture the adult man as a teen playing games with his friends. He'd calmed down. Once again, Ollie was impressed with Kaylie's tact. If she hadn't stopped by, he and Devin wouldn't have ever approached the topic. They would have talked about anything but what happened long ago.

"Was Colin the only one with a girlfriend?" Kaylie asked.

"Yes. We all always had dates for the formals, but none of us had a long-term girlfriend like that. She became part of our group."

"Was she nice? Sometimes girls can be bitchy to their boyfriend's friends. I think it's because they're jealous of the time they spend together. I've seen it a dozen times. They try to guilt the guy that he doesn't need friends anymore because she should be enough."

"She wasn't like that. Not at all. She was new to the high school our senior year. All the guys instantly wanted her for a girlfriend. She was smart, and being new gave her an air of mystery that was also appealing. Colin fell hard for her. We all accepted that they were a couple, but I was happy that she became my friend. I think she needed friends, not just a boyfriend." Devin's gaze was distant. "I remember thinking it must suck to change schools and leave all your friends behind when you're almost finished."

Devin has no problems remembering things from before his accident.

Ollie was curious why Kaylie was continuing the conversation in this direction. Maybe she was trying to show Devin that his memory wasn't totally useless and could still remember good things. Devin was responding positively and appeared relaxed.

"I was lucky to never have to change schools," said Kaylie.

"Same," said Devin. "I went to school with the same kids all my life."

"Were the four of you always friends?" she asked.

Devin thought hard. "No. I'm not sure when we all came together and it actually stuck. Maybe our freshman year?"

"I'm sorry you lost your closest friends," said Kaylie.

"Thank you," said Devin. "I've never had a group like that since." Emotions flickered across his face.

He's lonely.

Ollie wondered what it was like to have your mind betray you. And your body do the same. Devin had gone from being a healthy, social teenager to one with memory loss and an arm that wouldn't obey. Now that he'd spent time with the man, Ollie didn't notice his physical limitations the way he had when they first met. He bet other people would feel the same way. Maybe Devin needed to meet people with common interests.

"Are you on Xbox?" Ollie asked.

Devin looked startled. "Xbox Live? No. I don't have a headset or subscription."

"I have an extra headset you can have. If you get a subscription, we can play online. And you can also play with anyone all hours of the day. I've played with people around the world."

Devin's face lit up. "That would be great."

Ollie was pleased.

That was easy. He just needs friends.

24

It was after 10:00 p.m., but Mercy and Noelle had caught a second wind as they went through the binders of notes from the old cases. The chocolate cheesecake might have had something to do with it.

"Tyler Hynd—the murdered teen—lived with his maternal grandparents," said Noelle as she paused to lick her fork. "They've both passed away."

"Where were his parents at the time?" asked Mercy, setting down her cup of decaf coffee. She knew better than to have caffeine late at night, but the cheesecake had begged for coffee.

"Hmmmm." Noelle studied the notes. "His parents weren't married. Dad had a Texas address at the time, and the grandmother had said he was never involved in Tyler's life. Mom was serving time in Coffee Creek."

Coffee Creek was a women's prison on the other side of the Cascade Range.

"Where are they now?"

Noelle focused on her computer. "Mom was in and out of prison." She sighed. "She died from a drug overdose in Portland a few years ago. Had been homeless. Tyler's dad died five years ago, according to follow-up interviews."

"Who's next?"

"Colin Balke's parents live in Prineville now."

"That's not too far. We can call them tomorrow too."

"Mia Fowler had lived with her dad here in Bend. The current address I have for her dad is in Wenatchee. Looks like Mia's mother has been unreachable for several years. The last contact detectives were able to make was more than ten years ago, and she'd said she hadn't seen her daughter since the girl was eight." Noelle hesitated. "Looks like Dad is an asshole. He has a lot of domestic violence charges going back over two decades."

"Sounds like a great guy. Maybe that's why Mom split."

"And left her daughter with him?" Noelle was skeptical.

"She might have had no choice. What do her previous interviews say?"

Noelle was quiet for several seconds as she flipped pages. "They're short. Simply say she hadn't seen her daughter or her ex in years. No explanations."

"Sounds like someone who fears stirring up trouble."

"Maybe. Or she simply didn't care."

"Let's try to find both and call."

Noelle nodded and added them to her growing list.

"We know Devin's current situation, so that leaves Alex Stark's family," said Mercy.

"Foster kid since he was three."

Mercy held Noelle's gaze. "Is it just me, or did these kids all come from shitty situations? Maybe that's why they stuck together."

"Devin and Colin both lived with their parents at the time. I don't see anything indicating a bad situation in those interviews."

"But the other three . . ."

"Yeah, they definitely had some struggles. Follow-up calls over the years didn't contact anyone related to Alex Stark. Here's an interview with his foster parents, who said he was a good kid that didn't cause any problems. He lived with them for four years." Noelle continued to skim the interview. "They seemed genuinely upset about his disappearance. All the cold case follow-ups say the same. They hadn't heard from Alex."

Mercy studied the five kids' photos that Noelle had put up on the wall.

Did some of them feel abandoned?

She knew what it was like to lose family as a teen. At the direction of her father, Mercy's family had essentially shunned her for fifteen years. Mercy studied Mia's blue eyes, searching for signs of heartbreak or fear. She saw none.

Was your relationship with your father a tough one?

I'm projecting.

Mercy looked down, annoyed with herself. She flipped the pages of the binder in front of her, determined to focus only on facts. "Colin Balke's parents would have known Rob Newton pretty well as a kid since he lived next door."

"Most likely."

"Move them to the top of the list to call tomorrow. They might have heard from Rob if he was doing research."

Noelle nodded. "He might have contacted any of these kids' relatives."

"Do we have his cell phone records yet?"

"I submitted the request yesterday. Hopefully soon."

"And we don't have anything from his computer to indicate what he'd been working on exactly or any notes he'd made?"

"Not yet. Forensics has his computer and phone. I requested it be made a priority, but you know how that goes."

"Every case is a priority," said Mercy. "Didn't Rob have some research notebooks? We should have received copies by now." Mercy checked her computer as if the copies might have appeared since she last checked her messages five minutes ago. She fired off a polite but firmly worded email requesting they hurry the fuck up. "I know the investigators eventually ruled out all the family members as suspects back then. Who else did they focus on?"

"A high school teacher and a neighbor of Mia Fowler." Noelle pushed an open binder toward Mercy.

Mercy's skin crawled at the thought of the five teenagers being attacked because of a neighbor's fascination with Mia Fowler. She eyed the photo of the neighbor, Jason Slade, and read the detective's notes. Slade had been renting the home three houses away from Mia and her father. He was a registered sex offender and couldn't account for his whereabouts during the first few days after the teenagers had disappeared. He said he'd been sick at home without any visitors.

Slade acknowledged that he knew Mia Fowler. He'd met her several times while walking his dog, and she usually talked more to his German shepherd than to him. She'd fed and walked his dog when he'd had to go out of town several months before she disappeared. "So there'd be a reason if her prints or hair turned up in his home," Mercy commented. "Convenient."

"But there was no evidence to connect him to the crime," said Noelle. "This guy was only questioned because he was a registered sex offender living near one of the victims."

"I can't say I have much sympathy," said Mercy.

"I don't either. Mia's father pushed hard for the detectives to investigate him further when it was revealed he was a sex offender. Neither he nor Mia had known that before. The detectives couldn't find any evidence to justify a warrant to search his home or vehicle, and Slade refused to let them."

It was on the tip of Mercy's tongue to ask what Slade had been hiding to deny a search, but she suspected he'd learned how to protect his rights after being arrested years earlier. She skimmed the notes to find what he'd been previously convicted for. "He assaulted a teenage girl." Fury made her look up at Noelle, who nodded.

"His cousin."

"I would have looked hard at him too," Mercy said. "Where is he now?"

"Living in Redmond. He's a long-haul truck driver."

"That's not too far away. Our list of people to contact is getting longer." Mercy turned the page. Suspect number two back then had been Erick Howard. A high school physics teacher. Colin, Devin, and Mia had taken his classes. Howard had been questioned months before the disappearances, after two students reported that they'd had sexual relationships with him. The two girls had later retracted their stories after admitting they'd been angry that they were failing his class. But the murder investigators had taken a close look at Erick Howard anyway.

Mercy shook her head. "What makes a teenager believe they can create a story to ruin someone's life and get away with it?" She looked at Noelle. "Did you read this?"

"I did. My mother would have said they did it because their frontal lobes weren't fully developed. She used to say that to me every time I did something stupid with no regard for the consequences."

"They could have ruined his career."

"I guess the rumors didn't die away," said Noelle. "Follow-up calls indicate he continued to be harassed, so he moved to a different school the following year. He's still teaching at one of the Bend high schools."

Mercy flipped through several more pages in the binder. Dozens of tips had come in about the disappearance of the teenagers, and they'd all been investigated. "They also looked into whether the missing three could have attacked the other two." Mercy skimmed the notes. "It appears the investigators felt this was a very strong theory. But friends and family denied it could be possible. Thoughts?"

"It's possible," said Noelle. "But the crimes feel advanced for teenagers to carry out. Slicing the throat of your friends? And according to the medical examiner, the cuts weren't made by a hesitant hand.

Whoever did it used a confident stroke. I can remember having arguments with friends at that age, but to be angry enough to carry out murder?" She frowned.

"It does happen," said Mercy.

"But usually someone—either a family member or another friend or a teacher—confirms that there was something going on with the suspect. That the attacker had emotional issues or was under the influence of another violent personality. There is nothing like that in all these interviews from their family, friends, and even teachers at school. And I feel like people really knew these five kids. They weren't loners; they were social and appeared to be good students."

Mercy closed the binder in frustration and glanced at Noelle's long list. "Are we wasting time by digging into these cases? Is this going to help us find who killed Rob Newton?"

"I think we need to talk to Rob's wife next," said Noelle. "And do an initial interview with the podcaster who confronted Truman yesterday about Rob." She pointed at the business card on their board that Truman had given Mercy. "Paula Jupp. *Paula's Pursuit of Truth.* She came all the way out here from Minnesota for some reason."

"Did you verify her flight here?"

"Yes. Paula's flight came in early yesterday, and I established that she was on the plane, so she couldn't have been here when Rob was killed."

Mercy stood and walked over to the board. She eyed the card for a moment, checked the time, and dialed.

If she's so into the truth, she won't mind a phone call at 10:00 p.m.

"Hello?" Curiosity filled the female voice.

Mercy put her on speaker. "Paula Jupp? This is FBI Special Agent Kilpatrick. Your card was passed on to me because you have information in the murder of Rob Newton. I heard you mentioned something about a cover-up?" She raised her brows at Noelle as the detective grinned back.

"Oh! Well . . . I don't think I have any really important information."

"You thought it was relevant enough to bother the police chief."

"It's just that I knew Rob was investigating those kids who disappeared. He talked about that old case all the time."

"And?" Mercy projected boredom into her tone. "Do you know why he picked that case?"

"He told me he knew the kids. Said one of the missing had been a neighbor. I know he'd been questioned at one point back then, and he'd told the police he didn't know anything, but he'd heard that other people were scared to cooperate. He said he'd been scared too."

"Why was he scared?"

"He didn't say specifically but alluded that people were keeping information to themselves. But who has the power to make people scared to cooperate in an investigation? Law enforcement? Parents? The actual killers?"

"You were friends with Rob?"

"Sort of. We knew each other online because we were in the same business, and we've talked for years."

"Why did you fly here when you heard Rob had been murdered? That seems extreme for just a business friendship. A phone call would have been sufficient to pass along any concerns."

Paula was quiet for several seconds. "There's obviously a big story here. A podcaster was murdered in the same way as the victim in the story he was investigating? That's gold," she said flatly. "It's going to capture the media's interest."

She wants the inside scoop.

Noelle made an expression of disgust and gestured for Mercy to hang up.

"Thank you, Ms. Jupp. We'll be in touch." Mercy ended the call without waiting for Paula's reply. "Cross her off the interview list. That was a waste of time," she said. "People will say the most stupid things trying to get a story. Truman thought she was just nosy, and I think he was right."

"She might not have known Rob. She could have made that up and used it to convince people to talk to her."

"We can ask Rob's wife if they knew each other."

"I'll text her now," said Noelle, picking up her phone. "And I'll remind her she said she'd give us his social media passwords."

Mercy rubbed her eyes. It seemed like all their work was bringing up more questions.

"Who has the power to make people scared to cooperate?"

Paula's question rattled in Mercy's mind, and she wondered if people close to the teenagers had truly held back information or if that had simply been the gossip making the rounds. The name of the original Deschutes County investigator was on Noelle's call list. He was retired, but she wanted to touch base and get his impressions. Mercy had found his notes to be thorough and well thought out.

But deep in his heart, did he suspect one person?

"Sara says she doesn't recognize Paula Jupp's name or her podcast," said Noelle. "But she's not surprised. She says Rob had a social network of podcasters, but he rarely mentioned anyone by name to her. Sounds like she didn't get involved in Rob's work that much. She promises to send the social media stuff tomorrow. She's in bed."

"Paula is probably right that the media will grab hold of this story. I'm surprised it hasn't happened yet." Mercy dreaded fielding the questions.

"I think we've been lucky so far because of where Rob was found," said Noelle. "The location was just outside most local news coverage of Portland and north of news coverage around here."

"And I had the impression the sheriff would protect as many details as possible," added Mercy. "If the story gets out, it will originate from someone who got a look at the bodies."

"But they'd have to make the connection to the old murders to really catch the national media's interest."

"It can happen," said Mercy. "I talked with a man at the scene who remembered. But I agree the remote location is working in our favor at the moment. I wonder how long we have before we're bombarded." She looked at the binders spread across the table and the stacks of boxes on the floor.

We need to work faster.

25

In my dream she's whispering. Her eyes are wide, her face close to mine.

She's scared, and I want to protect her.

Protect her from what?

Then Colin's face appears, blocking Mia's.

He's talking urgently, pleading with me, but I can't hear his words.

He grows frustrated. I can tell he's shouting, but I can't hear him.

I look to Mia, desperate for an explanation.

Now she's crying.

Something horrible has happened.

Spinning around, I see Tyler.

He's on the ground.

The dirt around him soaked with blood.

Blood that moments before had pumped through his arteries and veins.

An arm comes from behind and lifts my jaw, exposing my neck.

I can't breathe.

I wake. Heart racing.

A knot of fear in my throat and I close my eyes, breathing it away.

And again—everything I saw evaporates into the dark.

26

Ollie stood outside his motel room door in the freezing temperature and looked one way and then the other, searching for a sign that would point him toward ice. It was still dark out, and Ollie had woken early even though he didn't have a morning shift at the warehouse that day. The previous night had gone well. He and Devin had watched TV until 2:00 a.m., bingeing the *Star Trek* series. There were still episodes left, but they'd struggled to stay awake and finally agreed to stop.

Devin had held a gel ice pack from the emergency room on his head several times during the evening. This morning he'd complained that his head was still tender, but he'd forgotten to put the gel pack in their kitchenette's freezer the night before. And of course there were no ice cube trays, so Ollie had promised to round up some ice.

Ice bucket in hand, he wandered to his left toward the motel office, passing several other room doors, watching so as not to trip on the uneven concrete. He'd left Devin in charge of making coffee, both of them craving it desperately. He wondered how long Devin should stay in the motel. No one had said when it would be safe for him to return home.

It'll be safe once they catch who attacked his mom.

Following a rattling noise, Ollie found the ice machine. He eyed the buildup of corrosion and dirt on the machine's air vents and wondered how clean it was inside. He scooped enough to fill his bucket, made a mental note to tell Devin not to use the ice in drinks, and headed back to the room. He paused outside his door, reached for the handle, and frowned, eyeing something dark on the ground right in front of the door.

Is that . . . ?

He squatted to get a closer look, confirming what his mind hadn't wanted to see. It was a small puddle of blood. No more than three inches in diameter. At first he thought it must have dripped after he left the room, but it was already dried along the edges, so in his uncaffeinated, cold haze, he hadn't noticed the spot earlier.

There's a smaller drip. And another.

There was a definite trail leading to the right of the motel room door. If he hadn't already seen Devin that morning, he would have thought the man had wandered out of the room.

Maybe he left before I got up but came back?

Ollie hadn't seen any blood inside the room, and Devin hadn't mentioned that he'd gone outdoors. He'd come out of his bedroom yawning and complaining about the lump on his head when he heard Ollie prepping the coffee maker.

Ollie took a few steps, following the drips, wondering if they were from an injured dog. He passed two more rooms and reached the end of the motel complex. He looked around the corner of the building and squinted into the dim light, seeking the source of the blood.

There. A body on the ground.

She's hurt!

Kaylie?

Adrenaline racing, he stumbled to the body.

Not Kaylie.

Relief made him drop to his knees next to the woman, spilling the ice.

Thank God. But who is it?

She was on her stomach, her hands tied behind her.

An X of black tape crossed her mouth.

Her throat had been sliced open.

◆ ◆ ◆

Truman squatted next to the dead woman as he stared at her face, a range of emotions ripping through him.

Dammit, Paula. You got too close to someone.

Guilt surged through him for blaming the victim, and he wondered if he should have taken the podcaster more seriously that day in the diner. But nothing she'd told him had made him think she could be in danger.

Should I have warned her?

Linda hadn't been attacked at the time Paula had approached Truman, so there had been nothing to warn her of. No one had suspected that other people, besides Rob Newton—whose murder had occurred miles away—were on the killer's list.

Or is he simply erasing his tracks?

Ollie's early-morning phone call about the body had come through just as Truman was parking at the Eagle's Nest police station. Minutes later, Truman had been at the dumpy roadside motel a few miles from town. After Ollie had told him that the victim was tied up and her throat had been cut, he'd called Mercy and asked her to inform Detective Marshall. Both women and Deschutes County sheriff's deputies were en route.

Shock had nearly knocked him over when he recognized the dead woman.

It can't be a coincidence that her body was left near Devin's motel.

Truman wasn't up to date on what Mercy and Noelle had uncovered about the case, but it seemed to him that someone was sending a warning to Devin.

Is he lying about how much he can remember?

It appeared the blood trail had been deliberately started outside Ollie and Devin's door. Truman doubted the blood had dripped from the body so perfectly in a neat trail. Somehow the killer had created it, possibly hoping Devin would see it.

Truman had told Ollie to pack. He was moving the two men. Truman deeply regretted choosing this motel—he'd focused on convenience instead of security. Granted the door and windows had strong locks—which he'd tested—but the sole camera was in the lobby. None of the areas outside the motel had coverage.

Where is a safe place for Devin?

If Truman put him up at his own house, he risked bringing danger to his front door. He wouldn't endanger Kaylie and Mercy. Or Ollie. Had he been wrong to allow Ollie to stay with Devin? Clearly the man had some sort of target on his back. Truman ground his teeth, remorse swamping him because he hadn't taken Devin's safety seriously enough.

What if he'd attacked Ollie?

Truman shoved the vision of Ollie lying in Paula's position out of his head.

Another hotel? One with better security? Maybe Mercy's cabin.

He mulled over the idea. The cabin was a mini fortress with state-of-the-art security. But it was also in the middle of nowhere. That was an advantage in keeping someone from finding it, but a big disadvantage if a quick response was needed.

"Including Ollie's, only three of the motel rooms had occupants, boss," Officer Samuel Robb said as he stopped behind Truman. "I've talked to the people in the other two rooms, and no one heard anything overnight or saw something odd. The desk clerk is still freaked out that someone died here. Seems to be worried he'll lose his job. Pisses me off when someone makes a tragedy all about themselves." The burly officer glowered.

Samuel had arrived moments after Truman and helped set a perimeter around the scene. The desk clerk was a droopy-eyed, thin man in his thirties. Shock had stunned the clerk as the police arrived at the quiet motel and got him out of bed. He'd been sleeping in a small room off the locked lobby. There was a doorbell to ring for service, but he said no one had ever rung it at night in the six months that he'd worked there.

Until Truman had rung it a dozen times.

The clerk's hands had shaken as he called the motel owner, who lived in Nevada, and then handed the phone to Truman. A woman's rough pack-a-day voice on the other end of the line had asked all the wrong questions. She'd been more concerned about cleanup and negative publicity than about the fact that a woman was dead.

Truman wondered if the steam coming out of his ears had been visible during the call.

Two deputy units and Mercy's Tahoe pulled up and parked at the edge of the lot. She'd slicked her hair back into a ponytail, which meant she'd run right out the door after Truman's call.

"Linda Bonner needs a guard at her hospital room," Truman said as a greeting, wanting to hug her but holding back since other people were around.

"I mentioned it to Noelle, and she's sent a deputy. We all had the same thought." She took a long look at the motel clerk, who was chewing on a cuticle as he watched them from behind the lobby's glass door. "Where is the woman?"

Truman led her to the body. Samuel had rigged a tarp on an upright collapsible frame to keep away prying eyes. One of the motel occupants had casually wandered out of his room to get a look at the body but changed his mind after encountering Samuel. The former military man presented an imposing figure with his wide shoulders and stern countenance.

Mercy studied Paula's face, throat, and bound hands. "Same style of zip tie as Rob Newton's. The black electrical tape. Throat damage looks similar too. *Dammit.* I don't want to use the phrase *serial killer* yet, but it's clearly related to Rob's murder."

"And the old murder. I'd say *serial killer* is the right term even though they're decades apart," Truman said quietly. "Although *copycat* might be more accurate."

"I know. I know." Stress filled her tone. "The medical examiner should be here soon. I woke her up. She should be able to tell us if it's the same." Her tone stated she knew the ME would confirm the similarities.

Another vehicle parked, and Noelle strode over to join them. "Well, fuck." She sighed and rubbed the back of her neck as she studied the body. "Did Mercy tell you we talked to Paula last night?" she asked Truman.

"Yes."

"Does she have her cell phone on her?" asked Noelle.

"I haven't touched anything," said Truman.

Mercy slid on a pair of gloves and deftly checked the woman's pockets with a minimum of movement. "No ID or phone. We'll get her cell records to see who else she talked to. Good thing you recognized her, Truman—otherwise she might not've been identified for quite a while. Especially since she's from out of town."

Mercy frowned as she removed her gloves. "I called Paula at ten p.m. last night. You'd think she would have told us if she was meeting someone regarding Rob's murder. I guess they could have contacted her after I talked to her."

"Or she wasn't meeting anyone," said Noelle. "They simply showed up. Do we know her hotel?"

"I called the few hotels in the immediate area without any luck. Most likely she stayed in Bend, I'd guess," said Truman. "Do you think the black X has something to do with the fact that she's a podcaster? That she talked about something that made the killer mad? Rob Newton had the X and his job was the same."

Mercy and Noelle exchanged a glance. "It's a solid theory," said Mercy. "Possibly something Paula and Rob said in the podcasts upset someone. Or maybe it was something the killer was worried that they were planning to say."

"Does she have family?" asked Noelle.

The three of them stared silently at each other until Mercy blew out a breath. "We'll do some digging."

"Did she get too close to Rob's killer?" Truman asked in a lowered voice.

"She stirred up some sort of hornet's nest," said Noelle. "And clearly Devin is on this person's radar. This makes three close encounters with him, if you count the Jeep being abandoned on his property."

"He can't stay at this motel any longer," said Truman. "Ideas?" He gave a quick shake of his head at Mercy as she immediately started to speak. She grimaced and nodded. No doubt she'd had the same train of thought about providing a place at their secure home but then considered the family.

"I think another hotel would work," said Noelle. "Sorry to say it, Truman, but I suspect you were followed here when you dropped them off. Either followed from the hospital or from Devin's home. It's the only answer that makes sense. We can get Devin to another hotel without being followed. Transfer him between vehicles at the sheriff's department a few times." She glared at the clerk standing indoors thirty yards away, startling him enough to make him take a step back. "And we evaluate the new hotel's camera coverage *before* we check them in."

Ollie approached the group, and Truman realized he'd been listening nearby. "I'm staying with Devin," he announced firmly. "He's rattled pretty good and blaming himself for this woman's death even though he has no idea how it happened." He looked from Truman to Mercy, his face resolute.

Devin has a protector.

"Do you have an update on his mother?" asked Ollie.

"No," said Mercy. "I was about to contact the hospital when Truman called me about this. I'll do it next." She paused, concern filling her face. "You realize how dangerous staying with Devin could be, right?"

"I think if someone wanted to hurt Devin, they would have done it by now," argued Ollie. "They could have attacked him instead of Linda at his house or gotten into our room last night if they really wanted to." He held up his hands. "Yes, there are good locks on the door, but we could have been drawn out. Like if there was a fender bender in the parking lot, or we heard someone yelling that they needed help."

"You're not strengthening your case to stay with him," Truman pointed out.

"Well, *now* I know not to trust anyone," Ollie said in a self-deprecating tone. "And I don't think he should be alone."

"He's got a point about Devin," said Mercy. "There have been several chances for this killer to get to him, but he hasn't. Why?"

Noelle and Mercy exchanged a long look. Truman glanced from one to the other, trying to read their minds. A car door slammed, and he turned and spotted the medical examiner.

"Truman, can you stay with Dr. Lockhart while she evaluates Paula?" asked Mercy. "Noelle and I are going to have a talk with Devin right now." She met Ollie's worried gaze. "You're to stay outside."

Ollie shuffled his feet, and an obstinate expression crossed his face, but he nodded.

Truman clapped him on the shoulder, knowing it'd been difficult for Ollie to agree. The teen was naturally empathetic. He was always the most concerned about a sick kitten and didn't like to see anyone treated unfairly. Devin had dealt with hard knocks in his life, and Ollie was doing what he could to ease his way.

Truman was proud.

That's my son.

27

Mercy knocked firmly on Devin's motel room door, determined to finish the interview she and Noelle had started the day before.

"Seat him where he can't fall and hurt himself," muttered Noelle, standing to Mercy's right. "I don't know how much we'll accomplish. It's obvious his memory isn't good."

"I want to hear it from him," said Mercy.

The door opened the slightest bit, the chain engaged, and Devin peered out. He looked from Mercy to Noelle. "Yes? Can I help you?"

"We'd like to pick up where we left off, if that's okay with you," said Mercy.

Confusion filled his dark eyes. "Left off?"

His head injury must have knocked the start of our interview right out of his brain.

"Yesterday at the hospital. Before you fell," said Noelle.

He still looked bewildered. And now a little fearful. He made no move to disengage the chain. Mercy couldn't blame him, considering a woman had just been murdered, but Devin knew they were law enforcement. He shouldn't have any fear.

"Ollie!" Mercy called past the other motel rooms toward Ollie, who still stood with Truman. He immediately headed in their direction.

Ollie took in the chain and Devin's anxious eyes. "Dude. Open up. Mercy doesn't bite."

Devin blinked at Ollie and studied Mercy for a long moment. The door closed, and the chain clanked as he slid it.

Ollie shrugged. "I'd say he has reason to be cautious." He strode back to Truman.

The door opened wide. "Sorry," said Devin, looking at his feet. He glanced cautiously at Mercy. "Agent Kilpatrick." He shot a quick glance at Noelle. "Detective Marshall?"

Mercy frowned. Noelle's name had sounded like a question.

"How's it going, Devin?" Noelle asked as Devin moved back and they stepped in the room. He wore thick sweatpants, a long-sleeved shirt with a Crater Lake logo, and socks. Mercy glanced around the small motel room and spotted his shoes. They were slip-on sneakers, which made sense since his left hand wasn't much help. The main room had a lingering hint of cleaning chemicals and old cigarette smoke. Exactly what she'd expected from a run-down motel.

Ollie's backpack was at the foot of the foldout sofa, and through a side door, Mercy spotted a duffel bag on a bed in what must be Devin's room. Judging by the pizza box and open chip bags, the two of them had enjoyed their evening.

With Ollie's bed in the way, it was tight quarters.

Noelle promptly tossed the bed pillows off the foldout mattress, maneuvered the bed frame into the sofa, and then arranged the cushions in their spots, immediately relieving the cramped aura of the room. "Sit?" she asked Devin, who'd silently watched her fold up Ollie's bed.

He sat. Noelle took the other end of the little sofa.

Mercy set her bag on one of the chairs at the little table and slid out her yellow notepad. She grabbed the other chair and sat directly in front of Devin. "Devin, I'm going to bring up something that upset you yesterday, but we need to talk about it," she said calmly, as if speaking to a spooked horse.

Fear flashed in his eyes.

"Do you remember what I told you yesterday?"

"A man was killed. Like we were."

He included himself as killed.

She wasn't sure what to make of that but was pleased he remembered their conversation. Maybe his short-term memory wasn't as bad as she'd thought. "His name was Rob Newton."

"You'd said he was writing a story about us when he died," said Devin, staring at his left hand resting in his lap.

"Close. He's a podcaster who talks about true crime." Mercy decided not to mention the conspiracy angle of his show. "He was working on the story about you and your friends, and one of the reasons he chose it was because he went to high school with all of you."

Devin straightened. "He did?" He thought hard as his lips silently formed Rob's name several times. "I don't remember him."

Mercy returned to her bag and pulled out a folder. She handed Devin an enlarged photocopy of Rob's senior picture. Devin studied it for a long minute.

"Sorry. He's not familiar."

"It was Rob's Jeep that was abandoned on your property the other day. It had been stolen from the cabin he and his wife had rented. At the time, we knew it was Rob's, but we didn't know that he was researching you."

"Researching me," Devin repeated.

"Digging into what happened to the five of you," said Noelle.

Devin moved his right hand to his throat, touching the faint scars. "This man's throat was cut?" he asked.

"Yes." Mercy didn't mention the gunshot to the head.

"I don't remember any of it happening to me," Devin said slowly, still touching the scars. "I was told later about my throat and the zip ties and being found on the riverbank."

"What do you remember of the time while you were kidnapped?" Mercy asked. "There are five days unaccounted for. It was obvious that you and Tyler had been starved and beaten during that time."

"I don't know." He stared through Mercy, his eyes unfocused.

"That's not 'I don't remember,'" Noelle stated. "There's a difference in those statements."

"Yes," said Devin. "You're right." He turned to Noelle, studying her for a long moment. His every movement was slow, as if he were slightly removed from their conversation.

"Can you explain what you mean?" asked Mercy. So far Devin was holding it together. His color was normal, and his anxiety seemed under control. She no longer worried that he would pass out again, but she was on the edge of her chair in case he did.

"I have dreams," he started in a soft voice. "Hazy, confusing dreams, and I don't know what's real—maybe none of it is. In the dreams I'm scared, and the people I'm with are scared too." He swallowed hard. "I can see Mia's face and she's crying. I know she's upset about her father." He looked at Mercy. "Her dad was an asshole to her. *That* I remember clearly." He grew thoughtful. "So maybe what I remember about her is from before we were taken.

"I hear voices in my head when I wake, and I feel I should recognize them by their speech, but my brain can't match names to the voices. But while I'm dreaming, I *know* them. I know they're my friends, and I feel connected with them. It's when I wake and try to remember that the people are faceless and even the words are gone. Except the emotions continue to linger around me; when I'm conscious, I can feel how strongly everyone was scared." His plaintive gaze met Mercy's. "It's nauseating—a twisting in my gut. Their fear—and mine—makes me sweaty, and my skin is hypersensitive, as if it's on guard against something, creating a shield."

He's telling the truth.

Mercy sympathized. Even though his body had physically healed, he still experienced the internal turmoil without knowing who had caused it years before.

"Have you ever been hypnotized?" asked Noelle.

His face crumpled. "We've tried three different times. It doesn't work because . . . because . . ." He bent over, a hand pressed to his face. His spine was a long, bony ridge under his shirt.

Noelle touched his shoulder, compassion heavy in her gaze. "Why doesn't hypnosis work for you?" she prompted softly.

Devin shook her hand off his shoulder and lunged off the sofa. Mercy nearly grabbed for him, thinking he was falling, but realized at the last second that he was in full control. He paced across the room into the kitchenette and back again, his face showing a mixture of anger and pain.

I haven't seen him angry before.

"Because I can't see the faces," he spit out as he paced. "Ever. Almost every face is a mystery to me. *Every face.*"

Mercy caught her breath, realization sweeping over her. "Devin—do you have face blindness?"

He halted and put his right hand over his eyes. "Yes. Ever since *then*. I can't recognize anyone!"

Everything makes so much sense now.

28

Noelle looked at Mercy, confusion in her expression. "Face blindness?"

Mercy nodded to her. "I looked it up recently when a celebrity admitted he struggled with it. It's exactly what it sounds like. The inability to recognize faces. It can be caused by a traumatic brain injury, but some is congenital." She looked to Devin. "I assume you didn't have it before the accident?"

He nodded, his hand still covering his eyes. "That's correct."

"When Noelle and I came to the door a few minutes ago, you had no idea who we were until Ollie said my name."

"Mercy," he said. "Mercy Kilpatrick. Special agent. FBI. Long, black hair," he recited as if reading from a book. He lowered his hand and studied Noelle. "I linked your names together in my head. Noelle Marshall. Detective. Deschutes County. Blonde. Sometimes I can't remember quickly enough. I write notes if I think I'll see people again."

Mercy remembered how at their first meeting he'd asked for their business cards and laid them in front of him on the table. She'd noticed he'd kept glancing at the cards and then at their faces.

How does he function in public?

She sucked in a breath, remembering his blatant fear in the emergency room. He'd been frantically searching for a face he knew.

He can't *function. That's why he stays home.*

"Can you recognize your mother?" asked Noelle.

"Most of the time. She keeps those purple streaks in her hair to make it easier for me. It also helps that I simply know the woman in my house is my mother. If we're somewhere else and she steps away for a while, she always says 'It's Mom' when she returns. I rely a lot on spoken cues. Locations help, too, if I know a person is frequently in the same spot." He returned to the sofa and sat heavily. "It's just easier to stay home."

"You seem comfortable with Ollie," Mercy said.

"He has a few distinctive things about him that help me remember who he is. He's young—not many young people talk to me." He gave a faint but wry smile. "His teeth help. He always smiles."

"Did you tell Ollie about this?" asked Mercy.

"Not yet. I almost have a few times." He sat up straighter on the sofa. "Oh! Last night I learned Kaylie is your niece. I usually know who she is because she's always at the Coffee Café and has a nose piercing." He touched the side of his nose. "Those two things tell me it's Kaylie when she greets me. When she stopped by here last night, it took me a minute because she was out of place. But when she mentioned my usual coffee order, I put it together. She's always nice. The coffee shop is the one place I don't mind going because she's usually there."

Mercy was overwhelmed as she tried to put herself in Devin's shoes and imagine functioning in a world where everyone was a stranger. "What is the best way for us to help you?"

He shrugged. "Immediately tell me your name and what our previous interaction was. It'll take me a second, but I'll make the connection. My mother usually does this if we're together and someone stops by. She'll casually state their name first thing in conversation. But when things don't connect, I'll mention my bad memory, and people accept that because they know what happened to me. But truthfully, my memory is a big help in putting the pieces together to figure out who is speaking to me."

"This is crazy," said Noelle. "I had no idea such a thing existed."

"Me neither," said Devin. "At first I thought I was the only one with this problem. But I researched it. I was blown away that I'm not alone, and it's an actual affliction—sometimes without any brain trauma. There are varying degrees. Mine is at the worst level. Sometimes I want to hang a sign around my neck that says, DON'T BE CONFUSED THAT I CAN'T REMEMBER WHO YOU ARE. THAT'S NORMAL FOR ME." He shook his head. "Stupid idea. So I just smile at everyone whether they're speaking to me or not and cross my fingers that the people who know me feel they've been acknowledged."

"You said something earlier about remembering Mia," said Mercy. "Can you recall her face?"

His eyes went distant. "I can. Long, blonde hair. Striking blue eyes. And I'm not repeating that from memorizing a description. I can actually see her in my head almost as clearly as you standing in front of me."

"Who else can you recall like that?" asked Noelle.

Devin was quiet for a long second. "No one."

"What if I said George Washington?" asked Mercy.

Devin thought. "I can see him standing in a boat. Big dark hat. His hair is white or gray, but I can't really tell you what his face looks like."

"I can't say I could describe his face either, but I know it when I see it," said Mercy. "Sorry if I'm making you feel like a science experiment."

"It's okay. I know I'm weird."

"I'd say you're interesting, not weird," said Noelle. "If Mia is recognizable to you, it must be because you knew her before your injuries. I wonder why that doesn't work with other people you knew before."

"I've wondered a thousand times," said Devin. "It's sad that the only person I might be able to recognize on sight is . . . probably dead."

"You can't recall the faces of Tyler, Colin, or Alex?" asked Mercy.

"No. I've tried. I remember how I felt around them, though." He paused. "Alex was my best friend. When I look at a photo of him, I feel happy. I remember as kids we'd ride bikes for hours while we explored along the river. Tyler and Colin make me think of high school sports. We were on several teams together over the years."

"Does looking at the photos of those two make you feel happy?" asked Noelle.

Devin didn't answer; his eyebrows furrowed as he considered.

Mercy dug in her folder for photocopies of the two boys' pictures. She handed them to Devin. "Tell me how they make you feel."

He focused on Tyler's picture. "I feel bad. I know he died . . . and I didn't."

"No happy sports memories?" asked Noelle.

He tilted his head. "Yeah, I guess those are still there. We won a championship one year, and I remember getting drunk with Tyler that night."

He looked at Colin's picture and frowned. "I suddenly feel nauseated." He turned the picture over, his breaths coming quicker. "Looking at his photo, I feel a heavy guilt. Probably because I survived."

"But his body was never found," said Mercy quietly. "We don't have proof that your other friends died."

Devin held her gaze for a long moment. "Sometimes I worry I've seen them since then but didn't recognize them," he said softly. "One of them would have said something to me even if I didn't speak first, right? We would have known somehow if they're still alive. Why wouldn't they come home?"

"You called Mia's father an asshole," said Noelle. "We've looked into her father. He has domestic assault charges going back for two decades, so your feelings are accurate about him. Did he hurt Mia? Maybe that would keep her from coming home."

Devin looked at his feet. "I can't remember any specifics. But when I think of her father, I get angry."

Mercy handed him Mia's picture, and his face immediately softened as a small smile hovered around his lips. "She was really special."

"How does this photo make you feel?" asked Noelle.

"I want to protect her." He looked from Mercy to Noelle, bewilderment in his eyes. "It's almost overwhelming. I'd never put it into words before, but it's accurate." He went back to the photo. "I feel a lot of affection toward her too. She was kind, and she and Colin were perfect together."

"Any survivor's guilt like with the others?"

"That too." He stared at the photo awhile longer.

"Devin, take a look at these photos. Have you seen them before?" Mercy handed him enlargements of the messy campsite he and his friends had left behind.

His eyes widened. "No, I don't think I have. Or else I just don't remember," he said in a matter-of-fact tone. He pointed at the empty beer cans. "Tyler brought the beer. His grandfather would buy it for him."

Mercy's brows rose at the precise recollection.

Where did I read that he didn't have memories from after graduation? Or did someone just assume that?

The human brain is a mystery. And a damaged brain even more so.

"We made a mess, didn't we? If we could have, we would have cleaned it up. We never left anyplace looking like this." He continued to study the photos. "I remember Colin puking after too much vodka. We mixed it with orange juice. I know Mia was pissed that he'd gotten so drunk. We all were."

Mercy and Noelle exchanged a glance, and Mercy figured she was having the same questions about why certain things stuck in his mind. And others were completely gone.

"Devin, can I try something?" Noelle asked.

"Sure."

"Close your eyes. Can you picture the campground you were just looking at?"

"Yes."

"Okay . . . Colin is puking. Mia is mad. What else happened there? Do you remember eating meals? Did you hike?"

His eyes closed; Devin frowned. "I remember Alex made oatmeal for breakfast and it was nasty. No one brought sugar."

Mercy smiled in spite of herself.

"We hiked. Colin was hungover, and Mia was pissed at him. On the hike she told me . . ." He frowned. "She told me—shit. What did she tell me?"

"What emotion are you feeling as you try to remember?" asked Noelle.

"I'm . . . scared."

"Scared for her?"

"Yes." His brows furrowed again. "But I'm scared for myself too." His eyes opened, fear simmering in their depths. "I don't like it." He rubbed his right hand up and down his thigh. "I don't like it," he repeated.

His fear is definitely blocking something.

If only we could break past that wall.

"Devin, do you feel as if the fear you're having right now is keeping you from recalling other things?" Noelle asked.

"I don't know," he said emphatically, his hand still moving up and down his leg. "Maybe."

"You're safe here," Mercy said.

"I know, *I know.*" Agitation increased in his face.

"Let's try something else," Mercy said, wanting to calm him before he completely shut down. "Look at these two photos. Do you recognize these men?" She gave him the pictures of Mia's neighbor and the high school teacher who had emerged as primary suspects in the students' disappearances.

Devin frowned as he looked at the neighbor's picture, slowly shaking his head. Next he looked at the teacher's photo. He opened his mouth slightly, as if to speak, but then closed it, a perplexed expression in his eyes. "I feel like I know this guy. Who is he?"

Mercy realized Erick Howard's photo was recent. Devin most likely hadn't seen him since high school. "He taught physics at your high school."

Devin's face cleared. "Mr. Howard—he's a lot older in this picture. Great teacher. Class was fun."

Mercy made a mental note that even with his face blindness, Devin had felt he recognized a face from his past. And he'd done the same when she showed him pictures of Tyler, Colin, and Mia. He'd known who was who.

Maybe he still has the neural pathways to recognize people he was close to before his accident.

I wonder if his emotions help him remember. Clearly he had good experiences with his friends and the teacher.

She'd read about how scents could trigger memories. Perhaps with Devin, strong emotions were a trigger.

Devin looked at the neighbor's picture again. "I'm still coming up blank on this one."

Mercy's heart fell. According to detective interviews, Devin had been shown the photo of the neighbor several times since the abduction.

He first saw the image after his brain injury. Might confirm my earlier hypothesis about who he can recall.

"That's a neighbor of Mia's. Jason Slade."

He set the photo on the sofa and pulled his hand away as if he'd been stung.

Mercy tried to contain her surprise at the sudden reaction. "It appears you don't have a good feeling about the photo."

"No," Devin said firmly. "I'd been told about this guy. Mia was very uncomfortable around him. He didn't bother her at first, but then he started making inappropriate comments and touching her."

"Touching her?" Noelle asked sharply.

"Not like that. Just a quick touch on her shoulder or back—still inappropriate. It creeped her out. Colin wanted to break his truck's windshield." He grinned faintly. "We all supported Colin but agreed behind his back that we wouldn't do that sort of pointless shit."

"Devin, Jason Slade became a primary suspect when you kids disappeared because of his interactions with Mia and because he'd been a registered sex offender." Mercy watched him closely, searching his face for emotional clues.

Confusion was the most obvious emotion. "He was? But . . ." Distaste crossed his face and then more confusion. He took a quick glance at the photo. "Now I remember that investigators brought him up. I assume they showed me an image at that time, but he's not familiar to me. I've never seen him in person," he said hesitantly. "I think." His shoulders slumped. "If I have seen him, I can't remember. I assume there wasn't solid evidence since he wasn't arrested?"

"Correct," said Noelle.

Mercy felt Noelle's disappointment too. Devin's brain had a wall regarding Jason Slade.

Is the lack of memory because of something he doesn't want to remember? Or simply because he never met the person?

A knock at the door interrupted her thoughts. Devin stiffened on the couch, and Noelle hopped up to answer the door.

"Checking to see if you're at a good stopping point. I've got a hotel lined up that should work for what we need." Truman looked past Noelle and met Mercy's gaze, making her smile as always. Noelle glanced back, and Mercy nodded, agreeing they could stop for now.

Mercy turned to find Devin watching her closely. "That's your husband, right?" he asked.

"Yes. Truman Daly. Eagle's Nest police chief," she said, remembering how he'd asked for immediate identifications.

Satisfaction crossed his face. "I know. I put it together from your expression when you heard him speak."

She was simultaneously flattered and slightly embarrassed that she was so easy to read. And she became more convinced that Devin was their best tool for figuring out what had happened twenty years ago.

What is buried deep in his brain?

29

"I'm overwhelmed," stated Mercy, staring at her computer screen. "And I don't say that very often."

"I'm with you. There is too much information here," said Noelle. "I guess the logical way to start is to work back from the most recent."

After getting Devin and Ollie set up in a new hotel, the two women had dived into Rob Newton's email accounts and social media after lunch.

Snow had started to lightly fall as they'd returned to the sheriff's department, and Mercy checked the weather, preferring to not get snowed in. Thankfully, it was only supposed to last for two hours.

Sara Newton hadn't shared her husband's social media passwords as quickly as Mercy would have liked, making her wonder if the woman had cleaned up some things first.

Logically there was no reason for Mercy to think Sara would hold anything back. She wanted her husband's killer found. But Mercy knew people did weird shit during a police investigation. They hid things they were embarrassed about, convinced it wasn't relevant. Or tried to make their loved one appear perfect and kind when the opposite was true. They held back things they were uncomfortable talking about, and later law enforcement got the truth, but the damage had been done.

If Sara had cleaned up anything, computer forensics would immediately spot it. As Mercy looked at the thousands of comments on Rob Newton's social media, she couldn't imagine what Sara would bother to delete. It appeared Rob had just as many haters as fans. There was nothing to be gained from deleting a few posts or comments.

Or is there?

Mercy started with the social media, while Noelle dived into his email. Most of Rob's social media accounts had been created under his podcast pseudonym, John Jacobs. His alter ego was on every major social media app, but it appeared he would simultaneously share the same post on all of them. The posts were always a small segment of an episode to hook the listener and share links to the whole podcast. Mercy listened to a teaser about a murder in South Carolina and followed one of the links to the podcast at a major retailer. She scrolled, frowning as she looked at a few of Rob's episodes. "These are free. Doesn't he make money off subscriptions? Where's the income?"

Noelle looked up. "Haven't you ever listened to a podcast before?"

"No. I'm a fan of silence when I have a free moment. You listen to some?"

"I follow a few. Podcasters make money from advertisers, not the subscriber. Of course, the more subscribers, the more likely to attract advertisers. I usually listen while on the treadmill. The ones I like are about TV shows, where the actors talk about what happened behind the scenes on each episode."

"Well, I learned something new today," Mercy muttered as she refocused on her computer. She'd heard Ollie and Kaylie discuss certain podcasts, but the concept held little appeal to her. She'd rather read a book or watch TV than listen to someone talk.

Maybe I need a visual element for enjoyment.

According to the information they'd received from Sara, Rob also had a Facebook account under his legal name where all his posts and friends were private. First Mercy viewed this personal account from her own. Other than Rob's name, there was no relevant information available to anyone who wasn't his friend. She couldn't see his city or education, and even his profile photo was of a dog, not himself.

She approved.

Mercy then signed in as Rob, and his life popped up for her review. Looking through his timeline, she noticed he never mentioned his alter ego, John Jacobs. There weren't any posts about true crime or podcasts. Most of his photos were from hikes and bike rides. There were several pictures of him and Sara looking very happy. Beach photos and others from a trip to Palm Springs. This page had a few hundred friends, which was low as Facebook numbers went. Mercy went to his messages and found them empty, which was a little odd. Either he constantly cleaned them out or he rarely used them to communicate. Next she checked the Facebook groups he'd joined. There was a Bakersfield restaurant review group and another for his high school graduation class.

She clicked on the school group.

It wasn't very active. The last post was from three months earlier and had garnered two comments. She put Rob's name in the group search bar, and it pulled up one post he'd made a year ago.

She held her breath as she read.

> Anyone hear what happened to those three that disappeared after graduation? Mia, Alex, and Colin? Was that mystery ever solved? Are there any rumors about what happened to them?

It had eighty-two comments.

Most of the comments were speculation. Some posted that they believed Jason Slade or Erick Howard had killed them. Mercy noticed that the comments pointing at Erick Howard were widely contested, commenters saying how much they had liked the teacher. No one stated that they knew Jason Slade, so he received most of the negative comments. But other theories were plentiful.

> I heard the three of them got away from the killer and ran off to New Mexico.

> They're dead in the hills somewhere. I always expect to stumble across their bones on a hike.

> They attacked the other two guys, dumped their bodies, and then left.

That comment had the most replies:

> Yeah, I heard there'd been a fight.

> Colin was an asshole. This doesn't surprise me at all.

> No, they were all good friends. You're an idiot to even suggest this.

> I heard Devin still has brain damage. He's in a wheelchair and can't talk.

Mercy glowered.

> They'll never come back. They'd be arrested for killing Tyler.

She scrolled on.

I swear I saw Alex in Safeway in The Dalles about ten years ago. I almost said something but chickened out.

Mia was hot. It was probably that rapist dude.

"Asshole," muttered Mercy. She noted that even though Rob had created the post, he hadn't replied to anyone's comment.

Maybe he was hoping for leads to explore.

She exited the group and went back to Rob's personal page. She poked around for a few more minutes but didn't see anything of interest. She signed out and went into the public John Jacobs *They Were Wrong* Facebook page and checked his private messages.

"Ugh."

Nearly every message was bitter and angry. They called Rob/John a hack and a liar, claiming he made up all his stories. Mercy read a few, noting again that Rob never replied.

Most of the messages sounded hateful. Often the grammar and spelling were atrocious, making her worry for the future of the nation. Then she started to notice a similarity in many of the messages. The same phrases used in several different ones. Complaints worded the same way. Similar threats and even some word-for-word matching threats.

"Bots."

No wonder he didn't reply.

She slowed down her reading speed, looking for messages that seemed legitimate. A few were interspersed among those from the angry bots and the other bots stating John Jacobs had been left a million dollars in Dubai to claim or that he could buy fifty thousand more followers for $500.

Yeah, those followers will be real people.

She went back to the posts on the John Jacobs Facebook page and paid attention to the comments, now spotting the repetitiveness and poor grammar of more bots. "Why? Why do these stupid things even exist? What is the purpose? They're not going to sway opinions by spouting on a small podcaster's page."

"What?" asked Noelle without looking up from her screen.

"Nothing. Just thinking out loud."

"Mm-hmm."

"You finding anything interesting?"

"Not yet. You?" asked Noelle.

"Just that people like to share unfounded rumors."

"That's not new. I suspect gossip goes back to when the first humans spoke."

"It's making me feel as if I bathed in slime," said Mercy.

"Want to start with his research notebooks? The photocopies are available now."

Mercy was ready to change gears. She found the computer file with the notebooks and opened it. "There are two hundred and thirty-six pages. And he has the worst tiny handwriting."

Noelle finally raised her head. "That's a lot. Maybe some isn't related to the missing teens' case?"

"I guess I'll find out." Mercy sighed. "I'll print them and separate the pages that aren't relevant. I'm tired of looking at my computer screen anyway." She hit PRINT, stretched her back, bought a bottle of water from a vending machine, and then went to get her pages.

She sat back down, wondering why the paper in her hands made her happy when computers were more fluid and efficient for her work. She quickly numbered all the pages with red ink to keep them in order and then started to read.

It took her eyes a few minutes to adjust to his cramped handwriting, but she was pleasantly surprised that he wrote in full sentences and made good use of bullet points when needed. Overall the notes were well organized. Although there was a plethora of question marks. It appeared every question Rob came up with led to five more.

Just like police work.

She removed multiple pages that clearly addressed research on other topics. After a quick skim, the pile was down to 148 pages. A little easier to process.

Rob had explored all the theories presented in response to his question to his high school group and more. He'd looked into sightings of the trio reported online as best he could and had decided against traveling to most places, including North Dakota and Tennessee, to pursue the wide variety of sightings.

Research can get expensive.

Mercy noted he had planned to go to The Dalles and follow up on the suggestion in the Facebook group that Alex Stark had been seen in Safeway.

What would he do? Stand outside Safeway and stare at customers?

If Alex Stark was still alive, he must be using someone else's identity. The data analyst at Mercy's office had already searched for the missing three under their old identities, seeking new activity or name changes. There was nothing. The trio had vanished.

Many of Rob's notes indicated that he'd done the same type of searches. He'd also searched thousands of online photos of family members and other friends on social media, hoping to see one of their faces.

Smart move.

She turned a page, appreciation growing for Rob's determination to find the three. Her eyebrows rose as she realized he'd recently staked out the homes of Erick Howard and Jason Slade. The other day Sara had listed the locations she and Rob had gone to while staying in the area. She had not mentioned these homes.

Maybe she didn't know?

Mercy recalled that Sara had mentioned Rob had gone cross-country skiing some days. Sara hadn't gone because she hated the sport. Mercy suspected these were the days Rob had gone to the homes. His notes reported no sign of Slade, which seemed logical to Mercy since he was a long-haul truck driver. Rob had followed Erick Howard to Target and even approached him, pretending to stumble across him and reminding Howard that he'd been a former student. He'd received a pleasant greeting from the teacher but could tell Howard didn't remember him. The teacher had run a few errands while Rob watched his house but spent most of his time at home.

What did he expect to see at these men's homes that had anything to do with twenty years ago?

She shook her head and kept turning pages, reading slowly. Had Rob expected Mia or Colin to walk out one of the front doors? Mercy didn't see the point of the stakeouts. Her gaze locked on a name on the next page. Rob had staked out Colin Balke's parents' home in Prineville. And he'd seen two men separately leave the home that day who appeared to be in the right age range to be Colin. He'd used binoculars but lamented that hats had kept him from making a positive identification.

He listed two license plates.

That's where his notes ended. If he'd found the owners of the vehicles, he hadn't written it in his notes. The date he'd staked out the Balke home was the day before he'd been found on the banks of the Columbia River.

Did he approach one of the drivers and get himself killed?

Mercy immediately popped the first license plate into the system. The registered owner was Frank Balke, Colin's father.

What man around age thirty-eight would drive Frank's vehicle?

Colin had a sister who'd been close in age. Perhaps a son-in-law had used the truck.

She ran the other plate. The registered owner was Josh Bole, who lived in Prineville. Mercy pulled up his driver's license and felt a sting of disappointment. The age was about right, but the man looked nothing like Colin Balke. She ran a quick search on the name. Josh Bole was a plumber.

Most likely on a job at the Balke home. Or an acquaintance.

Mercy pulled up Frank Balke's license. She didn't see a resemblance to the photos of Colin, but perhaps Colin took after his mother's side of the family. She leaned back in her chair as she thought. Interviewing Colin Balke's parents was already on their list. Now she had a question to add to the interview.

"I'd like to interview Colin Balke's parents today," Mercy said. "Rob Newton had staked out their home and saw a man of Colin's age drive off in a vehicle registered to Colin's father."

Noelle sat up. "No shit? Rob thought it was Colin?"

"He couldn't get a clear look."

Noelle tilted her head, her gaze curious. "Do you think these kids are still alive? Why wouldn't they come forward? Finding them alive seems the most unlikely result of our investigation."

"Rob was certainly pursuing the theory."

Noelle glanced at her screen. "Do you mind going to the Balke home on your own? I'm still wading through these emails." She frowned. "I think you should take a deputy with you. Let's agree not to do any solo interviews. Too many bodies are turning up."

"Good idea, but I'll see if Truman is available instead. I know he'd planned to take the afternoon off."

"He's taking the afternoon off, and you'll make him work?"

Mercy grinned. "Spending time with me doesn't count as work. Even while conducting interviews."

Noelle rolled her eyes. "Newlyweds."

"We've been married almost a year."

"You're still newlyweds. Trust me. I've been one twice."

"When will be the third time?" Mercy had never asked the detective about her love life but suddenly was curious. She thought Noelle was stunning. Not traditionally pretty but someone who always got second looks. And she was cool and smart. The type of person everyone wanted to hang out with.

"Ha! Not happening."

"Never say never," said Mercy, noticing the detective had dropped eye contact.

Noelle shrugged. "Men my age carry a lot of baggage."

"Like two previous marriages?" she said in a teasing tone.

"Yep. Or two little kids, two felonies, two bankruptcies, or two current girlfriends. Dating at my age is like walking through lava. It's impossible to not be burned."

"I know I got lucky with Truman, so he's proof there are good ones around. You're only a few years older than me, so you could find one."

Noelle raised a single eyebrow in an elegant gesture Mercy wished she could imitate when Kaylie said something ridiculous.

"I'm forty-two."

She's eight years older than me?

"You could easily date a thirty-year-old," Mercy told her.

"Thirty-year-olds are children. Don't worry about my love life." She made a shooing gesture with her hands. "Go find your perfect husband and talk to the Balke parents."

Mercy stood and packed up her things. "I'll let you know what they say."

And ask Truman if he knows anyone for Noelle.

30

Parked along a street in a tiny older neighborhood in Prineville, Truman waited in his truck. The homes were simple shapes—like things a first grader would draw. Most of them were painted traditional whites, grays, and browns, but Truman had spotted a Pepto-Bismol pink home and another that was a very bright purple. He wondered what the neighbors thought. Clearly there wasn't an HOA.

Passing vehicles had dirtied the snow piled along the edges of the road. There were no sidewalks to shovel, but each of the driveways had been perfectly cleared. Between each two simple homes, a single towering tree stood like a sentinel, its evergreen branches coated with a thin layer of white.

Mercy had asked Truman to meet her to interview Colin Balke's parents and had shared a few case updates, including the sighting of a man Colin's age driving a Balke truck. Truman suspected that the missing three teens had died, but this information made him wonder why a survivor would stay hidden, making him want to dig deeper into the case. Watching Ollie interact with Devin had sparked Truman's need to find the person who had injured the man. Devin was a good guy; he deserved answers.

All the families did.

Ollie had driven Devin to the hospital that morning to see his mother. The doctors were now more optimistic about Linda's recovery but were keeping her heavily sedated as they monitored her head injury. Her stab wounds were healing, and she was very lucky Mercy had been there.

Linda hadn't woken to say who'd stabbed her.

The Balke family didn't know Mercy was coming for an interview, because if it had been Colin Balke who'd driven the truck, she didn't want him warned. Truman approved of her surprise pop-in approach.

He'd been watching the Balke house for a few minutes. A sedan and a Ford pickup sat in the driveway, so it was likely that someone was home.

Will we find a survivor here?

Mercy's Tahoe stopped behind him. Truman got out and met her in the street. She was dressed head to toe in her usual snug black, and Truman wore jeans with his hat, boots, and heavy coat with the Eagle's Nest Police Department logo. Her intense green eyes stood out in the gray day, distracting him for a long second. She looked eager to get started.

"Ready?" she asked. "Did you *see* that bright-pink house?"

"It's impossible to miss." He pointed down the street. "There's another in a shade of purple Ina would like."

"Kaylie would too."

As they crossed the road, Mercy snapped surreptitious photos of the vehicles and plates. "The truck's plate matches the one Rob listed," she said.

She knocked on the front door and stepped aside to where bricks covered the outer wall but she was in view of whoever opened the door. Truman waited a couple of yards back, his coat unzipped, his hands ready as he watched the windows.

The unexpected could happen when law enforcement knocked on a door.

A tall older man with a slight stoop in his shoulders opened it. He looked cautious but politely greeted Mercy. His hair was slightly disheveled, as if he'd just removed a hat.

Truman focused on a subtle bulge under his shirt.

He's armed.

Not uncommon around here . . . but why in his home?

She held out her ID. "Mr. Balke? I'm Special Agent Kilpatrick. We're doing a follow-up on your son's disappearance."

His mouth opened the slightest bit. His gaze shot to Truman and then immediately back to Mercy.

"That's Police Chief Daly from Eagle's Nest," she added.

"Why is the FBI at my front door after all these years?" he snapped, standing straighter. "Usually the most we get is an occasional phone call asking the same questions they've asked from day one."

A petite woman in jeans and a Rudolph the Red-Nosed Reindeer sweater appeared beside him, the top of her head barely reaching his shoulder. "Frank. Let's listen to what they have to say." She held out a hand to Mercy, subtly poking her husband with an elbow in what Truman recognized as a be-polite move. "I'm Yvette."

Frank stepped back, a glower still hovering around his eyes, but he gave a polite nod. "Please come in," he said robotically.

Truman removed his hat, shook both of their hands, and followed Mercy into their living room, highly aware of the weapon Frank Balke was carrying. The living room had a lived-in feel, its walls painted in warm colors and the older furniture upholstered in bold prints. Bookshelves stuffed with hardcover novels lined one wall, and along another stood an upright piano. The redbrick fireplace with a gas insert put out a welcome warmth in the room.

Truman sniffed. The home smelled faintly of bacon.

His stomach rumbled.

Yvette gestured toward the sofa while she and Frank sat in chairs across from it. She offered drinks, which both Mercy and Truman turned down, and then there was an awkward moment as they all silently looked at each other, the tick of the clock on the mantel sounding exceptionally loud.

"Do you have new information about our son?" Frank asked bluntly.

"No," said Mercy. "But there has been recent activity that has made us revisit the case."

"It was that man, wasn't it?" asked Yvette. "The one with the radio show. He's called us twice in the past few weeks, and I wouldn't talk to him. I looked up his website. It's trash. I told him if he had questions to go to the police."

"John Jacobs. He's actually a podcaster," said Mercy. "He called you?"

Both parents nodded.

"Just another snoop looking for a story to exploit," said Frank. "They come out of the woodwork every few years."

"Did you know he was in the same high school graduating class as your son?" asked Mercy. "His real name is Rob Newton. I believe he lived next door to you in Bend."

Eyebrows rose, and the parents exchanged a look. "Well, why didn't he tell us that?" asked Frank. "I might have actually talked to him. I remember Rob well. Quiet kid. He and Colin were friendly, but not friends, you know? Different interests."

"What sort of questions did he ask?" Mercy had a yellow pad on her lap, a pen ready to take notes.

Yvette cleared her throat. She had a small face with features that made her look like an elf. But a warm, mothering elf. "He was brusque and immediately asked if we'd had contact with Colin." She blinked rapidly and wiped her nose. "I refused to talk to him. I threatened to call the police if he contacted us again."

"But he called a second time?" asked Truman.

"Yes. I told him to talk to the police and then I hung up. I don't understand why he didn't say who he really was. Instead, he was rude."

Her husband gently rubbed her lower back, a troubled look in his eye as he gazed down at his wife.

Mercy took a deep breath. "Rob Newton was murdered three days ago. He had actively been researching the disappearance of your son and the other teens."

Yvette's eyes widened. Her husband's hand halted on her back, and his eyes narrowed as Mercy's words sank in.

"I'm sorry to bring up bad memories," said Mercy. "But you should know that Rob's body was found in the same location as Devin Bonner and Tyler Hynd—and the cause of death was nearly identical."

Yvette grabbed her husband's other hand as she gasped. "His throat was slit?"

"Yes. And he was bound the same way."

"What does that mean?" asked Yvette. "I don't understand." She exchanged confused looks with her husband.

"We're not sure," said Mercy. "That's why we're looking at the old case again."

"I thought they were very thorough with their investigation back then," Frank said slowly, his eyes distant. "They turned over every rock looking for those kids. It took us several years, but we finally accepted that they are dead. The follow-up calls every few years just stir up pain that we've tried to bury. If Colin was alive, he'd contact us. I've heard all those theories about the three running off; they're bullshit. Colin is dead."

Truman had been watching Yvette's face as her husband spoke. Her expression had gone blank as Frank stated they'd accepted their son's death.

Yvette will always have a mother's hope.

He suspected that deep down Frank felt the same.

But humans take on the mindset that is most comfortable. Waiting years for a child to come home is painful. They adopt a belief that it will never happen in an attempt to function and move on.

"What was Mia like?" Mercy asked, abruptly changing the subject. "How long did she date Colin?"

Frank looked at Yvette. "They'd been dating for about eight months," answered Yvette. "She was a nice girl." Frank nodded in agreement, looking from Mercy to Truman.

Mercy let the answer hang in the air. Truman said nothing, knowing she wanted the parents to feel they should fill the silence.

"She was a nice girl," Yvette repeated. "Good student. Sweet. Colin had a low opinion of her father, and both kids preferred to spend time at our home instead of hers. We didn't speak much with her father. Even after the kids vanished, but . . ."

Mercy raised both brows. "But?"

Yvette shot Frank an uneasy glance. "Mia didn't like him. I think he was unpleasant to live with."

"She told you this?" asked Mercy.

"No." Colin's mother thought for a moment. "Colin alluded to it. I can't remember exactly what he said about her father, but I inferred a negative situation several times. Do you remember what Colin said?" she asked her husband.

"No."

Frank Balke sat stiffly, his manner growing icier by the second. Truman wasn't sure if it was because of the topic or because Frank was holding back his opinions. Truman sensed that Frank and Yvette hadn't approved of their son's relationship with Mia.

"Colin was always looking out for others," Yvette continued, her voice quavering the tiniest bit. "I think in his subconscious he wanted to rescue Mia."

"Rescue her?" repeated Mercy.

"Well, yes. Her upbringing was rather rough. Her mother was out of the picture early on for some reason I was never told. The girl had a wounded look in her eyes, you know? Colin had a weakness for that."

They definitely didn't approve of Colin and Mia.

Mercy hadn't written anything on her notepad, but Truman was certain she was coming to the same conclusion. There was a condescending aura around the parents as they spoke of Mia, and it rubbed Truman the wrong way.

"What about the other boys?" asked Mercy. "Who was Colin's best friend out of the group?"

"Alex," said Yvette as her husband said, "Tyler."

They turned to each other with surprised expressions. "I'm sure it was Alex," Yvette said emphatically. "He was always over here."

"Tyler and Colin had played sports together since they were little," argued Frank.

Yvette looked back to Mercy and shrugged. "Both, I guess."

"And Devin Bonner?" asked Mercy.

A sudden chill filled the room, beating back the warmth from the gas fireplace. Both parents sat silent, the faintest hint of distaste appearing in their eyes.

Truman tamped down a flash of anger. Devin didn't deserve this.

"Devin?" prompted Mercy.

"I think he knows exactly what happened," Frank said, clipping his words. "For some reason, he won't tell anyone."

Disagreement crossed Yvette's face. "He's got brain damage. His memory is gone. I've talked to his mother. She says Devin wants more than anything to be able to remember what happened and who attacked them. But—"

Mercy and Truman waited for her to finish.

She shifted on the sofa. "Colin was mad at him for a while. I know at graduation they had some sort of conflict going on. I think Devin did something. Colin was very upset about it."

There was no disagreement in Frank's eyes.

"Devin did something to your son?" Mercy clarified. "You appear to feel very strongly toward Devin twenty years later—even though you don't know what happened. Why would Colin go on a camping trip if he was angry at Devin?"

The parents didn't have an answer.

Truman wondered if there was more than bad blood between Colin and Devin that colored the parents' current attitude toward Devin. It seemed excessive to hold a twenty-year grudge. He met Frank's gaze for a long moment. "What did the boys fight about?"

Frank didn't break the stare. "Dunno."

He's holding back.

"Why are you here, Chief?" Frank asked sharply. "I don't see your connection to any of this."

"You're right," said Truman, mildly surprised it'd taken that long for one of them to question his presence. "I'm not involved except on the periphery. My son is staying with Devin Bonner because his mother is in the hospital with severe knife injuries from an attack."

Yvette drew in a breath. "Linda?"

"She was attacked yesterday morning at her home," said Mercy. "We're investigating the possibility that it's related to Rob Newton's murder."

"How?" asked Yvette, concern in her eyes. "Why would you think that? Will she be okay?"

"She nearly died, but her condition is improving," said Mercy. "As for the connection to the murder, you'll have to trust that we have a reason to look." She cleared her throat. "Does anyone else drive either of your vehicles? The two out front are all you own, correct?"

The swift topic change took a moment to register with the Balkes.

"Our son-in-law borrows my truck occasionally," said Frank. "I keep telling him to get one of his own."

"They can't afford another vehicle right now," said Yvette, gently reprimanding her husband. "Why do you ask?"

"Did he borrow it within the last two weeks?" asked Mercy, not answering Yvette.

Frank frowned. "Yes. He hauled something to the dump. I'm not sure of the exact day."

"Thank you." Mercy finally made a notation on her pad.

"Why?" repeated Yvette.

Mercy gave her a sympathetic smile. "I can't comment on that element of the investigation at the moment."

Frank shot to his feet. "If you have a lead on my son's disappearance, I want to know about it." He glared laser beams at Mercy.

Truman slowly stood. He said nothing, but he held the other man's gaze while being aware of his hands.

Mercy set a hand on Truman's leg. "Mr. Balke, if I had anything concrete, I would share it with you. You know how many tips and leads go nowhere. I'm not going to waste your time and energy on things that pan out to nothing." She stood and tucked her pad into her bag. "You'll hear from me if there is news. I appreciate your time today."

Truman exchanged one more look with Frank, and they both headed toward the door.

Outside, Mercy poked him. "Turn down the testosterone indoors, okay?"

"You saw he was wearing a shoulder holster under his shirt, right?"

"I did. But still—"

"A man who wears a weapon inside his house is nervous about something."

"Maybe he just got home."

Truman shrugged. To him Frank Balke had felt on edge through the entire interview. "What's next?" he asked as they walked to her vehicle.

"I'll check in with Noelle and decide, but I'd like to talk to Mia Fowler's father and to the physics teacher. Would you mind checking on Devin and Ollie?"

"Will do." He surprised her with a quick kiss in the street and headed to his truck, thinking over the interview. His gut feeling told him Frank and Yvette had never heard from Colin.

The kids still being alive is just a theory.

A son would contact his family, right?

Unless he had a good reason not to return home.

31

As Truman sped back to Eagle's Nest, the police department popped up on his phone. He hit the ANSWER button.

"What's up, Lucas?"

"Hey, Chief. I just sent Ben to a report of shots fired." Lucas's voice filled the cab.

Truman frowned at the concern in his dispatcher's voice. Shots fired was rarely a serious dispatch call in their rural area, unless it happened in downtown Eagle's Nest.

"I think you should get over there," Lucas continued. "Grandma called it in."

Truman immediately pulled a U-turn, heading toward Ina's home. "I'm two minutes out. What happened?"

"She called a minute ago and said she thought it came from the Bonner home next door. Ben was the only person available for me to send."

"Dammit! Let him know I'm on my way." Truman pressed the accelerator. Ben Cooley had decades of experience with the Eagle's Nest PD. He knew everyone and most likely had known their grandparents, too, but Truman preferred to send the seventy-year-old out on calls that would use his people skills instead of to situations that could turn physical.

"You'll probably beat Ben there. He was out on Old Miller Road."

"Copy." Truman ended the call, and Ina's name popped up on his phone two seconds later. "You okay, Ina? I'm almost to your place."

"I thought Ben was coming," she said. "And yes, I'm fine. I've got Jolene right beside me."

Jolene had been her husband's revolver. Truman wasn't sure which husband. There'd been a few.

"Don't shoot anyone," Truman ordered. "Unless you really need to," he awkwardly amended.

"I've known how to handle a gun since before you were born, Chief."

"I'll arrive before Ben," said Truman. "What happened?"

"All I know is that someone is firing a rifle over there. I've heard four shots so far, and I'm certain they're outdoors. Usually I'd ignore a few shots, but I know what happened there yesterday."

Truman's hand tightened on the wheel as Linda's face flashed in his mind.

"I can't see the house from here," said Ina. "You want me to go look?"

"*No!* Stay inside."

"I'm just foolin' with you, Truman. How stupid do you think this old lady is?"

"I don't appreciate jokes when bullets are flying, Ina. I need to make a call unless you've got more information for me."

"Nope, that's it. Be careful." She ended the call.

Truman called Ollie. The phone rang. And rang. Truman ended the call when his voice mail answered and dialed again. Voice mail. "Answer, dammit."

If those two went back to Devin's home to get something . . .

He spun the wheel to turn into the Bonners' long driveway, feeling his tires slide and then immediately grab in the fresh layer of snow. He accelerated, noting a single set of vehicle tracks had already driven up to the house. The tracks stopped at a small Ford crossover he didn't recognize parked in front of the Bonners' garage.

Not Ollie's.

Relief swept over him.

But whose? The shooter's? Or a victim's?

He parked behind the vehicle and let Lucas know he'd arrived at the scene. He yanked his rifle from the dash and listened for a long moment. No shots. No one came running out of the home. He stepped out of the Tahoe. Active-shooter protocol meant he was to go straight in, not wait for backup.

But Ina was positive the shots happened outside.

He recalled how Mercy's quick response had saved Linda Bonner's life and cautiously headed toward the side of the house at a slow jog. He stopped at the back corner of the home and surveyed the land behind it. There was a large clearing for the yard and a small shed set farther back before tall pines took over. He knew Mercy had found Linda a hundred yards or so into the woods.

Clear the house first.

His radio crackled. Ben.

"You here?" Truman asked.

"Yep. Right behind your vehicle. What do you got?"

"Ina heard four rifle shots that she believes were outdoors. I haven't heard anything since I've been here. I'm outside at the northwest corner of the house checking the backyard. All quiet so far."

"Does this Ford belong to the home?"

"Unknown. I'd like you to knock on the front door, and I'll cover the back. Keep your eyes open."

"On it, boss."

Ben didn't need Truman telling him to keep his eyes open; he'd probably entered ten times the number of homes that Truman had.

His rifle ready, Truman took a few steps so he could see the glass slider and windows at the back of the home.

Ben's voice carried over the house. "Eagle's Nest Police Department! Anyone home?"

Truman moved closer to a window and quickly peeked inside from an angle. It was a bedroom; no one was visible. He ducked under it as he jogged past and rapidly glanced inside the next window. Kitchen.

"Hello!" shouted Ben. "I'm coming in the front door!"

Truman held his breath and heard no sounds.

"Front door's locked, Chief," came over the radio.

Truman replied that he'd check the back door.

Keeping close to the house, he went to the slider. He quickly looked inside from several angles, not seeing any movement. He took a deep breath and gripped the handle.

Locked.

He was standing on a small covered concrete patio. The new snow had only dusted its outer edges.

Footprint?

A partial print was visible at the patio's border. He narrowed his gaze, spotting parts of what could be prints close to the house. They'd come from around the other side of the home. He darted past the slider and checked the east side of the home. There were more prints. Someone had walked to the backyard along the east side of the house and possibly tried the slider as he just had. He looked across the white backyard. Headed toward the woods, someone had walked under the trees that lined the yard, a partial print here and there.

He asked Ben to join him, and he scanned the yard, his eyes straining to find returning footprints. There were none.

Ben appeared at the east corner of the home. He had his rifle in hand and his duty pistol in his belt along with a Taser. The Taser's electrodes were unlikely to be successful if a suspect was wearing a thick winter coat. And the officer had to be decently close to reach the target.

"If the footprints didn't come from the Ford, I'll eat my hat," Ben told Truman. "There aren't any prints by the car because the house blocked the snowfall, but they pick up just past the garage."

Truman pointed to the faint prints leading along the edge of the backyard to the woods.

A rifle cracked, and they abruptly lunged around the corner of the house.

As a second shot sounded, their rifles went up and they flattened against the home. Truman's pulse pounded in his head as he took a quick inventory of his body and glanced back to check his officer.

No bullet wounds.

"He's not shooting at us," Ben whispered. "But he is definitely in the woods."

"Ready?" asked Truman.

"Always," answered Ben. "Announce first?"

Truman wished he had his megaphone. *"This is the Eagle's Nest Police Department!"* he shouted. *"Put down your gun!"*

He held his breath, listening hard. From their current position, they could only see a small portion of the backyard and the shed near the edge of the woods.

"Someone's running," said Ben just as Truman picked up on the sounds. Faint crackles and the brushing of branches.

Moving farther away.

"He's leaving," Truman said quietly, noting the sounds were going in the opposite direction of Ina's home. He updated Lucas with his radio and had him request county backup to check the homes in the area.

"Let's go," he told Ben. They moved across the backyard in unison, Ben slightly behind and to Truman's right, providing each other overlapping coverage as they'd drilled dozens of times before.

When they reached the cover of the small shed, Truman announced them again.

"I'm unarmed," yelled a female voice from the woods. "He was shooting at *me*!"

"I need you to come out. Your hands over your head," Truman shouted back. He kept his gun pointed in the direction of the voice and sensed Ben shifting as he covered all other angles.

A long minute passed before Truman spotted a figure in the woods. She darted from tree to tree, keeping on the west side of each. Her hands were up, but she was clearly being cautious. She stopped at the last large pine trunk, about thirty yards away, hesitant to enter the open space between the woods and the shed.

Truman wanted her fully out of the woods. He moved forward slightly to peer around the shed to the right, taking in the woods to the east. "I've got you covered," he yelled to the woman. "I need you to come forward."

"I can't." Her voice quavered. "How can I be sure he's gone?"

She had a point. If she was telling the truth, he'd shot at her several times, and now Truman was asking her to cross open ground.

While he stayed behind a shed.

We need to go to her.

"Ready?" Truman asked Ben as he slung his rifle over his shoulder and took out his pistol.

"Yep." Ben kept his rifle ready.

They automatically fell into the same formation that they'd used to cross the backyard. Truman was thankful he had officers he trusted to securely cover his back.

Truman heard Ben's gasp before he heard the crack of the rifle. He spun and saw his officer falling backward, landing on his hip and shoulder, his shocked gaze locked with Truman's.

He's shot.

"Go!" Ben shouted and then screwed his eyes shut in pain.

"*Dammit!* Like I would leave you behind!" Truman lunged to grab the shoulder of Ben's coat and dragged him back to the side of the shed. "Officer down!" he shouted in his shoulder mic. "Get an ambulance here *now*!" Truman saw the hand he'd grabbed Ben's coat with was wet with blood. He stared at it a second and then at Ben. His officer was writhing on his back, swearing under his breath.

His wife is going to strangle me.

"Where are you hit?" Truman cast a quick glance around for the shooter and tried the shed's door handle. Locked.

This is the best cover we've got.

Ben didn't answer, his heels digging into the snow, but he continued to curse. Truman ripped open the officer's coat and wrenched it back to see Ben's left shoulder. He was bleeding near the top.

Not arterial.

One good thing.

Truman rolled Ben to his side, making the officer threaten to castrate him, and pulled the coat back farther, searching for an exit wound on the back of his shoulder.

There it is.

Blood continued to ooze and seep from both ends of the wound.

Awkward place for a tourniquet.

He'd have to use pressure. If the bleeding didn't let up, he'd reconsider the tourniquet.

"Put the tourniquet around my neck," Ben said through clenched teeth. "That'll fix everything."

Truman froze. Then exhaled heavily. "If you're telling jokes, it can't be that bad."

"Hurts like a motherfucker!"

"Then I'm sorry because this is going to hurt worse." Truman slipped out of his coat, folded up one of its arms, and shoved that between Ben's shoulder and the ground. Then he doubled the other coat arm, laid it against the entry wound, and pressed.

Ben shrieked.

Sweat trickled down Truman's sides. His heart was pounding and his lungs were working overtime. "You're gonna be fine, Ben. Your wife would have my head if anything happened to you."

The officer was rigid with pain, but his gaze met Truman's and the corners of his mouth turned up the smallest bit. "Damn right she would."

Far off, sirens sounded.

Thank God.

"What's your status, Chief?" asked Lucas through the radio. "Deschutes County is en route. Two minutes out."

Truman cast a look around the yard and at the woods. "Ben has a through-and-through in his shoulder. I've got pressure on it. Don't know the location of the shooter." He remembered the footsteps he'd heard running away. "There may be two shooters."

"I'm fine, Lucas," Ben hollered. "Don't call Sharon."

"You're not fine," Truman snapped. "A bullet went through you."

"He sounds normal," came Lucas's dry reply.

A choked laugh burst out of Truman as tears threatened, and he hung his head as he continued to press on the wound, sirens and Ben's cursing ringing in his ears.

It's not fucking funny.

Ten minutes later, EMTs had taken over Ben's care. Exhausted, Truman had sat heavily on the ground as they elbowed him aside, his gaze locked on the older officer.

Did I screw up?

His brain was confident he hadn't. They'd both followed protocol. But that didn't stop the emotional doubts and blame raging through him.

Four Deschutes County deputies, two Bend officers, one state trooper, and Truman's two other officers had shown up. Most had been sent into the woods to find the shooter and the woman. "Officer down" was a call that made everyone drop what they were doing and haul ass to a scene.

Truman pulled himself to his feet, determined to join the search in the woods. Ben was speaking in normal tones with the EMTs, and they'd placed an IV and packed his wounds and were waiting for a stretcher. Truman wondered if they'd given him painkillers.

"I can walk," argued Ben. "Don't need to be carried like a baby." He tried to elbow himself up to a sitting position.

Truman saw his face go white before an EMT firmly pinned him back to the ground.

"We'll wait for the stretcher," the EMT stated.

Ben didn't protest.

He'll be fine.

Royce had taken Ben's equipment back to his vehicle. The young officer had looked terrified when he first arrived on the scene and rushed to check Ben. Pale and with his hands shaking, he'd hovered over the man until Ben had told him his fly was down.

It was.

"He's too stubborn to die," said Royce as he returned and joined Truman, his hand subconsciously checking his fly again.

Shouts came from the search in the woods.

"On the ground! On the ground now!"

Royce and Truman automatically crouched and set their hands on their weapons as they turned to the trees. Another voice joined in, ordering someone onto their stomach.

Truman exchanged a look with Royce, and they headed into the woods, joining another deputy moving in the same direction as the shouts. A minute later they came across the state trooper covering Officer Samuel Robb as he checked the person on the ground for weapons.

"She's clear," said Samuel as he stood back up.

The woman was on her stomach, her wrists zip-tied behind her back. She wore a navy knit cap pulled down over her ears and a heavy winter coat. It was the same woman who'd stopped at the edge of the woods, not wanting to move into the clearing. She turned her head as Truman approached, her chin grazing the dirt. One cheek was bleeding, as if someone had scratched her. As he got closer, he recognized her.

Sara Newton.

Rob Newton's wife.

"Sara," he said out loud.

The woman squinted up at him, but his face was shaded by the trees. No doubt it was too dark for her to recognize him.

"I'm Chief Daly. I met you—" he started to say.

The day your husband died.

"You know her?" asked the trooper.

"Yeah. I met her a couple days ago." Truman squatted by her head. "What are you doing here, Sara?"

"You were there," she said, craning her neck to see him. "After Rob . . . vanished. The kid with the snowmobile was your son."

"Correct. Sit her up," he told Samuel. He helped his officer haul Sara to a cross-legged position. "Now tell me why you're here."

She stared at the dirt for a long moment, frowning as she thought.

"It can't be that hard to remember how you ended up here," said Truman. "Is that your Ford in front of the house?"

"It's a rental. I came here wanting to talk to Devin," she finally said. "Rob had said he believed Devin knew what happened all those years ago. Which meant Devin might know what happened to Rob."

"Devin's not staying here. How'd you end up behind his home?"

She squirmed a bit. "I walked around the house to see if he was out back when no one answered the door."

That seems rather ballsy.

"You thought he'd be outside in this thirty-degree weather? How did you get this far into the woods?"

She met his gaze. "I heard someone talking in the woods and I thought it might be him, so I walked up a path. I called his name, and that's when the shooting started."

"Who was shooting?"

"I don't know. I didn't see them. I ran at the first shot."

"Why would they shoot at you?"

"I don't know why I became their target. Fucking pine practically exploded next to me when a bullet hit it. I think I've still got bark stuck in my cheek." She shuddered. "When they started shooting at you, I ran back and hid next to a downed tree. I was there until I heard these guys coming." She glared at the trooper. "I told you I wasn't the shooter."

The trooper shrugged one shoulder. He'd done his job appropriately.

"You used the terms *they* and *their*—you think there was more than one person?"

Sara blinked. "Maybe. Someone had to be talking to another person. Or I guess they were talking out loud to themselves. I didn't actually see anyone. Was Devin the shooter or one of them?" she asked Truman. "You guys caught the shooter, right?"

"We haven't caught the shooter, and I know it's not Devin," he said firmly and then remembered Ollie hadn't answered his text. He checked his phone. Still no reply.

Devin can't handle a rifle.

But he could shoot a pistol.

"Anyone have something to clean up her cheek?" Truman looked at the officers standing around. No one said anything. "If the paramedics are still here, we'll get it looked at." He helped Samuel lift her to her feet. "Are you taking over your husband's research? Are you going to keep nosing around?"

"Can you take off the zip ties?"

Truman checked them. They'd been linked with a loop so they wouldn't pull on her shoulders too badly. "In a bit." He wanted more answers from her before removing the ties. "Rob's research?" he prompted.

"I don't care what happened twenty years ago," said Sara, bitterly. "I care about finding who killed my husband. So far the police haven't done anything."

Truman bristled. Mercy had been working sixteen-hour days to find the killer. "Believe me, they've been doing something, and I'm sorry they haven't found his murderer yet. What information did you think you'd get from Devin? It's been clear that he doesn't remember anything."

A miserable look crossed her face. "I had to do something. Rob was convinced he's pretending."

"What convinced him?"

"He'd said Devin had reasons back in their high school days to hate Colin. Some sort of incident Rob had heard gossip about when they were in school together. I'm not saying Devin is behind Tyler's death and the disappearances, but he doesn't have any motivation to say who was."

She is out of line.

Truman had seen the deep torment in Devin. It'd felt sincere to him.

"Why didn't you tell the investigators this?" he asked.

"I've got no proof. It's just something Rob had said. Why should I pass on something like that?"

Because you want to find your husband's killer.

"They need to know everything, whether you have proof or not. Let them decide what is relevant," he told her.

They'd been making slow progress back toward the house. Two more deputies immediately approached Truman as they came out of the woods. Judging by their grim expressions, they had news.

"There are fresh tire tracks in a driveway at a house to the east—probably two or three hundred yards from here," said the first deputy. "No one's home. In fact there is a For Sale sign at the street and a lockbox on the door. It's a big property like this one—maybe two or three acres. Someone parked in front of the home, and there are multiple boot prints in the snow that lead to the back of the house and farther into the woods."

"I wonder if they knew the property was empty and have been using it to keep watch on this house by coming through the woods," said Truman, thinking of how Linda and now Ben had been attacked. "See any outdoor cameras we could check?"

"No," said the second deputy. "We looked. The house isn't the nicest place."

Truman instantly knew which home it was. The owner had died, and the home had been for sale for more than two years. At least three times, kids had broken in and had parties, so the windows were boarded up. If anyone bought the property, they'd probably tear down the house. He wondered if the shooter had been inside the home.

"Tape off the driveway," said Truman. "Detective Marshall will want to have a look. I'll text her in a minute."

Ben was gone, but one of the EMTs was packing up their equipment. "How was Ben when they took him?" Truman asked the EMT as they approached.

"Very talkative," said the woman. "Is that normal for him? Sometimes the medications do that."

"Normal. His bleeding stopped?"

"Yes. And his vitals were good. He's doing well for someone who was shot."

Truman gestured at Sara. "Can you clean up her cheek?"

The woman peered at Sara's face. "Is that bark or dirt?"

"Both," said Truman.

She nodded. "It's going to hurt. Some of it looks deep," she warned Sara.

Sara grimaced and gave Truman a side-eye. "Undo my wrists now?"

"Okay." He didn't think she was a threat to anyone.

The EMT studied the zip ties. "I can snip them."

Truman stepped away and pulled out his phone, keeping half an eye on Sara as the EMT released her wrists and addressed the bark embedded in her cheek. Sara's story about confronting Devin didn't feel like the complete truth to Truman.

He texted Mercy and Noelle about the shooting—immediately assuring them that Ben was in good shape. Then he explained about Sara and the tire tracks at the other property. The forecast was for snow again that night, so they'd need to check the tracks before the sun went down in an hour.

They said they would be there as soon as they could.

Truman had just put his phone back in his pocket when it buzzed again. Ollie was calling.

"Sorry, I didn't see your call until now," Ollie promptly said.

"Have you guys left the hotel?"

"No. We've been here the whole time but had on headphones. I went down to the lobby to get our tacos. That's it."

"I got you lunch before I left. It's not quite dinnertime yet."

"We were hungry again."

Picturing Devin's gauntness, Truman suspected Ollie had been the hungry one. He never stopped eating.

He updated Ollie on what had happened behind Devin's home and emphasized *again* that the two of them needed to stay put in the hotel.

"Will Ben be okay?" asked Ollie, deep concern in his tone. Ben was like a grandfather to him.

"I think so. I'm headed to the hospital next. I'll let you know."

Truman ended the call and felt exhaustion swamp him. The emotions of the day had physically caught up with him.

But overall it had been a good day.

Any day I don't have to deliver deadly news to an officer's spouse is a good day.

32

Mercy watched the evidence tech take careful measurements of the vehicle tracks left at the scene. The tech had set up her own large lights, flooding the driveway with their beams. By the time Mercy and Noelle had arrived at the run-down house for sale, the sun had set, and officers from multiple law enforcement agencies continued to mill around, watching and talking, upset that an officer had been shot; it'd struck home. Their presence was how they showed their support.

But Mercy was ready for most of them to leave. Twice she'd been interrupted with random questions, the officers wanting the backstory for the events at the Bonner house—all the events.

The evidence tech sprayed a large section of tracks, and Mercy remembered how she had done the same at the substation shootings. Keeping an eye on the technique, she stored away pointers for the next time she had to work with tracks and treads. The officer shooting had triggered an in-depth response to collect evidence, unlike her rural substation shootings, where no one had been harmed.

Noelle was interviewing a state trooper who'd responded to the shooting, so Mercy walked over to the tech, digging deep in her memory to recall her name. It wasn't the same one who'd processed the Jeep.

"Cynthia, right? Agent Kilpatrick. I think we've crossed paths a couple times." Mercy braced her hands on her thighs as she peered at the section of tracks the woman had just sprayed.

The tech met her gaze. "We have." And refocused on her work.

Okay.

"Are there any distinguishing marks in the treads that will help us out?" Mercy asked in a friendly tone.

"Possibly," said Cynthia. "This vehicle has different tires on the front and rear. The front tires are much newer, and the rear ones will need to be replaced soon." She pointed at a faint line that crossed an entire tread. "The wear marks are very obvious. And the right rear tire has a nail or screw in it." She indicated a small oddity on the tread. "It has a nice big head on it. Should be easy to spot if you find the vehicle. Distance between tracks indicates this is a full-size truck."

"That's very helpful. Thank you."

Almost everyone around here had a full-size truck in their household. But the two different types of tires would help narrow things down.

Tires can be changed. Nails removed.

It wasn't a slam dunk.

Noelle joined her. "The house is still locked and boarded up. I don't think anyone has been inside. The path from here through the woods to the Bonner home has been thoroughly searched. They found several shells, some food wrappers, and a bullet in a tree trunk where they shot at Sara Newton. Want to walk it?"

"I do. Any other prints besides these?" She gestured at the prints that indicated two people had exited and returned to the parked truck. Apparently Cynthia had already collected the prints because several had been sprayed with the gray primer.

"Only the same two sets of boot prints were found between here and there," said Noelle. "But I was told that closer to the Bonner house,

Sara's show up." She grimaced. "Along with a lot of mishmashed prints from the law enforcement response."

"Understandable." Several white flakes fluttered to the ground in front of Mercy, and she looked at the sky. "Here it comes. I'm glad forensics got here when they did." She gripped her powerful flashlight, and she and Noelle took to the path, their lights shining wide beams on the ground ahead of them.

Path was a strong word. The two people who had made the boot prints had essentially followed a trail of least resistance through the woods, so the boot prints zigged and zagged around pines and brush. The pines had kept a lot of the snow from reaching the ground, and the dirt was frozen solid. The best prints were in the shallow covering of snow, but an occasional heel or partial print could be seen in the hard dirt.

"It's been a long day," said Noelle after they'd walked in silence for several minutes, scanning the ground and the trees above them.

"Started early," said Mercy, remembering the discovery of Paula Jupp's body outside Ollie's motel. The podcaster's autopsy was scheduled for the next morning. "Truman got a call right before he left that Linda Bonner had a complication late this afternoon," she told Noelle. "She had to go back in for surgery. It sounds like she has a serious infection that isn't responding to antibiotics."

"That poor woman," said Noelle. "And Devin."

"Truman was going to run Ollie and Devin back to the hospital. I don't know how late they'll be there." She was glad Ollie had Devin around and vice versa.

"We need Linda to identify who stabbed her," said Noelle. "Or at least get a physical description. Hopefully she knew the person."

"There's a good chance she didn't." Mercy stopped to examine one very clear boot print in the light coating of snow. Someone had left an evidence marker near it. "But I'll put money on the fact that the same person who stabbed her also shot at Ben. Or at least that it was one of the two people here earlier today. I wonder why they used a knife on Linda instead of a gun."

"Trying to be quiet?"

"They didn't care about being quiet today."

"Maybe they're getting sloppy—or desperate," said Noelle. "All the better for us. They'll make a mistake."

"I'd say they already made a few mistakes," said Mercy. "Number one being the tread and track evidence being gathered."

"Everything seems to center around Devin," said Noelle. "They've clearly been keeping an eye on his house for a while. Why would they spy on the Bonner home?"

"Even Sara was looking for him," said Mercy. She'd read Sara's statement from the shooting. The woman had asserted that she was only there to try to figure out what had happened to her husband, and that her husband had been convinced that Devin knew something he wasn't sharing. "I'm tired of people pointing fingers at Devin's memory. There's got to be another way to figure out who murdered Rob and Paula."

"And attacked Linda, Sara, and Ben," added Noelle.

They came across more evidence markers near two pines growing close together. The ground around the trees had several scuff marks in a frozen bed of pine needles.

"The markers are where they collected the shells," said Noelle.

Through the pines, Mercy spotted a faint light far off in the distance. "That light is at the rear of the Bonner house. They must have used this as their primary lookout spot."

"They picked up empty Red Bull cans and beef jerky bags here too. Our shooters are sloppy and rude."

"Clearly they spent quite a bit of time watching the Bonner home." Mercy wondered what they would have done if they'd spotted Devin instead of Linda or Sara.

He has to be the target.

The two women made a wide perimeter around the two trees, stepping carefully, checking the ground for anything the searchers might have missed. "Maybe we should come back during daylight hours," said Noelle.

"Forensics will be back tomorrow," said Mercy. "Frankly, I feel like I can see quite well with our two flashlights. The beams lit up the entire area."

The occasional boot prints from the shooters stopped several yards past the pines. That was as far as the shooters had gone that day, and Mercy knew they weren't far from the clearing where she had found Linda. A minute later they reached that spot. The snow was thicker here where the pines had thinned, exposing the sky. Many different boot prints crisscrossed the snow, most likely from the responders, as the prints came from the direction of the Bonner home.

"Truman said Sara was found just past this clearing," said Mercy.

They followed the most obvious trail of boot prints until they reached a spot where the searchers had separated into a small circle. "Looks like that's where they ordered her to lie down," said Noelle, moving the beam of her light back and forth across the scene.

Mercy nodded and started to circle the spot, moving farther out each time until she spotted a trail of smaller prints that must be Sara's. "Sara came from this way." She followed the tracks away from where the woman had been surrounded by law enforcement.

"She said she'd hidden near a fallen tree," said Noelle, following Mercy. "The only prints over here are hers. I guess no one went to verify her story."

"They were focused on the shooters, who'd left," said Mercy. "Understandable."

But my job is to look at everything.

Thirty seconds later, they spotted the downed tree, its rotted trunk nearly a yard in diameter. Mercy climbed over it to search the other side. She and Noelle followed the tree for a few yards, seeing no boot prints in the frozen dirt.

Mercy stopped.

That's where I'd hide.

Rot had carved out a deep area in the trunk near the ground. It was protected from the snow, but someone—or something—had disrupted the carpet of dead pine needles. Mercy squatted and shined her light under the trunk, positive that this was where Sara had hidden from the shooter.

"Find it?" asked Noelle from the other side of the trunk.

"I think so. It's the only place she could have scrunched up to hide, and the pine needles have been pushed around."

Mercy had started to stand when something metallic caught the light of her flashlight. She brushed some pine needles out of the way and found a small flip notepad with metal wire binding. It was similar to the tiny notepads that cops tucked in their pockets.

"A notebook?" Noelle asked as Mercy stood, surprise in her tone. "She dropped it? Or one of the officers did? It looks like what I used to carry on patrol."

"It was hidden, not dropped," said Mercy. She flipped it open, recognizing the tiny, cramped writing. "This was Rob's."

33

The next morning Truman stopped in the Coffee Café on his way to work. Kaylie was off that day, so her aunt Pearl was making lattes and pushing muffins behind the counter along with her son. Truman took off his hat and scanned the small store, and his gaze locked on a woman at one of the tables. It was Mercy's other sister, Rose, with her toddler, Baby Henry.

Just Henry.

The nickname was proving hard to shake.

Instead of joining the long line to order, he strode toward Rose's table. Her face had already turned his way, and by the tilt of her head, he knew she was listening to his footsteps.

"Morning, Rose."

"Truman! I thought that was you. Take a seat." She indicated a seat next to Henry's high chair as Henry beat his fists on the table in excitement, probably not recognizing Truman, but thrilled to have another person pay attention to him. The toddler picked up a half-eaten cookie and offered it to Truman. His eyes were bright, and gooey cookie had been smeared around his mouth and between his fingers.

"No thanks, Henry. That's your cookie." Truman took his seat, staying out of reach of Henry's hands.

Henry crammed as much of the cookie in his mouth as possible, delight in his eyes.

"How are you, Rose?" Truman asked, studying her face, which was so much like Mercy's.

"Good, thank you. Do you have an update on Ben?" She wrinkled her forehead in concern. "I didn't want to bother his wife today with questions."

"He'll be released this morning," said Truman. "There was no need for surgery, but they kept him overnight to keep an eye on things. Loaded him up with some painkillers, antibiotics, and fluids. He was very lucky."

"He was," Rose agreed. "Knowing him, he'll enjoy telling the story for many years."

"Yeah, I don't need to hear about it for a while. I can still see him going down." A small shudder shook his torso, and he was glad Rose couldn't see it.

"Here you go, Truman." Pearl had appeared and set a huge to-go cup in front of him. "I assumed you'd want the usual."

"I do. Thanks." He took some bills out of his wallet, but she waved them away. He gave her a stern look and tucked them in her apron's pocket.

"I caught what you said about Ben," said Pearl. "How is Sharon holding up?"

"Okay, I think. I didn't witness her chew him out in the emergency room, but I heard about it from three different people. She told him to duck faster next time."

"I've organized neighbors to deliver meals to Sharon and Ben," said Rose. "I'd wanted to do the same for Linda's son, but Mercy said he's not at home and that it would be a better time when Linda is released from the hospital."

"She'll be there a few more days," said Truman. "She had surgery again yesterday, but her doctor sounded optimistic when I spoke with her this morning." He paused. "How well do the two of you know Devin, her son?"

"He's in here about once every other week," said Pearl. "Nice guy, but always seems a little confused and lost. He reads at a table while waiting for Linda to grocery shop."

"I don't know him," said Rose. "I just know *of* him. He's never spoken to me, but I understand he has memory issues."

"Actually his recent memory isn't that bad," said Truman. "The real problem is he has face blindness." The two women listened, rapt, as Truman explained.

"That explains why he seems disconnected when I greet him," said Pearl. "I've been seeing him in here for two years and wondered why he treated me like a stranger each time. I didn't think I was that unmemorable."

"He recognizes Kaylie because of her nose stud," said Truman with a grin. "Maybe you should pierce an eyebrow or get a tattoo on your cheek."

Pearl swatted him on the shoulder. "How about Coffee Café name tags?"

Truman was surprised he hadn't thought of it. "I think that would work. He does know *who* you are, so he should easily make the association if he sees your name."

"That poor man," said Rose, her shoulders slumping a little. "I sympathize. People know I can't see them, so they automatically help out by identifying themselves. I connect the names to voices and sounds. Even how they smell." She frowned. "How could we make it easier for him around town? They don't wear name tags in all the stores."

"He says quickly introducing yourself and adding a tidbit of how he knows you fixes the problem."

"But how do we get the message out that everyone needs to do that?" asked Pearl.

"Mom!" Behind the counter, her son signaled that he needed help, and Pearl hustled back to work.

"What about making up some placards that inform people what he needs?" asked Rose. She produced a wet wipe and proceeded to clean Henry's face and fingers. He squirmed and leaned away as far as possible over the side of his high chair, batting at her hands.

Truman watched, fascinated that Rose had known exactly what was needed even though she couldn't see her son.

She teaches preschool. She's dealt with a lot of sticky kids.

"Not huge ones, but not too small either. We could put his picture on them—him and Linda since she's known a little better in town—and put them up in busy places. Like on the counter in here. And the post office, the feedstore, the diner . . ."

"We're not a huge community," said Truman. "I think that would be sufficient to get the word out."

"Do you think it's rude?" asked Rose with a small frown. "Are we overstepping? I don't want to embarrass him, but I understand completely what he's going through. I'm lucky that I grew up here in town, so everyone knows I'm blind. I'd like to do what I can to help."

"I'll feel him out about it and ask Ollie to discuss it with him. He recognizes Ollie now. Around him Devin's a different person than the man I first met. I'd like to see him relax like that with more people." He smiled at Rose. "You're very thoughtful."

She sighed. "Ask Nick how thoughtful he thinks I am after I've spent the day with Henry while he's teething. Pearl swears her kids never acted like their mouths were on fire all the time."

"He looks happy now," said Truman. "Clearly he enjoys Kaylie's cookies."

"He's a good coffee buddy."

Truman's phone rang with a call from the office, and he excused himself. He grabbed his coffee and headed outside to take the call. The café was getting busier by the minute.

"What's up, Lucas? I'm just down the street."

"Someone left a weird letter on Royce's windshield overnight."

"Let me guess. Royce couldn't tell who left the letter because he hasn't put in that security system I got him, right?" Truman had gifted home security cameras to all his men last Christmas. Royce had yet to install his.

"Correct, he hasn't," Lucas said in an accusatory tone. Royce said something in the background Truman couldn't make out.

"How weird was the note? Was it a threat?" asked Truman. "Maybe that will motivate Royce to install the cameras."

"It's not a threat," said Lucas. "But it's about Mercy's case, and I figured I'd let you tell her about it."

"What does it say?" Truman's spine had stiffened.

"I'll read it word for word." Lucas cleared his throat. "'Mia Fowler died two decades ago. You'll find her buried in the Yellow Pine pioneer cemetery. She's on top of Willem Johnson's grave. She shouldn't have died.'"

Truman waited for the rest.

"That's it," said Lucas.

"She shouldn't have died"?

His mind raced. The note could be fake, but if it was real, it meant someone knew what had happened back then. And was possibly watching the investigation unfold. He needed to call Mercy.

"The cemetery is about ninety minutes from here in the middle of nowhere," said Lucas. "I searched online, and there is a Willem Johnson buried there who died in 1878. I even found a picture of his headstone. It's a tiny cemetery. Only thirty-seven people buried there."

"I'll be at the office in a minute," said Truman. "First I'll call Mercy. Can you text her a pic of the note and what you found out about the grave?"

"On it."

Truman ended the call, his pulse racing.

He tapped Mercy's name on his phone.

What does this mean?

34

"It's not an exhumation per se," Mercy pointed out to her boss on the phone. "We won't disturb Willem Johnson's remains. We'll just remove a few feet of dirt above it—and then put it back."

Her boss wasn't convinced. "I'll have someone look into the legal aspect of what you want. I imagine permits are also needed. And the cemetery probably has historical protections because of its age," said Jeff with a sigh. "My understanding is you might also need permission from family. Who knows if we can locate the right Johnson family, considering how old the grave is. It might take a while to jump through all the hoops."

"I want it done tomorrow." Mercy tensed, waiting for his answer. She'd already given a heads-up to Darby, the data analyst, who'd immediately jumped into research.

"Not very demanding, are you?"

"How about this afternoon then?" Part of her was completely serious. She wanted this lead explored. Something about it rang true.

"Very funny. I'll let you know what I find out."

"I've already contacted Dr. Peres," Mercy said quickly before he could end the call. "She said she'll make herself available whenever we need her. She's curious too."

"The forensic anthropologist? She'd drop everything for this?"

"It's winter. Her schedule is light."

"What won't be light is digging into frozen dirt. And who knows when we could get a backhoe out there."

"I don't think we need a backhoe," said Mercy. "What happened to Mia Fowler seems to be a secret, so I suspect someone dug her resting spot with a shovel—maybe even dug all by themselves. That's harder than people realize, so it shouldn't be all that deep. Maybe a couple of feet. All I need is a few people with shovels. And Dr. Peres."

"How do you plan to dig in frozen dirt?"

"The dirt won't be frozen that deep," said Mercy. "We just need to get through the top layer, and then it will be normal." She crossed her fingers, hoping that was true. "There's specialized heavy equipment for it, but since we're digging in a small area, hot water is our best bet. Another option is to build a fire—"

"*A fire on top of a grave?* No! Are you nuts? Absolutely not." He sputtered for a moment. "What does Dr. Peres think about the hot water?"

"She suggested it." Mercy had only mentioned the fire to hear Jeff's reaction, and it'd been well worth it. At the sound of a chime, she pulled her phone away from her ear and quickly read the text. "Darby says the graveyard is owned by a local historical society."

"They might be easier to deal with than a local government," said Jeff. "Less red tape. And yes, I noticed Darby gave you information before I spoke to her," he added sourly.

"I agree a historical society should be easier. She's going to contact them. Hang on." Mercy quickly tapped out a message to the data analyst. "I'm telling her to lay it on thick about a teenager missing for twenty years."

"I don't want this coming back to bite us in the ass," said Jeff. "You're pushing a lot of lines here."

"If necessary, I'll invite every member of the historical society to observe. They can't complain that they didn't know what we were doing."

"You're only doing this dig if everyone is agreeable—the society, any relatives, whoever."

Yes!

"Thank you, Jeff."

"Don't get me wrong. I want to find out what happened to those kids, too, but I don't like that this was an anonymous tip. Someone could be messing with the investigation."

"I agree," said Mercy. "But something about it also feels legitimate to me."

The plaintive comment that she shouldn't have died.

There were hints of guilt and grief in that sentence.

She ended the call and turned to Noelle, who was studying her laptop in the little conference room. "We can move forward," Mercy told her.

"I gathered that." Her nails clicked on the keyboard. "Does your boss know about the notebook you found at the shooting yesterday?"

"I emailed him last night."

"We need to ask Sara why she didn't turn it in with the rest of Rob's notes."

"That can wait," said Mercy. "I want her to think that it's still where she stashed it. I wonder how long she'll wait to go back to get it."

"You think she's not being up-front with us?"

Mercy pointed at the small flip notebook beside Noelle's laptop. "I *know* she's not."

The notebook contained phone conversation details of Rob's contact with the people involved with the missing teens. There weren't that many. Mercy had skimmed it, not seeing anything earth shattering. At the back of the notebook were several amazing sketches. Mostly of Sara.

Mercy assumed they had been drawn by Rob. There was a quality to them that indicated the artist had really loved the subject. The way he captured her profile, a tender look in her eyes. They were simple, using a minimum of lines, yet full of life.

Both Mercy and Noelle had been impressed with his talent.

But why hadn't the notebook been with Rob's other research?

Noelle picked up the notebook and read the entries. "Twice he talked to Erick Howard, the physics teacher," she said. "Rob called him a week before he arrived and then again on the day he and Sara got to Oregon. The next day Rob staked out Erick's home. He doesn't mention approaching him in person like he said in his other research notes, but he does state that on both calls Erick said that he wouldn't speak with Rob about the case.

"He also called Mia Fowler's father twice. Both times Rob was told to fuck off. Like with Erick Howard, one call was made a week before Rob arrived in Oregon, and the second call was made on the first day he was here."

"But he didn't stake out the father's home."

"Maybe because the father lives in Washington? It's definitely not convenient."

"We still need to talk to Mia's father *and* Erick Howard," said Mercy, making her own note.

"He also listed that he spoke to Frank Balke twice," said Noelle. "That lines up with what Frank said during his interview. Again Rob called a week before he arrived, but the second call was on the day after he arrived. Rob noted that he was told not to call again."

"Just like Frank and Yvette said." Mercy thought for a moment. "Frank Balke said it was John Jacobs who called him. He didn't know it wasn't his real name. I bet Rob used his pseudonym for calling the others too. He was keeping the fact that he'd gone to school with the victims under wraps."

"Looks like he was unsuccessful in finding a phone number for Jason Slade, the registered sex offender who was Mia's neighbor. His notes indicate frustration that Rob couldn't speak to him and that his stakeout was unproductive."

"I have a cell number for Slade," said Mercy. "I'll find out if he's in town or on the road for a job."

"What's missing from this list is that Rob didn't contact Linda or Devin." Noelle looked up at Mercy. "He tried to reach out to everyone. Why not call or visit those two?"

"Maybe they were next on his list."

"They're not even listed in here. Rob wrote that Alex Stark's foster parents had both passed away and the same about Tyler's grandparents. He labeled them as not being relevant." Noelle raised her head. "Relevant to what?"

"Maybe they aren't relevant because they all have passed?"

"He notes that he was pleased with his contact of the Balkes, Erick Howard, and Mia Fowler's father."

"I didn't understand that when I looked through it," said Mercy. "He didn't get any information out of these people. What was there to be pleased about?"

Noelle flipped the notebook closed. "We've gone through all Rob's notes—I assume—and I'm still not certain what his game plan was."

"He may have not had one in place. I feel like he was searching for a direction to take his research." Mercy picked up her cell phone. "Since it's Saturday, Erick Howard won't be teaching school. I'll call him right now." She keyed in the number from her notes and put the call on speaker.

"Hello?"

"Good morning. I'm FBI Special Agent Kilpatrick. Is this Erick Howard?"

There was a long pause. "It is. What is this about?"

"I'm doing follow-up on the disappearances of Mia Fowler, Colin Balke, and Alex Stark. Have you heard from or had any contact with them?" Mercy rushed right into the question instead of asking if Erick had time for the call. She'd found most people said no when asked if they had time.

"No, I have not." Erick sighed loudly over the phone. "Someone calls and asks the same questions every few years. It's bordering on harassment, especially since I was in no way connected to the case. Don't you think I'd contact the police if I'd heard from one of them instead of waiting for you to call?" He paused. "But the FBI has never called before," he said in a different tone.

"We're offering assistance to Deschutes County, who originally investigated the disappearances and death," Mercy said. "Weren't some of them students of yours?"

"Yes, they were. Are you calling every teacher they ever had?"

Mercy ignored the question. "Have you been recently contacted by a podcaster named John Jacobs about their disappearances?"

"I was," Erick said slowly. "He called me recently. Twice. I refused to speak about it. Why do you ask?"

"Did you know of Mr. Jacobs before he contacted you?"

"No, I don't follow podcasts. I'd never heard of him."

Mercy waited a split second to see if Erick Howard would fill in that John Jacobs had revealed he'd been a student of his. He said nothing.

Rob kept his true identity from him.

She wondered if Rob would have had a successful conversation with the teacher if he'd identified himself. He'd said Erick Howard had been pleasant when they'd met in person.

"Is there new information in their cases?" Erick asked. "It seems like the investigations have been cold for years . . . decades."

"We're always seeking new information," Mercy said, deliberately keeping her intentions vague. "You never know what could crack a case wide open."

"Well, I hope something turns up. I didn't like how my name was pulled into their cases, but I have always hoped those kids would be found."

"Thank you, Mr. Howard. You know where to find us if you think of anything to help."

Mercy ended the call and shrugged at Noelle. "They're always curt until they want to know if we have new details. Then suddenly they're very helpful, hoping for some gossip. I'll try Jason Slade while we're on a roll here." She dialed and waited until the call went to voice mail. She left a message with her name and phone number but didn't state why she had called, knowing curiosity would get the best of most people and they would return her call.

She tried Mia Fowler's father with the same empty result. "So much for being on a roll."

"You spoke to one person. I don't think that qualifies as 'being on a roll,'" said Noelle. "I just got an email from a woman at the historical society that owns the pioneer cemetery. She is very suspicious of what we want to do," she finished with a grin. "Darby must have piqued her curiosity for her to email us so fast. I'll give her a call. Maybe I'll have better luck than you with calls."

"What's her name?" asked Mercy.

"Carolee Gubler."

"Hello?" The voice that came through the speaker was older and sweet.

"Ms. Gubler? This is Detective Marshall. Also in the room is FBI Special Agent Kilpatrick. I just got your email, and I'm calling to clear up any questions you have."

Mercy gave her a thumbs-up for using her title. Hearing *FBI* tended to make people pay attention and be more helpful.

"Oh yes. I can't say we've ever had a request for an exhumation at Yellow Pine before," said Carolee. "And the FBI is involved? You've got all of us very curious."

"Us?" asked Noelle.

"There are five of us on the board. An odd number so we don't have tie votes, you know."

"Of course," said Noelle, giving Mercy an amused gaze. "You understand it's not an exhumation, right? We just want to remove a few feet of dirt on top of one grave."

"And you hope to find another body in that dirt?"

"That's correct. We've recently received a tip that a girl who's been missing for twenty years may be buried there. We'd like to move quickly on this, and we'll have a forensic anthropologist leading the dig. She is very respectful and particular about procedure, and she will strictly follow any rules you have."

"That poor child," said Carolee. "But the ground must be frozen solid, and there is at least six inches of snow up there. Maybe you should wait until spring."

Noelle grew very determined, but her tone softened. "The anthropologist has dealt with frozen ground before. She won't even need any big equipment. We'll only use what we can carry in, and of course we'll be considerate of all the graves. It's very important that we investigate this lead as quickly as possible. Is there someone from Willem Johnson's family to inform?"

Mercy liked how Noelle hadn't asked for permission from the Johnsons.

"And your board is welcome to watch," added Noelle. "It might be very interesting to learn about the delicate process of uncovering bones."

"Hmmm. I know Virgil Malloy would be fascinated by that. I don't know if your forensic anthropologist would appreciate the constant questions he always asks. I swear he has an outboard motor for a mouth."

That would be an absolute no.

Dr. Peres ran a tight ship. No outsiders were welcome at her digs. Especially chatty outsiders.

"I'm sure she'd love to make it a learning experience," lied Noelle, lifting her hands in a "What else could I say?" gesture to Mercy.

Dr. Peres will understand. I hope.

"As for the Johnson family, there are no primary descendants," said Carolee. "There might be some very distant cousins, but they've never bothered to contact us, so I don't think reaching out to them is necessary. Especially since Willem's remains won't be disturbed. I'll put this to a vote of the board and get back to you."

Mercy leaned toward the phone. "Ms. Gubler, this is Special Agent Kilpatrick. Can you please contact your board for a vote immediately? We'd like to investigate tomorrow. There is a family waiting for answers."

If Mia Fowler's father ever gets back to me.

"Tomorrow? Oh . . . well, Virgil is currently out of town. So we won't—"

"He must have a cell phone," Mercy interrupted. "Your vote doesn't need to be in person, does it?"

"Our rules say it does. But we do consider extenuating circumstances. I'd say this qualifies. I'll make the calls."

"Thank you so much," said Mercy.

Noelle ended the call and held up her hand for a high five.

"Well done," said Mercy, slapping her hand. "I think we're going on a dig tomorrow!"

35

Ollie is here, and I'm confused to see him.

He's not one of us. He's not a musketeer.

He sits on the ground, his arms wrapped around his legs.

His face looks like that of an innocent child.

The others are arguing and don't see him.

Except for Mia. She sees him.

She looks to me, perplexed by the stranger.

I don't know what to tell her.

She sits next to Ollie. The others still don't see him.

Why is he here?

Ollie stares straight ahead, not seeing Mia. Or me.

Mia speaks to him, but he shows no sign of hearing her.

Concern fills her face, and she looks to me again.

She speaks earnestly, but I can't hear her words.

What is she saying?

She touches Ollie's arm, and he vanishes.

She screams. And screams.

I wake with her screams still ringing in my ears. They shear through the center of my skull. Panting hard, I get up and walk silently into the other room. Ollie is asleep, his breathing loud.

Relief swamps me at the sight and sounds.

As my lungs return to normal, I realize the young man has become my friend.

Ollie is a piece of good in the world.

While so much of it is evil.

36

Ollie had texted Truman a few times that morning with no response, but he and Devin had been warned that he and Mercy could be out of cellular range while they went to see if Mia's remains were buried in the Yellow Pine pioneer cemetery.

Ollie had Googled the cemetery and realized he'd been aware of it but hadn't known its name. The few times he'd passed by, there hadn't been a sign. Just a few dozen gravestones. It'd always felt peaceful, but he'd never wanted to linger.

Ollie had trekked through acres and acres of that area when he'd lived in the woods. At first with his grandfather and then on his own after his grandfather had died.

Not my grandfather.

Dozens of times the DNA results had broken into his thoughts like an intruder since Truman had told him the news. Ollie's emotions were still all over the place about it. He'd even discussed it with Devin, surprised that he'd grown close enough with the man to reveal how the results had torn him apart.

Devin had been supportive, echoing Truman's words that Ollie's grandfather was still his grandfather. "If I'd learned my mother wasn't my mother, you bet I'd still love her more than anything," Devin had told him. "I'd be confused and have lots of questions, but I wouldn't feel differently in the way that matters."

"At least she could answer your questions," Ollie had said. "I've got no one to ask."

They'd visited Linda the previous night. She'd recognized Devin and spoken a few words to him, but was mostly incoherent from being heavily medicated. So far she'd been unable to remember the stabbing, let alone who had done it.

Just like Devin can't remember.

Devin sat on the sofa in the hotel room, engrossed in a book on his Kindle. Ollie was struggling to sit still and wanted to get out of the room, but he felt an obligation to stick close to Devin. And Truman had ordered them to stay put. Someone wanted to harm Devin. Ollie didn't think anyone wanted to hurt him, but someone might, since he'd been with Devin nonstop the last few days.

Ollie had decided against keeping a gun in the hotel room. He'd weighed his decision carefully. He didn't want to face the instant decision of whether to take someone's life. What if a repairman for the hotel abruptly walked in? Uniforms could be faked or stolen. People lie about who they are.

Accidents happen. At the worst times.

Ollie didn't mind carrying when he was in the wilderness. He would fire at any animal that threatened Shep.

I miss my dog.

It was doubtful Shep missed him. The dog adored their cats, Dulce and Simon, and in the kitten room, he'd lie down to let the kittens crawl all over him. He liked to wash their ears.

"Ollie, I don't know how I'm supposed to feel if they find Mia."

Devin had set his Kindle aside, a lost expression in his gaze.

"I wouldn't think about it until it's confirmed," said Ollie, knowing without a doubt he'd be thinking about it, too, in Devin's place.

"She's been in my dreams a lot lately." Devin rubbed the back of his head.

Ollie didn't know what to say to that.

"I feel like I'm missing something during my dreams. That answers are right in front of me but just out of reach." His mouth sagged in a sad frown. "I'm so frustrated."

"That's understandable," said Ollie. "You were there. You probably saw what happened to them, but now it's buried deep in your brain." He sat on the sofa next to Devin. "It's not your fault."

"I repeat that to myself a thousand times a day."

"Maybe if Mia is found, that will help bring things to the surface."

"I've pretended that they find her. Trust me—nothing new popped up in my brain." Devin lifted his left forearm with his right hand and rested it on his thigh, massaging the fingers of his injured hand. "You're a good guy to hang around and keep me company. I know you've got better things to do."

"Nah. I've had a good time. You're better at *Fortnite* than anyone I know."

"If it's Mia, do you think Colin and Alex are in the graveyard too?"

Ollie shrugged. "Dunno. Maybe the anonymous tipster will leave another note saying what happened to the other two. If that's Mia, someone still knows what happened."

"Someone who possibly wants me dead," Devin said softly, his gaze on his injured hand.

The words had finally been said out loud.

Ollie didn't disagree; he suspected Devin was right.

37

"Virgil had the nerve to vote no," Carolee said to Mercy with an indignant sniff as the historical society member adjusted her thick scarf. "And he didn't admit it, but I know the only reason he voted no was because he wanted to be in town for this." The other three women next to Carolee nodded solemnly. "Then he suggested we FaceTime during the dig, so he could ask the anthropologist questions." She rolled her eyes dramatically.

Mercy bit back a laugh, imagining Dr. Peres's reaction. "That wouldn't have worked. There's no data service out here," she said, her breath hanging in the cold, crisp air.

Dr. Peres got lucky.

No . . . we *got lucky because Noelle told them Dr. Peres could make it a learning experience. The doctor would have kicked all of us off the site.*

"That's what I told him," said Carolee. "So he asked me to record it—which I'm not going to do either. I'm not going to film the unearthing of someone's bones. That's private. It'd probably end up all over the internet." She shook her head. "I swear, that man. He always thinks of himself first. No wonder his wife left him decades ago." More solemn nods.

Carolee and two of the other women from the historical society were colorful sights in the snow-covered graveyard. Bright shades of red, blue, and green were shown off in their thick, padded coats, knit scarves, and hats. The fourth woman—whose name had slipped Mercy's mind already—was dressed head to toe in black, but they all wore the same hiking boots, which were now caked with snow. Gloved hands were shoved in pockets, and their eyes were serious, but an air of anticipation hovered around them.

Mercy felt it too.

The Yellow Pine pioneer cemetery was far from any main roads. Carolee had explained that most of the people buried there had lived in a tiny nearby settlement during the 1800s. "It was hard to survive out here. It's so isolated," she had said. "Pioneers had a tendency to be stubborn, so the community thrived for a little while, but most of them eventually packed up and moved closer to big towns."

Mercy scanned the thirty-seven headstones. They appeared small and insignificant, poking out of the pristine snow at all angles. She had felt like an intruder when they arrived, interrupting the tranquil woods and leaving tracks in the smooth blanket of snow. Willem Johnson's headstone was near the center, his name almost vanished, a victim of decades of weather. She'd passed a dozen other Johnson headstones before finding his. Extremely short lifetimes were engraved on some of the stones.

She and Truman had spent the early hours of the morning heating water on their stove and in the microwave. They'd poured the hot water into gallon jugs and then set the jugs in Styrofoam coolers Kaylie had warmed up with electric blankets. They'd packed towels around the jugs for insulation. Noelle had done the same thing at her home and so had Royce. Altogether they had seven large coolers of hot water.

By the time they'd reached the cemetery, the water was no longer hot. But Mercy suspected that any water warmer than the ground would help.

Truman had grown quiet as they'd driven closer to the cemetery. He'd been studying the landscape, and she saw him give the passing pines several sharp looks.

"What is it?" Mercy finally asked. "I don't think the trees deserve your disdain."

He swallowed hard and pressed his lips together.

Something is up.

She waited.

"Do you know where we are?" he asked.

"I know the general area."

"We're coming in a different way, but not far from here is where . . . where . . ."

Then it hit her. This was sort of near where Truman had been beaten and held captive in a shed by men who were angry that he'd arrested one of them. He'd gone missing for weeks, and Mercy had despaired that he'd never return. He would have died if Ollie hadn't broken him out and cared for him. It'd been more than a year and a half since then, but he still had physical scars and clearly still had emotional ones too.

They rarely spoke of that dark time.

"Oh, Truman," she breathed, setting her hand on his arm as he drove.

"I've not been up here since."

"They were all arrested." Mercy had been present for it.

"I know." He'd smiled at her and squeezed her hand. "Let's not talk about it anymore."

Mercy had nodded, but she'd struggled to put it out of her mind as they parked along a snow-packed road.

As they'd walked to the cemetery, Dr. Victoria Peres had helped distract her by issuing curt instructions. The tall forensic anthropologist was a natural leader who expected things done her way—and *only* her way. The scene was hers, and she ran a tight ship. If someone didn't follow her rules, they'd be put on the spot and risk immediate ejection from the scene. Mercy had worked with Dr. Peres a few times and respected her passion and attention to detail. The doctor's assistant, Keri, moved fluidly beside her, knowing what the anthropologist wanted before she asked for it.

In front of the headstone, Royce and Truman had used snow shovels to clear a large rectangle in the six inches of white fluff. Dr. Peres had set out small posts and thin rope for making a grid and laid out several tarps. Stacks of buckets, two large, framed screens, and small hand tools were ready. Under the snow they found frozen clumps of thick grasses with twisted roots. Dr. Peres poured water over a small area, let it sit for a minute, and then poked around the dirt with a small shovel. Satisfied the water would make the ground manageable, she demonstrated how to loosen and remove the packed grasses.

It took much longer than Mercy had expected. The roots were thick and tough, but the water worked well to soften the icy dirt. Dr. Peres wouldn't let more than two people work at a time because the area was relatively small, and she wanted to supervise every movement. It seemed like forever before they were looking at a cleared rectangle of dirt.

"Okay," said the doctor after creating a grid of wide squares over the rectangle with string and small posts. "Every scoop of dirt is to be set on that tarp in the spot that coordinates with the grid. It'll be filtered as we work. First we'll go about six inches deep in a wide area. It's cold out here, and I know you don't want to be here all day, so we're going to work quickly at first to see if we're on a wild-goose chase. If we find signs that something is here, we'll slow way down."

She assigned Royce and Noelle to filtering the dirt into buckets. Then she handed Mercy and Truman shovels while she and her assistant each picked up a jug of water. "I'll pour water for you, and Keri will for Truman. Then we'll trade off."

Mercy dug near the foot of the grave where the doctor had poured water; Truman and Keri worked closer to the gravestone. It was muddy and cold, but the constant movement helped her stay warm. She glanced occasionally at the four women from the historical society waiting several yards away. Dr. Peres had shoveled a line in the snow that they were not allowed to cross, and they were impatiently respecting it.

Only Dr. Peres and Keri spoke as they worked, carefully watching every shovelful removed by Mercy and Truman and giving advice or instructions to Noelle and Royce as they filtered. The group quickly shoveled and filtered six inches of muddy dirt with no results. At least the dirt wasn't as hard and frozen deeper down.

"Okay. Let's go down another six," said the doctor. Royce and Noelle took the shovels while Mercy and Truman sifted mud. She soon wished she were shoveling again. Mud did not sift. She had to push it through the tiny spaces while wearing kitchen gloves over her winter gloves. It was messy and frustrating.

Mercy wiped mud spatter from her cheek with her wrist, and Truman grinned, his eyes lighting up.

"I made it worse, didn't I?" asked Mercy, fighting the need to wipe the area again.

"It's very charming."

"Mud is not charming. It's dirty."

"Stop for a second, Royce," said Keri. "Dr. Peres. Take a look."

Mercy and Truman set down their screens and joined the others. Keri slowly poured more water onto the gravesite, and the pale, knobby end of a bone came into view.

"Holy shit," said Royce. He glanced up at the four board members, who were curiously watching. "Excuse my language, ladies."

"What did you find?" asked Carolee, straining to see but not daring to step over her snow line.

"It's the head of a humerus," said Dr. Peres. "Now we're going to slow everything down and work more carefully." She looked at Mercy, her dark eyes pleased. "Not a goose chase after all."

A half hour later, Dr. Peres had a muddy skull in her hands. "I don't want to thoroughly rinse it here," she told them. "It needs to be done indoors, where I'm sure nothing can be lost."

"But is it female?" asked Mercy, anticipation making her grip her trowel tightly.

"I'm nearly positive it is female and Caucasian. The long hair found underneath could support it being female too. I need to look at some other things before deciding."

It'd been odd to find the hair. It was long and brown—not Mia's blonde, but Dr. Peres said it could have absorbed the color from the dirt.

"It's got to be Mia Fowler," said Royce.

"No jumping to conclusions," ordered Noelle. "Someone could have known there was a body here and decided to screw with us by reporting that it was part of our investigation." She looked at the doctor. "Do you have an age guesstimate?"

"It's too muddy. I need to be able to see the fissures better," said the doctor. She turned over the skull, studying the teeth, and then picked up the mandible to check the teeth there. "I don't see third molars, but that could mean they're still in the bone or have been removed. I'll need to take films." She glanced at Noelle. "You have dental films for comparison, correct?"

"Yes. They're in the original case files."

The next few hours were spent painstakingly removing each bone. The site was continually photographed, and sketches made of where each bone had been found. The doctor dried a tiny spot on each bone and labeled it with the case number and then added it to one of a series of small tubs.

The board members got too cold and went home after promising not to talk about anything they'd seen that day. Mercy watched them leave, wondering if they'd truly be able to keep it to themselves. No doubt Virgil would call, pressing for information.

"What is that?" asked Royce, gently nudging something in the grave with his trowel.

Dr. Peres dripped a few tablespoons of water on it. "A metal donut button. Most likely was on her pants or jeans. This was where I removed her pelvic bones. Keep looking. You'll probably find more or a zipper."

The woman had been buried on her back, and the remains were completely skeletal. Since the small bones of her hands were found adjacent to her spine, the doctor suspected her hands had been resting on her chest. Mercy's first thought was that her hands had been tied behind her, but the doctor pointed out that the long bones of her arms were on top of the ribs.

They could have been tied in front of her, but Mercy wondered if the notion of the hands placed on the chest might be accurate. It felt like a position arranged by someone who cared.

Dr. Peres said the pelvis also indicated the body was a woman's. She showed them the subpubic angle along with the sciatic notch, stating both were wider than she'd find in a male. Four stud earrings had been found, along with a simple silver ring. Royce quickly found four more donut buttons, and Dr. Peres commented that she was surprised no shoes had been found. The buttons indicated she'd been clothed, but for some reason she had been buried without shoes. Her clothing was gone, completely decomposed.

Keri had been keeping a record and announced when all bones were accounted for. But Dr. Peres asked the investigators to keep digging because sometimes things were buried with a body. Another hour of careful dirt removal found nothing, and she called an end to the dig.

Everyone was filthy. They slowly packed up the tubs and supplies. They'd worked through lunch, but Noelle had brought a dozen deli sandwiches, which they'd munched on during short breaks. All the sandwiches were gone, and Mercy was starving. It would be dinnertime by the time they got home.

They'd been completely out of contact all day—which Mercy hadn't minded. No phones. Even Truman's radio had been useless. Several times she'd caught herself checking her phone, but after the fourth or fifth time, she'd embraced that she was cut off from everyone and found it oddly quieting to her brain. The area was truly remote. As she passed by the old gravestones, Mercy tried to imagine living in the area during the 1800s.

She knew how to live outside the modern world. She'd been born to preppers, and she had her own cabin that was stocked and ready in case the world went to hell. But only because of modern inventions did she consider herself well prepared. Simple things like plastic food buckets, gas cans, and glass canning jars had made it possible. More modern things like her generator, solar cells, and Wi-Fi had made it comfortable. Not to mention a top-notch security system.

None of that had been readily available in Willem Johnson's world.

I don't know how long I would have lasted.

Truman caught her reading a young woman's headstone and accurately guessed her thoughts. "You would have done just fine back then. You're a survivor. And stubborn and smart."

"No antibiotics. No modern birth control. I probably would have died in childbirth," she replied, feeling morbid.

"Maybe." He took her hand and squeezed it.

Her eyes searched his, and all thoughts of a life without current-day medicine evaporated. She lived in the here and now. With a man who made her pulse quicken every time she looked at him.

How did I get so lucky?

38

The next morning Mercy's shoulders ached from the digging. She'd taken Advil an hour ago but still felt several twinges. She wasn't out of shape—not at all. But clearly the digging had used her muscles in an unfamiliar way.

She and Noelle were working in their usual room at the Deschutes County sheriff's office, trying to not think about the identity of the bones they'd uncovered the day before. There was no point in speculation until they received a confirmation from Dr. Peres.

Dr. Peres had promised that the forensic odontologist would examine the teeth from the remains that morning. Mercy checked the time every few minutes, impatient for the call. In the past the odontologist had told Mercy that with two sets of good X-rays she knew within thirty seconds if teeth were a match. Recording her findings and writing her report were what took the longest.

"Stop sighing," Noelle said, eyeing Mercy over her laptop. "And by the way, I left a voice mail for Sam Durette, one of the retired detectives who worked the missing kids' cases twenty years ago. I met him a couple months back when he came in about another old case. He's a straight shooter."

"Good to hear. His notes in the binders are meticulous, but I would like to hear his personal thoughts." Mercy sighed again, and Noelle raised a brow at her. "I'm impatient to hear from the forensic odontologist," she explained.

"Clearly."

"I feel like we can't move forward until we know their results. My brain keeps analyzing what it means if Mia Fowler has been found."

"Mine keeps speeding off on a dozen tangents because of the same thing. I'm sure we'll hear from them before noon."

That's three hours away.

Mercy's phone rang and she snatched it up, her heart rate accelerating. "Kilpatrick."

"Agent Kilpatrick? This is Cynthia Parnell in forensics. We spoke while I was collecting tire tread evidence at the shooting where Officer Ben Cooley was injured."

Mercy remembered the all-business forensics tech. "Of course. You have the tread results already?" It would be a very fast turnaround if they received the make of the tires this soon. Mercy knew the forensics department always had a backlog of evidence to process.

"I wasn't working on that evidence. I was processing tread evidence from a substation attack in Wasco County."

"I collected those treads about a week ago."

"This is different. What I'm looking at is from a substation shooting more than three weeks ago. Your name is not attached to the investigation."

Mercy recalled that Wasco County had experienced two substation shootings. She'd attended the second one. "You're right. I went to a second one in that county. You probably haven't gotten to the evidence from that one yet."

"Well, I will look at it when I get off the phone with you because while I was processing the tire treads from the first substation investigation, everything felt very familiar—as if I'd seen the treads recently. I immediately pulled up the evidence from Officer Cooley's shooting and the treads match. Remember how the truck had old and new tires? And one had a nail or screw embedded in it? The same vehicle was at the substation shooting and at Officer Cooley's shooting a few days ago. I'll email you the specifics."

Ben's shooter also shot up a substation?

Mercy couldn't speak as her brain tried to catch up. Every muscle in her body had frozen at the tech's revelation. She'd expected Cynthia to tell her the first substation shooting was related to the one Mercy had processed—not to tell her that it was connected to the shooting behind Devin Bonner's home.

What does this mean?

"There was a third substation attack," Mercy finally said, as her mind continued to spin. "There was one in Crook County two days after the Wasco County one I attended. I processed its tire treads too."

"I'll add it to my list to compare to Officer Cooley's shooting and get right back to you." Cynthia sounded as if she were discussing a grocery list. No emotion at all.

Mercy's heart was ready to explode out of her chest. "Rifle shells were also collected from all those locations," she pointed out. "Can we get them compared ASAP?"

"I'll make the recommendation."

"Thank you," she forced out and ended the call. She set down her phone, staring at Noelle.

"What is it? You look stunned."

"I am." Mercy ran a hand through her hair as she stood and paced around the small table. "The vehicle that was at Ben's shooting was also at one of the electrical substation attacks. She's checking the treads from the other two recent attacks."

Noelle blinked. "Holy crap. *Those substation attacks are connected to our investigation?*"

"At least one is. But my gut tells me that they all will be. The two I went to were identical in method." She reversed her pacing direction. "I want the ballistics reports on the shells from the attacks and Ben's shooting. I want to know if they back up the tread evidence."

"What does it mean if the same men committed all the crimes?" Noelle mused. "I have no idea what electrical substation attacks have to do with Devin Bonner or Sara Newton. Or anyone we've been dealing with."

"I don't either." Mercy's phone rang, and she stared at its screen for a long second before understanding why Victoria Peres would call her.

One startling phone call from forensics made me forget I'm expecting an identification on yesterday's remains.

She shook her head and hit the SPEAKER button. "Dr. Peres?"

"Good morning, Mercy."

"Detective Marshall is here with me. You're on speaker."

"Morning, Detective. Is it possible to switch to video for this call, Mercy?"

"Yes. Moving you to my laptop too." She suspected what the anthropologist wanted to show them would be easier to see on the larger screen. A few seconds later she and Noelle were looking at Dr. Peres and a blonde woman Mercy recognized as the forensic odontologist, Dr. Lacey Harper. "Hi, Dr. Harper." She introduced Noelle.

"I've met Detective Marshall," said Dr. Harper. "That case with the remains of a child found in the woods last summer."

"I recall," said Noelle. "You were very helpful."

"First I'll let Dr. Harper share what she's found," said Dr. Peres, her dark eyes serious. "Then I'll explain my information."

Something is up.

"You found Mia Fowler yesterday," Dr. Harper simply stated, a pleased expression on her face.

"I'll be damned," exclaimed Noelle. "After twenty years!"

Exultation rolled through Mercy, but it was immediately followed by a sense of sorrow.

Now we know for certain.

Dr. Harper's gaze filled with sympathy. "I understand," she said to Mercy. "It's normal to feel excited and disappointed at the same time when someone is identified. I'm sure her family will be happy to have answers."

Mercy and Noelle exchanged a glance.

Will her parents care? Assuming we can reach either one of them?

"Walk us through your identification process, Dr. Harper," said Mercy. "In layman's terms, please."

The odontologist gave a wide smile. "As you wish." She cleared her throat and moved the cell phone to show a large computer screen that displayed several digital X-rays. "Mia Fowler had good dental care, which makes my job much easier," said Dr. Harper. "The bite-wing X-rays from her dentist were taken just a few months before she disappeared. There was also a panoramic film from her orthodontist that was about four years old, taken after she had her braces removed." She indicated the large film, which looked like a smiling mouth. "It shows the patient's entire mandible and the maxillary sinuses. The first thing that caught my eye was that Mia Fowler had all four of her first premolars removed. This was sometimes done in certain cases before braces."

"My first ex-husband had that done," said Noelle. "He was told his mouth was too small. I disagreed," she said, raising an elegant brow.

Off-screen, Dr. Harper snorted and continued. "This morning I took new films on the skull." The image on the computer changed to enlarge two rows of the small films, the ones that showed the top third of the upper and lower teeth. "Mine are the top row. Her old ones below. All the films show missing first premolars." She tapped each one.

Mercy wondered how she knew which teeth were missing when they all were in perfect rows without gaps, but that was why the doctor was the expert.

"The old films also show two composite fillings. One on the distal of number three and another on the mesial of thirty." She indicated whitish blobs on the films. "They are identical in shape to the films I took today. They were the only restorations in her mouth back then and today. I can see them when I examine the actual skull too."

"Two fillings don't sound like a strong identification," said Noelle.

"It's not just the two fillings," said the odontologist. "It's the identical lack of fillings in twenty-two other teeth, the identical crown shapes of all the teeth in the films, *and* the four missing premolars. I can take it even further and match the bit of bone loss where her premolars were removed. Even the sinus shapes are identical." She paused. "It's a positive identification. There are no doubts in my mind. At all."

"Thank you, Dr. Harper," said Mercy. "I appreciate you explaining for us."

The camera shifted to show Dr. Peres. "My findings confirm that this was a young Caucasian woman," said Dr. Peres. "According to Mia Fowler's father's interview back then, she'd never broken a bone, and I found no evidence of breaks. But I found one thing that doesn't show up in her medical history from her father. I'm ninety percent sure Mia had given birth at some point."

Mercy was speechless for the second time that morning.

When did she have a baby?

"Why ninety percent?" asked Noelle.

"Because it isn't an exact science. I found dorsal pubic pitting, which most of the time can indicate a pregnancy, but it can also have been caused by other stressors. I've seen women who had several children but don't have the pitting, and I've seen women who've never had children who show the pitting. But both of these examples aren't the norm."

"What kind of stressors could cause it?" asked Mercy.

"Trauma, inflammation, or weight gain, for example. But this is a woman who died young. She had less time to experience those other possible factors than, say, a woman in her forties. Dr. Harper didn't mention it, but the root formation of her third molars indicates that she most likely died close to the age at which she disappeared. Maybe within five years."

"If I hadn't known Mia was eighteen when she disappeared," added Dr. Harper, "I would have estimated an age range of fourteen to twenty-three based on her third molar roots. I've seen fourteen-year-olds with them fully formed and twenty-three-year-olds whose root growth is behind schedule, but both of those are definitely out of the normal curve." She shrugged. "The tooth development schedule is slightly different for everyone. It's why I suggest an age range when looking at teeth."

"Dr. Peres, you suspect Mia had a baby at some point." Mercy brought the discussion back to the unanticipated fact. "It could have been before she switched high schools, correct? She was new to the school her senior year."

"That's correct," said Dr. Peres. "I also look at other things in the pelvis, and with all those taken together, my findings lean toward pregnancy. But I can't say when."

"Don't you think her father would have stated she'd been pregnant in the past when she went missing?" Noelle asked Mercy.

"I don't know," said Mercy. "You're talking about a man with a history of domestic abuse and who a few people have said wasn't liked by his daughter. He may have not wanted it to be known that she'd been pregnant in the past or didn't think it was relevant to her disappearance. Or she was pregnant when she vanished, and he didn't know."

"Or it happened after she vanished."

"Or, as Dr. Peres pointed out, there is a possibility she was never pregnant." Mercy raised her hands. "If she *was* pregnant, is it related to why they vanished?"

"Because one girl was pregnant, four other guys were taken too?" Noelle was skeptical.

Mercy turned back to the screen, where Drs. Peres and Harper had been listening to the discussion with interest. "Is there anything else we need to know, Doctors? What about cause of death?"

"Since the remains were completely skeletal, I didn't have a lot to go on. I found no damage. No indications of choking, stabbing, or gunshot. But of course all of these things could have happened and not left a clue on the bones . . . It's not likely, but it's possible."

"Shot in the abdomen or stabbed in the abdomen," added Noelle, "could have left no trace on bones. Even choking doesn't guarantee that the hyoid bone will break."

"Correct," said Dr. Peres. "So that is all I have for you at this moment. I'll let you know if anything else turns up."

Mercy thanked both doctors and ended the call.

She rubbed her neck, noticing Noelle was deep in thought.

Now we have more questions.

39

Mercy watched Noelle take a bite of the chocolate croissant and regretted ordering just her usual coffee with heavy cream. They sat outdoors at a French bakery and coffee shop as they waited to meet with retired detective Sam Durette on the sunny but chilly day. The heaters above their heads made it bearable, but her feet were cold under the table.

"I should have got the almond croissant," Mercy said.

"Yes, you should have." Noelle broke off a piece and passed it over, and Mercy reluctantly accepted.

The bittersweet chocolate surrounded by buttery croissant melted in her mouth. "Jesus," she muttered.

"I know." Noelle grinned. "The French know how to do pastry right."

Mercy sipped her coffee and the flavors vanished.

Maybe I'll get a few pastries to go.

"When do we tell Devin that Mia has been identified?" Noelle asked around bites of pastry.

The same question had been bouncing through Mercy's mind. "I'm not sure."

"Maybe finding out will trigger something in his brain," said Noelle. "Push forward those memories that are hovering behind his walls. Asking about a pregnancy might help too."

"It's possible."

They sat in silence for a long moment as Mercy pondered possible outcomes of telling Devin. Judging by the lines on Noelle's forehead, she was also thinking hard.

"I'd like to tell him in person," said Mercy. "That isn't something you share in a phone call."

Noelle checked the time. It was nearing 10:00 a.m. "We've got a lot to deal with today."

"I know. What do you think about having Truman tell him? He was going to stop by there this morning." Mercy hated not to be there, but if she couldn't, then Truman with Ollie by his side seemed a good substitute. He would know when to gently prod to help Devin with any emerging memories.

"I think that's a great idea."

Mercy picked up her phone. She'd talked to Truman right after Mia's identity had been confirmed, so he already knew the details.

"What's up?" he answered. Road noise sounded in the background. He was in his vehicle.

"Are you on your way to see Devin?"

"I am. What do you need?"

"Would you be comfortable telling him about Mia? And asking about a pregnancy? We're waiting to talk to one of the previous detectives. I don't know if I have time to get over there today, and I feel it should be done in person."

"It should. I can do that for you."

"I don't know how he'll take it," Mercy said. Noelle nodded at her words, her mouth tight.

"I'll handle it. Ollie being there should help."

"Thank you."

"I'll let you know what happens. Pulling into the hotel now."

She ended the call with a "Love you," pulling her gaze away from Noelle.

"Y'all are cute," said Noelle as Mercy set down her phone. "Don't be embarrassed for people to hear you tell your man you love him."

Noelle had read her accurately. "It's not really embarrassment. Just feels awkward to say when I'm working."

"Get over it."

Mercy snorted. A movement caught her eye, and she studied a man crossing the parking lot toward the coffee shop. It had to be Sam Durette, the retired detective. Everything about him said lawman.

Lawman as in law enforcement from a different era.

He was tall and lanky with wide shoulders, and a cowboy hat hid some of his white hair. He moved with confidence but seemed to favor a hip, and Mercy noted the faint bulge under one arm, indicating he was armed.

"That's him," said Noelle, wrapping her scarf more snugly around her neck and raising a hand to the man. She wore warm gloves, making Mercy regret leaving hers in her Tahoe.

"Morning, ladies." Sam touched the brim of his hat and took a seat. Noelle pushed a large cup of coffee toward him. "Bless you," he said. "Black like my heart?"

"Yes, it's black coffee, but I doubt that's the color of your heart," said Noelle, giving him a fond smile.

Mercy instantly liked the retired detective. His eyes were shrewd but kind, and he comfortably wore the years of lines on his face. He had returned Noelle's phone call not long after they'd received Mia Fowler's identification and had agreed to meet to discuss the old case. He hadn't been informed about Mia Fowler. Yet.

"Glad to see you found practical footwear," Sam said to Noelle with a wink.

Mercy grinned, realizing Sam was familiar with Noelle's penchant for expensive heels on the job. The cost of the sensible-looking boots on Noelle's feet was probably equal to Mercy's mortgage payment.

Noelle introduced Mercy, and the keen gaze studied her for a long second. "I've heard of you. You went undercover in that remote militia compound. Nearly lost your life."

Mercy swallowed hard. That had been a little over a year before but was fresh in her memory. "Yes, that was me."

"Good job." He gave her a nod, and his approval touched her. "Now," he said, including Noelle in his gaze, "what did you want to know about the kids' cases from twenty years ago?"

Mercy jumped in with both feet. "Who did you suspect for their disappearance?"

His white brows rose. "You don't hold back, do you?"

"I've read all your notes. At least twice," said Mercy. "You're thorough and deliberate, all the *i*'s dotted and *t*'s crossed. But I want to know what you felt in your gut." She glanced down at her coffee. "I know it's been a while. Take your time to recall."

He snorted. "The minute I got off the phone with Detective Marshall, I reviewed the case."

It was Mercy's turn to raise her brows.

"Don't get me wrong," said Sam. "I would never remove materials from the department or photocopy some things from unsolved cases that I couldn't get out of my head. Not supposed to do things like that when you're about to retire." He blinked slowly, an innocent expression on his face.

He totally photocopied notes.

Mercy could see herself doing the same when she retired.

"I never liked Jason Slade. The registered sex offender neighbor whose past offense was against a teenage girl." His gaze grew grim. "I could never get past the feeling that the entire case centered around Mia Fowler—which made him very likely in my mind. Her father—man, he was a piece of work—kept pointing at Slade too. I agreed with his assertion that the neighbor'd had more than the normal amount of contact with the girl. Something about Slade didn't sit right with me. But we couldn't find a shred of evidence against him."

"What didn't you like about Mia's father?" asked Mercy, sipping her coffee. Her feet no longer bothered her. Talking with Sam Durette had gotten her blood pumping.

"He was an asshole. By all accounts ignored the fact that he had a daughter until she vanished."

"If the case centered around Mia, why would the four other teenagers vanish too?" Mercy asked.

Sam sat back in his chair, frustration in his face. "I don't know what happened during the days before those two boys turned up on the banks of the Columbia River. Nothing made sense. You asked for my gut feeling and that was it. Didn't say it was logical."

Noelle and Mercy exchanged a glance as Noelle gave a slight nod.

"We found Mia Fowler's remains yesterday," said Mercy. "She was buried in a shallow grave in a pioneer cemetery. We found her from an anonymous tip that stated exactly where she'd be. The forensic anthropologist said she was still young when she died, maybe five years older at the most."

His mouth had dropped open as Mercy spoke. He snapped it shut and rubbed his chin. "I'll be damned. I'd long given up hope that more of those kids would turn up. Cause of death?"

"Unknown."

"No mention of the other two missing boys?"

"No."

His gaze went distant as he thought. "You couldn't determine that she died at the same time as the two were found on the river."

"Correct."

"But for some reason she ended up—where was this cemetery?"

Mercy shared the general location and that it'd been unused for more than a hundred years.

"That's a hell of a long ways from the river." Sam continued to rub his chin, deep in thought.

"More than a hundred miles," added Noelle.

"I feel like that supports my theory that the case revolved around her," Sam said slowly. "The other two might have been dumped somewhere else around the same time as the first two. Maybe she was kept alive a little longer."

"We have a strong reason to believe that Mia Fowler was pregnant at some point," said Mercy, watching surprise enter his eyes.

He didn't know.

"What we don't know is if it was before or after she disappeared. We're also not completely certain she had a pregnancy. The forensic anthropologist suspects she did but has said the science isn't precise."

"I don't remember hearing anything about that. I wonder if it happened after she disappeared." His eyes narrowed. "It just paints more arrows pointing at Slade in my mind. At the time it was obvious to me that he found her attractive."

Mercy's stomach churned. "The boys were killed so he could get at Mia? Seems excessive. And a lot of work. He could have grabbed her when she was alone."

"Where is he now?" asked Sam.

"He lives outside of Redmond, about a half hour from here. He's stayed out of trouble, and he's a long-haul truck driver," said Noelle. "And hasn't returned our calls."

Sam made a noise in the back of his throat that Mercy interpreted as him not being happy with this update. "When did he move from Bend? Did he buy? Rent?"

"I'll look." Noelle pulled out her laptop and started typing.

"What kind of person was he?" asked Mercy.

"Angry little guy. Especially angry that he was interviewed when those kids vanished."

"Little?"

"Well, almost everyone is shorter than me. So that was unfair for me to say," Sam said. "It's just that he expressed a lot of bitterness that you wouldn't expect from looking at him. Seemed like a normal guy, slight, nondescript, but then he starts talking and the quantity of hostility surprises you. Don't know if he was always like that or if it came after his conviction."

"Jason Slade became the Redmond property owner six years ago," said Noelle. She looked up. "But the owner before that was his father. I assume it was willed to Jason or something."

"What kind of property?" asked Mercy.

"Let me Google it. It's got thirty acres," said Noelle. "Here's a satellite view." She leaned closer to her screen. "House and a few outbuildings. Few trees. I don't see an indication of crops of some sort." She turned the laptop for Sam and Mercy.

Mercy eyed the outbuildings, which were set far back from the small home.

He could have kept five teenagers for a week at his father's. And kept Mia even longer.

A glance at Sam's face told her he was thinking the same thing.

"There's no evidence that points at Jason Slade," Noelle said firmly, looking from one to the other. "Sam, even you stated that."

"I did," he said flatly.

The three of them were silent for a few seconds.

"After twenty years, I doubt we'd find anything at this location," Mercy said slowly.

"Ground-penetrating radar," said Noelle. "Those other two boys ended up somewhere."

"You'd have to search thirty acres," said Mercy. "But I still want to talk to Jason Slade. If he won't return our calls, maybe we need to knock on his door." Without evidence, no judge would give her a search warrant for his property. She'd have to start with an interview—assuming he'd talk to her.

"But who gave the tip about Mia Fowler?" asked Sam. "Clearly someone knows what happened."

"Devin Bonner is the only survivor—that we know of," Noelle pointed out. "What were your thoughts about him back then?" she asked Sam.

Pity entered his gaze. "That kid went through hell. I spoke with him several times once he could speak."

"Did it feel like he was hiding something?" asked Mercy.

"Trauma fucks with the human brain," Sam said grimly. "That kid had been starved, beaten, had his throat slit, and been left for dead. Doesn't surprise me one bit that he has barriers in his brain—whether they're mental from the experience or physical from his beatings. I assume he's still the same?"

"Yes," said Mercy. "He remembers nothing. He's said he feels like answers are just out of reach sometimes." She glanced at Noelle. "We believe he's been the target of some recent deadly attacks. The first put his mother in the hospital, and a second time a murdered woman was found outside his hotel room. And a podcaster doing his own research about the killings was recently murdered."

Sam's eyes had opened wide as she spoke, their intensity growing. "John Jacobs?"

"He contacted you?"

"He left a voice mail requesting an interview. I didn't call back. Looked him up online. His podcasts were bunch of nosy crap."

"Sam wasn't listed in his research notebooks," Noelle pointed out to Mercy. "Maybe there are other people Rob contacted but didn't list." An odd look came over her face, and she started to type on her laptop.

"Shit," said Mercy, wondering who else they didn't know about.

"Back up a few steps," said Noelle, scanning her screen. "Jason Slade has a Chevy half-ton Silverado. We've got tread evidence from the shooting near the Bonner house. At the scene, the tech said it was a full-size truck, right? Let's start with a visit to Jason Slade's home. Maybe we'll get lucky, and his truck has a set of new tires on the front. If he's on the road with his semi, his truck should be at the home."

"It's a shot in the dark," said Mercy.

"You have a better idea?" asked Noelle with a shrug. "If we find the truck, we can get a warrant for weapons and search his property for one that matches the ballistics we're waiting on."

"Colin Balke's father has a full-size truck too," said Mercy. "We can make that our second stop."

"The father?" Sam asked, eyebrows shooting up. "You suspect Colin's father was involved?"

"I don't know if he was involved twenty years ago," said Mercy. "But I think Rob Newton suspected he was involved more recently. He was watching the Balke home and saw a man Colin's age driving a vehicle registered to the father. When I interviewed Frank Balke, he said it was his son-in-law. But he was very squirmy during the interview. I felt he was holding something back. He may be involved on the periphery somehow."

"Colin Balke could be alive?" Sam asked. He blinked several times and scowled as he analyzed the assertion.

"I don't know," said Mercy. "But the only new piece of physical evidence we have is the tire treads from the shooting." She stood and looked at Noelle. "Let's go find the vehicle."

40

Truman stepped into the hotel elevator and pressed the button for the third floor. When he'd texted Ollie that he'd arrived, Ollie had said he and Devin would be right down, but Truman had told him to stay put. He was there to escort the men to the hospital to visit Linda, but first he wanted to tell Devin about Mia.

To avoid being followed, Truman had taken a winding route to the hotel, even pulling over a few times to observe the cars behind him, but hadn't seen anything suspicious. He couldn't hide the Eagle's Nest logo and light bar on his SUV, but at the hotel he had found an out-of-the-way parking spot where few people would notice his vehicle.

He'd reluctantly rented a small car for Ollie while his red truck sat hidden in Truman's garage. The old truck was too distinctive for Ollie to drive at the moment. It was like a big sign stating OLLIE IS HERE. If someone tried to follow him and Devin back to their hotel, he'd be obvious. Truman had moved several items in his garage to make room for it; no vehicle had been in the garage since he'd bought the home.

Truman and Mercy preferred to drive the men but had acknowledged one of them might get called to work, which could leave Ollie and Devin at the hospital, and they didn't like the idea of using a rideshare service. After much discussion, Truman had agreed he or Mercy would follow Ollie's rented vehicle for hospital visits.

Truman stepped out of the elevator, strode to their room, and knocked sharply. A shadow moved behind the peephole, and then Ollie opened the door. He wore his coat, prepared to head to the hospital.

"We're ready to go," he told Truman.

"Sit down for a minute. I want to talk."

Ollie studied his face for a long second, and then his eyes widened the smallest bit.

He knows I have an answer about Mia.

Ollie stepped back and waved Truman into the room. Devin stood at the end of the short hallway in a coat.

"Let's have a talk before we go to the hospital, Devin. I have something to discuss."

Devin's face went blank, but anxiety lurked in his eyes. The three of them took seats at the little table. Ollie unzipped his coat, clearly understanding they weren't going outdoors for a while.

Truman met Devin's gaze. "It was Mia that we found yesterday. It's been confirmed with her dental records." He set a hand on Devin's arm. "I don't know whether to say I'm sorry or that I'm relieved a twenty-year-old question has been answered."

A mix of emotions flooded Devin's face. "I'm feeling both." His eyes grew wet and tears started down both cheeks. He wiped them with his good hand. "I don't know why I'm crying."

"It's a huge thing," Ollie said, leaning toward the older man. "You've been in limbo for two decades, not knowing what happened. Anyone would feel overwhelmed at finally finding an answer." He patted Devin's shoulder. "Whatever you're feeling is exactly right."

Devin blew out a long breath. "I always knew she was dead."

Truman stilled. "You did?"

A memory?

"Of course. She would have come back if she'd been alive." Devin continued to wipe his face, and Ollie fetched a towel from the bathroom.

"Thanks." He dried his eyes. "She was special to all of us, you know? She was genuine."

"Was there some jealousy of their relationship?" Truman watched the man closely, wondering if Mia's news would lead to some new recollections. He'd subtly prod and question, hoping Devin's brain would open some doors.

Devin thought for a long moment. "I don't think so. We respected the relationship. If one of the other guys felt that way, I didn't know about it." He shifted his sad gaze to Truman. "How did she die?"

"They can't tell."

Emotions flickered across Devin's face. Again he appeared to struggle with relief and dismay at the answer.

And now I'm going to add to his struggle.

"There's one other thing, Devin." Truman paused to plan his statement. "The forensic anthropologist believes there is a good possibility that Mia had been pregnant at some point in her life."

Devin sucked in a breath at the same time that Ollie's mouth fell open. "Pregnant," Devin stated hoarsely. "When was she pregnant?"

"They can't tell. And like I said, they're not one hundred percent positive."

Devin slowly shook his head, keeping his eyes locked with Truman's. "If she was ever pregnant, I didn't hear about it." He broke eye contact, lowered his head, and pressed the heel of his palm between his eyes.

Truman waited, wondering if this would open something in Devin's head.

Devin rocked slightly in his chair a few times. Then he grabbed the towel and pressed it against his eyes, his face still turned down.

"There is a possibility Mia died a few years after she disappeared," Truman told him. "The forensic anthropologist said she was close to eighteen but could have been as old as twenty-three at her death. It's hard to tell."

Devin threw the towel on the table and pushed up out of his chair. He paced the small room several times before halting to meet Truman's gaze. "That would mean she was *kept* somewhere, and that's possibly where she got pregnant." His voice cracked, and he spun around and continued pacing. "This is really shitty information you're giving me," he snapped. "It just raises more questions and puts horrible images in my mind!" He shook his head, disbelief on his face. "There has to be a mistake, and she actually died at the same time as the others."

"Others?" Truman seized the word.

"Well . . . me and Tyler." He stopped. "I want to kill someone right now," he spit out. "Mia might have suffered horribly for *years*. Shit! How am I going to get these thoughts out of my head?"

Ollie moved to stand in front of Devin and placed his hands on his shoulders, looking him earnestly in the eye. "It's okay. I want to kill someone, and I didn't even know her. I guarantee Truman has had the same thought. You'll work through it, and they'll find more answers to all these questions."

"I'm *shaking*, I'm so angry."

"I feel it," answered Ollie.

"She might have been tortured and raped," Devin said in a harsh whisper. He pulled away from Ollie. "Dammit!"

"I can tell you her bones don't indicate any physical abuse," said Truman, suspecting the fact would be of little comfort.

"She didn't deserve this. None of it," ranted Devin.

"None of you did," said Truman.

"Maybe I did." Devin hung his head.

Truman held his breath.

What did you do?

"Why the fuck would you say that, Devin?" asked Ollie, anger clipping his words. "No human *deserved* what happened to you."

Devin pressed his palm between his eyes again. "I don't know why I said it. It just came out. I feel so guilty about Mia. So damned guilty about all of it."

"It's survivor's guilt," said Ollie.

Devin shook his head but said, "Maybe."

"Devin," said Truman slowly. "Are you remembering other things?"

He exhaled. "Snatches of things. Bits and pieces like I've had before."

"But they're new bits and pieces?" asked Truman.

Devin was silent a long moment. "They're familiar. I recognize them. Maybe they're pieces of my dreams, not reality."

"Or they're from what actually happened to you," said Ollie. "Describe these fragments."

"Mia crying and whispering to me, but I can't make out her words. Images of Mia happy, tilting her head and smiling. Colin is happy, but then I see him mad. Mad at all of us." His eyes were clenched shut.

"Where are you when you see this? What's in the background?" asked Ollie. He shot a questioning look at Truman, who nodded back at him.

You're doing good.

"Outdoors. All of the fragments are all outdoors." Devin lifted his head, eyes still shut. "I see the tents behind Colin," he said in wonder. "It's the campground." He opened his eyes, stunned.

"Good job," said Ollie.

"Maybe it's in my head because I was shown the campground pictures the other day." Devin grimaced.

"Or the pictures helped break something open," said Ollie.

Devin seemed to sway a little, and Ollie grabbed his shoulder. "You okay?"

"Yeah." Devin sat back down at the table. "Suddenly exhausted." He glanced at Truman. "I don't remember anything else."

"It'll come," said Truman, knowing he had no way of promising that. "You've always said you didn't remember anything after graduation, so it's a step in the right direction."

"Yeah." Devin didn't sound convinced.

"You ready to go see your mom?" asked Truman. The man was clearly wiped out, and Truman hated to push for more memories. It might be counterproductive.

"Definitely."

"Let's go, then. I'll follow the two of you to the hospital. Ollie, make sure your phone is readily available."

Since his mother was attacked, Devin hadn't expressed much fear about the possible danger to his life. Truman didn't know if it was a coping mechanism or if Devin didn't fully believe he could be a target.

Truman wasn't sure either, but bad things seemed to happen around Devin Bonner.

41

"I left another voice mail for Mia's father," said Noelle, sitting beside Mercy in her Tahoe on their way to Jason Slade's rural home.

"I hate to send local law enforcement to his home to do a death notification," said Mercy. "But it looks like we might have no choice." She sighed. "Not that he's shown any interest anyway." More digging by Noelle had turned up a six-year-old death notice for Mia's mother in a tiny Louisiana town.

Mercy's heart ached for Mia. She'd had little family support in her short life.

What happened to you?

She couldn't imagine what Mia's last days had been like. How had she died? Had she lived a few more years? Had she watched her friends die?

Mercy suspected Mia's had been a horrible death.

Dumped in a shallow grave.

But someone had cared enough to remember where she'd been buried. And possibly the same someone had placed Mia's hands on her chest before covering her with dirt. Probably a sign that someone had known her or had at least cared a little.

The GPS told Mercy to make a left turn. They were far outside Bend in a rural area with few pines, and gentle slopes shaped the land.

Mercy knew homes were scattered through the region, but they had been built out of sight, hidden by the rise and fall of the country. This was a place where people wanted privacy.

Mercy understood. She valued privacy. But after studying the layout of Jason Slade's property, she'd wondered if he'd used the remoteness of his father's home to hurt those teenagers.

I have no proof.

And twenty years later she was now unlikely to find proof. But maybe, just maybe, Jason had a full-size pickup with new tires on the front wheels.

A needle in a haystack.

The left turn took her off the rural two-lane highway onto a dirt road. The snow had mostly melted, but small white piles had lined the highway, stained with red dust from the ground rock used to sand the roads.

"It's about five hundred more yards," said Noelle, studying the GPS.

The rough road arced up and then eased down, with several wide curves along the way. Scattered igneous boulders sat in the fields, poking up among sparse sagebrush. The landscape lacked color. Muted tans, greens, and grays made the area seem washed out. The only intense color filled the sky.

"So much of the countryside makes me feel as if I'm the first person to ever see it," said Noelle, looking out her window. "It seems untouched."

Mercy felt the same.

The feeling vanished as a home came into view. It was a double-wide mobile home set in a shallow valley. Behind it the dull-brown land sloped up a few hundred feet to a small craggy peak dotted with snow. To the home's west were three outbuildings, different sizes and distances from the house. The rest of the long valley was flat and rocky.

Mercy drove closer and realized the home had seen better days. It was weathered and aged, its paint chipped and peeling. The wooden stairs to the front door sagged.

"There's the eighteen-wheeler," said Noelle as part of the cab came into sight. It was parked on the far side of the largest outbuilding. "He's definitely not on the road. I wonder if he's home right now."

"I don't see a pickup."

"Could be in that building by the semi. It has a roll-up door."

"Unless he's willing to raise that door for us, we're not going to get a peek at his tires. Dammit. I'd hoped this would be easy," said Mercy. "This is a guy who won't return our phone calls, so I suspect he won't give us a guided tour of his property." She pulled a sharp turn and parked.

"Ready?" she asked Noelle, checking her weapon in her shoulder holster and pasting on the friendly smile that was always her first offensive play.

"Ready."

42

Ollie kept an eye on Truman's black SUV in his rearview mirror. He noticed Devin occasionally glancing at his side mirror. Driving the tiny rental car was odd compared to driving his old truck. The seats were so low, it felt as if he were inches above the ground. And the car's engine was a whisper compared to the roar and growl of his truck. When they'd stopped at a light, he'd even checked to see if the car was still running.

There'd been an awkward silence between the men during the ride to the hospital. At one point Ollie had finally asked Devin if he was okay, and Devin had said he was but didn't want to talk. He'd kept his gaze directed out his side window, but the lines on his forehead and the clenching of his jaw were apparent.

A lot had been thrown at Devin in the last hour. If Ollie's brain was running wild with things that could have happened to Mia, Devin's speculations had to be ten times worse.

As Ollie pulled into the hospital parking lot, his phone rang with a call from Truman.

"Yeah?"

"I need to get back to Eagle's Nest. Royce is struggling to handle three fighting drunks on his own."

"Drunks? It's not even noon."

"Doesn't matter to some people. You good from here?"

"Yeah. Go ahead. I'll drop Devin at the hospital entrance and then park."

"Okay. Call if you need me."

In the mirror Ollie watched Truman pull a U-turn and speed away.

"Don't take me to the entrance. I can walk," said Devin.

"Okay. It's best if we stick together anyway." Ollie drove past the hospital entrance and turned down a parking lot row. The lot appeared to be full.

"There's one." Devin pointed as a Subaru's backup lights came on. Ollie stopped to wait.

Spot is too narrow.

He snorted. He wasn't driving his truck. The tiny rental car would fit just fine, even though the SUVs on either side were parked nearly on the lines.

Small cars have some advantages.

But he'd never part with his truck. Truman had bought it for him. That alone made it his most prized possession.

He pulled in and parked. Ollie grabbed his phone and stepped out of the car. He was about to close his door when a sudden movement happened behind him. Pain rocketed through his head and he fell to his hands and knees, smashing his face against the inside of the car door as he went down.

I was hit in the head.

"Devin!" he squawked. He blinked hard, fighting the pain.

Another blow to his head knocked him to his stomach, his lips and teeth grating against the coarse blacktop. Glass shattered and metal scraped, and something skittered past him on the ground.

Fuck! Devin!

Pain ricocheted through his skull. Everything hurt. His teeth. His lips. His head.

I fucked up. I should have dropped Devin at the entrance.

My fault.

He fought to push up to his hands and knees. Blood dripped from his mouth, creating shiny dark spots on the ground. They blurred, and he struggled to refocus. His vision was reduced to a narrow, fuzzy tunnel.

My head is going to explode.

"Devin." His speech was a wet whisper. On the other side of the car, a struggle was happening. Muffled shouts. Scuffling.

Get Devin.

His right arm collapsed, and then his cheek flattened into the blacktop. He stared at the underbody of the vehicle next to him. The smell of dirt, blood, and engine oil assaulted him, and he closed his eyes as the world spun.

Push through the pain.

But rest first.

"You kill him?" said a voice.

"Does it matter? Let's go."

Ollie breathed hard as he mentally took inventory of his body. Legs were fine, but his knees complained from hitting the ground. Stomach good. Lungs good. Arms good but palms stinging.

Head. Not good.

He took a deep breath and opened his eyes, blinking to clear his blurred vision. He pushed up to sitting and leaned to one side, spitting blood and fighting to keep down the bagel he'd had for breakfast.

Devin?

Ollie turned and lurched upward, pushing with his feet until his elbows were on the driver's seat. The passenger door was open. "Devin?"

Did they kill him?

Ollie couldn't see the ground on the passenger side.

He held his breath and turned until he sat on the driver's seat, his feet on the ground outside. His vision tunneled and then widened, making his stomach churn. The pain at the back of his head was a throbbing constant. Same with his mouth. Once his vision stopped wavering, he stood and steadied himself. He moved around the front of the car, bracing himself against it as his legs trembled with every step.

There was nothing on the other side. Devin was gone.

Ollie pushed the passenger door shut.

Call 911.

Where's my phone?

He stumbled back around to the driver's seat. His phone wasn't in the cup holder or on the seat or floorboards. Memories of a small crash of glass and metal and then skittering sounds flashed.

He lowered himself to the blacktop and looked under the car, spotting his phone underneath the front bumper. Not wanting to stand again, Ollie crawled around to the front and picked up the crushed phone. The glass screen was a spiderweb, and the phone's bottom edge had splintered off. Small chunks fell into his hand.

Someone stomped on it and kicked it.

He pressed the screen and all the side buttons. Nothing.

Find help. Get to the hospital.

A vehicle approached, and Ollie forced himself up, leaning on the car's hood, intending to wave his arms. But they wouldn't lift. A silver truck passed.

The driver.

The driver's profile stuck in his mind. Before Ollie had been hit, he'd seen the face reflected in a rear window of the rental car. It'd lasted a nanosecond, but Ollie was positive he'd just seen him again.

They took Devin.

He pushed to his feet and stumbled to the back of his car to see the rest of the parking lot. No people were in sight, and the hospital entrance was at the distant end of the lot. It felt impossibly far.

It might as well be a mile.

But a silver truck was waiting for traffic to pass so it could turn out of the parking lot and onto the street.

If I go into the hospital, the truck will vanish.

Indecision tore at him, his head and vision spinning.

Follow them. See where they take Devin and then find a phone.

He darted to the driver's seat, started the car, and backed out of the space. He fought to focus: it took all his mental strength, his fingers tight on the wheel, and he strained to see ahead of him.

Am I okay to drive?

It was the only choice.

He sped down the lot and turned onto the road without stopping. The truck was several blocks ahead.

Don't let it out of sight.

Ignore the pain.

I can do this.

43

Mercy rapped on Jason Slade's door for the second time.

"Mr. Slade?" she asked loudly. "I'm Special Agent Kilpatrick. We've been trying to reach you."

Thirty feet to her right, Noelle kept an eye on the front and down the west side of the home. "Nothing moving in the windows," she told Mercy. "Feels empty to me."

Mercy agreed but would make no assumptions. "Let's walk around to the back. I'll go to the other side." She went down the steps, placing her feet at the sides of the sagging boards, keeping a tight grip on the railing. Noelle watched until Mercy reached the east side of the house, and then they both headed toward the back.

On Mercy's side of the home were two windows. Both too high for her to see in. She rounded the back corner of the home and spotted Noelle as she did the same. On the back of the house was a sliding glass door, but its deck had collapsed, leaving a pile of weathered boards and concrete blocks under a thin layer of snow. Risking a step out the sliding door could break someone's arm or leg.

"Nice," muttered Noelle as she stepped through the deck debris. She stood to one side of the glass door, angling her head to peer through. "It's quiet. I can see a kitchen. A table and chairs."

Mercy lifted her leg over a stack of boards and moved to the other side of the glass door, checking indoors in the other direction. "Couch. TV." She crouched down and pulled aside a loose piece of skirting to look under the mobile home. Light filtered in from several places where the skirting had fallen off. She saw nothing underneath but support beams and more blocks.

"Let's check the outbuildings," she told Noelle. They crossed the fifty yards between the home and the large building with a rolling door. Mercy rapped on the big door, creating a booming sound, and identified herself again. Silence. She tugged on the handle. The door didn't move.

Noelle eyed the 18-wheeler beside the building. The black cab had a sleeping compartment, and a trucking company's name was printed in an arc on the door. Noelle pounded on the wall of the sleeping compartment. "Hello? Mr. Slade?"

Mercy did a quick circle of the building. No windows. She checked one of the remaining buildings while Noelle did the other. Their doors were locked.

"You could easily keep someone in one of these," said Noelle with her hands on her hips as she eyed a locked door. "Several someones."

An engine sounded in the distance.

"We've got company," said Mercy. They both moved to the side of the building, where they could watch the road but not be easily spotted. A moment later a silver pickup came around a curve. It continued a hundred feet and then abruptly stopped in the lane, still far back from the home. Its engine idled, the driver impossible to see through the angled windshield.

"He's wondering about my Tahoe," said Mercy. "Let's see what he decides to do."

The truck turned, pulled to the side of the lane, and then backed up, starting a three-point turn on the narrow road.

"He's taking off!" Noelle cried.

In sync they dashed across the property to Mercy's vehicle. Jumping inside, Mercy floored it after the pickup, which had sped away after completing its turn. Noelle was on her phone, requesting backup from Deschutes County. The rural highway came into view, stretching across the landscape, and the pickup fishtailed as it took a hard left onto it, barely slowing.

Mercy took the turn with ease and pressed the accelerator, determined to close the distance. The truck sped up.

"A deputy is a few minutes out," said Noelle, gripping the handle above her door. "I wonder why this guy ran?"

"He could've at least asked what we wanted," said Mercy, her heart pounding in her chest. She took several long breaths, focusing on the road, enjoying the chase.

"Oh, shit! That *asshole*!" yelled Noelle.

The truck had passed a sedan and cut back to his lane too quickly, forcing the sedan off the road, where it slammed to a stop on the shoulder.

"They're okay," Noelle said, checking as they sped past the sedan. "But the driver is pissed."

"That makes two of us. That truck needs to get off the road before he kills someone." Mercy punched the gas pedal again and drew closer as Noelle snapped a picture of the license plate.

"PIT?" asked Noelle.

"Yep." Mercy had already decided to do a precision immobilization technique (PIT) maneuver to stop the truck. She waited until the two vehicles were on a long, straight stretch with no oncoming traffic. She moved into the oncoming lane and accelerated as she veered into the truck's rear left fender with her front fender. Knocked off course, the truck spun across the road in front of the Tahoe and slid down the snowy sloped shoulder of the road, where the driver hit the brakes. Mercy turned and stopped in front of the truck, blocking it from returning to the highway.

"Yes!" said Noelle. She slid out of the Tahoe and raised her weapon, her arms resting on the hood, the engine block between her and the driver. She yelled for the man to get out of the vehicle. Mercy waited in the cab, ready to block the truck again if he tried to maneuver out of the snow.

The truck's rear wheels spun in the snow as he tried to back up. The spinning dug him deeper into the snow, scattering mud. He finally gave up and turned off the engine.

"Deschutes County sheriff's office!" Noelle yelled. "Let me see your hands, and then get out of the truck!"

Mercy stepped out of the Tahoe, covering the pickup driver from a different angle. The pickup door opened and the driver stuck out his hands, fingers splayed, and then stepped down into the muddy snow.

"Step out where we can see you," Mercy yelled.

The driver moved from behind his door, his hands still raised.

Mercy recognized Jason Slade from his license. "On your stomach, Mr. Slade. Keep your hands in sight."

The man looked down at the dirty snow. "Fuck." He awkwardly knelt and then flopped to his stomach, keeping his hands above his head. Noelle quickly cuffed him and checked his pockets while Mercy covered her and checked the truck for more occupants. Finding nothing of interest, Noelle hauled Jason to his feet and politely brushed the snow from his front. "Seriously?" he spit out, scrutinizing them both with angry eyes. "Two women?"

"You'd prefer three?" asked Noelle with a sugary sweetness in her voice. Her smile dared him to continue.

Jason Slade had a shaved head, and a little hair growth outlined the pattern of his baldness. His face was long, and the huge puffy bags under his eyes needed luggage tags. He wore Carhartts that were stained at the knees and a denim jacket lined with wool.

"What made you run, Mr. Slade?" Mercy asked, putting away her weapon.

"*You* chased me." Fury rolled off him.

Mercy remembered how Sam Durette had described Jason Slade's anger and bitterness. "You ran first," she pointed out. "We were waiting outside your home to have a neighborly chat, and you raced off like you'd seen White Walkers."

"White what?"

"Never mind." Mercy took a few steps to get a side view of his truck, eyeing the front and rear tires.

The treads were packed with snow, so she dug some out from a rear tire, searching for the indicator bar. She eyed the strip that ran the width of the tread. She was no expert, but she'd checked her own tire treads' wear over the years and recognized that the rear tires still had a lot of life in them. She dug the snow out of a front tire, the wear appearing nearly identical to that in the rear. A quick walk around the pickup showed the same with the tires on the other side.

"What are you doing?" Jason asked, scrunching up his forehead.

Mercy pressed her lips together. The pickup had four tires with several thousand miles left on them. Not two new tires and two nearly worn out.

But again. Tires can be changed.

She'd proven nothing.

"You never gave me a good answer about why you ran when you saw our vehicle," said Mercy, ignoring his question.

Jason looked away, lifted his chin, and then shifted his gaze back to her. "You know why."

"Pretend I don't."

He shook his head and glanced away again, annoyance in his eyes. "I didn't know what was in it."

Mercy exchanged a glance with Noelle. "You didn't?" Mercy asked, having no idea what he was talking about.

"No. He asked me to drop it off since my route would take me there anyway. That's all. I didn't ask any questions. I've known the guy for years. Asshole."

"But you looked to see what was in it," said Mercy to get him to expand on his odd statements.

Where is he going with this?

"No, I didn't," Jason said firmly. "And I only did it once for him—well, twice." He shrugged.

"Where did you drop it off?" asked Noelle.

"Georgia."

She must have looked confused because he added, "It's my usual route."

Frustrated with the odd back-and-forth, Mercy asked, "Where were you this past Monday?"

"Georgia," he said with emphasis. "Like I said, it's my route. I got home yesterday." He looked from Noelle to her. "The trucking company's GPS tracker will confirm my location."

"It will confirm your *truck's* location," clarified Mercy.

"Well, who else would be driving my truck?" he said, staring at her as if she'd lost her mind.

If Jason was telling the truth, he'd been out of state for all the attacks. Including Rob's.

But what made him run from us?

"And that's where you dropped it off," Mercy said, searching for answers.

"Yeah." He glared. "I knew when I saw that black government SUV that you'd found out."

Mercy took a stab in the dark. "Fentanyl?"

"I think so."

He ran because he delivered fentanyl.

A Deschutes County vehicle pulled up and parked on the edge of the road. The deputy stepped out and headed their way.

"Look at that," said Noelle, patting his shoulder. "Lucky you. Three women."

The deputy had put Jason in the back seat and was speaking with Noelle beside her vehicle. Mercy wasn't sure if there was enough to charge him, but someone should question him about the fentanyl.

It'd be simple enough to track Jason Slade's location over the last week. Besides his company's GPS, there were credit card purchases and cell phone towers to indicate where he'd been.

I don't think he's involved.

Sighing, Mercy ran her fingers along the scrapes on the fender of her Tahoe, hating the sight of the marred paint and metal.

At least I did the PIT move this time.

A PIT maneuver had been pulled on her vehicle nearly two years ago, causing it to spin off the road and roll down a bank. Her SUV had been totaled, and she'd had vivid nightmares for months. No doubt today's action would make the dreams return.

Her phone rang with a call from Truman.

"You're immobile on a highway in the middle of nowhere," he greeted her.

She smiled. He was tracking her, a necessary evil. "That's correct. I'm fine, but I'll tell you about it later."

"Can you see Ollie's signal?" Truman asked. "He's not showing up for me."

"Hang on." Mercy lowered her phone and opened the tracking app. It showed Kaylie at her coffee shop and Truman on the highway between Bend and Eagle's Nest. No Ollie.

"He's not showing up for me either," she told him.

"I followed him and Devin to the hospital," said Truman. "I know sometimes it's hard to call out from inside. Maybe something is blocking his signal."

"I located him when he visited Linda the other day," said Mercy. "The app showed you there with him."

The long silence on his end of the line unnerved her.

"I'm going to call the hospital," he finally said. "See if he and Devin are still with Linda."

"Get a deputy to escort them back to the hotel," said Mercy.

"I'm headed back to Bend. I'll do it." His tone was odd.

"Everything okay?" she asked.

"I regret not watching them walk into the hospital," said Truman. "Royce was in a pickle and I had to help, so I left after they turned into its parking lot."

"I would have done the same," said Mercy.

"I don't like it." His voice was tight.

"I know." The tracking was supposed to give them peace of mind. Not being able to see Ollie made her antsy too.

"If that kid turned off his phone, I'm going to strangle him."

"Ollie knows the rules," she assured him.

I'll strangle him first.

"I'll let you know what I find out from the hospital." They exchanged I-love-yous and ended the call.

Mercy studied the wallpaper of her phone. A wedding photo of her and Truman. She was looking directly at the camera, happiness on her face, but Truman was staring at her, wonder in his eyes. She never tired of looking at him in the picture.

They never skipped the I-love-yous. With their professions, any time could be the last time they spoke to one another. Truman's "I love you" had sounded more intense this time, more emotional. The situation had made him emphasize his declaration to her.

He worries he won't have the chance to say it to Ollie again.

I'm worried too.

44

The head of hospital security scanned the video feeds as Truman stood behind her chair, digging his fingertips into its leather. "It happened just after noon," he told Janice for the third time.

"Hang on. We'll find it." Janice scrolled on her touch pad.

Time was slipping out of Truman's hands. He needed to know *now* what had happened to Ollie and Devin after he drove off.

After talking with Mercy, Truman had called the nurses' station of Linda's hospital floor. They'd confirmed that no one had visited Linda that morning. In fact Linda had asked several times when her son was coming because he wasn't answering his phone. Stress simmering in his stomach, Truman had asked to be connected to security. The head of security had promised to check the video feeds, and Truman had told her he was on his way.

When he'd arrived at the hospital, he'd had to wait ten agonizing minutes for the head of security to appear. Janice had finally jogged down the hallway. She was a petite woman with a long, blonde ponytail. "I'm sorry, Chief. I had to take a report from a visitor whose tennis shoe got hooked by a revolving door. Ripped a hole in her shoe and knocked her to her knees." The woman shook her head. "She's lucky she didn't break something. She refused to be checked into the ER."

My son is missing, and she's dealing with a ripped shoe.

Janice had led him to her small office, where four screens rotated among different views of the hospital. To Truman's surprise, no one had been in the office monitoring the screens. He mentioned it. "I've got two guards walking the property during the day and one in the evenings," said Janice. "I like to have them out and about for visitors to see, but they're usually bored out of their brains. When I'm not taking reports, I'm in the office doing paperwork and keeping one eye on the cameras."

She scrolled through a feed that included the parking lot entrance where Truman had split from Ollie and Devin. Truman watched several vehicles turn in. "That's their car. And I'm right behind them."

He watched his SUV stop at the side of the entrance, knowing he was calling Ollie. Then the SUV pulled a sharp turn and drove off. Ollie's car moved out of view.

"That was at 12:23," said Janice. "Let's check a different angle and see if we can catch them again." Suddenly the screen switched to a camera that covered the hospital entrance and the drive right in front of it. Ollie's little compact drove through the view, and Truman caught a glimpse of Devin. "Switching again," she said.

The next camera shot covered most of the parking lot. Ollie was stopped in a lane, waiting for another car to back out. "He's about as far away from the hospital as you can get," Truman muttered. The rental car swung into the spot, its front end disappearing from their sight. The back half of Ollie's door was visible, the rest blocked by a big SUV in the next spot.

"Oh, shit," Janice and Truman uttered at the same time. They'd spotted two men moving furtively among other vehicles, making a beeline for Ollie's car.

"Do you have a camera that's closer?" he asked.

"No." Her answer was grim. "And I'm zoomed in the maximum."

Ollie's door swung open, and he stepped out of the car. Truman held his breath as one of the men rushed Ollie, swung something, and hit him in the back of the head.

Truman's heart stopped as his son went down, out of their view.

Ollie. Oh my God.

"What the hell?" Janice stopped the feed, backed up, and watched Ollie get hit again.

"Keep going," Truman ordered through clenched teeth. He didn't need to see it happen any more.

On the far side of the car, a second man tackled Devin, and they went down, out of the camera's sight. The man on Ollie's side swung his arm again, apparently taking another hit at Ollie. Truman was thankful he couldn't see the weapon strike Ollie, but then his brain immediately conjured up the most painful images possible.

Ollie's head split open.

Ollie bleeding to death.

"Can you tell what he was hit with?" asked Janice, distracting Truman from his morbid thoughts.

"Something red. A wrench?" suggested Truman. "One of the big plumber ones?"

Janice nodded, her gaze glued to the screen as the man who'd hit Ollie darted around to help the second man with Devin. A moment later they hustled Devin between several cars and out of camera view.

Janice switched to a different camera. The men had stopped at a silver pickup.

"He's still on his feet," Janice commented. She played with the keyboard, trying to zoom in on the pickup, but shook her head. "I can tell it's a Dodge, but I can't read the plate."

At the truck, Devin suddenly fought back. His arms were tied behind him, but he kicked with both legs and swung his head. He landed a headbutt to the chin of the man who'd struck Ollie.

Good man, Devin.

A blow to Devin's jaw stunned him, and the men pushed and shoved him through the back door of the truck. One man crawled in after him, and the other jogged around to the driver's door. There seemed to be another struggle inside as the driver turned and lunged toward the back seat to help with something. After a long minute the truck backed out of its spot and then drove off out of sight. Janice switched feeds and the truck reappeared, headed toward an exit. Each second moving farther and farther away.

"That's the best we've got," said Janice as the truck paused at the exit, waiting for a break in traffic.

Truman pulled out his phone and texted Lucas to put a BOLO on a silver Dodge Ram crew cab pickup. He didn't know the year, but he guessed it was nearly ten years old.

"I'll go back to the other guy." Janice dragged her fingers on her pad.

"He's my son," Truman said quietly. Bile had burned up his esophagus as he watched Devin get shoved in the truck. He was terrified of what they'd see happen next to Ollie. Truman knew his rental wasn't in the hospital lot; he'd checked.

Janice sucked in a breath. "I'm sorry. I didn't know," she said sincerely as she returned to the partial view of Ollie's car. She'd backed up to where the two men shoved Devin out of range. Truman held his breath again. No one was visible at Ollie's car. He checked the ticker in the screen's corner to be certain she hadn't paused the video.

How hurt is he?

"Something moved," said Janice. "The car dipped the littlest bit. Like something happened inside."

Truman agreed, staring as hard as possible at what he could see of the rental car. There was more movement. Partial glimpses of an arm, a shoulder, and the back of a head. He couldn't tell what was happening, but he was nearly certain it was Ollie.

He's not dead.

"Both doors are still open," Janice said.

Truman nodded. He couldn't speak. His heart was in his throat.

Do they come back for Ollie?

Suddenly they saw Ollie stand, but then he vanished as he moved toward the front of the car and reappeared on the passenger side. He paused, leaning heavily on the hood, and then he pushed the passenger door shut. "He was looking for Devin," said Truman, his voice rough. "He thought Devin was on the ground on the other side of the car."

Janice nodded as Ollie made his way back around to the driver's door. He seemed to drop down for a long moment, making Truman panic at the thought that he'd passed out.

Stand up, Ollie!

The silver Dodge passed through the camera view. Seconds later, Ollie lurched to the back of the car, bracing his hands on the trunk as he looked up and down the parking lot.

Thank God.

Ollie stared in the direction the silver truck had gone, frozen.

"I think he knew that was them," said Janice.

Abruptly Ollie staggered to the driver's door. A few seconds later, the car shot backward out of the parking spot and then sped toward the exit.

He's weaving. He shouldn't be driving.

Truman cursed as Ollie pulled out into traffic without stopping.

Janice leaned back in her chair. "I don't think he should be behind the wheel. He's got to have a concussion if he was hit as hard as we think. But clearly he went after the pickup."

"Looks that way. His phone must have been damaged in the fight, or else the other guys took it and powered it down." Truman rubbed his forehead.

What do I do first?

He sent Lucas another BOLO with a description of Ollie's rental car and asked him to call the rental car company to see if it could track the vehicle. Truman knew not all rental companies used trackers, but it was worth a try. The he called the Bend Police Department to request an evidence team to the hospital parking lot.

Next he called Mercy and gave her a quick recap of what he'd seen in the videos.

His phone still at his ear, Truman thanked Janice, left her his card, and headed toward the hospital doors.

"Ollie's okay?" Mercy asked.

"More or less," said Truman. "He's clearly hurt and probably shouldn't be driving. The two men that grabbed Devin might have been the ones who shot Ben. I wouldn't be surprised if their big pickup left those tire treads."

"Which means they also shot up the substations," said Mercy. "I have no idea how that connects to Devin." She sighed. "Maybe we don't need to collect Jason Slade's weapons. That's what we're doing now. He thought we stopped him because he was trafficking drugs. When I told him we were looking to connect his truck and weapons to a murder, he practically handed me a written invitation to take his guns. He wants to prove that none of this has anything to do with him."

The hospital's automatic doors opened in front of Truman. He stepped out into the cold sunshine and put on his cowboy hat. It was slightly surreal, walking into the parking lot where he'd just seen Ollie and Devin attacked. "I'm headed out," he told her, and they exchanged I-love-yous.

He strode across the lot to where Ollie's car had been. A new car was in its spot, but the SUVs on the sides were the same. Truman slowly paced around the car, studying the ground.

There were drops of blood on the driver's side. He looked away.

He's okay. I saw him drive.

But it killed him to think that the teenager had been hurt. If Ollie had been hit in the head, medical complications could crop up soon.

He bent over, shined his phone's light under the car, and then did an awkward hunched walk around it. Near the front he saw some tiny pieces of metal and glass on the blacktop.

Those could be anything.

But they looked a lot like phone pieces to Truman. He snapped a photo but didn't touch them, leaving a forensics team to collect the evidence.

He wanted to check where the silver truck had parked, and was halfway there when a man stopped him in the lot.

"Chief Daly?" he asked hesitantly. He appeared to be about forty, and his clothing suggested that he worked a ranch or a farm or in some other sort of outdoor industry. Thick canvas pants, scuffed boots, a snapback cap that used to be red, and a thick coat. His dark beard needed a trim, and his shoulders were hunched against the cold.

"That's me. What can I do for you?" Truman quickly scanned the man, noting at least three places he could have a handgun. He tried to place the man's face.

The man looked around and then at his feet. His gaze reluctantly came back to Truman's. "I need to talk to you."

"I'm pretty busy at the moment. I'm in the middle of an investigation and expecting the Bend police any minute."

Never hurts to mention that law enforcement is on its way.

"You'll want to hear this, Chief." The man's chest rose and dropped as his shoulders hunched a little. He seemed reluctant to say what was on his mind.

Impatience roiled through Truman.

I need to find Ollie.

"My name is—well, my name used to be Alex Stark," he finally said as he looked hesitantly at Truman.

Truman held the stranger's gaze, feeling the name was familiar but not recalling where it fit.

Then it clicked into place.

No. He can't be.

"Alex Stark," Truman repeated. "You sure of that?"

"Yeah."

One of the missing teenagers from twenty years ago.

45

"If you're Alex Stark, you need to explain where you've been for twenty years," said Truman with a hard stare at the man's face. He glanced around the parking lot and spotted a Bend police SUV pull in. He lifted his arm and flagged it down. Once Bend had control over the kidnapping crime scene, he'd go search for Ollie and Devin.

But he had no idea where.

"I know I do," said Alex. "That's why I followed you here. I was going to tell you in Eagle's Nest, but you headed out of town."

"I'm not who you should talk to," said Truman. "That'd be the FBI. Or county."

The man paled and blinked.

Truman narrowed his eyes at him, suspicion rising. "Do you know what happened in this parking lot today? You have something to do with that?"

Confusion crossed Alex's face. "What happened? I followed you here and then waited for you to come out of the hospital. I didn't see anything."

He seemed sincere, and Truman's gut believed him.

"Why'd you pick me to talk to? Whatever happened to you twenty years ago has nothing to do with the Eagle's Nest Police Department."

"I know." Alex shoved his hands in his coat pockets. "It's that they're just . . . so big."

Truman knew he didn't mean height. "'They'?"

"Sheriff's department."

A thought occurred to him. "Did you leave the note on my officer's car?"

Alex's gaze flicked to the side. "Not sure what you mean."

"I think you do. Mia Fowler."

Alex winced. "I know you found her," he said softly. "She didn't deserve that."

The Bend police unit parked nearby.

I've got to call Mercy. She needs to know this.

Two Bend police officers got out of the SUV, and one raised a hand at Truman.

"Give me a minute while I explain to these guys what needs to be done," said Truman. "Then I'll take you to the people you really need to talk to. They'll appreciate that you came forward." Truman joined the two Bend officers and rapidly briefed them on what had happened in the lot, showing them where Ollie had parked and where Devin had been shoved in the pickup so they could preserve the scenes.

When he turned around, Alex Stark was gone.

Heart pounding, Truman scanned the lot. Nothing.

He wanted to come clean. Why would he leave?

"Hey," Truman said to the two officers rolling out crime scene tape. "The guy I was talking to . . . did you see where he went?"

One of them pointed toward the edge of the lot. "He headed that way."

Beyond the last row of vehicles were the densely packed trees and shrubs of a green space that stretched for at least a hundred yards and circled the hospital grounds. Alex could have gone in any direction.

Truman glanced back at the two officers, tempted to ask for help. But protecting the scene of Devin's kidnapping took priority over a search for a man who'd made some wild claims.

Did he distract me for some reason? Or was he trying to change the direction of Mercy's investigation?

"Dammit." He'd believed the man was Alex Stark, but now he had his doubts, wondering if he'd been lied to.

Was he working with the kidnappers?

But Truman couldn't think of a motivation for a kidnapper to boldly approach him in the parking lot not long after the crime had taken place. It made no sense. He pulled out his phone to Google an old photo of Alex Stark to compare to the man he'd just talked to, and the phone rang in his hand with a call from Ina.

"Ina. What can I do for you?" he asked distractedly, continuing to search for a photo.

"I think it's what I can do for you, Chief. Your boy is here, and he looks like hell spit him out."

Truman's fingers froze on the screen. "Ollie?"

"Yep. He's got two huge lumps on the back of his head, and his mouth is a bloody, scraped-up mess." She lowered her voice. "He seems confused and not quite with it. Keeps talking about a silver pickup and trying to find Devin Bonner. He's pretty upset. I've got him holding bags of peas against those lumps."

"Does he need an ambulance?" Truman strode toward his vehicle.

"I remember you knocking your head worse than this on that little motorcycle of yours, taking jumps all over your uncle's property. You did just fine."

Something might be bleeding inside his skull.

"Ina, call 911. I want him to go to the hospital."

The hospital's emergency department entrance across the lot caught Truman's eye. This was the hospital where Ollie would most likely end up. It was at least a half hour from Ina's.

Do I wait?

He didn't know if he could stand still for that long.

"Ollie wants to talk to you first," she said.

"No, Ina—"

"Truman?" Ollie's voice was shaky.

"You okay, son? I saw what happened in the parking lot on the hospital feeds. You got hit hard." Visions of Ollie going down took over his brain again.

"You've got to find the silver truck. *They took Devin.* I tried to follow—but I lost them. And I can't remember where I was. Then I realized I was near Ina's, so I stopped." His voice dropped to a whisper. "I might have blacked out, Truman. I can't remember how I got here."

Ina was right. Ollie sounded genuinely confused. If he had blacked out, his head injury could be worse than it appeared. "Ina is going to call an ambulance as soon as we're off the phone. If you blacked out, you need to be checked at the hospital."

"But what about Devin?" He spoke in a stumbling cadence. "Have you found him? Do you know why they took him?"

"We haven't found Devin yet, Ollie. We will."

"He can't protect himself!" Ollie sucked in rattling breaths.

Truman's heart cracked at the teen's distress. "Then you didn't see Devin fight and headbutt the men who took him. We've got a BOLO out on that silver truck. Someone will spot it and we'll find him. Now give the phone back to Ina."

"I love you, Truman." A wet sniffle sounded. "I don't say it enough."

"Love you too, son."

"What's going on?" Ina asked sharply. "What's this about the Bonner boy?"

That "boy" is almost forty.

"I'll explain later. Call 911. *Now.* Ollie needs a doctor."

"On it." She ended the call.

His Google search for Alex Stark was still open. Putting his worry about Ollie on hold for a second, Truman scanned until he found an article with all five of the teenagers' old photos. He enlarged Alex Stark's.

Maybe?

He pressed his lips into a line and closed his eyes, trying to call up the face of the man who had claimed to be Alex. He opened his eyes and studied the photo again. He still couldn't tell.

He exhaled and called Mercy.

"Are you still at Slade's?" he asked at her greeting.

"Just leaving. Any word on Ollie and Devin?"

"Yes. Ollie is at Ina's. He's got two big lumps on the back of his head and tore up his mouth. Somehow he drove there from the hospital, but he thinks he may have blacked out."

"How did he not go off the road?"

"Maybe he did at one point. I don't know, and he's hazy on details. Ina called for an ambulance. I want him checked out right away. He wasn't speaking quite right."

"Oh, Truman."

"He'd followed the truck that took Devin but somehow lost them and got turned around, I guess. I haven't gotten any hits on the BOLO for that pickup, but I have one other thing I need to tell you. Is Noelle handy? Put me on speaker. She should hear this."

Mercy spoke in the background, and a second later Noelle greeted him.

"I had a man walk up to me in the hospital parking lot minutes ago and tell me his name was Alex Stark."

Silence answered him.

Truman gave them a brief description of his encounter with the man. "Honestly, I believed him. His reaction to my question about Mia felt genuine." He took a breath. "But when he vanished, I wondered if it was simply a distraction to sway your investigation."

"Sway from what?" asked Noelle.

"I don't know. Change the direction somehow. It seemed the only logical answer. If he wanted to finally come forward, why would he decide to vanish? After he left, I pulled up an old picture of Alex, and I can't say with certainty that it's him. But I can't say it's not him either. I thought that the Bend police showing up made him nervous, but maybe it was an act."

"It doesn't make sense," said Mercy. "Why would he hide for twenty years? And now come out of the woodwork?"

"I don't understand it either. But my gut is still telling me that was Alex Stark."

"Maybe he'll approach you again," said Noelle. "Hang on to him this time."

Truman thought back over the meeting. "I feel like he wanted to get something off his chest."

Mercy humphed. "Yeah. Twenty years of secrets."

46

Devin sucked in air as the bag was ripped off his head.

He sat on the floor in an empty house, breathing deep, struggling to stay calm.

A thick plastic grocery bag had been put over his head after he'd been shoved in the truck. He'd been able to get glimpses out around the bottom but unable to see his captors during the ride. The two men had argued as one drove and the other lay on top of Devin in the back, smashing his head into the seat cushions. The man was heavy and constantly ground his elbow into Devin's back, making pain shoot up his spine. The driver wanted his throat cut immediately, but the man on his back refused, saying he had to wait until he got what he needed from Devin.

Who are they?

Every muscle hurt. Now he stared at the two men before him in the barren house, studying their clothing and trying to glimpse their eyes through the holes in their ski masks.

Ski masks. Seriously.

"You know what a stereotype is, right?" Devin asked, trying to keep his voice from shaking. He knew they wanted him dead.

But why?

The men glanced at each other, but neither spoke.

Is Ollie okay?

He'd seen the young man be struck and then fall to the ground. But before Devin could react, the second attacker had tackled him to the ground and wrenched his arms behind him, quickly binding them. Then the two had hauled him to his feet and dragged him away. He'd strained to see over his shoulder but hadn't spotted Ollie.

There'd been no ski masks when the men attacked, but Devin couldn't recall anything he'd seen of their faces. They'd pushed his head down as they darted toward their truck and worn caps low over their eyes. At the truck Devin had fought back, hoping it would slow down their getaway and that a passerby would question what was happening. Thrust into the back seat, he fought again, thrashing and kicking, swinging his head and baring his teeth. The plastic bag was shoved over his face and pulled tight at his neck. Devin had stopped. He'd quickly grown dizzy, seeing spots in his vision.

Now he sat on bare plywood in the old house, his back against the wall. The carpet had been ripped out, but sections of old, moldering carpet pad had crumbled and piled in the corners. The windows of the deserted home were boarded up, and only a single camping light poorly lit the room. As they'd dropped him to the floor, the men had argued about tying his ankles. One had wanted to, but the other had pointed out how unsteady Devin was on his feet. "He's not going anywhere," he'd scoffed. "Especially with his hands behind his back. We can walk faster than he can run."

They aren't wrong.

Devin knew his physical limitations. There were many. But he couldn't focus on that now. He had to rely on what he did have: his brain and words.

He was in trouble.

He had no doubts that these two men had murdered the two podcasters.

And stabbed my mother.

Dizziness hit him, and he focused on a beam that was exposed through a hole that had been ripped in the ceiling. Because of him, his mother had come close to dying.

What do they want from me?

The heavier of the men had thick, fleshy hands, and his stomach hung over the belt of his khakis. Devin suspected this one had used his body weight to pin him in the back seat of the truck. The second was taller and leaner. His jeans were faded and the knees had big holes. They stood close, towering over him.

Don't show fear.

The heavy man crouched next to Devin. Because of the shadows from the camp light, his eyes were black smudges behind the mask. "I heard your memory is making huge strides these days, Devin."

"From your lips to God's ears," said Devin. "I wish it was so." He fought to keep his voice even. His heart was pounding, his anxiety spiking, but he was determined to maintain a cool head.

I fervently wish my memory had returned.

"That's not what I've been told."

Devin shrugged one shoulder, masking the fear that had permeated every bone. "I would know better than anyone."

What does he want?

"Maybe you just don't want to admit it," said the taller man.

The venom in his voice surprised Devin. So much anger. He took another look at the taller man in the poor light. His arms were folded across his chest, and irritation rolled off him.

Should I know him? Is that why they hide their faces?

He was tempted to say there was no point to the masks, but he suspected the less they knew about his disability, the better.

"Why would I hide that my memory improved?" asked Devin.

Keep them talking. Surely someone saw the attack in the hospital parking lot.

"To get back at me," said the heavy man.

Do I admit I don't know him?

"You'll need to expand on that," said Devin. "I don't have any revenge plans that I'm aware of."

The man snorted and stood. With a jerk of his head, he motioned for the taller man to join him across the room.

Devin exhaled. Sweat ran down his ribs as he watched the men talk in low voices. He couldn't make out the words. The tall one made curt gestures as he argued, and the heavy one threw several glances Devin's way.

"Get what you need, and I'll take care of him," said the tall one.

Devin doubted "take care of" meant a warm bed and tea. His stomach gave a slow roll, the contents threatening to reappear.

The men returned. This time the heavy man didn't lower himself, making Devin crane his neck. "You have something I need," he told Devin. "The car accident. You have the stuff."

Devin was lost. He shook his head emphatically. "I know nothing about a car accident."

"Maybe you don't have the stuff, but you know where it is," he clarified. "Tell us where, and once I have what I need, you can go."

Bullshit.

Devin thought hard. "Do you mean the Jeep that was left on our property? I didn't know that was an accident. The police thought it'd been dumped."

The men both snorted as they exchanged a look. "We left that for you," said the tall one. "A word of warning."

"Warning about what?" Devin was lost, and his fear ramped up.

My fucking shitty memory is going to get me killed.

His words angered the tall one, who took two steps, grabbed Devin by the upper arms, hauled him to his feet, and shook him, banging his head against the wall. "Stop lying to me!"

His fingers dug into the flesh of Devin's arms as he continued to shake him.

Déjà vu swamped him.

I've been here before. I experienced this recently.

One of my dreams. Colin shaking me. Screaming at me not to lie.

"I won't tell anyone!" Devin shouted at the man. "*I won't.* I know you're scared, Colin!" Pain radiated from the back of his skull where it had been slammed into the wall.

The tall man froze, still holding Devin's arms.

Why did I say that?

Colin is dead.

Devin met the man's dark gaze. "Colin?"

47

Truman spoke with the crime scene team, explaining again what had happened in the hospital parking lot. He checked the time, wondering how long it would take the ambulance to arrive with Ollie. Impatience shot through him as he saw that only ten minutes had passed since he'd spoken to Ina.

Dammit.

He slid the phone back in his pocket, and it rang two seconds later with a call from Ina.

"Is Ollie okay, Ina?" Truman asked.

"He's gone, Truman! He was resting on the couch, and I went to use the bathroom. When I came out, he was gone! I'm going to throttle that boy!"

"He drove away?" Truman clenched his phone. Ina would have to get behind him in line to throttle Ollie.

"No, his car is still here, but I don't know where he went. I've checked everywhere."

Truman rubbed his chin, stress shooting through his nerves.

He's got a head injury.

"I'm on my way, Ina. When the ambulance arrives, have them help you look."

"Do you think he got confused?" asked Ina. "He must be outside somewhere."

"I bet he went to Devin's house," said Truman. "He was looking for Devin, so that might make sense to him if he's not thinking clearly."

"That poor boy—both of them."

"I'll call the station too. They can get there quicker than me."

Truman had a vision of Ollie collapsed in the snow between Ina's and Devin's homes.

"I'll go outside and look around," she said.

He didn't like the thought of that. Ina used a cane for good reason. If she fell, she'd break something. "Stay put." He opened the door to his SUV. "Let someone else search the property. If you fall, you'll need an ambulance too."

"Oh no—shit! That boy!"

Truman turned on the engine. "What happened?"

"Jolene is gone."

It took a second for the name to register. "Your revolver? Are you sure?"

"Since the goings-on next door, I've kept it on the kitchen counter during the day. It was by the toaster when I made lunch. It's gone."

Truman sped out of the hospital parking lot.

Would Ollie take her gun?

"You and I are going to talk about weapons storage when this is over," Truman said.

"I've had guns since before your daddy was born," she snapped back.

And now one's missing.

"Sit tight and stay inside, Ina. Someone will be there soon." He hung up and called Lucas.

"Hey, boss."

"I need someone to get over to Ina's and search outside between there and the Bonner home for Ollie. He's got a head injury and just vanished on foot from her home."

"Both Royce and Samuel are helping get cattle off the highway about ten miles east of town. I'll pull Samuel."

"The Sedgewick cattle again?"

"Yep. I'm glad to hear Ollie turned up, even if it was briefly."

"Let Samuel know that Ollie most likely has a gun on him. His head injury is making him a little erratic, so he needs to be careful. Tell Samuel to check the Bonner home too."

"Check because Devin is missing?" asked Lucas. "There's still nothing on the BOLO for the pickup."

"I'm en route. ETA in twenty-five."

"Copy."

His next call was to Mercy.

"I've never had so many calls from you in one day," she answered.

"Ollie's vanished from Ina's. It appears he took her revolver, but his car is still there." Truman reminded himself to breathe.

"He can't have gone far," said Mercy. "Why would he take her gun?"

"He's not thinking straight. I suspect he went to the Bonner home, looking for Devin. He must have thought he needed protection."

"Could someone have taken Ollie from Ina's home?"

That hadn't occurred to Truman. "It's possible. I like to think Ina would have heard, even though her hearing isn't the best."

"Would you like us to meet you there? Noelle and I are on the road back to town."

"Please. I'm still pretty far out from Ina's. Samuel is on his way too."

"Will do. Keep me updated."

They signed off with their I-love-yous.

Truman merged onto the highway, pressed the accelerator, and turned on his overheads to warn people out of his way. At the moment he had no patience for slow drivers.

Ollie, what are you doing?

48

Ollie ran through the woods, panting hard, his breath heavy in the cold air, Ina's revolver tight in his hand.

What will they do to Devin?

He'd tried so hard to keep up with the silver truck. But one second it'd been in front of him, and the next it'd vanished. Suddenly he'd looked around, and he'd been on the shoulder of the road, the rental car's engine still running but the gear in park. It'd taken him a minute to get his bearings and realize Ina's home wasn't that far.

He could kill someone if he continued to drive.

Ollie had no idea how long he'd been on the side of the road or how he'd had the presence of mind to get off the road. It'd been a blur.

The attack. The pain. The blood.

Then the realization that they'd dragged Devin away.

It was too easy to see Devin in the position of that murdered podcaster he'd found at the hotel.

Ollie grew dizzy and stopped running, resting his hands on his knees, breathing deep.

Uh-oh.

He took two steps and vomited into a bush. Then he spit and spit, trying to get the nastiness out of his mouth, wishing he had something to rinse with. Shards of pain stabbed his brain, and he wanted

Ina's frozen peas for the back of his head. He spotted a patch of snow, scooped up a handful, and pressed it to his head.

"Owww!" Pain made his eyes cross, and he dropped the snow.

Bad idea.

He knew he should have waited for the ambulance, but he had to check a hunch. Based on the direction his car had been pointed when he'd woken on the side of the road, he'd assumed he'd followed the truck until that point.

He hoped.

If he had, there was a small chance the truck was headed to the abandoned home on Ina's road. Ollie knew Mercy suspected the men had used it as their base for spying on Devin's home. The investigators had finished processing the home, collecting the tire tread evidence and whatever else the men had left behind.

Does it make sense to return to a place the police are done with? Like hiding in plain sight?

He was going to find out.

He straightened, wiped his mouth with his sleeve, and pushed on.

I should have called Truman instead. Too late now.

His phone was in pieces.

He walked now, still feeling rather light-headed. He focused intently, trying to put one foot in front of the other. Going in the right direction wasn't a problem. He'd spent years in the woods, and his sense of direction was second nature.

He'd passed Devin's house a few minutes ago, taking a quick detour to see if a truck was in the driveway. It wasn't. And the drive was covered with a pristine, thin layer of snow.

There was little snow in the woods, and the ground was frozen and unforgiving when he stumbled. He'd fallen a number of times, catching himself with the hand not holding the gun. His palm was scraped and bled in spots. He ignored it; the real pain was in his head.

Not stopping me.

A corner of the abandoned house came into view. He slowed to move from tree trunk to tree trunk, keeping an eye on the home for any signs of habitation. Plywood covered every window, and the backyard was overgrown with wild grasses and berry vines. He continued to skulk through the woods, wanting a view of the far side of the home.

There it is.

A silver truck was parked where the drive wrapped around to the garage, out of sight of anyone coming up the driveway.

Ollie blew out a breath. Devin had to be inside the home.

Now what?

He looked at the revolver in his hand. He hadn't thought ahead. He'd just acted. Now he was outside a house with two violent men, a gun in his hand, and no cell phone.

The sound of an engine made him crouch behind a tree, hoping it was the police.

The motor grew louder, and a small, beat-up truck parked next to the large one.

Not police.

A man got out, strode to the side door of the garage, pulled it open, and walked in.

Now three men. At least.

The house wasn't completely boarded up after all. If the man had gotten in, then Ollie could. He crept closer, wishing it were night instead of midafternoon. At the home, he flattened himself against the wall and pressed an ear against a boarded-up window. Voices. He couldn't tell if any were Devin's. But one definitely sounded mad.

Ollie moved to the side door of the garage, held his breath, and quietly opened it. No one was inside the garage, but it stank like an outhouse, and garbage covered the floor. Mostly broken beer bottles. An old mattress that'd been slashed open. Graffiti littered the walls with band names, racist slurs, and crude drawings. He knew kids had partied here for years.

No thanks.

He stepped cautiously around the mess. The door between the house and the garage was missing, so he kept to one side until he was near the opening and listened. Someone was pissed.

"This isn't what we agreed on! You kept this from me on purpose!"

"Because we knew you'd be a pussy about it!"

"You grabbed him in broad daylight! Are you trying to get caught?"

"What happened to you? You used to be on our side!"

"I am on your side. But you're doing *stupid* shit! We've stayed quietly under the radar for decades, but now you've killed two people, which is making the police search everywhere. And you tried to murder Devin's mother!"

"I told you she saw my face when I was waiting to spot Devin! She recognized me! I had no choice!"

"You're the one recklessly destroying everything. We were safe! Devin doesn't remember anything!"

"That's not what that podcaster told me. He was digging, planning a story. He said Devin knew what had happened back then and was working with a lawyer to go to the police."

"I don't know what you're talking about."

That's Devin!

Relief flowed through Ollie, quickly swamped by determination to get Devin out. But he'd heard three other voices besides Devin's. The odds weren't good.

"I'm not having anything to do with this!" said one of the other men. "You're going to kill a man who knows shit about nothing because you're paranoid! Don't you think you've done enough?"

"What happened to you, Alex? When did you go soft?" The tone was menacing, making Ollie shudder. "You've dragged your feet at every turn."

"Because this is over! It was over decades ago! All we had to do was stick to the plan and our lives would be fine!"

"Things change."

"Well, I'm done. I'm outa here. I won't have his blood on my hands. He's a fucking innocent, you assholes. He doesn't know nothin'. And *you* know that's the truth."

Boot steps headed Ollie's way.

Panic shot through him, and he darted out the garage door, closing it quietly behind him.

I've got nowhere to hide.

He scooted six feet away and made himself as flat as possible against the wall, hoping the man would turn toward the trucks without glancing in his direction.

The door swung hard, slamming against the outer wall. The man came out, swearing under his breath, and turned in the opposite direction.

Ollie couldn't breathe.

Thank God.

Then the man spun back to close the door, and his surprised gaze met Ollie's.

49

Devin was in shock.

Colin removed his hands from his shoulders but gave one last shove, slamming Devin into the wall again. He spun away but shot a glower over his shoulder.

That's Colin.

He still wore the ski mask, but that had helped Devin recognize him. The name was connected with memories of Colin's movements and posture. The way he walked and held himself. A face wouldn't have helped.

I know we were camping. It was on our hike that he got mad at me.

But why?

The young Colin had merged with the bitter man before him. Tall. Athletic.

"You're alive," Devin said softly. "Why are you so angry with me? I'm not the one who hid for twenty years."

Colin didn't answer.

Devin turned his attention to the heavier man, trying to see Alex in his bearing and body shape. Suspicion burned from the man's eyes, and Devin couldn't sense Alex in him at all. "Who are you?"

"You don't remember?" the man asked.

Devin studied him a moment longer. "No. Which is normal for me. Whoever told you I've regained my memory of what happened lied to you."

The two masked men exchanged a glance.

"He *knows*," said Colin. "*He's* the one who had the photos. Maybe he got rid of them, but I'm sure he knows enough for the police to connect the dots if he goes to them."

I do?

What have I forgotten?

Devin slumped against the wall. "I don't know what photos you think I have because it is all locked behind the fucking walls in my brain. Along with everything else that happened after graduation. I'd love to give you what you want, but I can't." He shrugged. "It's impossible." He eyed Colin. "I don't know why Tyler was killed, or who tried to kill me back then. Or why two people were killed in the same way this past week." He paused. "But I suspect you know all the answers." He struggled to maintain eye contact. "At least tell me what happened back then," he said softly. "Alex, Tyler—Mia. They found her remains yesterday. But I don't know—"

"Stop saying you *don't know*!" shouted Colin.

"I don't!" Devin shouted back. "All I remember is how furious you were, and you telling us not to tell anyone. *But I don't know why!*"

The heavy man pulled off his mask and glared. "Does that help?"

Devin searched his face. He was older, his hair gray. Like every other face, his triggered no memories.

"No," Devin whispered.

They won't believe me.

50

Ollie pointed Ina's gun at the man standing outside the garage.

His hands shot up as fear filled his eyes. He wore a faded red snap-back cap and a thick, heavy coat. "I'll give you whatever you want. Don't shoot. *Don't shoot.*"

Ollie's hands shook, and he heard Truman's voice in his head.

Do not point a gun at a person unless you are willing to shoot them.

Ollie knew he was incapable of shooting anyone. "Get Devin out of there." His stomach swirled and cramped.

I'm going to vomit again.

The man squinted at him, his hands lowering a fraction. "You're the other one. The guy who's always with him."

"Hands up."

"They're not going to let him go," the man said earnestly, lifting his hands more. "They think he's got evidence they want."

"He doesn't. He doesn't remember *anything*." Ollie struggled to keep his voice steady.

"I know that, but they don't believe him. You've got to trust me. I'm on your side."

Bullshit.

"Explain." Ollie concentrated on his breathing, grappling to stay focused. The man's face kept blurring.

"I went to Chief Daly today." The man's words poured out. "I was gonna tell him everything those two had done. They sucked me into this, but I refuse to hurt anyone. I don't care if I go to prison if everything comes out now. That's better than looking over my shoulder for another twenty years."

Realization hit Ollie.

"You're one of his friends who disappeared." Ollie was stunned. "Who are you?"

"Name was Alex Stark." The man stared at his feet.

"Devin liked you. He told me you played a lot of sports together."

"We did. He was a good guy—I'm pretty sure he still is," he added emphatically.

"Then why the fuck have you been hiding for *twenty years*?" Ollie emphasized the words *twenty years* with little jerks of the gun. "Devin believed you all were dead."

"It's a long story."

"Devin doesn't have time for a long story," Ollie snapped. "What will they do to him in there?"

Alex was silent. But his eyes said everything.

Sweat ran down Ollie's temples.

They're going to kill him.

"Before we graduated Erick killed a little kid in the street when he was driving drunk, but the police never solved the case. Tyler knew about it; Tyler had been in the car during the accident and then tried to blackmail him with photos." Alex looked miserable. "That's why Tyler was killed. Erick believed that Devin knew where the photos were hidden, so he cut Devin's throat, but somehow he survived. With Devin's memory gone, Erick felt safe all these years, but he recently found out Devin was remembering things from back then. He believes Devin will get him sent to prison." Alex paused. "But I know Devin never had any evidence about the little boy's death. Devin doesn't know anything about the drunk driving."

"Did you tell them that?" Ollie wanted to shout.

"I tried! But Colin . . ." He looked away. "Colin knows Devin doesn't have it because Colin is the one who always has had the proof and photos, not Devin."

Ollie didn't understand. "Who was driving drunk?" he asked, tightening his grip on the gun.

Shouts inside the house made Ollie and Alex flinch.

"You've got to get him out of there," Alex whispered loudly, his hands still in the air. "He doesn't have long."

Desperation swamped Ollie.

I don't know what to do.

51

Mercy sped up Ina's long driveway and spotted an Eagle's Nest PD vehicle parked at the house next to an ambulance. A moment later Samuel appeared from around the back of the home and raised a hand at Mercy and Noelle. Mercy lowered her window as the officer approached.

"I asked the EMTs to check out Ina," Samuel said. "She's worked up about letting Ollie slip away and was pale and breathing hard. They put her on some oxygen and are trying to calm her down." He pointed toward the back of the house. "There are footprints going from the back door, through the yard, and to the woods. I've yelled for Ollie but no answer. I was about to start through the woods when I heard you pull up."

Mercy put the Tahoe in park. "We'll come with you. We can call the EMTs if we need them."

She grabbed her duffel of medical supplies from the SUV, not knowing what sort of shape Ollie would be in. Then she and Noelle followed the officer to the backyard.

Please let him be okay.

"Find that boy," Ina shouted from the back door. She had an oxygen mask in her hand, and two frustrated EMTs were trying to get her away from the door. "And make sure he's got Jolene!"

"We'll find him, Ina," Mercy called back as they continued their trek. "Go sit down!"

"Jolene?" asked Noelle.

"Ina's revolver," said Mercy. "Ollie—or whoever took him—will be armed."

"Great," muttered Noelle. "A teenager, a concussion, and a gun. Always a good combo."

Ollie's footsteps were easy to spot through the thin layer of snow in the backyard. But once they moved into the shade of the pines, the snow cover became patchy, and tracking became more difficult. "He's most likely gone next door to the Bonners'," said Mercy. "Let's spread out a bit and head in that direction. Don't want to miss him if he's collapsed under a bush."

They made short work of the hundred yards to the backyard of the Bonner home, constantly calling Ollie's name. Twice they spotted footprints that seemed to be Ollie's. Memories of finding Linda hit Mercy when they reached the path that led to where she fed deer. "Let's check the house." She turned down the familiar trail toward the home.

"There's no point," said Samuel a minute later as they stopped at the edge of the Bonner property. He pointed at the fresh tracks in the Bonners' snowy backyard, which led nearly to the house and then turned around, returning to the woods.

Ollie made it this far.

"Why didn't he at least knock on the door?" asked Noelle.

They followed the tracks toward the home, and as they grew closer, they saw the driveway arc. It was completely smooth with snow.

"He didn't stop because no one has been here since it snowed overnight," said Mercy. "He must have kept on through the woods—toward that abandoned house where we found the tire treads." She pulled out her phone and called Truman.

"Did you find him?" Truman asked.

"Not yet. We followed tracks to the Bonners', but it's clear he turned around before reaching the house. I think he continued on to that abandoned house. Can you meet us there?"

"I'll be there in a few minutes."

"We'll approach through the woods and probably meet you in the middle somewhere."

"Copy."

The three of them immediately headed back to the woods. Ollie's path through the snowy yard wove back and forth, making Mercy's chest ache at how injured he must be.

Noelle squeezed her shoulder. "He'll be okay. He hasn't been missing for that long. He couldn't have gotten into too much trouble."

"Said by someone who clearly doesn't know Ollie that well," said Samuel, making Mercy snort.

He was right. Ollie had a way of stumbling into trouble.

"Agreed, but weaving and making poor decisions isn't like him," said Mercy, not saying out loud what she feared: his head injury was severe.

"He'll turn up," said Samuel. "He always does eventually."

Mercy mentally crossed her fingers.

We've got to find him before his head injury gets worse.

52

Ollie pointed his gun at Alex outside the garage. His mind was racing.

How do I get Devin away from them?

His brain scrambled for an answer.

Instead, get the men away from Devin.

He met Alex's gaze. "If you give half a shit about Devin, listen up. I'll fire and you yell for them to come out because you shot someone who was snooping. Got it? And then run for the woods. Get them to follow you."

Alex's mouth dropped open, but he nodded.

Before he could talk himself out of it, Ollie lifted Ina's gun and fired twice into the air.

Alex paused for a split second, then ran, yelling back over his shoulder, "Guys! I got him! Get out here!"

Ollie ran toward the far side of the home, darted around the corner, and plastered himself against the siding, listening hard. His eyes struggled to focus, the pain in his head getting worse. A moment later he heard the garage door open.

"What the fuck?" said a voice.

"I got him!" Alex shouted from the woods. "It was that teenager! Get over here!"

"Let's go!" said another voice.

"What about *him*?"

"He's not going anywhere."

The sounds of running footsteps grew fainter. Ollie risked a peek around the corner in time to see both men vanish among the trees.

Trying to keep his balance, he darted back through the garage and found Devin on the floor in the house, his mouth and nose bleeding. Devin's eyes went wide at the sight of him. Ollie shoved Ina's gun in the waistband at the back of his jeans and hauled Devin to a sitting position. "Let's get you out of here. Can you stand?"

Shit. His wrists are bound.

Devin nodded, and Ollie helped pull him to his feet. The man swayed, and Ollie braced him under the shoulder, hoping his own legs could handle the extra weight.

I need someone to brace me.

"Is there something to cut those off your wrists?" Ollie scanned the dirty room.

"Check in that." Devin nodded at a paper bag on the other side of the room.

Ollie leaned him against the wall and scrambled to the bag. Inside he found a hammer, pliers, two box cutters, and more zip ties.

What were they going to do to him?

He grabbed the box cutter and ran back to Devin. Focusing hard, he made short work of the zip tie, his hands shaking as he tried not to cut Devin's skin. Devin's arms fell to his sides, and he rolled his shoulders. "Hands are numb," he muttered.

"Let's go."

"Not so fast."

Ollie spun around at the new voice and lost his breath. A tall man stood at the door to the garage, his pistol trained on them.

One came back.

What can I do?

They want Devin dead.

And now me too.

Ollie was hyperaware of Ina's gun in his waistband, pressing against his back.

If I reach for it, he'll shoot.

53

Truman immediately spotted tire tracks in the driveway of the abandoned house as he turned off the rural road.

Those could be anyone's tracks.

Two gunshots echoed through the air. Truman hit his brakes and listened for more, scanning his surroundings.

Shit. Mercy? Ollie?

He hit Mercy's name on his phone. It rang and rang and then dumped him into voice mail. He tried again. Voice mail.

As his heart tried to beat its way out of his chest, he called in his location to Lucas and asked for county backup.

Taking a deep breath, he sped up the long drive but slowed as the house came into view. The tracks led around to the side of the home, the vehicle that had created them out of view. He followed at a snail's pace and then stopped as the tailgate of a silver pickup came into sight.

That's the truck.

His senses in high gear, he grabbed his rifle from the dash and climbed out of the truck, his gaze sweeping the area.

What am I going to find?

He ran toward the back of the home.

◆ ◆ ◆

Two gunshots sounded, spiking Mercy's adrenaline.

Still deep in the woods, she, Noelle, and Samuel broke apart and took cover behind thick ponderosa pine trunks. She listened hard, but there were no more sounds.

Did Ollie shoot?

Why?

"Everyone okay?" Mercy called quietly, her chest heaving, her back pressed against the rough bark.

"All good."

"Clear."

"How far away was that?" Mercy asked.

"Close," said Noelle. "But definitely closer to that old house."

Faint shouts came from the same direction.

That's not Ollie.

"Let's go," she said. She dropped her medical duffel and took point while Samuel and Noelle fell back and to her sides, the three of them covering all 360 degrees. She ignored the phone silently vibrating in her pocket.

"I got him!" shouted a man. "It was that teenager! Get over here!"

He shot Ollie?

Fuck.

Behind her, Noelle sucked in a breath.

"Eyes up," muttered Mercy, pushing forward. They had to reach Ollie.

"He's over here!" the same man yelled, his voice closer.

How many men are there?

Mercy raised a fist, signaling for Noelle and Samuel to stop. She stepped behind a tree, her eyes and weapon trained in the direction of the shouts. The faint crunching of steps behind her told her Samuel and Noelle did the same.

"Where is he?" shouted a different voice, farther away.

"Here!" yelled back the first, closer than ever. "He's over here!"

A man wearing a faded red cap jogged into view, looking over his shoulder. Mercy saw the movements of another person not far behind him.

"Hold," she whispered, lifting her fist again. She wanted to see all the characters in play.

Where's Ollie?

How badly is he shot?

The closest man stopped and spun in a circle, deciding which way to go. She squinted at his heavy coat, wondering if he was hiding a weapon.

His hands are empty.

The second man came into sight. He was older than the first, and his belly spilled over his belt. He raised a rifle to his shoulder and trained it on the first man's back.

He will kill him.

"Stop! Police!" shouted Mercy.

Light flashed at the end of his rifle, and Mercy fired at the second man, her vision tunneling on him, faintly aware that Noelle and Samuel had fired too.

The first man dropped to the ground, and the second man's torso jerked before he fell to his knees, his rifle tumbling out of his hands.

We hit him.

Heart racing, Mercy ran forward and trained her weapon on the first man in the dirt, who had his hands over his head, his red cap near one elbow. Noelle and Samuel went to the second. Noelle kicked away his rifle and checked the man while Samuel covered her.

"Don't shoot, don't shoot," shouted Mercy's man, his face pressed into the ground.

She didn't see any holes in his coat. "Are you hit?" she asked, panting hard.

There was a long silence. "I don't think so," he finally said.

"Stay there," she ordered. "Don't move."

Noelle secured her man. "He needs medical," she shouted over to Mercy.

"As soon as mine is secured."

Samuel knelt next to the shooter while Noelle checked the pockets of Mercy's man and cuffed his wrists behind him. "No weapons. I'll get your kit." She ran back to where Mercy had dropped her duffel.

"Where's Ollie?" Mercy asked her man, pulling out her phone to request help.

He twisted his head, looking up at her in surprise. "Back at the house."

"He's okay?"

"He was when I left." Fear flashed in his eyes. "But he's probably not now."

Mercy's heart stopped.

54

Devin knew it was over.

A volley of gunfire had sounded outside, and then the tall man with holes in his jeans had returned.

That's Colin.

He must have shot the other men.

And now he would shoot him and Ollie.

Devin's wrists, arms, and shoulders ached, but his face hurt worse. The heavy man had hit him several times.

My fault Ollie is involved. I should have pushed him away on day one.

I've got to convince them to let him go.

"Colin," said Devin.

"Shut up! Erick may be stupid enough to think Alex shot someone, but I know what a spineless wimp Alex is. Looks like it's a good thing I came back."

Erick?

"Who's Erick?" asked Ollie.

"The fat fuck running after Alex," said Colin. "He was our physics teacher."

Devin inhaled sharply.

Mr. Howard is Erick.

That's why he expected me to recognize him when he took off his mask.

He started this.

"I'll tell you what you want to know, Colin," said Devin, his mind scrambling for a solution. "You're right, I was keeping it to myself. But you have to let Ollie leave first."

Colin gave a slow, wide smile. "Is that so?"

"Yeah. Let him go first."

"You fucking idiot," said Colin. He sneered and stomped closer. "I *know* that you know *nothing*. You never did. The same stuck-up gallantry almost cost you your life twenty years ago, and now you're doing it again. You think lying to me can save this kid's life and yours?"

Devin's heart raced. He'd had one hand to play, and Colin knew it was a lie.

"I don't understand," said Devin.

What did I do twenty years ago?

"'I don't understand,'" mimicked Colin in a high voice. "I'm sick of hearing you say that. You don't know anything because Tyler didn't tell you about Erick's car accident."

"Tyler?" Devin breathed. Next to him, Ollie tightened his grip on his upper arm.

"Erick was giving Tyler a ride when he hit and killed a little kid with his car and didn't stop. Tyler blackmailed Erick for a lot of money after that, threatening to tell the police. Tyler had pictures of the damage to the car and told Erick that he'd passed on that evidence to one of his friends in case something happened to him."

Devin held very still, trying to make sense of the story.

Our physics teacher killed a child?

"Tyler blackmailed Erick for tens of thousands of dollars." Colin snorted. "Then Erick decided to kill Tyler during our camping trip, figuring the other person that had the photos had to be one of us. He surprised us while we were hiking and at gunpoint made us tie each other up. Then loaded us up in a van. Remember?"

Hands are tied behind me again.

Pushed into the van, I land on Mia, who is crying.

Colin is yelling at Tyler, blaming him.

Why is Mr. Howard doing this to us?

"Erick will take care of Alex now," Colin continued. "He's never had a problem when it comes to protecting himself. He does whatever it takes, and Alex has proven to be a risk. After the kidnapping, he tortured all five of us for days. And when Tyler wouldn't admit who else knew about the evidence, he killed him."

Spinning around, I see Tyler.

He's on the ground.

The dirt around him soaked with blood.

Blood that moments before had pumped through his arteries and veins.

"Then he said he'd kill us one by one unless we told him who had the photos. You—being the chivalrous asshole you clearly still are—stepped forward and admitted you had the photos."

An arm comes from behind and lifts my jaw, exposing my neck.

I can't breathe.

Colin gave Devin an odd look. "You should be dead, man. We saw him slice your throat like he did with Tyler. Fucking prick. Mia flipped out. She'd always had a soft spot for you."

I always know her in my dreams. I know her by her hair and her eyes.

Her voice. Her laughter.

I can smell her scent. She always smelled faintly of sunshine and the outdoors. It's fresh and warm. When I meet her gaze, I'm happy.

"And now here you are again, trying to save someone else by lying." He points the gun at Ollie's head. "You've got nothing to tell me, Devin. *I know that.* Because Tyler gave *me* the blackmail photos of the car. You had nothing to do with it."

Devin's ears started to ring.

Colin let me die that day.

He hated me back then, even though he'd been one of my best friends. Everything had changed between us. Why?

Colin looked from Ollie to Devin and back, clearly struggling with a decision. He pointed the gun at Devin. "This is for Mia, asshole."

Devin closed his eyes, waiting for the gunshot.

Maybe he'll let Ollie go if I'm dead.

"No!" Ollie shoved Devin, stepping into his place, and Devin crashed to his stomach as four gunshots filled the room and Ollie landed on top of him.

I can't breathe.

Devin sucked for air. Ollie had knocked the breath out of him. He pushed and shoved until Ollie slid off and air finally entered his lungs. Devin rolled over and stared at Colin on the floor, bleeding heavily from several shots in his torso but still blinking.

"Oh, my God," said Ollie. "Devin, are you okay?" He pushed up to his hands and knees.

Ollie's not bleeding.

Devin's gaze went to the door. A man stood there with his weapon still trained on Colin but his gaze locked on Ollie.

That man shot Colin.

"You okay, son? Devin?"

That's Truman. Truman shot Colin.

"I'm okay," said Ollie. "I don't know about Devin. I landed on him pretty hard."

"I'm good," Devin finally said. "Not hurt." He crawled across the floor to Colin, using only his good hand.

"Careful, Devin," ordered Truman. He kicked Colin's gun away as he dialed his phone.

"Colin," Devin said, staring into his eyes, trying to commit them to his faulty memory. Blood rapidly flowed across the plywood.

Even now, I don't recognize his face.

Hate shone in Colin's eyes. "You're such an asshole. No wonder Mia loved you best," he hissed. He gave a sputtering, wet, bloody cough and closed his eyes.

Devin covered his face with his hands.

It's over.

55

Three days later

Mercy and Noelle sat across the table from Alex Stark in a small room at the county jail. Behind them, retired detective Sam Durette leaned against the wall, his cowboy hat in hand. Even though they'd been introduced, Alex continuously shot apprehensive looks at the tall man, making Mercy wonder about Sam's expression.

Colin Balke and Erick Howard were dead.

Alex was the only source of answers to their many questions.

After hearing the shots from the old house, Mercy had been terrified of what she'd find inside, visions of Ollie dead and bleeding running through her mind. Instead, she'd been shocked to find Truman had fired the shots. He'd emerged from the home as Mercy, Noelle, and Samuel had entered the yard, their weapons ready, only to discover the threat had been eliminated.

All three—Truman, Ollie, and Devin—had been shaken by the events and revelations that had occurred in the abandoned home.

Taking a life created a huge burden. One Truman would forever carry. Even though his actions had saved Devin and Ollie, it still weighed heavily on him. Mercy could feel how rattled he was as he embraced her in the backyard, whispering over and over that he'd had to shoot, that he'd had no choice.

She understood.

Three of them had fired at Erick Howard as he tried to shoot Alex Stark in the back. Mercy didn't know whose bullet—or bullets—had killed him. It didn't matter. The burden was slightly lighter because it was shared with Noelle and Samuel, but it still gave her sleepless nights.

Mercy focused on Alex Stark. She and Noelle had read the reports and interviewed Ollie and Devin, learning what Colin and Alex had revealed during that horrible day. But there were still holes in the two-decade timeline.

I have so many questions.

Noelle started first, lobbing Alex a soft question to get him talking. "What's life been like for you for the last twenty years?"

"Life wasn't great. Especially at first. We were practically slaves for those guys."

"What guys?" asked Noelle.

"SCs," said Alex.

"Sovereign citizens," added Mercy, thinking of all the headaches sovereign citizens had given her in the past. "It explains how you were able to disappear—on paper anyway. Nothing those folks hate more than having a government involved in their lives."

"You have no idea," said Alex.

"Tire tread and shell evidence have linked you to three electrical substation attacks," said Noelle. "Was it you and Colin each time?"

"Yeah. It was more him. He heard about accelerationist theories from one of the guys we lived with for a while—not all sovereigns were into that. Most just wanted as much space as possible between them and the law. But Colin was really fervent about creating disruption, believing it would bring an end to our current government. He talked all the time about how it wasn't fair to the little guy and it was our duty to bring about a change. I went along with him because it was just easier than arguing with him."

Mercy wasn't sure she believed him. Alex appeared to be forthcoming, but it was easy to blame the dead guy for everything.

"I don't understand why Erick Howard let you three live in the first place," said Noelle. "He'd already killed two of you. Why stop there?"

Alex grimaced and shrugged. "I've asked myself the same question. I don't think he expected to actually kill any of us at first. He thought Tyler would give him the photos and feel threatened enough to not go to the police. But Erick got a little more nuts as the days went on and no one was giving him the information he wanted."

"Where did he keep all of you for five days?" asked Mercy.

His shoulders twitched, revulsion on his face. "A fucking shed. No food. Hardly any water."

"But where was it?" Mercy asked pointedly.

"I have no idea," said Alex. "Didn't dare ask him afterward. I was just thankful he let us live."

"Which you still haven't explained yet," Noelle stated.

Alex was silent for a long moment, his gaze distant. "I think killing Tyler and Devin was harder than Erick expected. Takes guts, you know—or an evil soul. It's not an easy thing to do. Physically or mentally. I think back then—after killing the two of them—he'd suddenly had enough . . . maybe overwhelmed. Seeing that he would have to kill three more of us was too much." He grimaced. "But then he started again with that podcaster."

Mercy thought of all the murders she'd dealt with. She knew she'd brushed shoulders with evil souls.

But killing seems easy for some people.

"He put my prints, Colin's, and Mia's all over the knife he killed Tyler and Devin with. He took pictures of us with the bodies, making us pretend to cut their throats. He promised to kill Colin's sister, his parents, every member of our families if we told anyone. And we knew he'd do it—he'd proved he wasn't afraid to kill. If we never went back to our lives, he'd let us live."

"Jesus," mumbled Noelle.

"Mia didn't care if we disappeared. She hated her father and had planned to leave after high school anyway. I was a foster kid and didn't feel like I had anyone I'd miss. So we left that day. With nothing. Erick dropped us off in bumfuck nowhere. We were taken in by a group of people who lived off the grid. They needed strong backs, so we worked for our keep. Learned how to live off the grid.

"After a few years, we were pretty much accepted by them on equal footing. But Erick knew where we were. Every few years Erick would show up to remind us of his promise. He'd bring recent pictures of Colin's parents and sister to prove that he was watching them. Mia's father too. He still had the knife with our fingerprints and the photos."

"When did Mia die?" asked Mercy.

Alex thought. "It was our first year there. Early spring, I think."

She got pregnant right away . . . or was pregnant when they were captured.

"She was scared," said Alex. "Scared of giving birth and angry at Colin. Blamed him for her pregnancy." He lifted one shoulder. "Didn't seem fair. It takes two, you know. They fought all the time after Erick let us go.

"Colin and I buried her," Alex was saying, his gaze on his cuffs. "It'd been horrible. Colin wouldn't let Mia go to a doctor, and the woman who was helping with the birth didn't know what to do. Mia screamed for hours. By the time the baby came out, it was dead, and she wouldn't stop bleeding." He shuddered. "I begged Colin to take her to a hospital, but he refused. Said it was too dangerous for us." He lifted his head to look Mercy in the eye. "He sacrificed her and the baby to protect his own ass."

The image of the dying pregnant girl stuck in Mercy's mind. She recalled how she'd walked the pioneer cemetery and told Truman how dangerous it was to be pregnant back then. It was almost fitting that Mia had been buried there.

"She shouldn't have died."

Alex's words on the note.

"A common theme I'm seeing in Colin's history," said Mercy. "Selfishness . . . narcissism."

"Looking back, I realized it too," said Alex. "When we were in school, everything centered around what he wanted to do. He was good at making it feel like we all made decisions, but truly it always came down to him.

"Mia said it was Colin's fault Devin had been killed—for a long time we thought he was dead. Erick didn't tell us until years later that Devin had survived but had brain damage.

"I was glad to hear he lived," Alex said. "But Erick added Devin to his list of people that he'd kill if we didn't keep his secret." He looked at his hands again. "That meant something to me. I didn't want Devin hurt. He'd been through hell."

"Who killed Rob Newton?" Mercy asked.

"Erick and Colin," said Alex. "I drove them to that cabin in the middle of nowhere. When Rob called Erick, asking for an interview for his podcast, he told him that he'd already interviewed Devin and he'd regained his memory of what happened. That scared the shit out of Erick. He got in contact with Colin and said something had to be done before this guy put the truth out there."

In order to shake the trees and see what fell out, Rob Newton had told everyone he'd called that Devin was getting his memory back. Jason Slade hadn't been threatened by the comment because he wasn't involved. Rob's phone call had just made Colin Balke's parents more suspicious of Devin.

But Erick Howard had seen Devin's returning memory as a threat. And taken action.

No doubt Rob Newton hadn't expected to lose his life during his investigation.

"Who stabbed Linda Bonner?" The small woman lying motionless on the cold ground would forever be burned in Mercy's brain.

"Erick. He was headed to watch the house that morning and accidentally came across Linda in the woods. He said she recognized him from the past and was immediately suspicious about why he was at their home." Alex paused. "I don't know how true that is. Erick might have overreacted when he came across her. I'm sure Linda was aware that Erick was a suspect in her son's attempted murder back then, but frankly I don't think he looks much like he did back then—so I suspect he stabbed her anyway, knowing who she was."

Fury rolled through Mercy at his answer.

That poor woman.

"Who fired at Sara Newton behind the Bonner home?" asked Noelle.

"Colin," Alex said firmly. "We'd used that old house a few times to park at while we kept watch on the Bonner house, waiting for Devin to come back. We recognized the podcaster's wife when she entered the woods, and Colin decided she probably knew the same things her husband did. I got out of there, but Colin later told me he shot a cop."

"And the other podcaster? Paula Jupp?"

"Erick said she called him, asking nosy questions. He gave the order and said to leave her near the hotel where Devin was staying. She was another warning like Rob Newton was, for Devin not to speak up."

"So you're saying you were involved in that murder," said Mercy, slightly surprised he hadn't put all the blame on Colin.

Alex looked away and said nothing.

Mercy had heard enough for one day. Her heart was heavy at the image of what Mia had gone through. They asked a few more questions and then wrapped up the interview.

◆ ◆ ◆

A half hour later, Mercy took a large drink from a glass of wine. Sam Durette sat across from her and Noelle in their little workroom. He'd gifted them each a dozen bottles of a local red wine. A thank-you for solving the case that had been on his mind for twenty years.

She and Noelle had exchanged a long glance and immediately opened a bottle.

Mercy leaned back in her chair and took a smaller sip of the pinot noir, letting it sit on her tongue before she swallowed. She sighed.

It's a good one.

She needed it to wash the distaste of Alex's interview from her palate.

Mercy and Noelle had repacked all the old records and added their own, stacking the boxes along one wall in the room. The table was empty for the first time in a week. Except for the wine bottle and three glasses. Noelle had closed the conference room door. Drinking in the building broke several rules.

Neither of them cared at the moment.

"I never dreamed those teenagers would end up living with a bunch of sovereign citizens," said Sam. "No wonder they were able to vanish. Did Alex tie up all your loose ends?"

"I think so," said Mercy. "We'll find out if he was as hands-off in the murders—including Paula Jupp's. There were only two men at Rob Newton's murder at that cabin. We'll see if Alex's fingerprints show up or if it was done by Colin and Erick as he claimed."

Rob's wife, Sara, had finally admitted that she'd taken some of Rob's Xanax before going to bed the night he'd been murdered. Like many witnesses, she'd held back information she was embarrassed to admit. She also hadn't given Mercy and Noelle Rob's little notebook they'd found in the woods. Believing the investigators had enough of his research, she'd kept it because of the amazing sketches he'd made of her.

"I believe most of what Alex told us," said Mercy. "Even if he didn't admit his full role, he'll be in prison for a very long time once the government gets through with him. They are taking the substation damage very seriously."

Sam spun his wineglass, studying the deep red as it swirled. "It sounded like he was affected by Mia's death," he said. "But why didn't he fight Colin harder for her? They could have taken her to a hospital or done *something*." Fury colored Sam's gaze as he looked from Mercy to Noelle. "I suspect Colin Balke knew how to control Alex."

"I can't understand how such fundamentally different people had been friends," said Mercy. "Devin lost so much memory but never lost his core values. He was willing to be shot to try to save Ollie. Just like he'd stepped forward for his friends. But Colin—" She wrinkled her nose. "A true narcissist. Only thinking about himself and allowing a grudge to fester for twenty years. Two very different men."

"To Devin," said Sam, raising his glass. "I hope he has a better life after this."

Mercy and Noelle joined the toast. "He will," said Mercy. "We've put some plans into motion. And he's got Ollie as a buddy. Ollie makes everyone's life better."

"He's a good kid," Noelle agreed.

Mercy checked the time. "I hate to drink and run, but I'm meeting Truman for our anniversary dinner."

"I forgot!" said Noelle. "Happy first anniversary!"

"Happy anniversary." Sam held up his glass again. "May you be as happy as my wife and I were as we celebrated our fortieth last month."

Forty years?

Mercy couldn't imagine.

Truman is who I want by my side for forty years.

"Any plans after dinner?" asked Noelle.

"He's booked a couple nights in a hotel. The kids aren't allowed to call unless the house is on fire—and that's only after they call the fire department." She frowned. "Kaylie said something about pita chips. I have no idea why." She stood up and put on her coat. "Sam, good seeing you again, and Noelle, I'll talk to you in a few days."

Mercy left them to finish the bottle of wine, a smile on her face.

She had better things to do.

56

Two weeks later

Truman read the email for the third time and eased back in his chair, keeping his gaze on his computer screen, his fingers tapping his leg.

The signs hadn't been obvious, but there had been enough to prod him to investigate. Mercy had offered support, but she worried about how it would affect him. Truman had worried too. He'd spent many days and nights thinking about it.

How do I feel?

Anxiety wasn't present. His stomach was fine. In fact there was a relief brought on by finally having an answer. A relaxation that went bone deep.

I'm okay.

Part of him had expected to be devastated, but oddly he wasn't. This wasn't about him. It involved him to a degree, but not the way it did other people.

"Hey, Mercy?" he yelled in the direction of their kitchen. "Can you come in here for a minute?"

Their house had been full for Ollie's twentieth birthday that afternoon. Mercy's parents had come, along with her siblings and their spouses and kids. Baby Henry had toddled around the house, weaving among everyone's legs, determined to catch Dulce or Simon. The cats toyed with Henry, allowing him close and then suddenly jumping out of reach.

Everyone from the police department and their families had come, including Ben and his wife, Sharon. Ben's gunshot wound had healed, but he'd gotten accustomed to keeping the arm immobile. Now he attended physical therapy to restore his motion and strength.

Ben hated therapy. But Sharon made sure he didn't miss an appointment.

Noelle had shown up early and helped Kaylie decorate the home with cheesy SpongeBob decor and balloons, wanting to embarrass Ollie—which it had. Devin and his mother, Linda, had come. Truman thought Linda looked good for having been nearly killed three weeks before. Her sparkling personality was back, but like Ben, she was taking it easy.

Three of Ollie's friends had been banished to the kitten room after Truman caught them ogling Kaylie. He'd told them to clean the litter boxes, but last he'd checked, the young men had decided to stay and dangle toys in front of the kittens.

The party had wound down. All the presents had been opened, all the pizza eaten, and all the candles blown out. Now a few stragglers were left on the back deck, sticking close to the big patio heaters as they talked and drank.

I can't believe Ollie is twenty.

Truman couldn't imagine not having Ollie in his life.

I almost lost him.

Time with the young man was suddenly more precious.

My son. No matter what.

Mercy appeared at the door to his office. "You shouted for me?"

"Yes, sorry about that." He took a breath and discovered he couldn't state what he'd found, so he gestured at his computer screen. She stepped close and set her hands on his shoulders as she read.

"Oh, Truman." She squeezed his shoulders. "You were right. Are you okay?"

He swallowed. "I am. It's just weird. Now that it's in front of me, I don't know what to do. But it's not about me."

"It changes nothing."

"It changes some things."

Mercy spun his chair around to face her and held his gaze, her hands taking his. "A lot has happened the last few weeks," she said softly.

He knew what she was referring to.

Shooting Colin Balke haunted him. Truman could still see the man's accusing and shocked expression as he realized he'd been shot. Each passing day made the image fade a little more, but he knew it could lunge from a corner of his mind at any moment.

"I'd do it again," he told her.

He had no doubts.

But it doesn't take away the images burned in my brain.

"You would do it again because it was the right thing to do. If you hadn't, Devin would be dead, and probably Ollie too," Mercy stated firmly. "It'll get better."

He cupped her face in his hands, putting all his love for her in his gaze. "It will for you too. We'll get through it together."

"I know," she whispered. She pressed her forehead against his, and they spent a long moment simply appreciating each other's presence.

She gets me.

She gave him a quick kiss. "Want me to bring in Ollie and Devin?" she asked.

"I need to make a phone call first. Might take some time. Then I'll talk to them." His mind was spinning.

How will Ollie take this?

Ollie sprawled on the comfy old couch in Truman's office. Devin sat on the other end, and Shep hopped up between them. He shoved his nose into Ollie's armpit, then turned to curl up against Devin, closing his eyes with a doggy sigh.

Traitor.

Actually he liked that Shep had immediately taken to Devin. The man had been over several times for meals and video games. He was comfortable with Ollie's friends, who'd been very understanding when Ollie suggested they all wear name tags when Devin was with him. It had worked. Devin's gaze often went to the tags, and he'd tease them about the trouncing he'd given a friend last time they played.

They hadn't put pictures of Devin up in Eagle's Nest stores, but the word had gotten out to the locals that they needed to say their names when greeting him. Ina had worked the gossip train to let everyone know. Local businesses had added name tags. Employees who'd worked the same job for thirty years—and whom every customer knew—happily wore them.

It'd made a difference; Devin wasn't as nervous about venturing out into public.

Some of his old memories had come back since the deaths of Colin and Erick Howard, but the face blindness was still fully present.

Ollie studied Truman, who was perched in his computer chair. He'd smiled when they entered, but something had seemed off. His smile didn't reach his eyes.

He's nervous.

This immediately made Ollie nervous. Truman was a rock.

What did I do?

Ollie thought back. His friends had been immature around Kaylie, but Truman had immediately handled it, speaking quietly to them so that no one else heard. No one had noticed—except Ollie—when the guys slunk away to the kitten room.

He can't be mad at me about that. And he wouldn't have asked Devin to come in.

Mercy leaned against the edge of Truman's desk, her arms folded across her chest. But she smiled. A genuine smile. She looked happy.

It can't be too bad.

"What's up?" Ollie finally asked.

Truman scratched his jaw. "A lot of stuff has happened over the last few weeks," he said slowly. "Devin, it's been great getting to know you and Linda. Eagle's Nest is a better place now that the two of you are more involved. And I especially appreciate the friendship that's grown between you and Ollie."

Ollie agreed. He'd gotten a little ribbing from his friends about Devin being almost forty, but they'd grown to like him too.

"I just got off the phone with Alex Stark." Truman paused. "Clearly you don't remember this, Devin. But you were seeing Mia Fowler. Alex said the two of you started dating before she called it off with Colin. When Colin did find out, Alex said all his anger was directed at you."

Ollie glanced at Devin. The man was frowning and concentrating intently on Truman's words.

"We went behind Colin's back?" Devin asked, disbelief in his tone.

"According to Alex. That would explain the falling-out between you two that Colin's dad brought up. Alex didn't think you deliberately sought Mia out; he thinks it just happened."

Devin was silent for a long moment.

"That would explain Colin's anger that I've seen in my dreams," he said slowly. "And why I felt so much guilt when he was mentioned—more than I ever felt about Tyler and Alex. It went beyond survivor's guilt." He grimaced. "Now I know why. I stole his girlfriend."

"You don't know that," said Ollie. "Mia could have pursued *you*. But either way, I can see why Colin was mad back then, but it's ridiculous that he carried that bitterness for twenty years. He wanted to shoot you because of it."

How can someone carry that rage for so long? And kill because of it?

"Whenever you talk about Mia, your face lights up, Devin." Ollie thought hard. "You're sad, too, but this explains why you look dreamy eyed when you talk about her. You loved her—more than a friend."

Devin looked a little shell shocked, his eyes dazed. "That makes sense. It's depressing to think that I can't remember the one time I was in love."

Ouch.

"You sacrificed yourself for her back then," Ollie said, respect and reverence filling him. "You told Erick that you had the car accident photos. You *knew* he'd kill you for that. You probably hoped he'd let the others go."

"I don't remember." Devin's shoulders slouched. "I don't feel like I sacrificed anything."

Ollie looked at Truman and Mercy. "Why did Alex let everyone believe that Colin and Mia were still a couple at that time?"

"I asked him that," said Truman. "And it wasn't the only thing he was untruthful about. He said he thought some things were best left in the past."

"So he decided the narrative. Unfair. Devin deserves to know what happened back then."

"He does," said Truman. He glanced at Mercy, who gave him a small nod.

Truman met Ollie's gaze, love and concern in his eyes. "You deserve to know, too, Ollie. I had a comparison done between your DNA and Devin's. He's your biological father."

Ollie stilled. "What?"

Truman nodded. "You heard me."

A faint buzz sounded in Ollie's ears, and he held on to Truman's gaze as if it were a lifeline. Ollie reluctantly broke away to look at Devin, who stared back at him, his mouth open the slightest bit, his eyes wide.

"How—how can that be?"

Truman's pulling a joke on me.

Ollie studied Truman's expression. And then Mercy's. Both were full of affection and love.

They're dead serious.

"I had to prod him and tell him I had genetic evidence, but I got Alex to admit that the baby didn't die with Mia." Truman cracked his knuckles. "I'm not sure when I became fully aware that I had questions, but every time I saw you and Devin together, I sensed similarities—I didn't actually *see* them, but subconsciously my brain had slowly lined things up side by side. You're both tall—and Ollie, you used to be as thin as Devin at one point. Looking back at when we met, I saw your frames would have been almost identical."

Ollie rubbed his sweating palms down his thighs. Truman was right. His legs used to be bone thin like Devin's. Now he had muscle.

Truman continued. "You both get the same look in your eyes when you talk about gaming and TV shows—and your eyes are physically similar."

Simultaneously Ollie and Devin turned to study each other's eyes.

He's right.

"It's so obvious to me now," said Truman. "But because Devin came into our lives out of the blue, we didn't expect it or notice it. But something deep in my brain saw it."

Ollie's head spun.

Is this really happening?

"The woman who'd helped during Mia's birth offered to take the baby and find it a home. Alex couldn't tell me her name or even what she looked like, but I believe that woman gave you to your grandparents, or else she was your grandmother, Ollie."

Ollie stared at Truman, memories of his grandparents filling his mind.

"Either way, Devin fathered Mia's baby. Devin is your dad, Ollie."

"That means you have another grandmother—Linda," added Mercy. "You've suddenly grown a family."

"I already have a family," Ollie stated, apprehension churning his stomach. "All of us."

Are they going to ask me to leave?

Mercy leaned forward, concern in her eyes. "You still have us, Ollie. We're not going anywhere, and neither are you. You're our son—mine and Truman's. But now you've got another important person in your life. Although I think you valued Devin already," she said, turning a fond gaze to Devin. "Your family circle has grown. That's never a bad thing."

"Holy crap." Ollie didn't know what else to say.

"Holy crap," repeated Devin. "You're my *son*?"

Ollie turned to look at him. "I don't know." His head was spinning.

"You are," said Truman. "It's the truth."

Ollie studied Devin's face, looking for more signs of himself. Devin was gazing at him, doing the same.

Maybe the chin?

"This may be your birthday, Ollie," Devin said slowly, never lowering his gaze. "But it's the best present I've ever gotten." He tentatively put a hand on Ollie's shoulder, and a wide smile covered his face. "My best bud is actually related to me!" he said, wonder in his voice.

Ollie grinned. A million questions ricocheted in his mind.

This is a good thing. But . . .

Ollie's gaze flew back to Truman and saw tension in his eyes. "You're my dad," he said firmly. "This doesn't change that."

"No, it doesn't," agreed Truman. His shoulders visibly relaxed.

"I still want you to adopt me," Ollie told him. He turned to Devin. "That's okay, right?"

"You don't need to ask me," said Devin. "You two need that. Everyone can see it. And it changes nothing between us." An odd look crossed his face. "Son." He grimaced. "That didn't feel right. Might stick to Ollie for a while."

Ollie agreed. "We'll figure it out."

Devin's gaze went distant. "Mia was pregnant. I wonder if I knew that. She might not have been aware of it before we were separated."

"Mia was my mother." Ollie tried out the words, but they felt foreign. He'd seen a few pictures but didn't feel a connection. "What about her parents?" he asked.

"Her mother passed away," said Mercy. "Her father is alive . . . but he's been hard to get ahold of. We can talk about that later."

Mercy doesn't like something about him.

They could discuss it later. Right now Ollie was overwhelmed by the thought of Devin as his father.

My father.

"Mercy had a good point," Ollie said. "My family circle can easily stretch to add you and Linda." He blinked rapidly. "I went from having no one after my grandfather died and now I have more family than I'd ever dreamed of." Tears burned in his eyes. "You don't know how badly I've wanted people in my life. I was alone for so long."

Devin slid closer, squeezing Shep between them, and leaned to put an arm around Ollie's shoulders. "We'd already established that we enjoy hanging with each other. This just slapped a title on it."

"Yeah." Ollie wiped his eyes. "And you're stuck with me now. No going back on this."

Devin laughed, his arm tightening on Ollie.

My family has suddenly expanded.

He could get used to that. Easily.

Mercy had moved to Truman's lap, her arms wrapped around him, both their gazes on Ollie, full of love and deep affection.

But they're my parents. Always.

Acknowledgments

I can't seem to stay away from Mercy and Truman. But according to the emails I receive, my readers love them too. I adore these two characters and the little family they've put together. A family that expanded during this story. I suggested in the acknowledgments of *The First Death* that this book might star Noelle Marshall, but Mercy and Truman—and Ollie especially—had more to tell me. But Noelle is still on my radar. She will get her story told.

This is my twentieth novel. I never dreamed I'd write so many books. I had no idea I'd create a world in the Pacific Northwest that readers want to drop into over and over. I love to revisit previous characters and pull them into current books. I never know who will pop up, and it delights me as much as my fans when a familiar face appears on the page.

I'm lucky to work with a dream publisher that lets me choose what stories to tell. They've supported me from my very first book, always enthusiastic and eager to see what I turned in next. I've been with my acquiring editor, Anh Schluep, and developmental editor, Charlotte Herscher, for a long time and wouldn't be where I am without their brilliant guidance and support. My agent, Meg Ruley, does amazing things for me and is such a lovely person. I'm very blessed to have these three women in my life.